# THE MADWOMAN
# OF EL MALPAIS

*J.D. —
To my favorite
storyteller — Never get tired of
the Mississippi Riverboat and Ozark
ramblers, as well as New Mexican Urban and
Outback tall tales and Musings —*

# THE MADWOMAN
# OF EL MALPAIS

*A Mysterious
New Mexican
Adventure*

P. J. CHRISTMAN

Highgate Lane Press

**Highgate Lane Press**
Santa Fe, NM 87501

**FICTIONAL WORK:** This is a fictional work. While some real place names are used, others are purely fictional. The characters in the book are also fictional. Any resemblance of the fictional contents or characters of this work to those of real life are purely coincidental.
**WHERE/WHEN WRITTEN:** in Boulder, Colorado, in 2004
**COPYRIGHT:** TXu1-347-832
**ISBN-13:** 979-8-88895-131-6 (Paperback)
**COVER:** by iStock Photos
**FIRST PAPERBACK EDITION:** January, 2023
**USAGE:** Other than short passages for review purposes, no part of the content of this work may be used without the express written permission of the author.
**RIGHTS:** All publishing, motion picture and other rights for The Madwoman of El Malpais are held by the authorm, P. J. Christman, and are available.
**CONTACT:** runstats@aol.com

# OTHER PUBLISHED WORKS
## *by*
## P. J. (Paul) Christman

Lost in a Room Full of Dinosaurs
Santa Monica Dead Palms
Nothing More, Nothing Less
Skins of Lightning
The Purple Runner
Black Christmas Pudding (Play)
Sour Apples (Play)

# Kahlo in Santa Fe

(KAHLO)
I never say much, and that makes my Mom and Grammy mad. I can't help it. I used to talk more, until my aunt Ashleigh's death. She was always real nice to me. She let me read anything I wanted. I'm only nine, but she treated me like an adult. I didn't have to play with dolls, or do sports, or watch the Simpsons. Auntie let me be a real person, not just a kid in grade school in New York.

The problem is, Mom says I'm becoming a recluse. You're probably wondering if I know what a recluse is. I do. That's one of the problems for a precocious nine-year-old. Everyone thinks you don't understand a lot of things, when if you read everything you can, the only thing you don't get is sex. I know I'm not ready for what I've read about it. I leave that to adults. Grammy says one day it will be time, but then I'll wish it wasn't.

I like climbing up on things and surveying the surroundings. That's probably the only thing I like doing that Mom feels is normal for a young girl not yet five feet tall. Santa Fe means Holy Faith, and when I got to the Holy City of the Pueblos and Spaniards with Mom and Gram, I was excited. Yah, I liked the Georgia O'Keeffe Museum and the adobe buildings. But it was the feeling I got just being in an ancient city of magic and dancing and *farolitos*. I can't explain it, but I knew I was going to have another of my 'visions.'

I have no control over those things, just like Lecha in the *Almanac of the Dead*. I just see things. One minute I'm looking at a scene in the city or out on the desert and suddenly, the meaning of something there comes to me. It's not usually a vision of something specific. Mostly it's just an impression of what something means that nobody has been able to figure out. Sometimes my visions cause problems, like what I found out when Auntie was killed. I've never been able to speak about it, and sometimes I go days without saying anything to either Mom or Grammy.

I forgot to mention. Sometimes I stutter. I have tried everything and so have psychologists. But I can't help it. Sometimes I just can't get beyond the first word of what I want to say. That's another reason I can go for days or even weeks without speaking. My first name is Kahlo, which Mom says is appropriate because the famous Mexican painter walked with a limp, while I talk with a limp. The good thing is that if I really feel I know what I'm talking about, such as after a vision, my stutter goes away. And then my vocabulary soars. Gram says she doesn't understand where I get some of the longer words I suddenly use during an explanation of a vision. Sometimes I sound like a college professor, and I can't explain how I do it. It's probably all the reading I've done. I never spend much time watching TV. So, when I do talk, sometimes I stutter and sometimes I sound like a verbal genie has escaped a bottle. It's as if a Pueblo Kachina has given me back my speech. You probably wonder why I said Pueblo Kachina and not Christian or Jewish God, since Mom's half of both. It's because I'm adopted. I think I might be an ancestor of the Chacoans, but neither Mom nor Grammy is certain what tribe they got me from. Mom has red curly hair and I have long straight black hair and eyes like anthracite coal, like Aunt Ashleigh had. Some say I have the eyes of a shark. Mom tried to get pregnant when she was married. But she couldn't. All the storks were away somewhere else.

Anyway, Mom went off this morning to rock hunt. She never finds much, but I think it's like fishing, for boys: it doesn't matter if you catch anything. Once both of us went to the mineral museum in Denver's City Park, we were hooked. It's hard to imagine that many colorful minerals and gems are somewhere out there in the West. And you can understand how expeditions set out from the Old World in search of gold, silver, and precious stones. Cortés and Coronado just had gold fever like many others who dig around in the deserts and mountains today.

Gram still isn't awake. Every night she usually drinks a whole bottle of vodka disguised as vodka tonics, or sometimes just with ice. Then she sleeps it off, and when she gets up, I always hope she'll have lunch with me. Because I worry about her. She has been a widow so long, I think it's her loneliness, particularly at Christmas, that causes her to drink so much. Even though she limps after Aunt Ashleigh pushed her down the stairs, she walks a lot. But if she doesn't start eating more, the doctor told her cirrhosis is going to set in. Fortunately, she is witty, and Mom says that may save her.

I was just walking along the empty Santa Fe River thinking about the book I had just finished, *Somewhere South of Here*, which takes place in Santa Fe. I like romances, even though the only boy that ever paid attention to me moved away from Manhattan to help his asthma. Gram let me go to the factory outlet bookstore way south on Cerrillos Road and let me get a stack of books about the West. Books are my only friends because we are on vacation. Actually, even if we weren't on vacation, books would be my main friends. It's my own fault because I don't like talking.

Anyway, I was just hopping from one sidewalk square to the next when I had a vision that Mom was talking to someone south of Chaco Canyon. It wasn't the friendliest of conversations, but I wasn't afraid for her. It seemed like Mom was beginning a great adventure.

# Jungles and Coasts

(KALIBER)
My first encounter with New Mexico gave no hint of what was to follow. Beautiful sunsets, undernourished cacti, monolithic rock mesas, and even the endless harbingers of drought, none of it telegraphed the change in store for escapists from coastal urban frenzy. Having endured humidity, terror, and the startlingly different mindsets of Viet Nam was wholly different than the challenges faced in trying to figure out the Anasazi world of Chaco Canyon. Then there were those three Gotham women and their own confounding complexities. Yet being from two cities couldn't prepare any of the four of us for the fabled magnificent seven. And as for Nam, well...it had been nothing more than ideal preparation for insanity.

I never did adjust from the dismal days of the jungle. It had been tropical hell, a mixture of sounds and silence and sun and rain that caused the polarized behavior of good and evil. It was easy to blame your state of mind, or the cause, or the color of their skins, or the smells of death and mayhem, or Republicans. You could even blame it on dominos. But at some point, your mind went. Schizophrenia is too simple a term for the devolution of the brain's vacillations during tropical combat. To relate my fits-and-starts insane behavior at age 17 doesn't translate into any contemporary description. I was demented and mean at times. I got hurt so bad Purple Hearts meant nothing...The shrieking. The shrieking of human screams, bombs, missiles, 50-caliber bullets, wild parrots. None of it mattered. And all of it mattered. Like everyone, I counted my days. After I was patched up and dropped back into that seething, boiling cauldron of death and the unpredictable, again, I counted my days. Oh yah. Every second, every hour, every day, I counted and prayed. To Christ, to Allah, to Mohammed, to anyone I could conjure up in intervals of silence.

Then an encounter with punji sticks turned my arm and leg into a haven for maggots. My own private Apocalypse Now during half-conscious ferrying across rice paddies and down the Mekong in a helicopter. A different world just a Pan Am flight away. And yet when that Pacific redemption finally came, there were no slaps on the back, no thanks, no job, no nothing. A rest and recuperation lull in idyllic, transitory Honolulu before the storm. Then suddenly the silent unspoken gunfire of the real world hit with the same force as the metal and phosphorous they dropped from B-52s. Arrival in the lower 48 was hauntingly empty. Back in the USA to nothing but memories of behavior tacitly demanding *omerta*. Two years of your worst nightmare, and you had to forget it as if it had been an evil mirage. Adjustments? Fitting in? Types like me remain eternal pariahs.

The tail end of San Francisco's flower child thing, and me with hair no longer than new-mown grass. The Dead, the Airplane, the Fish. It had all happened while I was saving people in straw hats for democracy. The hippies in tie-dyed shirts looked right through me. Long hairs ignored me or glared contemptuously; short hairs found my presence embarrassing. Of course, it's easy to blame maladjustment on the shell shock of war. I felt sorry for myself. But there was no exclusiveness to my self-imposed plight. Many riding the buses to the financial district had the vacant stares of the living dead, as well. It was a time of national search for individual identity.

I smoked a lot of dope and did a bunch of construction jobs during which you either bite your lip or kill someone. Orders on construction sites mirrored those from fresh lieutenants who got fragged. The sounds of pounded nails were like tracer bullets all around you. Months passed in many a bay area fog. There was the occasional woman, the serendipitous conversation, or uncommon sober moment in the marine air during which I thought I could make it. But this different form of survival all seemed no more than a bag of meaningless commercial shit. I had the attitude of an ex-con with the disparate emotions of helplessness and anger. A high school education and two Purple Hearts merely gained me the ability to buy the *Chronicle* and look at the ads for bus boy, laborer, telemarketer, short-order cook.

I found a guy willing to rent me a loft above his garage north of Mill Valley, and before I knew it, years had gone by and I had nothing more to show than a stack of paperback classics, a lot of empties, and a tattoo of a palm tree and a small desert isle on my hip. It didn't seem right that I could slip beyond my 20s with no more direction than sipping a few Coronas in the afternoon sun somewhere in Marin County.

During one of those alcoholic epiphanies when you suddenly feel destiny is turning your way, I decided that Hollywood beckoned. I drove the old beater down Route 1, stopping a lot on majestic Big Sur cliffs to contemplate how life on one side of the Pacific could be so different from the ineluctable melange on the other.

When I rolled into the Los Angeles valley, it became apparent that citizens of Southern California have a different approach to the essentials of life. Where San Franciscans did as much alcohol and drugs as they could while partying in a series of high-ceilinged Victorian rooms overlooking the Bay, those in the City of Angels with an unpublished script, a bit part in a TV series, an audition with a blockbuster producer, or a job delivering mail at Fox Studios, did the same thing and a few lines around somebody more successful's pool. You talked a lot of smack and got laid by doing it. Aids hadn't intruded its gargoyle-like presence yet, and many misguided sexual interactions with almost anyone led to stardom, fame, riches, or a major studio producer's phone number. Instead of a casting couch, it happened in swimming pools, on NBC Burbank's Johnny Carson set, or out in the sand dunes somewhere along Pacific Coast Highway. Free love. Erotic and exotic episodes perennially seducing those pretenders to Hollywood thrones with brief interludes of dim lights in bright surroundings.

These diversions of booze and sex did wonders during my negotiating year after year while increasingly sublimating unspeakable past jungle behavior. And held at bay that interminable wait for the siren of success finally to appear. Of course, for most, she never does. But more alcohol and never-ending sexual encounters convince you that the elusive pot of gold is still just the other side of UCLA, nearby Schwab's Drug Store, or at that chance encounter in one of a thousand Santa Monica, Marina Del Rey, or Malibu bars frequented by kindred lost souls.

You might ask what happened to the rest of the 80s and 90s. And I might just give an unexpected answer akin to a convoluted Joe Eszterhas screenplay. Everyone expects a miracle, and those great expectations can take decades if not a lifetime to dissipate. I don't know how many halcyon moments I had when something I wrote nearly got put onto celluloid or video tape, or some woman I fell for nearly became involved with the dreamer I continued to be rather than the someone who is paid real money for services rendered. Sure, it was close. Close but no cigar. Cipher, and even the new BMW from the studio union job got older. I got older.

It's hard to explain how at some indefinable point in time the need for accomplishment finally is overwhelmed by an admission that it may never happen. How you downsize to a city the size of

Boulder and then how even that progressive metropolis spawning myriad open spaces along with JonBenet Ramsey mysteries and college football scandals grows too crowded, too expensive, and too sophisticated.

The brief depiction of my odyssey doesn't unravel the slow, insipid details of how a Viet Nam vet ends up in a canyon somewhere in northwest New Mexico. Gradually, not suddenly, a return to the simplicity of the vast outdoors began to make more and more sense. Like a summons to the great unknown, when all past friends evolve from the familiar to disappear into the vapors of family life, careers, relocations, or reclusion like my own. One day I said goodbye to my apartment in Boulder and goodbye to all those middle-aged Friday dreamers from the Mediterranean Café. I even gave away a lot of the stuff of life-long collections. Gradually all those time-honored photos and letters you would one day reexamine, faux furnishings you are going to replace when you make it, and other pack-rat flotsam are let go through garage sales and Alcoholics Anonymous store donations or given away to those still collecting with an obliviousness to their gathering storm of detritus. I felt lighter with each giveaway or disposal. Change is life, even if it does threaten the stability of a repetitive existence during which one avoids the acknowledgment that time is finite and no longer to be wasted.

Life within a little more than an hour of Chaco Culture National Historical Park was simple. It could have been complex because of my former brief job as a National Park Service Smokey ranger. But my relocation south of the Canyon was just isolated enough that even the very few who came upon my old mining shack kept their distance. Only a rare adventurer made the serendipitous discovery. And that was only because in parallel fashion such explorers also were seeking a similar mysterious destination offering escape.

New Mexico requires a certain mindset. Maybe my being of part Welsh and possibly Diné descent near a Navajo reservation about the same size as New England had its own atavistic allure. I don't know, and the reasons remain impenetrable, even with a non-military moniker like Kaliber Ristraverdé. It wasn't my real name, but who cares? A lot of *cerveza* has been unable to extract the truth of this strange transmutation.

But there I was with a stack of dog-eared paperbacks, one gallon plastic bottles of distilled water, bags of dried comestibles to cook up over a Coleman stove each day, a contractor's belt with all the tools of rock and gem hunting, and enough self-prescribed anesthesia of 100% agave tequila, Corona 12 packs, and the remnants of a bottle of Myers's rum to drop in cold water in a nearby stream.

Winter would be another matter, as once you've experienced Southern California and the tropics, even dry cold has little appeal. Then I thought I'd probably go to Santa Fe and paint interiors of art galleries or help plaster adobe walls for the rich and famous. At the same time, I might finally put to use all those countless hours of reading into disgorging that one Hollywood script or compelling novel for those who still value the written word. Promises like that, though, particularly given my proclivity for procrastination, have as much chance at completion as keeping the Rio Grande filled in the third millennium. I guess I still would blame my laziness and incapacity for finishing projects on a mind that long ago was blown out of all possible communion with my fellow man.

What happened next seemed out of character in an odyssey becoming increasingly hermetic. I still felt angry enough to split rocks with a miner's hammer; distraught enough with the current political and economic climate to throw a tantrum. I had made self-involvement into a jaded art form. Hope seemed an esoteric concept one finally lets go of after a lifetime of foolish fancy.

I had no idea that soon the three Dupíns, the two Indians, and that quixotic treasure hunter Cantrell would somehow invade my quiet existence. Seep into my life like alcohol and infect far more than my liver. Then how could three women ranging from 9 to 70-something affect someone so intent upon solitude?

It all began on one of those New Mexican spring days when the sun calms your awakening from another nocturnal blast of past torment. I was boiling up some Allegro dark-roasted coffee. Just reading a few lines from Edna St. Vincent-Millay to disabuse the old brain with a non-alcoholic substance fueling one's privately created unreality.

Then there she was. A woman in white muslin blouse and jeans, her necklace of polished turquoise jouncing as she bounded between rocks in the distance. The old approach-avoidance syndrome infected a mind I had been happy to give over to caffeine and Millay. Yet just seeing her somehow piqued a sublimated curiosity for contact with another human being of the opposite gender.

The thing was, I couldn't tell if the woman was going to come toward my cabin or not. Strangers had ventured within range once or twice before. But most of them felt the vibes of remote occupancy and kept their distance. I wasn't sure about this one. All I could see in the distance was a mop of unkempt carrot hair exploded above chin level and skin far too milky to be out in even the late March high-altitude UVRs. She had a ragged white canvas sun hat dangling from one hand and what looked to be a magnifying glass in the other. What in the hell she was doing 50 miles off the interstate lumbering around by herself in Doc Martens?

I figured I'd just go on about my morning habits. After all, it was my place, and she was the intruder. Not really, but that was the way I thought at the time. Maybe the way I've always thought, and that's why I'm alone. But I think you get the drift of how screwed up my attitude about any extra-New Mexican reality had deteriorated. I was happy. Then suddenly I felt as if I needed a drink. In case. In case the woman invaded my space and obtruded the sorts of questions people always asked more out of a weird need for human encounter than for genuine answers. I tried to concentrate on the Saint's poetry, honest I did. The last thing I wanted was to have to make conversation with some female hiker with a jaunty attitude that comes from some Eastern school and a few years as a professor of humanities at a private college. Or she could have been a geologist for all I knew. But somehow I sensed she would have been dressed differently then. Hiking boots and some sort of jacket in case the winds suddenly brooded up the valley. A geologist would be moving with a different intent look, maybe one connoting a predetermined mission for some mineral, and a rock formation lending credence to the search.

This woman appeared more inquisitive, much like she had pulled into a rest stop, then thought a quick hike within a half mile of the parking lot to be just the ticket to getting her legs stretched and mind uncluttered from the whirring of 20-tire juggernauts. She had a look, though, I'll say that. Something inscrutable, more like Marlene Dietrich blowing smoke and daring you to guess her true sexuality. The woman was tall and leggy, yet moved with the alacrity of a Knopf book editor or the founder of a dot.com firm already having made her fortune but unable to decelerate from warp speed. Abruptly she would pick up a stone, look at it with the same brevity of Lovejoy scrutinizing a fake antique, and then toss it back to Mother Earth as if no more than a wadded-up paper airplane. Occasionally she would bound from one rock to another, as if missing a step and cracking her noggin were as likely as being hit by claymore mine pellets in some godforsaken thicket of hanging vines and men so recently dead they still had color in their faces. Glimpses of her side-lit face made her more mysterious than ever. It was almost as if the woman permanently wore the smirk of one who knows she regularly gets checked out by some enchanted observer.

The enchantress didn't wink in my direction, but she tarried here and there as if in a giant pretense of being completely alone, like I normally am off Highway 9.

Just as suddenly, she evaporated. It was as if a mirage had disappeared amidst the sedimentary rocks, and my mandate was to return to Millay and Allegro bean early morning lofty ambitions. I stumbled down a ways from the shack so that I could survey the highway and see if she had left some large four-wheeled beast beached alongside. She must have left it further down the road. Then I settled into a metaphysical ellipse like those the Diné often let evolve during non-conversations. Wait. The mirage will return.

I temporized by picking up a rock I had hoped would be a geode and hit it with the point of my miner's hammer. Unfortunately, it just chipped. It was far less hollow than my dreams of finding that huge array of purple amethyst inside such a sphere. The whole procedure mirrored my life. Constantly hoping for a miracle instead of working a real steady job that provided you mythical American prosperity. It had been more than 50 years since I had popped out to face life in the land of dreams, and that one watershed point of separation from normality never really had made itself apparent. A few thousand drinks, a few hundred books, a few score of missed opportunities, and more than a few fleeting interpersonal relationships with the gender of Venus, and then the unidentifiable slow unobtrusive slide into reclusion.

Very much like the sudden ghost around a corner in a haunted house after someone shouts 'It looks like there's no one here!' there she was. Like an apparition with a nimbus of the morning sun behind a diaphanous dress, suddenly this redheaded succubus was gazing down at me from a rock not far enough away to avoid contact. I knew I would have to say something if she didn't, and for several seconds, like the eternity of waiting for a whistling bomb to land in 'Nam, we remained in place.

Yet there was no way I was to know how this aging vamp as well as her *enfant terrible* daughter, and *grande dame* from Gotham would besiege my tranquility, nor how all of us would further come under the mystical spell of the Anasazi and their Chaco civilization.

# Off Highway 9

(AURORE)

*This is all I need*, I thought to myself. Two hundred miles from Santa Fe, in the middle of a remote canyon in which I believed the serenity of isolation could be found, the pursuit of gems assayed without conflict. And suddenly I'm confronted with some guy who looks like Dennis Hopper just having climbed off his chopper in Easy Rider. I had seen him from a distance. But as I hiked farther up into the canyon, this escapist apparently from a Grateful Dead time warp, thankfully, had disappeared. In fact, when I set out, I believed I could safely spend an hour or so wandering about in hopes of finding some sort of semi-precious gemstone to make my morning. Without encountering any human, jackalope, or other animated oddity of the desert. A brief diversion before my real quest to figure out the meaning of the Chaco civilization. I was wrong.

The whole westward migration to escape the alluring madness of Manhattan and find my sister's killer was probably a sure path to insanity. But if I could do ten things at once in New York, certainly a disparate pair of pursuits in the New Mexican desert seemed reasonable. A dual purpose, a bizarre quest for perhaps a guilty party within the realm of the known. A different sort of search for the Great Western Meaning of Life. Not that the duality made any sense. But then the life I left behind of editing books, with its endless critical scrutiny, conversational duplicity with desperate authors, and merciless excisions, every word of which they held dear, all suddenly seemed vestigial, and to be sublimated by new untold natural surroundings.

Then again, the whole cathartic panoramic scene discovered during my impromptu search had been invaded by some transient character reminiscent of a mix of Kit Carson and Billy the Kid. In the distance and from above I could see him standing in dusty jeans and black T-shirt, arms akimbo, probably wondering just who the hell this woman was having appeared as a potential disruption to his rustic approach to northwest New Mexican life. Unfortunately, I couldn't just summon a First Avenue barman juggling a cocktail shaker to provide me with a Bombay martini. I had decided, anyway, that drinking before noon, whether occurring in the sophisticated East or parched West, was to become a bygone memory. I quickly feigned being unaware of his distant presence and veered off out of sight.

In a nearby arroyo there was quartz in profusion, sometimes a sign that gold is nearby. *Shoo-ure.* Just like those famous mythical mines New Mexicans were always looking for, or the gold rather than turquoise of the Seven Cities of Cibola. They were probably there all right. But if they were readily accessible, why hadn't they been discovered in the past 450 years? Enough Navajos, Apaches, Hopis, and Utes had romped over the area in the 20th Century alone, that any such secret cache should long ago have been revealed.

Still, Kahlo and that despot Katarina were probably treading water in some Santa Fe spa, while I was now alone and unencumbered by a precocious daughter with a propensity for botanical discovery, and a garrulous mother whose didactic deliveries often increased with her daily consumption of alcohol. They were two gems from the Dupín dynasty, ever remaining a bit rough and uncut like a real diamond underfoot northwest of Fort Collins.

My Manhattan short attention span hadn't yet been dispatched. The image of Coyote Bob or whoever he was kept reappearing like threatening thunderheads. I needed to get on with the day's investigations, however vague they might be. Time to get on with the quest. And I knew that to get back to the car through that narrow canyon might well find Mr. Reclusive again within range.

I was just ambling over a ridge with traces of green mineral content here and there, when Coyote Bob suddenly was too close to avoid.

"You won't find much up here," he said as if a geologist decanting an ultimatum to a freshman field tripper. He did manage one of those smiles in which the upper lip may be held down to conceal missing molars.

Nothing came out of my mouth. I didn't know whether to answer, nod, or disagree. I chose a perplexed shrug.

"Nope. I've had my head down, up and down this canyon, hoping to find that one undiscovered rare nugget or rock laced with turquoise," this possibly feral discovery added without gesture. "But all I've found was a little quartz and a lot of sandstone."

The thought occurred to me that his shack might be a laboratory for mail bombs or fertilizer explosives or whatever else someone who finds society off-putting might conjure up with endless time on his hands. Then again, I was a master at hasty judgments, a notion to be overcome by just such a bizarre opportunity.

"The find ruins it anyway," I suddenly found myself responding. "The endless pursuit is more important. I mean, what if one of us did find even the Seven Cities out here in this remote corner of Western nirvana? There'd be a McDonalds here within 30 days, and a Wal-Mart within six months."

"Oh, the minerals and the ancient cities are out there, all right. More silver and turquoise than you can imagine. One of the great secrets of mining and rock hunting keeps anyone from *finding* them, however. The secret is sometimes to share your discoveries, but always to underestimate the size of the find and never to divulge their locations. It's sort of like a hot stock. By the time you hear about it, it's gone—at least at the price to make a killing." He put his mining hammer back into a belt worn and faded as if he had many times made just such discoveries.

I was nonplussed. I didn't want to continue a conversation leading nowhere and risk conveying nervousness to this socially remote canyon man unexpectedly transforming into someone far more dangerous. Then again, he had a certain compelling way about him. Perhaps the sort of masculinity a man develops from self-reliance and self-education. Or maybe like being an orchid thief. He appeared fit, as well, his whole persona perhaps a disguise for something quite different. Like the orchid man.

Anyway, I looked for an exit line from a potential confrontation of inexplicable allure, in contrast to those recent ones with men in Armani suits and half-baked lines borrowed from Billy Crystal. "Any such mineral revelations will have to wait. People are expecting to meet me for dinner in the town of Cuba east of here. I'll have to come back with a burro for the silver ore," I threw over my shoulder as I stumbled quickly down an incline leading back to the highway and an escape from a reality far different than that of sharks devouring Gotham power lunches.

"If you're going to Chaco Canyon," he yelled to get in the last word, "the south road is passable right now."

To say that I had no idea how this man and others, as well as the mysteries of the area, would infect my tranquility, gravely understated just exactly what destiny had in mind. I knew little of the Anasazi, archeo-astronomy, or the mystically analytical powers of my own daughter. But if Deadwood had only the quick and the dead, and New Mexico the slow and alive, I would learn.

# Katarina of the Desert

(KATARINA)
There is something about the West. An intangible, ethereal quality that captivates even an urban pseudo-sophisticate in her 70s such as myself. It's not just the majestic vistas, exotic desert plants, and daily dose of solar infusion. It's more a quality of well being that invades one's delightful self-pity connected to the ongoing battle of light versus darkness. And I mean for someone in her 70s, given the life I have enjoyed, diurnal deterioration of both the physical and mental realms is not easy to accept as an irremediable fate. Yet serendipitous tiny wildflowers, the sun on certain strata of sandstone, or a miniature green lizard's revolving eye are just the sort of desert phenomena that force me to brighten my outlook.

I can say, for instance, that my daily consumption of vodka alleviates a lot of the pain. It isn't easy to accept old age gracefully, you know. One gradually watches beauty change into a disturbing visage quite unimaginable for someone who in her day beside her Steinway in Carnegie Hall often was confused with being a stage actress of marvelous radiance. One who possessed a magnetic allure not only for media and audiences of one to a thousand alike, but also a vamp whose list of eligible bachelors before marriage proved extensive enough to create the consistent illusion of an eternal royalty of physical beauty. I could feel the pulse of audiences as I finished the last note of a Beethoven concerto or a more contemporary musical piece with just the right manipulation of the ivories. Arrivals at late night Manhattan bistros were always made with panache and to an indiscreet reception of admiring stares.

Yet time becomes the one parameter over which there is no control. One may exercise until blue in the face, consume massive quantities of vitamins, antioxidants, and numerous elixirs of repute, only to discover that there is no true fountain of youth. That youthfulness, while it may indeed be reflected by slenderness or by being able to move with alacrity and an exuberant spirit, does nothing to conceal the inexorable deterioration of the physical body. Old age in the United States of America, with its thirst for instant gratification as well as relentless glorification of the beauty and vibrancy of youth, has all the status and allure of poverty. The veneration like that accorded to retired janitorial staff. You are invisible, as one friend so aptly put it. And it is that distressing gradual deterioration alone which I use as an excuse for my drinking.

When I was young, dancing and walking alone dissipated the substantial amounts of alcohol I imbibed. A martini here, a bottle of Châteauneuf-du-Pape there, and I was none the worse for youthful wear. But slowly over time, the eyes begin to reflect such perennial excesses. One's senses become dulled and less responsive. Boundless energy gradually escapes, and with each year, becomes less available throughout fewer and fewer hours of each day. Not a pretty picture, you might say. And if I weren't so assured of my resilient charm and wit and how I can still transform five guests at dinner into mirthful admirers, I might tell you I no longer have redeeming qualities.

Even my late daughter Ashleigh pushed me down a flight of stairs in the same year she met her untimely death. I can't really blame her, though I do. Because I am what some might stereotype a lush. Oh, not in the sense of luxury being a vice I engage. But rather in the nature of the recurrent uttering of some alcohol-induced *faux pas* to just the sort of person not knowing you well enough to ignore the remark. One of the traits of old age, of course, is that you feel you have earned the right to say what you think. To risk offending anyone, anytime, with a cornucopia of esoteric knowledge put forth as unwelcome advice to those who will listen. Like the daily condescension I extend to my granddaughter, Kahlo. A sweeter, kinder child one will never meet. Yet even with all her delightful ingenuous energy, she still must suffer the indignity of continually hearing vodka-fueled deprecating remarks from a grandmother whose opinions are delivered in unpredictable staccato fashion.

Please ignore the entire whining on the dissipation of later years. One of my weaknesses is the ability to whine about anything, when really the lament has nothing to do with anything more than the disappointment of being unable to be noticed for one's youth. Yet I must come to grips with it. After all, a certain level of wisdom and analytical powers contrastingly come with the territory of having spent more than 70 years at urban war. I may be cranky or eccentric in sudden bursts, but I can rarely be accused of being boring. Kahlo, for instance, who is out walking along the Santa Fe River near our Inn at Loretto digs, can attest that even I in my dotage provoke her into torrents of internet investigations and deep delves into books which would prove far more challenging to other prodigies beyond the age of nine.

Soon we will be driving some sort of rented gasoline-powered desert marauder into northwest New Mexico, Kahlo in the hope that she will make discoveries igniting further visions, and I that I shall rekindle a spirit of youth avoided in hotel rooms with a surreptitious bottomless glass of clear unreality. I think that may be her drifting into this southwestern accommodation just now.

"Hi, Kahlo. Discover anything along the empty creek? Interesting transients, newspaper salesmen, or poets spouting modern-day cowboy rhymes?"

Those obsidian eyes merely glanced briefly in my direction. Kahlo rarely says much, even when questioned by relatives. But I shall try again.

"You can afford to practice with me, Kahlo. Imperfection in your speech eventually will disappear in tandem with your developing genius."

"I s-s-s-saw...a vision."

And with that Kahlo quickly slipped into a chair that appears to be upholstered with an Indian blanket, and madly began pushing a computer mouse around in front of a lap-top screen as if her life depended upon an ability to discover the Seven Cities of Cibola before lunch.

"I won't bother you further with my somewhat unorthodox commentary, Kahlo. I'm going to walk to the Aztec Café for a strong espresso before we take off for Grants and the great unknown of northwest New Mexico. You know that my own brand of curiosity has not yet meshed with the world of electronic information. See you soon."

That interchange was around eight o'clock—far too early as you might imagine for someone of my age and residual blood alcohol content to be up and around. Yet concessions must be made when your granddaughter's mother has already taken off on some adventure in these desert surroundings, and the prodigy is soon to be tugging at your sleeve to head out into the Wild West.

It is now around 12:30 p.m. in the remnants of the formerly vibrant railroad depot, Grants. And while I would be content with simply checking into one of those hotels with the Route 66 signs that let you know you are not at the Four Seasons but rather at a run-down abode more appropriate to the 1950s, Kahlo has us watching videos in the colorful NW New Mexico Visitors Center just on the fringe of El Malpais. The name in Spanish, of course, refers to the Badlands, though nothing untoward seemed to be going on in the vicinity on that given cool and bright early spring day.

On the way into the center one merely need look out the massive cathedral front windows to see the sprawling black carpet of desiccated lava beds stretching a great distance to a horizon of red mesas. I'd be just as happy on my Santa Fe hotel balcony in the winter sun, nursing a vodka tonic while gazing out over the sleepy State Capitol and surrounding adobe enclaves and dreaming of unattainable future romance.

Within this enchanted center of the desert world, Kahlo soon was raptly watching a video of Chaco Canyon. She was sitting in a large theater chair of about a hundred in rows of 10, and we had already sat through another video on Acoma. It is an easy way to learn something about the area geologically, anthropologically, and pictorially. The videos ensnare you much like the terrain itself, insidiously destroying any sort of melancholy with an ongoing reminder that life as most know it pales in comparison to southwestern desert phenomena. It's the sort of stuff that has Kahlo fiddling with strands of her hair without missing a single narrative phrase or factual explanation on obscure Eleventh Century places such as Pueblo Bonito or Kin Kletso. Apparently, the Anasazi walked as far as they could into the center of the northwestern New Mexican desert until they discovered a canyon with a dominant single central butte as well as a creek that for at least several centuries provided them with enough water.

There's no telling what impressions Kahlo was receiving and how she was transforming such information into possible visions. We almost took her out of school in New York. Her teachers said that few of the subjects normal children embrace interested her much. But that she could write extensive lists of minerals, plants, and stellar patterns from remote U.S. areas. Kahlo one minute may drift off into a reverie, then the next intently focus upon something at hand, whether the contents of a video or a desert tableau.

A half hour later my granddaughter was churning through the variety of non-fictional as well as fictional portrayals of the history and lore of this vast arid landscape. We were in the tiny book area adjacent to the ranger desk behind which two Smokeys were talking softly in their khaki and olive-green uniforms.

"Gram."

"Yes, dear."

"C-c-could we b-b-buy this?" she stammered, holding up a large coffee table, show-and-tell book called *Chaco, A Cultural Legacy*. Kahlo has a way of staring up at an adult with those imploring eyes that weakens even a tough old nut such as myself. I knew she'd have devoured the contents within, at most, 48 hours. While her stutter may inhibit her ability to talk, she compensates for this inability with a voracious appetite for reading at a high-speed internet rate of absorption.

"Can I answer any questions?" inquired a ranger from underneath his Smokey hat. He looked an Indian of some sort, the striking kind who has pockmarked high cheekbones and straight black ponytail that one sees so much of in the drier and more remote areas of the Four Corners States.

"I think so," I responded, looking down at my granddaughter with the gold book under her arm. "Kahlo, are you sure you want me to buy this book?"

She just nodded. In terms of her speech impediment, the addition of a third unknown party generally further assists her into social purgatory.

"Headed out to Chaco Canyon, are you?" asked the Indian ranger, whose hammered silver nametag read Chichilticalli Aldebaran. "You might be starting out a little late if you are. Of course, you could try going in on the south road. It's a little bumpy and has a few ruts and cattle grates. But it should be dry enough now to make it if you feel adventuresome. My advice would be to wait until you can start early, though. It's a long way in and out. It took the Anasazi more than 800 years to leave," he added with the trace of a raised eyebrow.

Kahlo's face already was expressing disappointment, an expression she quickly attempted to conceal by starting to flip through the pages of her new book.

"Is there another ruins nearby which might be a better choice, given it is already early afternoon?" I inquired, wondering if the mint I had put in my mouth outside was successfully disguising the alcohol vapors discharged from someone habitually under the spell of distilled grain spirits.

A smirk crept across the ranger's face, almost as if there is nothing he enjoys more than revealing a secret location to someone having shown more than a typical tourist's interest.

"Yah," he answered, stepping over so that he was positioned with hands on the glass-topped desk casing right in front of yours truly, Katarina Dupín, late of Manhattan and soon to be resident of Santa Fe. "There are several ruins which are a little off the beaten path and can be missed unless you are familiar with them. But I can tell you how to get there."

He then leaned in a little and glanced back and forth between the diminutive Kahlo, now held spellbound, and the doting grandmother, attired in black cowboy hat, turquoise blouse, and black jeans in an attempt to recapture youth. "I'd meander over to Pueblo Pintado. It's easy to miss if you're not careful," he added, opening a map and turning it 180 degrees to face the pair separated by almost 70 years of disparate knowledge and experience. "But you take 605 13 miles north out of Grants until you come to highway 509. You take that 36 miles to where it T's into highway 9. Then you take that about 10 miles northeast until you can see a water tower. Just beneath it is a sign pointing left to Pueblo Pintado. You drive up a dirt road appearing to lead nowhere, and you'll come upon it. It was an outlier of Chaco in the 1100s, and it has some reasonably well-preserved walls. If you go now, I can almost guarantee you will be entirely on your own there."

Kahlo was starting to squirm, afraid to glance too long at the mysterious Indian ranger, yet not wanting him to think she lacked interest. Knowing her as I do, I can tell you she was much more excited than most nine-year-old's would be at the prospect of touring the remnants of an ancient civilization. There was another reason for her excitement, but anyone else learning about that was to come much later.

To say that much of the West appears as good as spectacular Doug West scenarios doesn't do it justice. It makes you realize that while things may be a bit crowded in Manhattan or Hong Kong, there remains plenty of breathtaking space in the western USA. I mean, after a while the intermittent mesas, meandering gulches, casually lingering cattle, and huge fenceless parched expanses seem almost commonplace. We came upon few other cars. Apparently, most visitors are tied to their children's school year, and other than about two months of summer, much of the high desert terrain sees only the occasional vehicle pass by or rabbit hop off into some sagebrush.

Ranger Aldebaran's instructions were perfect. When we came upon the water tower, it was if he had made a mistake. There were no more than occasional scattered farm buildings in the area. Yet the small sign was there, and within a minute or two we had driven the nondescript dirt road to the Pueblo Pintado outlier.

Kahlo set off from the car with her usual enthusiasm, while I applied sunscreen and repositioned my hat to try to avoid further sunspots that are telltale signs of those of chronological distinction.

Pueblo Pintado definitely possessed an aura. You couldn't actually see Chaco Canyon some 20 miles or so to the northwest. But it felt as if the Anasazi still somehow were influencing your visitation, even though they had departed centuries earlier. The early spring sun illuminated the ruins in a manner that almost gave it life. Everything was as still as a ripple-less pond, though the scant water in the area probably was up in the tower. Only the intermittent sounds of Kahlo's climbing throughout in her limitless curiosity broke the stillness of a thousand years. We were the only humans, the only car, and we saw no wildlife. Kahlo spent several minutes sitting on a wall examining a sandstone-encrusted arrowhead she had discovered on the mineral-strewn sacred ground.

Signs in more than one spot entreated visitors to stay on appointed trails and off out-of-bounds perishable walls. Yet children such as Kahlo cannot usually be restrained as adults might be. She honored the most delicate-looking areas yet scampered here and there amidst stone remnants once having held the denizens of a unique first and second millennium civilization.

I'm not quite as agile as my granddaughter, as you might imagine. Vestigial alcohol content always makes me wary of falls, as well. While nine-year-old's may suffer merely a scraped or sore knee, an elder stateswoman such as myself might break a hip and find herself confined to a hospital bed without the requisite pain-numbing liquid palliatives mediating the acceptance of physical decline.

"Be careful, Kahlo. I know you want to see and touch everything. But the signs make it clear that if everyone repeatedly handles or walks upon stones and masonry, it eventually crumbles and wears down. And that doesn't even mention the destruction from wind, snow, sun, and rain. We must honor the Anasazi. They might have been your ancestors."

Kahlo stopped fondling a piece of quartz she had picked up as if an ancient treasure and stared at her grandmother. You can always tell when her nine-year-old ego has been offended. Silence can be just as effective as words. She hates enforced discipline, the kind that a child with the knowledge of a 40-year-old still must endure.

It wasn't more than several minutes later when I felt I could decipher nothing more from these piles of stones, even considering the certain historic majesty they exuded. A breeze had come up, and I decided that I might just rest in the car rather than upon an off-limits ancient wall of some sort. Maybe even turn the car heat on, probably an anathema to those used to outdoor life on the high plains. In truth, I had a small Starbuck's thermos with my favorite liquid refreshment in it under the seat.

"I'm just going to take a short rest in the car," I threw out to Kahlo, who at that point was staring off to the northwest as her hair swirled round that miniature face. She knew my remark to be duplicitous, aware of my true medicinal beverage needs by this point in any given day. But I knew she wouldn't say anything.

She didn't. Kahlo was turning a piece of quartz over and over in her hand, just when a large raven alit on a wall not far from her. The bird's one eye seemed to revolve to focus upon my granddaughter, and she too permitted just the slightest diversion of her glance to acknowledge the raven's presence. Twice it cawed as if demanding she pay attention, much like Poe's raven's 'Nevermore.' Yet Kahlo's glance remained affixed in a northwesterly direction.

Meanwhile I reached the rental car and slipped into the driver's seat for a nip. A gust of wind caused the vehicle to sway. A minute later I turned on the ignition and depressed the accelerator. The car merely sounded like one of those nearly battery-dead junkers of someone in a film trying to flee a mass murderer. After several more attempts I decided that the battery might run down and desisted.

In the distance Kahlo and the bird both seemed to be gazing out over the dry rolling plain. She obviously had heard that I had been unable to get the car started. But when a nine-year-old prodigy is in the process of physical as well as mental discovery, there is little to be done by anyone who believes in the curiosity and optimism of youth.

I debated on what my next move should be. Trying to start the car might wear down the battery. Not doing so meant two non-desert dwellers possibly remaining at unpopulated ruins in the middle of nowhere as dusk descended upon them. The light began to fade, illuminating the Pueblo Pintado ruins and my granddaughter with the sort of side-lit aura one often sees in television travel ads.

Finally, I decided I might prevail upon her to use her cell phone to summon automobile help of some sort. When I had walked back to her fixed position alongside the north wall of the ruins, Kahlo still appeared to be concentrating on what only she alone can envision.

"Kahlo, can you see anything unusual in the distance?"

She made no reply, still lost in her reverie.

"Kahlo?"

She began to fiddle with a lock of hair finally having subsided during a calm, a sign that she might be about to say something.

"S-s-s-s-Seven Cities," she suddenly blurted.

"What about them?" I returned, unsure whether she was referring to the Seven Cities of Cibola or something else.

"In the d-d-d-diary, l-l-l-leagues and Hawikuh are confusing p-p-p—people."

I hadn't a clue what she was talking about. But before I could try and extract more from my precocious descendent, an old beat-up Ford truck pulled up alongside our car perhaps a few rabbit holes away. Out slowly climbed an elderly Indian who gave the impression that his destination was well known. He stopped briefly to look over at the two of us, then began to walk toward the ruins fence entrance. There was something about his white ponytail portraying a dignity of wisdom and an ability to rescue two females possibly in distress.

# Ketl Drives to Cuba

(KETL)

What in the name of Geronimo is that old woman doing sitting in her car? I asked myself. When you live in a hogan and an attached tipi on the Diné reservation, you see a lot of strange things. And what you see often involves white folks out trying to discover just what it is we Navajos do on our vast property.

I don't do a lot at my age. At least the sort of things I did when I was a sixteen-year-old who lied about his age to enlist in the U. S. Army as a code talker back in the early 40s. Now I content myself with watching and listening. That may seem a little simplistic. But there is a lot to be said for sitting and listening to some of the young Diné tribal members drumming. The sounds of prey being put out of its misery by a cunning coyote as you gaze up at a crescent moon. Or watching the shadows climb up a nearby red mesa wall in late afternoon. You've pretty much seen it all before anyway, when you've lived in northwest New Mexico as long as I have. I'm too young to have attacked stagecoaches full of arriving white settlers, and too old to spend time learning computer skills that change faster than the patterns of light in the Land of Enchantment.

I had driven my old truck to the ruins of Pueblo Pintado to do nothing more than meditate as the sun went down. To watch the fiery globe's illumination on the ancient stone walls, and to listen to the large raven who sometimes comes and caws as if we have been related for years. Edgar Alan Poe, one of the Anglo writers I have read, seemed to put great stock in a raven as an omen. He was probably right. Usually, I can detect when the bird is trying to convey something to me.

In fact, I think I see him sitting on that wall not far from a little girl who looks like she could be a Pueblo. Then again, she must be with the old white woman staring at me from her car window. It occurred to me that as much as I had planned on being alone at Pueblo Pintado, I had company, even if it was a visiting paleface and a child who might be Native American.

"Afternoon," I said in my usual fashion when I don't wish to be rude to those you cannot ignore when you come upon them in remote places.

"Do you live around here?" the old woman who had rolled down her window asked.

I could vaguely smell alcohol of some sort—probably vodka because it has the least aroma. There was no point to telling her that alcohol is not permitted on Navajo reservations since many of the Diné have some of their own purchased from off the Reservation, anyway. And this was near the edge of *Dinétah* limits. It's kind of like the U. S. Army: don't ask, don't tell.

"Not far," I replied, not stopping in fear of being held in conversational ransom by someone unused to apparently empty and silent natural surroundings. As I continued walking, I could hear her trying to get her rental car started. You could tell by the sound of the starter than the chances weren't good. Normally I have jumper cables in my truck, but I'd lent them to a nephew of mine who works as a ranger at the Visitor Center in Grants.

I got about halfway to the gate into the ruins grounds that probably shouldn't have any fencing, when I decided that she was going to totally deaden her battery if she made one more attempt. I walked back with a solemnity I felt appropriate to what she thought an aging Indian should possess.

"Maybe you flooded it," I said as I came to a stop near her car window.

"I haven't a clue about cars," she answered. "Do you think it will still start?"

She popped the hood as if I were a mechanic, so I had a quick look. I bent a little this way and that to feign I could shed additional light on the matter after this cursory examination of her rental car engine. "Probably not."

The old woman looked at me like I was a bearer of bad tidings to be held accountable. I slammed the hood shut and shook my head a little bit to extend at least a shred of sympathy.

"We need to be in Cuba by six to have dinner with my daughter," she said as if it was the sort of statement implying responsibility to a rescuer.

"I wasn't going that way," I casually dropped while adjusting my faded jeans and belt to allow the remark to set in. "But I could take you up there, and you could come back with a tow truck and jumper cables."

She seemed to be weighing the thought of riding 60 miles with an unknown Indian, against waiting in a desolate location near sunset to see if anyone else happened by.

"You could wait and hope someone comes along with cables," I added with what I hoped to be a tone of resident knowledge. "But at this time of year, you might end up spending the night in your car. If you have a cell phone, I'd suggest calling a towing service in Grants or Cuba. Then again, with the sun going down soon, I doubt if they'd come out until tomorrow morning."

The grey-haired one just rolled her eyes. "That's my granddaughter up there. I don't think we'd do well spending the night in a car out here," she replied, as if she meant that they'd be spending the night in Indian Territory.

"I'm only going to stay for a half hour or so. I'm going up to sit in the pueblo ruins and watch the sunset. After that, if you want, I can give you and your granddaughter a ride into Cuba."

She smiled while staring at me, as if contemplating native assistance. There was no point in waiting for her to say something. She knew where I'd be, and I knew where she'd be. It was up to her whether to risk being alone with an Indian.

I made my way up to the ruins, trying to keep as much distance from the little girl as possible. She looked a Pueblo, as I said earlier. But I knew the old white woman would get anxious if I got too close. So I sat on the ground near a west wall and discreetly lit up, out of their sight. I can't drink alcohol, you see, even though most of those of European descent probably think every Indian is a drunk. In fact, there are signs everywhere in New Mexico about drinking and driving. A lot of Indians do drink and drive. Once they were warriors and squaws living a simple life in harmony with their environment. Now many of them work in casinos, sell jewelry, or perform, the focus being money, the great anathema to the spirit of our ancestors. Drinking clouds the need to escape from the white man's ways.

I still try to lead a simple life. It doesn't cost much when you're my age. You can't drink, you can't do much to accommodate the opposite gender, and you can't move about for as many miles as you once did. I'm lucky to be alive. After World War II I worked in a uranium mine up near Shiprock. People didn't know much about radiation in those days. Or at least they didn't care if their workers—many Pueblos, Apaches and Diné such as me—were exposed to the harmful invisible rays from the mines. Five of my friends died of cancer. But I relied upon a diet of cruciform and root vegetables as well as daily intake of tribal herbal remedies that my father had told me about.

I'm still here, though I went through a rough patch after I quit mining and became a waiter in a Santa Fe Chief dining car. Subservience is not my inclination. But I loved riding the rails with the silver settings and damask tablecloths, and I made pretty good tips and saw a lot of the country out the windows in passing. The display car they have at the Sacramento Railroad Museum is a pretty good rendition of what I walked up and down daily.

All that was long ago, and those fabled trains, just like traditional Native American life, went the way of dinosaurs too slow for modern times. The good news is that all those years earned me a nice social security check, and thanks to the same government that stole a lot of our Four Corners lands, I'm now provided with the means to smoke a bit and reflect upon sunsets.

On many a day I drive to Anasazi ruins in the area and take in the wonders of the light, the sounds, and the birds, lizards, rabbits, and other creatures I glimpse in the yellowish or orangish hues of dusk. At Pintado I found myself drifting into a contemplation of just how differently the distorted rays of the late afternoon sun illuminate the surroundings no matter how many times you gaze out across the desert, or how many pilgrimages you make over the years.

Then unexpectedly the little girl appeared from around the corner of the wall not much more than a jackalope length away. Her coming upon me sitting cross-legged startled her, but she quickly regained her composure as if having discovered nothing unusual. I was watching her examine rocks she was picking up like I was no more than a prickly pear cactus, when it came to me that this little girl has a quality like one I have, which is the ability to perceive things others don't. There was something in her eyes that told me, though we had only briefly made contact. Often when I meditate, things come to me that I can't explain. Not exactly clairvoyance, but very close to it.

"What does that arrowhead tell you?" I asked as she absent-mindedly turned over an encrusted flint piece she had found somewhere nearby.

She looked up at me, and our eyes met again for only a split second before she diverted her glance out to the horizon and then down to the sacred ground around us. Her mouth opened, but nothing came out.

"I know," I began to reassure her. "You are caught between two worlds, and it is just as hard to tell anyone about it as to decipher what you perceive, am I right?"

Again, she glanced my way and picked up another stone. Then she hesitantly nodded in agreement. Her eyes conveyed perception you rarely see in a child. And I knew from just this cursory encounter, that I had met a kindred spirit. I had no idea from which tribe she had come, but it was a good guess she was adopted, and probably from some Pueblo tribe. That she wanted to say something was obvious, yet at the same time, I knew the ability to do so to a stranger such as myself was hard.

"Your grandmother can't seem to get your car started," I said to change the subject and relieve the pressure upon her to talk. "I told her I was just going to sit and watch the sunset, and then if she wanted, I could give you a ride into Cuba. I hope I didn't interrupt your investigations. Sometimes when a stranger comes upon me in the ruins, I know I find it invasive." I said this to create an opportunity for the little girl to avoid dialogue beyond her grasp, and I further conveyed this by closing my eyes and raising my face toward the sun. I heard her footsteps dissolve away as she disappeared round the corner.

It was only a minute or so later when I heard the approach of footsteps again. By peeking with one eye, I could see her mouth open several times as she continued to scrutinize a piece of sandstone in her hand. But nothing came out.

"Can you ever s-s-see cities?" she was finally able to stutter while fiddling with a lock of her hair.

"Sometimes," I answered without opening my eyes or turning toward her. In the manner of a Diné, I waited to continue. "But more often I see spirits of friends and relatives who have departed the Earth."

"I see c-c-c-cities," she stammered while beginning again to distance herself from me. "But I c-c-can't—"

And those were her last words. I could tell the polarized forces of wishing to share, and of having to do so with a stranger, had enabled her to begin, but not to complete an explanation of what she had seen. Many times, I too had wanted to share visions with others yet found myself tongue-tied. But this particular ellipse didn't matter, especially since I am used to it among my fellow Navajo. I had a premonition she and I would talk again in the future, though I doubted if it would be on the ride into Cuba.

The old woman and child, introduced as Katarina and her granddaughter Kahlo, were uncomfortable during our journey into Cuba. The gray-haired one was gripping my rusted Ford truck door like we might at any moment be making a sharp right-hand turn. She kept her other hand in her lap and eyes fixed upon the darkening horizon. There wasn't much light left at that time in spring, and it seemed like the more the orange rays of the sun evaporated, the more nervous she was getting.

Sitting between us two elders, the girl named Kahlo alternately fiddled with a lock of her hair and several arrowheads and rocks she had taken from the Pueblo Pintado. Occasionally she would glance at her grandmother or me. And sometimes her lips would move, as she looked out through my cracked front windshield. The three of us jounced amidst the squeaks and bounces of the old truck, each lost in our own private thoughts. Earlier when *La Vieja* had asked my name, I had only told her Ketl, leaving off the Lizhiní-Shá part which means 'black sun.' They didn't need to know any more than the name Ketl because in less than an hour the three of us would part company.

"Kahlo sometimes sees things others don't," the old woman suddenly blurted as we rounded a corner near a large sandstone outcropping, which cast a long shadow. I could have revealed my own inclination to see things during this strange odyssey, but atavistic Diné heritage kept my tongue silent.

"It's almost like a curse, because when she has chosen to talk about what she sees, there is a magnetic attraction to quizzing her more and more, which she finds unnerving," the old woman prattled on as if her granddaughter wasn't even there. "Once in a while Kahlo will find someone to whom she can speak about her visions. But usually that brain of hers just keeps ticking over and I, for one, have no idea what's going on in there."

All the while the little girl continued to fumble with the rocks in her hand, replacing them in her pocket, taking them out again, playing with that long jet-black hair. Halfway to Cuba or so, I figured if I were to reveal a little of my own clairvoyance, maybe it would ease the tension of two city folks locked inside a vehicle with an Indian who doesn't say enough when the mood doesn't strike him.

"Sometimes at Twin Angels, or Acoma, or Chaco, visions come to me too," I said without looking at either of them. "What I see can be a blessing or a curse. But most of the time, I see no more than missing relatives and friends, rather than anything which reveals some mysterious history of the southwest. That same raven, for instance, that was perched on the wall near your granddaughter at Pueblo Pintado. Sometimes when it caws, it's as if it has descended from the Anasazis."

The old woman let go of the door handle. I could tell my remark was like an elixir for relaxation. Suddenly the Indian driver had a dimension with which both could identify. The little girl looked up at me, but just when she did, the truck went over a dip in the road, and the jarring tossed her up enough that she looked back out at the desert and distant mesas. I sensed Grandmother Katarina wanted to learn more about my own ability to see things others don't. But that tangible barrier between cultures made us much like three people in a canoe who must get to the other side of a river, but don't necessarily take to their traveling companions. The trip continued in silence.

It couldn't have been more than 20 minutes later, with the afternoon breezes having picked up, judging by a couple of plastic bags caught on a fence we passed, that our journey to Cuba was just about over. None of the three of us was in company of choice, though I'd have to say I might have gotten the little girl Kahlo to say far more than her grandmother could imagine if the two of us had been alone. And I knew that particularly the old woman would be relieved to see the first buildings of Cuba as a sign that her granddaughter and she both were going to exit my truck alive. She was very polite. It's just that an Indian with my wizened and tanned face, no matter what I say, often seems to daunt *belagaana* visitors forced by circumstances to say something to me. Particularly in remote spots like Pintado, where for all they know, I might try to scalp them or rob them of valuable plastic or other urban items. I'm harmless, of course, and old age has even brought out additional philanthropic concerns I didn't think I'd ever have in me. But it's the sort of notion Diné don't talk about.

"Would you like to join us for dinner at Casa Blanca?" the old woman asked as she readjusted her black gaucho hat upon her head. "We'd be happy to repay your kindness by buying you dinner."

I had the feeling that even if I had been able to accept, I would have been more a novelty than a true member of their party of three plus one. That's not the sort of invitation I'm comfortable with. When I have to spend time with more than one person other than relatives, I usually find myself wishing I was elsewhere. Now the old woman and her daughter certainly were different than most of the tourists I had met in the area over the years. But dinner with three city folks, one of whom rarely talks, and at least one other who probably wouldn't stop, even though I love Mexican food, wasn't on my low-key agenda. Besides, I had to get back to my hogan because my nephew, Chichilticalli, was probably going to be waiting there with the jumper cables I had lent him. He seldom drinks on his own. But I would pour him a shot of a special *Reposada* tequila I keep there for him. Then after I lit up my own form of escape, the two of us would talk a little at a time of the women of the Visitor Center and other tall tales.

Cuba is like a hundred other towns in New Mexico. It's not nearly as junky as Farmington in terms of those huge roadside fast food franchise signs. But it does have that mix of adobe, one-story homes, and no rhyme nor reason to business and residential areas surrounded by a lot of dust and occasional empty French fries bags and paper drink cups that remind you that you have returned from the great expanses of the desert to urban life of questionable value.

"This will be just fine," Katarina said as I pulled my truck over before the adobe walls of Casa Blanca right on highway 550. "We can't thank you enough, can we Kahlo," she added as she began to pull her granddaughter from the front seat. "You sure you won't join us for dinner?"

"The ride was no problem. But I have to get back home, because my nephew will probably be there waiting," I answered with a certain finality, since my engine was still running. "I hope you find a place in Santa Fe."

Kahlo hadn't let go of the door, even though Grandmother Katarina was doing her best to detach the young one with visionary powers from my Ford.

"Seven," the young girl threw out before a last-minute magnetic spell had been interrupted by her grandmother. Oddly, I figured she was talking about the cities many believe were no more than mythical, but which Kahlo and I undoubtedly believe still exist.

"There are seven cities," she began without stammering and before disappearing into the adobe confines of a good place for burritos with 'Christmas' red and green chilé sauce, "but not the ones in the Zuni pueblo."

# The Radon

(QUIVIRA)

I've always been a sucker for easy money. Scams, betting, Ponzi schemes, lotteries, and even non-card-sharping poker were siren-like adventures that appealed to me more than writing about football. Which is what my last legit job was in New York. Writing about all those heavyweights in the NFL. I was a hack, though, and what I really liked with the passion of a Buccaneers defensive secondary hit man was gambling. Particularly on college games. You opened the paper, examined the lines on every collegiate contest, and chose four or five you knew were dreamt up by some drunken sportswriter in a bar late on a night when he had first downed six gin-and-tonics. If you were good—and I was—you could augment any real-world salary with weekly dividends.

Eventually, however, every distorted mind reaches that one point in life when you are tired of the whole rat race. Not tired of making money. Tired of the process and all the unreasonable behavior associated with it. Burned out in Manhattan, was what I was. I knew that if I used one more bit of hyperbole about so-and-so's lateral movement dexterity, or had to distill just one more boring defensive game into a scintillating story of hearts of oak, I was going to go down on a combination of cocktails, cocaine, and high-maintenance women. It was time for a change, and I knew it. Time to get the hell out of a world where younger guys can write circles around you and party twice as hard. Time to leave the high-velocity stuff and related perks before you implode from nasty habits. And I was a master of the kind of indulgences that appear to be routine, with the necessity of spending the money you made and combating the sense that maybe there were more important things on the planet than a bunch of 300-pound guys beating the hell out of one another on astro-turf.

That's how I first heard of the Mogollon Cross. I was in some bar in New Orleans during a Giants/Saints game weekend, and I was feeling like I might even get to like filigreed iron and Dixieland music. The whole evening seemed to be waxing in a way that makes a visitor feel like a rich pirate in the Barataria bayous. And I don't even know how it was that I overheard two guys talking about treasure and how difficult the laws were to keep exploration legitimate. The pair had the swarthy skin of roofers who had been out in the sun too long, and each looked like someone you wouldn't want to confront over a political argument. Somehow, I got into their conversation without making them too defensive, probably because they weren't about to reveal anything about specific undersea valuables they were after.

I told them I was going to be driving out into the Southwest, probably at first to visit my sister in Durango, Colorado, but then to find something else to occupy a mind addicted to financially irresponsible challenges. And I made it clear that much of my time had been spent in the kinds of monetary adventure for those who were used to circumventing normal commerce. I didn't need to specify the nature of my past expeditions. They knew that I hadn't had to travel to put my thirst for financial reward into action. They also realized I was moving on, and that became a big part of their willingness to share any information, especially since I had no interest in underwater treasure.

The Seven Cities of Cibola came up, and the three of us had a good laugh about Vasquez de Coronado and how the Indians sent him all the way to Kansas. In fact, that's how I got my first name, Quivira. It's probably the most fruitless destination anyone's ever reached. But my mother liked the sound of the word, even so, and thus one of the Cantrells suddenly became monikered after the misguided barren plains turnaround point of a Spanish explorer.

The whole New Orleans bar evening ended amicably, which is good, because I have the sort of German/Irish temper that can flare up exponentially when the alcohol in me exceeds a certain level. And that doesn't mention the two of them, either of whom looked like a cutthroat or brigand from a Johnny Depp pirate movie.

Durango's the sort of town that mirrors the canyon it sits in. It still has that Western feel to it, the aura of honky-tonk piano bordellos and ranchers sophisticated enough to use a cell phone as well as a lariat. But not much sun comes into the canyon, at least in March, and the rock walls in daylight seem kind of confining. I didn't really want to visit my sister, who along with her psychologist husband teaches at Fort Lewis. Not that the campus isn't beautiful and the beer cold down on Main Street, but more that my sister has always considered me the outlaw black sheep of the family, and she's right. Still, their ranch a few miles southeast of town was a place to clear the cobwebs after a couple of lame attempts at chatting up women half my age from the Fort, and drinking more than enough to forget any such failures.

I got out of Durango, as I said, the kind of town in which someone of my nature probably would find trouble if he stayed longer than three days. I escaped without assault and battery on my sister's husband. He and I got into it over some sort of psychological bullshit he had attributed to my behavior. Neither of us had any warning. It was just the kind of squabble I'm always encountering without really trying. It's my nature, I suppose. That and the fact that I'm big. Certain people piss me off without doing or saying anything egregious. And there can be no doubt that if I have downed a few rum and tonics or shots of tequila, Dr. Jekyll's got nothing on me. The whole transformation can get ugly. Fortunately for the two of us, however, I ignored the invasive fact that suddenly I wanted to smash his chiseled face in, yet backed off before any real fireworks started.

One good thing was that I had left New York in my old Pontiac convertible with a considerable amount of cash. Most of it I had made playing the spreads on college games, but also because I had lived in a rent control apartment on the Upper West Side in Manhattan. I had saved a substantial wad that I could draw upon should I need to do so to successfully complete my combo find-myself-out-West and now treasure hunt.

A bad sign was that the cobalt blue Pontiac with the white top often attracts highway patrol buzzards like the roadrunner exceeding the limit in Yosemite Pete cartoons. I was pulled over more than once for some trumped up reason or another, but then finally in southern Colorado I got nicked for 75 in a 55. Cops love out-of-state plates. You know the drill. The speed limit had been 65 and suddenly when you're just trying to get into enjoying the rustic settings alongside the road, it has turned to 55. You miss the sign and don't make the adjustment, so a CHP helps you make a bigger adjustment to your bank account. I have to be careful over their questions, too. Not that I have anything to hide. But rather because of those inquiries they often make that seem overly obvious to the point that you get super-annoyed without much provocation. It was a female cop, however, and I concentrated on discreetly perving her well filled out starched uniform shirt. I even answered all the questions with a smile. The trouble is, with my size and the look of my car, any kind of law enforcement officer often gets suspicious. Luckily for me, before she answered a summons on a walky-talky attached to her belt, she handed me the ticket, and said, "Drive safely," before I had any sort of change in blood pressure. Man, she was good looking.

The original idea was to use my sister's place as a jumping off point to Southwestern nirvana. Just to see what develops in the desert States of New Mexico and Arizona. I had always loved John Ford/John Wayne movies, those sharply contrasted, black-and-white gems with a passel of cumulus clouds threatening, buttes intermittently giving a majesty to the colorful but parched expanses, and stagecoaches being the primary vehicles escorting nasty white folks among the wild Indians. Something about the young Wayne sitting on his horse with a whole load of Apaches up on the ridge and knowing you were in for some rollicking volleys of arrows and bullets. Trouble is only bad if you don't have the stomach for it. Otherwise as a journey it has a certain magnetism just like professional football. You can get hurt, but if you can play the game successfully, it's a rush like no other.

So, there I was piloting the cobalt beast through the thankfully warm March air, the top down, but my spirits up. I'm kind of a loner, anyway, though I have been married twice, and being out on those desolate roads to nowhere between spectacular mesas and buttes on top of which they drop four-wheel drives during TV commercials was just the sort of tonic I needed. I didn't even have a tape recorder or notebook with me. It was just me and the Western elements, more cathartic than your favorite drink in your favorite bar or restaurant at your favorite beach resort with the sun going down and an adventuresome attitude.

I had no plan. I had examined an atlas over cocktails in a Durango bar featuring a strangely relaxing Byzantine interior and traditionally nubile waitresses. But then decided upon nothing more than exploring Monument Valley as if scouting locations for my next Ford movie. There is just no easy description of how it feels to have your arm on American vehicle steel as you gaze out over a brown, orange, and yellow landscape still untarnished by fast-food chains and giant box stores. The gloam is like no other. Just when the sun is going down, it's as if you have privately discovered your own soul. I had even turned off the kind of top-40 country hits you find are your only radio station options in the still unfenced areas of wide-open spaces. Just wishing the day and drive could go on forever, each panorama more mesmerizing than a 70-yard touchdown pass in slow-motion video replay.

It was strange then, after I had driven a scenic loop of Monument Valley and continued south for considerably more than 150 parched miles, that I came upon what looked to be a few outbuildings of a ranch, and not far beyond them a place that was going to tear my mind up as to what's socially irresponsible without urban surroundings.

It was a bar like no other. I had just exited a reservation as large as all New England where alcohol is illegal. So it was with a sense of relief that somewhere near Geronimo a giant neon sign across the front like the old '50s motel roadside numbers simply blared: RADON BAR. Beside it was a margarita glass also lit up in fluorescent green, these electric attractions framed by a halo of ambient light to create an aura of invitation for suckers like me with a thirst for spirits both liquid and human. A whole lot of dusty flatbed trucks and four-wheel monsters were badly parked off to one side and in front of the place. As I turned into the lot, I could hear the original *I Only Have Eyes for You* coming from a jukebox, and suddenly it came to me that this was the type of place where you could have a balls-to-the-wall good time.

During the delay while I beached the old Pontiac in the lot and ambled inside, the music had changed to some country swing band melody. A few guys who looked like cowboys no longer with the slender waist of a James Dean were two-stepping with ladies in tight jeans and fringed blouses. All the crossed pine beams above gave the place the feel of a Yellowstone lodge, one that could be saved from burning down, though, by the spray of beer, if necessary. The bar was long enough that sliding a cold frosty one from one end to the other would require sober dexterity, and a strange mix of Western sorts along this distressed pine resting place were slugging drinks and shots or further establishing the mythology of the place. The whole cavernous room was lit up by every conceivable tequila and beer sign from Corona to Cuervo Gold, with the biggest halo coming from a huge old Wurlitzer juke box at one end of a dance floor crowded with the sort of folks who find desert living addictive. There were very few seats left at the bar.

I ordered a Myers's rum and tonic, specifying the three pieces of lime I once experienced in a concoction called 'Bob's drink,' in a bar called the Mediterranean in Boulder, Colorado. The bartender looked at me like I had just driven over from a UFO in White Sands. I smiled, unwilling to begin what promised to be an interesting evening with a contretemps at its inception. The place was rockin' and I needed at least three drinks to feel that I belonged in company with those who appreciated the great outdoors far more than urban exhaust fumes and skyscraper office space.

It took me an entire cocktail to quit looking in the giant antique mirror above the bar at myself and the reflections of dancers spinning behind me. When I started on a second liquid elixir, I finally began to get rid of the remnants of that ringing in the ears you endure from hours behind the wheel in an open car. It had been a little too chilly to have the top down, but I've never been the type to let weather get in the way of my favorite interaction with nature. So what if my face and left arm were wind-burned? They were minor afflictions evaporating with the effects of medicinal beverages and jukebox tunes varying from rock 'n' roll to Nashville good-old-boy stuff.

Looking too closely at those around you in a bar like this usually gives me the feeling that coming from an urban existence is all but meaningless in a place for those from open ranges where water is more valuable than tax-free bonds or Brooks Brothers ties. There was no doubt about it: getting drunk was the only way for someone who has never ridden a horse or thrown a lariat to find these citizens transformed into appealing characters.

The guy next to me, for instance, had that unique quality of minding his own business. His very being there proved that attitudes weren't necessarily red necked everywhere in the Wild West, as more than likely he was a Navajo or other Indian no longer riding bareback round the Four Corners expanses. He had a black ponytail and pockmarked face, but instead of a cowboy hat, he was wearing a baseball cap with a New Mexico flag logo on the front. The Indian sipped his beer and seemed content to let the day dissipate without benefit of talking to some alcohol-fueled stranger with attitude. But being the curious sort that I am, I was about to invade his tranquil existence.

It didn't happen right away. You see, having been a sportswriter for much of my life meant that I'd learned to enjoy watching almost anything involving action and whirling colors. The music never disappointed, nor did the cowboys and cowgirls and Native Americans twirling around in the white man's version of Western dance. The more rum drinks I had, the more I found the whole scene intoxicating.

All the while the Indian next to me calmly sipped his mug of beer. He might have adjusted his baseball cap once, but there seemed to be a good chance of the two of us spending several hours right next to each other without ever speaking. And although alcohol can be blamed for anything from domestic altercations to premature aging, it also does wonders for the inhibitions of writers and other introverted sorts who remain tongue-tied until their blood-alcohol level reaches a certain threshold.

"Is this place always like this during the week?" I asked the Indian, without much more than a glance in his direction.

"This is only the second time I've been here. But from what I hear from friends, this is a calm night."

"Excuse me for asking, but I couldn't help but notice that the entire time I've been sitting here, I think you've still been nursing the same beer."

He just nodded to agree.

"If you're short of money, I'll spot you one."

The Indian slowly turned and looked at me with just the edge of one side of his mouth curling into a smile. "I've got money. But I rarely drink more than one or two beers." I got the impression that's all his Native American medicine man would allow. Maybe he was weighing me up before saying anything much. He just sat there looking straight ahead before finally adding: "Sometimes I have a shot of tequila at my uncle's place, but I don't drink much anymore."

"Bad for the health?" I asked.

"If I worried about my health, I'd have been dead long ago. I smoke."

"Yah, cigarettes are probably no worse than alcohol."

He smiled again, then took another sip of his beer. "Who said anything about cigarettes?"

It was the kind of answer a writer likes: indirect, leaving you with a conclusion to be conjured up. Now that he mentioned it, his pupils were dilated. Inwardly I shook my head slightly while deducing one man's rum and tonic is another's doobie.

"It's probably cheaper in the long run."

"No hangover."

Now you hate to go with the stereotype of Indians not saying much, but this Native American's eyes and inflections told a different story. There definitely was a lot more under that baseball cap than he was revealing. I can't say why, but maybe my sports reporter mentality wanted to know more about a man from a culture completely foreign to me. Yah, O.K., so I was stereotyping him. But he did look the part of a contemporary Indian. And the look was reinforced by his apparent taciturn manner. Still, people like the Western citizen on the barstool next to me are always seen as opportunities when you've got the jaundiced brain of a pundit. It's as if they possess some amazing exposition of life that becomes your destiny to try and free up. That sounds nothing more than a load of crap, but maybe the rum was talking.

"Do you live on the Navajo reservation?"

"Nope," he answered in deadpan fashion. "I live in Grants."

"That's a long way from here."

"Yah. You might call this a recon trip."

"What are you reconnoitering?"

"Mm... I work at the Visitor Center just south of Grants, and they wanted me to check out some lodging recommendations in this area. We get a lot of tourists through asking our advice on the whole Four Corners area, which they think extends all the way to Phoenix."

"They think it's just your back yard."

He snorted a laugh which was its own answer. "Most of the people we get into the Center think they can see the entire area between Texas and California in two or three days. It's our job to try to convey there's more than one Saguaro cactus in the West or than standing on the South Rim of the Grand Canyon."

# Shadow Boxing

(CHICHILTICALLI)

Just one look told me the guy next to me was going to be trouble. We're not talking Milagro beanfield kind of trouble, just because he's Anglo and I'm a Zuni. It's more his coldly impersonal survey of the Radon shitkicker bar telegraphed that he didn't care what anyone thought of him. He was big, pasty-faced, and imposing. Which might do well in a Boston bar, but not quite as well with the kind of nightriders who cruise out of Farmington and other northwest New Mexican pueblos and barrios. He made an effort with me, too, and it was apparent that he had the same sort of big-hearted adventuresome spirit of Buffalo Bill or Billy the Kid.

The trouble is, not all the Native Americans and Hispanics in this area are as tolerant as I am of gringo invaders. They resent them. They even resent me because I was a Rhodes Scholar who once read astronomy at Oxford. When you have been raised in the Zuni pueblo, but somehow developed the ability through reading as a teenager to test like a rich white kid from Phoenix, you are somewhat of a pariah among your own people, but still a dark-skinned Indian to those of European descent. I didn't even play football for the Zuni Thunderbirds in high school. But I was one of the lucky ones who read a lot of the white man's stuff, a strange habit that got me from the red mesas of the Zuni Pueblo to the muddy heaths of England.

That's why I mind my own business in a bar like this. Not because I want to be mistakenly identified as the quiet, stereotyped Native American. But rather because I know when a lot of Anglos hear how I really converse, they don't know how to deal with me. It confuses them. They want the stone-faced cigar store Indian from the movies who says little, moves slowly, and projects the deferential behavior of a butler. That's not me, though I can be pretty quiet.

Then again, the stereotype is me when I'm in a white man's bar where simply to look once at some redneck's girlfriend has gotten me into deep trouble before. Well, maybe not too deep so far. Because I did some boxing as a Golden Gloves lightweight, I've been able to hold my own against much bigger dudes. Luckily, I haven't yet been knifed or shot. The trouble with bars like the Radon, is you never know exactly who you're dealing with when blood pressures start to rise, or the odd distasteful remark has been made to someone with a short fuse and a tattoo of a skull on the inside of his forearm.

Anyway, I decided it was best if I just kept my responses to a minimum with the curious big guy next to me. It wasn't just that he was pounding the rum and tonics like they were cups of water at a desert oasis, but more that his face was a road map with enough indentations, scarring, and discolorations to convey that you didn't want to provoke him—even in Indian Territory. His scrutiny of anyone and anything in the bar was fearless. I couldn't tell if he was accumulating courage through his rum drinks to try his luck on the dance floor, or whether he was the among the melancholy type that shows up in the great outdoors to drown his sorrows from romantic disappointment or financial disaster. The few interchanges we had had to that point were unremarkable in the sense that neither of us had revealed anything of mystery to the other. But that was about to change, as all things must in the destinations and temporary encounters of Great Western life.

"So, I guess Coronado never did find anything of value to take back to Spain," the Anglo who told me his name was Quivira Cantrell abruptly asked after a huge slug of distilled island cane drink.

"The Natives made sure he didn't."

"What do you mean by that?"

Intentionally I delayed my response, going along with the stereotypical need for many big city Anglo dudes to see us as a little slow on the draw, even though I think like a combination of unconventional Zuni, jaded British observer, and New Mexican pale-skinned minority.

"The word got out early on through the pueblos. The Zunis, Acoma, Laguna, and others discovered that this strange Spanish explorer wearing silver skin and riding a large four-legged animal wasn't on a goodwill mission."

"So, indigenous sorts developed an *ad hoc* plan when these Spanish types showed up?"

"They knew they had to placate the pale-faced arrivals sporting the facial hair of buffaloes with something. All the tribes realized they were intolerant invaders if gifts and surrender didn't come quickly."

"Sounds like a lot of young NFL players."

"Most of the time it was either surrender, or fight."

"Didn't many of the local Native populations get a preview with the earlier passing of Friar Marcos and the feathered Esteban?"

"Mm," I agreed, knowing the big man was still wondering just how much Anglo history on the sixteenth century I knew. "The Zunis and Acoma quickly learned these strange conquistadors were dangerous. The Acoma held them off as long as they could. But it didn't matter, anyway. Vasquez de Coronado couldn't be bothered staying in one prickly pear cactus-ridden place or another too long when there was no gold or silver just over the next horizon to take back to Spain."

"So, they gulled the Spaniards big time."

I nodded. "The trick was always to send them farther and farther on. His man who traveled briefly to Chaco might have recognized the value of turquoise but didn't. Then when the whole bedraggled group got to the Rio Grande and Tiguex, it became less costly to continue northeast, rather than fight any more battles and get hit with more arrows."

"So continued the wild goose chase."

"Exactly. Sending foreign treasure seekers to Kansas was the greatest historical gull since the many errant quests for the Holy Grail."

"So, you think the Seven Cities and all that is a load of crap."

"Not necessarily. The problem for Coronado centered upon the diversions he didn't see, and a lack of ability to recognize water and turquoise as two resources more valuable than gold."

By that time, I knew I had said more than this sportswriter wanted to hear. Then again, maybe he was entranced just like all the others who come to New Mexico in search of lost treasure or the Seven Cities of Cibola. If you wanted to put anyone on a jack, all you had to do is even hint about some story or another regarding ancient precious metals or gems. And I had a feeling I was going to have to play the same role tribal members have played for more than 450 years.

"I was in New Orleans and a couple of guys who were deep-sea treasure hunters mentioned something called the Mogollon Cross. Have you ever heard anything about it?"

His eyes betrayed an insatiable curiosity that often overcomes those with no intention of proceeding beyond modest inquiry. Some

Nashville band stuff behind me now felt like it was providing the pause I needed to decide upon just the sort of response the big guy named Quivira needed. An entire atavistic reality of several hundred years of calculated reactions thundered through my mind like off-reservation tequila or on-reservation secret smoke. Did I want to continue the illusion with Mr. Cantrell or not? On the other hand, I did feel compelled to honor my Zuni civic duty. And I knew I could give him a Native American ambiguous answer that would leave him preoccupied for days.

"Yah, of course. It's another of those local legends that some think outrageous, and others believe historical. How Captain Grijalva carried a silver cross he acquired in Arizona before the climb into high country. He supposedly then got some Hopi assistance in adding peridot stones to it. Naturally, it's never been found, and probably never will be...Or it might be the kind of story much like the ersatz ruby scepter described as bait in the novel, *Coyote Cowgirl*."

"You mean imitation stuff."

"Yah. Tourists love the legends, though. Our Visitor Center bookshop is loaded with more legendary fuel than you can get from the locals hanging out in Tesuque or spinning yarns in the square opposite Santa Fe's Palace of the Governors. All good stories if the mood strikes you."

"You don't sound like you've spent most of your life on a Navajo reservation."

"Nope."

"Been beyond Colorado, huh?"

I could see him wondering again. He just couldn't figure me out. "Not only been across the New Mexican borders," I replied after glancing his way in the mirror, "but also have made it across the big pond to the east."

The visitor fiddled with his drink a bit, then examined me in the mirror like he couldn't decide how seriously he should take me. It always perplexes visiting palefaces when an Indian doesn't talk like Geronimo as played by Burt Lancaster, or Crazy Horse just before taking advantage of Custer. I thrive on those kinds of misguided impressions, though, and so do many of my Native American amigos, even the ones who never made it beyond reservation schools.

Still, this guy Quivira was getting more loaded, and his quivering eyes told the story of a dude with a volatile temper probably held in check while he felt in control, and the number of drinks consumed didn't number beyond the transformative level of Mr. Hyde.

"You may think I'm nuts, but I'm going to spend some time trying to find that cross," he said, before lapsing into further contemplation of perhaps the sun glinting off a Mogollon silver and peridot number he might discover in some burned out canyon off El Malpais lava beds.

I didn't want to disabuse him. After all, I was working in a place promoting that sort of legendary stuff. And if it weren't for the gambling revenues and receipts from tourist indulgences and purchases, many of my friends would not be able to afford their smoking material or illegal hidden stashes of 100% agave Reposado and toolboxes full of cerveza.

"Yah, I'm the type of guy who is a sucker for that sort of apocryphal tale. It's kind of like betting on football. Lots of time all the shit you've learned, observations you've made, and wise-assed comments you've interjected into quasi-journalistic summaries of outrageous games, merely send you in the wrong direction. You think you know the Denver Broncos are finally ready to kick the asses of the Indianapolis Colts, but they're not. You still fervently believe your clever analysis gives you the edge on the spread. And 24 hours later, you've just lost the five hundred bucks you won the previous week. College games are one thing, but the Pro's are another." He paused to take another sip of his rum, before dashing a few dribbles from his mouth with his hand. "Yup. I'm sure all the wild adventurers having underestimated the indigenous populations in these areas spent an exhaustive amount of time, money, and effort on failed treasure hunts."

I pursed my lips, not knowing if it was time to agree with his accurate analysis or not. But Quivira was on a roll not even Wild Bill Hickok could better.

"I figure I've got enough money in the bank to spend as much time drifting around the Four Corners deserts as I want. I want to stay away from women for a while, drink when I feel like it, get up in the morning when I feel like it. I'm sure you've heard all of this before from the great white hunters who arrive in Indian Territory thinking they're gonna discover what no one else has been able to in 450 years. The difference is, I don't give a *shite* if I my brain turns to toast and my car becomes a burned-out hulk as the summer heats up or water runs low. Once I got used to covering football, strangely enough I knew the only way I was ever going to be truly happy was leaving my marriage and writing behind to attempt to rejuvenate myself out among the saguaro and sagebrush."

His rambling disquisition went on intermittently like this for a good 10 minutes. The whole process was part of an urban catharsis experience many passing tourists undergo when they've either been out in the sun too long, or the vistas in the early morning or late afternoon just plain overwhelm them. The desert has a way of doing that to folks, even if you were born here. The arid wide-open spaces are like a siren beckoning to all those with preoccupied minds from an overload of urban survival endeavors. Suddenly you're running through a canyon so spectacularly lit it's as if your spirit transcends the mundane existence you've led for days and weeks and months on end. The desert does that and more. It's probably the same as coastal folks staring out at the Atlantic with a light breeze and a Cosmopolitan or glass of Pinot Noir in their hands. You've seen the Corona ads. Sitting in a deck chair without a care in the world. In the high or low deserts, sometimes just one solitary saguaro or a single barren red mesa overcomes with the same tranquility.

Quivira man was soon to reach his own private spiritual transcendence in Indian territory. But then, when you've been a big city kind of survivor for as long as he has, and with the size he's carrying, there's always just that one last interruption to what could be a perfect afternoon or evening.

In this case, the whole place had been rocking for an extended period of up-tempo stuff from the juke box, when the ballad *Don't It Make Your Brown Eyes Blue* started crooning to fill the rafters and stir the two genders into the kind of close contact that goes with barroom dancing. Now it looked to me like the visitor, by glancing in the mirror from time to time, had been eyeing a woman on the dance floor. She had that dangerous sort of sexuality like the south end of a magnet when all the guys within range are polarized north. Quivira, apparently, was no different than any other male with a load of unused testosterone and his arms temporarily crossed until he could muster the courage to ask Calamity Jane to dance. Just like everyone else, Q-man could see the large, pointed breasts outlined in her tailored, brocaded cowboy shirt, and the spray-on jeans that didn't have to be Tommy Hilfiger to broadcast what was within. She was the 'it' girl of the moment. This curvaceous cowgirl had the attention of the nearby pack of desert coyotes, there was no doubt about it. The problem is, she had never stopped dancing because her combination of animal aura and rhythmic appeal created a constant demand for continuing.

Within a minute or two Q-man slowly careened her way, asked Calamity Jane to dance, and the pair engaged in a passable slow shuffle. I had this premonition that something ugly was coming. Yet I told myself that this character from the East had the body mass to avoid trouble. Who in the room was going to confront a guy well over 200 pounds?

Probably any number of alcoholic cowboys with enough friends to assume strength in numbers, that's who.

Anyway, the dance seemed to go just like part of an old Dick Clark saddle shoes TV re-run. That is, until Q-man decided to accompany the magnetic cowgirl back to her table. It wasn't exactly apparent what one of those New Mexicans with arms like tree trunks said to the stranger from the East, but I knew it wasn't good. Even though the Wild West is largely a term conjured for the 19$^{th}$ and early 20$^{th}$ Centuries, if at your own risk you enter certain bars in New Mexico or Arizona or Texas in these times, you 'goan' discover the same sort of spontaneous combustion that once killed Wild Bill Hickok.

That's why I keep my mouth shut most of the time. Native American or no, there are just no guarantees on how some dude will take your having scrutinized his woman, or that remark you thought to be innocuous. On many an occasion this Indian has seen chairs and fists suddenly flying and wondered how it all began. There's also a Grand Canyon-sized undercurrent of animosity between the Hispanics, Native Americans, and Great White Sharks in these parts. Not between everyone, of course. But among enough bigoted sorts that bar fights still erupt with the same frequency as verbal blather in certain Western establishments.

The next thing I knew, Q-man was being accompanied outside by four guys who looked like they might pull some serious iron from their flatbed truck toolboxes. That is, unless our visitor was unlucky enough to find one or several of them packing those exploding weapons which put holes in a person.

O.K., so call me crazy, but I had taken to this big guy's candor. He hadn't been the usual condescending Anglo, had listened to what I told him without acting as if a strange Native American park ranger is incapable of complex thought process, and he had made a real effort in terms of bar camaraderie. Besides, I didn't like the odds, the fact that four strutting posers were walking outside with him, making it almost a dead cert he was going to undergo some serious physical damage in the parking lot.

I headed for the door, not knowing whether I was going to regret getting involved in what promised to be one of those scenes outside in which more than one person, instead of an interchange of verbal abuse, decide upon the old stereotypical shit stomp. Sometimes a fight could be fair. Yet it was more likely one of a group was going to pull out a knife or gun to gain an advantage the British would term unsportsmanlike. Still, Mr. Quivira Cantrell might just possess a tolerance for alcohol that would allow him not to get any attitude bashed out of him. But I doubted it. And so I followed him into the night like a moth closes on a porch light.

The usual nonsense was in progress, where a bunch of guys who have been drinking say stuff they'd normally never mutter to a jackalope or even to an ex-wife who cost them their adobe ruins of a home. There was a toxic tension in the cold desert night air, what with the misty glow of the neon signs shining down upon the flotsam hulks of painted iron and into dried clay ruts with the occasional crumpled empties in them. The whole lot felt a bit weird, especially since more than a few folks from inside had come out to witness the kind of a confrontation from one or more locals under the influence of firewater who hold a lofty impression of their ability to knock a few heads in the night. I kind of shook my head and crossed my arms, still wondering if he started getting the crap beat out of him, whether I'd make any effort to reduce the odds.

With no more warning that a rattler gives early on before you get too close, two of the bigger sorts jumped on Q-man and started waling on him. There was no doubt his size was somewhat of a defensive advantage, that, and a tolerance for alcohol much like those who come down from ski resorts at altitude and can drink anyone under a table.

Now, most folks think fights are like movies, where a guy gets hit repeatedly but comes back for more and then some, picking himself off the ground for the ultimate retribution. That's a load of dried cow patty. In most fights someone gets a good lick in before his victim expects it and that advantage then leads to broken bones, contusions, abrasions and generally to one beat-up son of a bitch. And this one wasn't your James Bond no-one-gets-bloodied type of hoo-hah.

I mentioned before I had boxed in New Mexico and extra-mural at Oxford. But what I didn't mention is that because I'm a Zuni and of average height, I've been in a lot of street and bar fights. I never plan to be. It's just that particularly big Anglo characters often say real nasty stuff to me about either my skin color or going back to the reservation, or how ugly I am. It's the kind of antagonism that's challenging for a Zuni to accept with equanimity. So, often what happens is that I have to duck one or two punches or slashes by a drunk with a knife—if I'm lucky and the dude doesn't have a gun— and then I'm forced to let him have it with either a solid right jab to the jaw or a left hook. Well, maybe that's a distilled description just like motion picture violence. On the other hand, what comes down depends upon the situation. If the guy happens to be real abusive, I might kick him in the nuts, or break his arm. Basically, I'm a man of moderate temperament, until some wild-assed brain-dead bronco buster or other pushes too far. And that's what these two guys were doing while the other two laughed.

Their behavior's the sort of thing I was talking about before. Without thinking any more about it, I pulled one of the more aggressive pair off the big New Yorker and hit him real hard with a backhander, enough that he fell and dented his head on a monster truck bumper. One down. Then one of the two dudes watching came at me and swung. Piece a cake when you've got far less spirits in you than he has. I just leaned back enough so he missed and then smacked him real hard in the gut. When he leaned over to hold his stomach, my knee took care of the rest of his pale-faced temper. The fourth guy now began one of those slow exit dances during which you try to look as if you're not really part of the group at the center of the action. And old Q-man, of course, now had rallied to get the other cowboy's pearl buttoned shirt looking like it had been scuffed up real bad during an alligator-wrestling episode in a parched arroyo just west of Colorado's Great Sand Dunes.

My recollection is not real good on the next few minutes. But suddenly they were gone, the bar people had evaporated back inside, and the music was still blaring.

"You didn't have to do that man," the big fellow said while testing to see just how bad one of his ribs was.

"No problem. Although much of the world is still into religious war, I guess I'm still into cowboys and Indians."

"Yeah, but I'm a paleface."

"Believe it or not, I don't stereotype all Anglo dudes. And four mean cowboys with an attitude against one visitor—white or red-skinned—is the kind of arrogant macho stuff untamed ranch hands pull all the time on tribal dudes who find themselves a little too drunk and a little too late in a parking lot."

"Yah, well, neither of us would probably find a whole lot of friendly faces welcoming us back inside, especially since I'd misguidedly start chatting up one of their girlfriends again."

His face had red blotches and a bit of blood here and there, but Q-man was going to see another sunrise even if a rib or two left him with a poor night's sleep. It was strange meeting a guy from the big city like him. Usually, they talk at you as if you sit by the side of the road every day selling blankets. But this guy was different, and I figured somehow we were going to meet again. I didn't know how I'd encounter Q-journo again in two States with just one of its reservations thousands of square miles and lots of people trying to decide what it is they left to move to Santa Fe. But I knew the chance was as good as the constellations revolving spectacularly through the New Mexican night sky.

"I'm going to head over to Grants," I said, clearing my brain back to reality and stretching a sore neck a bit. "But you know, if you decide the Mogollon Cross treasure hunt notion keeps rattling around your brain when it cools down from those four nasty dudes, and you want to continue the search, you probably need to meet my uncle, Ketl."

# Kahlo at Aztec Ruins

(AURORE)
While I was driving up to Aztec, it was difficult to ignore the encounter I had had back in that canyon off Highway 9. When I decided to leave New York in order to get to the bottom of my sister Ashleigh's death, my intent was to try to learn how to reduce the pace of my own private urban insanity, to attempt to unwind enough to again experience the pulse of the earth daily. New York nightlife was exhilarating. But it could also infect you with a sophistication that eventually interfered with the simpler things in life, elements I hoped to reintroduce while I poked around northwest New Mexico.

And yet I had run into Easy Rider Man, or whoever he might be. I can't quite say why he visually reappears in my thoughts, but then maybe it's because I've always had an approach-avoidance thing toward men. The most acute minds often treat me poorly, call infrequently, and never quite make the transition to financial security. And those amazing thought processes often moving a nanosecond faster than my own observation rate have a magnetism invariably leading to disappointment. The conversations are better, the sex is better. But there is always that point beyond which the two of you perhaps atavistically revert to the male-female gender/

hormonal thing, in which testosterone never quite can accept the embrace, wisdom and cunning of estrogen.

So here I was out West, hoping more to find myself than the reason or person responsible for my sister's demise. Her death had been one of those enigmatic occurrences that superficially seem simple. The coroner had ruled it cardiac arrest. Yet my sister was the sort of woman who habitually watches what she eats, consuming little alcohol, and consistently rejuvenating her cardiovascular as well as skeletal muscle systems. She was the straight arrow in the family. Very few liked her, mind you. But then who, with a bright mind, is ever universally adored? Her death had come unexpectedly in the early afternoon, and ostensibly she had been alone when the spirits left her.

Aztec and its incorrectly named ruins built by the Anasazi were among the last places she had visited before her untimely death. Yet that said, what death is ever timely? Sometimes I wanted to kill her myself. For she and I had entertained an argumentative relationship, one in which each continually attempted to establish mental supremacy. However, as we all know, sometimes the glibbest or most extroverted easily gets the better of a brighter but introverted mind, particularly in public. Fortunately, I am far from introverted, and our resultant ongoing verbal skirmishing was well matched. My sister, however, had possessed a searing wit just short of perhaps Oscar Wilde. There was no stopping her once she got her talons into a weak adversary, particularly if it happened to be someone of the male gender.

Which meant that anyone in the family at one point or another held enough animosity for their often mentally cruel relative to at least think about assassination. The whole devolution of this singular family member, as far as I was concerned, remained far more than mysterious, yet probably far less than heinous. She had been out West on an extended trip to leave others including a recently divorced husband behind. Her postcards indicating a man she had met in Santa Fe, a rafting trip, as well as a newfound ability to tear through several books delineating a protracted wish list, had helped her reach a sort of high-desert nirvana. My acerbic sibling had seemed happier than she had been in a long time, never once even mentioning skewering anyone in her posted summaries and e-mails from obscure cyber-cafés. Yet with no witness save the maid who found her, the possibilities of foul play and nothing untoward at all remained two polar extremes between which the truth lay.

I left Cuba early, needing the time to be away from my mother and daughter. I got to Aztec and the ruins of what once was a thriving pueblo just when it opened. Two women in the town's tourist office had recommended several accommodations in which someone of my sibling's nature might have spent time. That early morning also was the best opportunity for a spring survey of what the Anasazi reputedly built when their water sources in Chaco Canyon began to evaporate into second-millennium oblivion. I accepted a handout guide to be digested upon the arrival at any in a series of numbered signs.

The light was perfect, as the morning sun at high altitude ever seems a companion of warmth no matter how dire anyone's circumstances. That sort of implies my own condition to be in question. However, my initial impressions of the Southwest acted much like an unexpected catharsis. Every day when thoughts of my real purpose crept in, the light from the Sun god kept my spirits from being dampened.

Upon a mound not far from the adobe headquarters, theater, and bookshop building in which I had first watched the obligatory historical video, several workmen were quietly tapping bits of rock. Judging by their appearance and short stature, any of the lot could have been an Anasazi warrior, but more likely a Hopi, Navajo, or

Ute from the area. A tent roof on four metal posts shielded them from the sun, and the relaxed pace of their approach to rebuilding a small component of the Ruins was remarkably soothing to observe. I only wish New York slowed enough at times to be like that.

"We're back," abruptly came the voice of my precocious daughter.

I turned and noticed the pair completing a chronological female triad within our family tree, the other arrival being my mother, Katarina Dupín. The two had driven up from Cuba to meet me, though Kahlo had been far more eager to delve into Chaco Canyon along the way.

"I'm t-t-t-taking my own t-t-tour," my daughter said before nervously adjusting her *Colorado Buffaloes* baseball cap in hopes of my answer becoming a mere formality.

"Very well, Kahlo. Far be it from me to impede the progress of a female explorer with the energy of Jeanne D'Arc."

"Ca-ca-calamity," she threw over her shoulder, and was off, skipping to the first numbered sign, a nine-year-old not yet afflicted with the more predictable languorous protocols of the middle-aged or elderly.

"You know your daughter," commented Katarina, whose face under a straw sunhat was powdered no differently than if she were on a shopping mission along Fifth Avenue. "Reverse psychology works best. It makes her feel like an adult. And makes me feel a child again playing a game."

"We both know my daughter to be no different than either of us was at her age," I answered, the pair of us slowly beginning to amble toward station number two. "Neither Dupín left a stone unturned, and still wouldn't if our energies were the same as someone her age. The main problem of life does not involve interpersonal issues, it's the inability to learn everything you want while you still have the energy and faculties to do so."

"And I'm doing my best to limit any such acquisition—not to mention the distressing passage through one's 70s—with a clear evil spirit."

"Don't get me going on that one, Mother. It's too nice a day to spoil."

This sort of mother-daughter rhythmic banter sporadically erupted much like it does in any similar eternal parent-child relationship in which each wrestles for control. Both of us maintained a mild interest in our historic surroundings, but far more toward the ongoing unspoken allure of defining our familial rivalry. Kahlo, on the other hand, appeared much like a whirling dervish just having discovered the Ancient World to be a cornucopia of show and tell. One minute she would be running her hand along the stones forming a perfect T-shaped doorway, while the next disappearing through a low door into a series of rooms perhaps once used for cooking, sleeping, and whatever Native Americans did for amusement in the $13^{th}$ and $14^{th}$ Centuries. All of Kahlo's expeditions require the same élan. Never have I seen my daughter dragged down by boredom, addicted to televised inanity, nor wanting to go home early. During one year she might have the inquisitiveness of Peter Pan, while the next that of Cortés or Coronado—without the armor, but with the same thirst for adventure.

My mother often walks with a pronounced limp. Yet the sun and survey of an ancient civilization much older than someone having seen fewer than 1000 moons were providing her with a physical rejuvenation she would continue until the first afternoon cocktail. You can well imagine that a woman once a piano virtuoso, even given her late-life proclivity for boozing, rarely during casual observation misses a trick. Katarina sometimes acts a Columbo, pretending that some concept or behavior is beyond her. Yet this is never really the case. Her dewlap and gray hair betray the aging process, but her eyes tell the story of a thousand adventures. Nothing eludes a woman of substance, not even the abuse of same.

As we continued our survey of the remnants of what was an ancient residence of unique complexity, my late sister Ashleigh's spirit without provocation blew through a brain desperately trying to concentrate on the beauty of the moment. On one of the last days she would grace the Southwest, my errant sister had sent a card mysteriously mentioning an unnamed male who had accompanied her, at least in touring the Aztec Ruins. It was unclear from her cramped cryptic printing on the card just how she had come to know this perhaps ultimate companion. Nor did the brief description of her impressions shed any light upon what had transpired shortly thereafter.

"You seem distant," mother interjected, the faint aroma of day-old alcohol coming from somewhere within a body barely able to fill out pants and a blouse. "If you're going to waste this magnificent expedition on nothing more than your sister's departure from the planet, you might as well get on with it instead of pretending to enjoy things more ancient than myself."

"You are so right, *Mamá*. And who better to point out this shortcoming, than the sage of upper Manhattan. I shall make an effort to pay more attention to these former residences constructed by men in headbands and macaw feathers who could teach the early third-millennium masons a thing or two."

The problem with each of the three of us is not an inability to frame several compelling sentences in a string. It's more that mental preoccupation that comes from our following suit in a long line of family readers and thinkers. Reading and thinking, particularly while coursing through the reviews of the *New Yorker*, or say, a biography of Isak Dinesen or Charles Dickens, conveys a sense of solitary joy those from the world of illiteracy never enter, one in which vicarious pleasures often outweigh those of the real world. Yet there is a penalty for behavior even remotely including a good laugh or moving experience. One becomes a bore to the loquacious, arrogant to males attempting a mating ritual, and secretive to those discussing their laundry or menstrual habits with anyone.

Take Kahlo, for instance. Off at a short distance among the crumbling stone, she was Dian Fossey among gorillas, or Amelia Earhart about to take off on a circumnavigation. Her curiosity, thankfully due to contrasting inhibitions with social skills, is boundless. She loves everything from watching a lizard scamper across a dusty trail, to the thought process delving into the very essence of massive early second-millennium building projects such as this.

Just now her hands were on her knees as she sat on the lip of an open round underground container of some sort or another. She was thinking, no doubt. Thinking of exactly what the Anasazi had in mind when they built this circular pit in the center of their city. And knowing my precocious offspring as I do, there was little likelihood of anyone disturbing this thought process until the mysteries revealed themselves.

Someone of Kahlo's curiosity, enthusiasm and spirit also exerted an inexplicable magnetic attraction to those encountering such a phenom. And she didn't have this effect just upon doting relatives, though doubtless I count myself one of her admirers. Katarina and I had come to a brief impasse while discussing another obnoxious relative currently threatening to break off communication. This pause in our parrying proved ideal for strolling over to see just what Kahlo had divined from her examinations.

As we approached, her fists never once strayed from her temples. She was deep in thought, a large pair of Candy-like sunglasses dwarfing her face, the miniature archeologist completely unaware of her surroundings, save the pit before her.

"Kahlo, has it come to you what that kiva or whatever it is was used for?"

There was no response. She hadn't heard a word I'd said.

"Kahlo? Are you there?"

She pulled her cap down lower upon her forehead. "W-w-water. W-w-water and b-b-b..." The last word she uttered slipped into verbal oblivion, an inability to say the complete word without a stammer. She had also tailed off her remark because of being unsure. Kahlo never completed a sentence when any doubt over an investigation remained.

Katarina and I followed our nine-year-old explorer into a huge partially subterranean kiva restored to what is believed to be its original appearance. To me kivas always seem like Kiwanis Club circles, or Kappa Kappa Gamma secret chapter rooms in which the members sit in a circle and convince themselves their surroundings lend weight to their decisions. The central rectangular stone firepits must have kept them warm when snow was covering all but the center hole of the roof through which the smoke tailed. And yet no one knows for sure what these ancient Native Americans did in these chambers. "It's a mystery," as a nervous thespian repeatedly mutters in the film, Shakespeare in Love.

Such challenges are just the sort of mental stimulation Kahlo needs to attack like a young boy throws himself into sport. One minute she was over by the firepits leaning down to examine the masonry more closely, and the next scampering over to sit on the curved bench surrounding the circular arena. She would fiddle with her braid, gaze fixedly up at the overhead pine beams, and then suddenly jump up and career toward another position along the edges of the endless seating arrangement upon which many an historic figure once perched.

A short time later all three of us were outside in the morning sun again, Kahlo obviously lost in thought while retracing her steps back among some of the largest ruins. Katarina and I followed at a discreet distance, not wishing to interfere with the youngest member of our bloodline's great gift of curiosity.

Minutes later a woman in the olive and khaki uniform of a ranger appeared to be on a walking inspection, but more likely making one of her rounds to ensure no one is vandalizing or further reducing any of these historic discoveries.

"Do you think you know what the Anasazi were up to?" the ranger inquired of Kahlo after noticing her scrutiny of a T-shaped doorway.

Kahlo nodded. "N-n-not completely. B-but I think I understand a few things that I haven't found in any of the b-b-b-books I've read."

"Have you read a lot of books?"

"Mm-huh. Grammy just let me g-g-g-get a few more from the S-S-Santa Fe Library and a f-factory outlet store."

"And what have you found different than the books speculated?"

"I c-c-can't say just yet."

"I see."

"P-p-people wouldn't believe me, anyway. I'm only nine. Who's g-g-going to believe s-s-s-someone my age?"

"Mozart wrote a symphony when he was younger than you are. Maybe you should give your theories a try."

"I w-w-will. Just not yet. I'm not r-r-r-ready, until I'm com...pletely s-s-sure."

"Well, let me know if I can answer any questions for you," the ranger added before adjusting her Smokey hat and continuing on her way.

Kahlo can be quite secretive. Yet much of her introversion results from the effects of her speech impediment. I was hoping the ranger's encouragement would unleash a torrent of information my daughter sometimes can release without flaw when the mood strikes, or a daunting situation fails to overwhelm her. Once in a great while all her neurons align in a certain fashion, the unexpected rewarding result several unhindered verbal paragraphs or a surprisingly mellifluous outpouring. It feels a miracle. And at the same time this brief respite from inhibition often breaks my heart. There is a great deal within that nine-year-old repository of stored information. Yet social limitations leave that same cornucopia of mysterious content locked inside my daughter's wonderful mind.

Kahlo, lost in thought and her step uneven, slowly walked back to the open kiva in the center of the main ruins. She definitely was onto something, because usually if any concept, location, or person is worth a second look to a nine-year-old, that same double curiosity is a sign Kahlo is attempting to confirm a conclusion already made. She sat back down upon the lip and swung her legs out a couple of times, lost in abstract thought. And again, her hands went up to her temples, so that she could rest upon her elbows during mental and physical reexaminations of the pit below.

"Kahlo, you shouldn't sit on the walls!" mother yelled, before quietly turning my way. "She lives in her own world, my dear, as you know"

She was right, of course, but the protective nature of motherhood toward a precocious daughter with few social skills always rears its armored head when I'm in range of my own overly solicitous mother. "It's the sort of thing any nine-year-old—male or female—undertakes. Most of the time young boys are stirring up anthills and young girls dressing up in adult clothing to see what it feels like. But they all grow up, and one must hope that during the process they get through all those childhood needs which if not satisfied, carry on into adulthood."

"I wonder how vodka figures into that."

"Now, Katarina, don't start. You've had your day in the sun, and at some future point, that sun will undoubtedly set. But two generations for which you are responsible stand or sit before you, and hopefully you feel pride in and are intrigued by both."

"All my life I've been intrigued by how blood conveys certain physical and mental commonality yet makes no guarantees regarding behavioral patterns. There has never been any telling what you'll do or think next. And Kahlo is no different. The decided contrast is that while you were already playing doctor at a pre-pubescent age, Kahlo more likely will have her nose buried in archeology or astronomy tomes and mysterious kivas way beyond adolescence."

The two of us had come to a halt very near a crumbling series of rooms that undoubtedly once contained Anasazi at work or play and the plotting of their defense against the elements or other tribes. We had also come to an impasse on what to say next, the sort of elliptical period occurring between blood relatives when silence is the best temporary solution.

Kahlo, in the interim, had twisted her baseball cap backwards on her head, gone back to some sort of intense peering into the empty stone chamber below, and then replaced her cap bill-forward in a manner less befitting a young person trying to be cool.

It wasn't more than several minutes of standing in the sun, when my mother and I began walking onward beyond a station from the guide booklet we had visited the first time by. With little warning I felt at peace with both my mother and daughter, and haven't a clue why, unless the ancient surroundings with the same marvelous eternal weather brightened my outlook.

Kahlo, still obviously preoccupied with her latest sleuthing, joined us, and began to skip ahead.

"You're up to something, K.," I threw out to her.

My daughter came to a halt and turned. The two relatives stared at her, guaranteeing an inability to tell us any of her canny deductions without stuttering.

"B-b-b-baths," she said, nervously adjusting her cap. "B-b-baths..."

# Quivira in Chaco

(QUIVIRA)

When I woke up in some god-forsaken Farmington, New Mexico motel, the room smelled like smoke and my head felt like it had been used as a soccer ball, post-guillotine. I was hung over big time, the traffic noise outside so irritating I pulled the thin blanket and sheet over my head and hoped it was all a bad dream. It wasn't. A few pathetic minutes of hiding, and I threw the covers off and walked the creaky floor to the door. Outside looked like Mars. Well, not really, but there's something about a distorted view of a million franchise signs in early brain-damaged morning that make you want to go back to bed and dream of someone like Salma Hayek.

An hour more of self-pity, a shower, and two cups of explosive local cyber café brew, and I was at least then able to read one of those tabloid throwaways advertising all kinds of entertaining ways to further achieve blimpdom. Yah, that was another thing I was constantly telling myself. That once you balloon up much over 200 pounds, your clothes sometimes begin to feel like they'd been machine-dried on high until shrunken to fit someone you used to be when you swam in high school. I was going to have to watch the calories a little better. But I was on holiday. In deference to that thinking, I wolfed down a huge cinnamonster roll with enough simple sugar, gluten, butterfat, and other nasty ingredients to shorten my brief span on the planet another year. But who cares? That's one of the best parts of self-loathing. You can get in a downward spiral and then exacerbate the process by indulging sugar blues.

Diving into a sweet roll also made it mandatory to go back to that motel with the chipped-paint-and-rusted metal sign and hide under the covers for another snooze. That's what holidays are for, anyway, and my distorted and dissipated behavior only reinforces the tawdriness and reputed laziness of the overweight journalist. I want to keep up the image. O.K., so the Mayo Clinic or Weight Scrutinizers Anonymous say I should give up the high carbs and fat and get into exercise. I know all that. Doing it, however, is another thing. Late night drinking and early morning exercise are not exactly a marriage keynoted in Wild Western lore. This is the desert, I told myself, and one needs to get into a mode of a cowboy or Indian who rides the range or drives some beat-up pick-up that has front doors that squeak, as well as needs plenty of calories to get him through the day. Besides, my face and ribs were going to be sore for a moon or two.

Anyway, eventually I did get going. It wasn't until close to 10, but I studied a map of the surrounding area, unusual since northwest New Mexico apparently has about one small town for every hundred you'd find on a survey of the East Coast. This discovery was soothing, because I knew for at least part of the day I could probably put the top down on the old cobalt Pontiac and enjoy seamless scenic driving in the Land of Enchantment. Arizona and Monument Valley were going to be hard to top, but then there was my quest for the Mogollon Cross—whether quixotic or not—and I'm the type of guy whose day doesn't have to be filled with much more than a few pleasant views, a good read or two, and then the requisite cocktails and a fulsome but filling southwestern feed.

'On the road, again,' as Willy Nelson would say. My first observation on that morning during which the shifting of my bulk on the

Naugahyde in the sun revealed the discomforting discovery of unexpected stabbing pains where those country gents had pounded my mid-section. Never mind, I told myself. It was time to get on with the rest of my dubious quest destined to provide more amusement than a Broncos/Chargers game.

There wasn't much out there in northwest New Mexico, at least in terms of the kinds of livestock you usually think of as grazing. Probably because it's tough to graze when there's neither much vegetation nor water. As I headed down highway 550, the occasional oil pump loomed as a slow-moving praying mantis out on a desolate rolling plain. The nature of these arid surroundings seemed a bad place to have car trouble, at least when you're my size and driving the sort of outmoded machine I pilot. And given the thought that it would be hard to attract any potential Samaritans driving at 75 mph or better to get to Farmington or Santa Fe as fast as they can. Yet the old beast had only blown once. Something about the close to 400 horses and low-performance engine that meant you used a lot of gas, but rarely came up with a dead machine. Everything else might break down, but some big Detroit engines went forever.

Driving into Chaco canyon from the northeast can only be described as a trip successfully negotiable by those with no kidney problems. After three or four miles of pavement to lull a visitor into complacency, any adventurer must then pilot 20 miles or so of gravel, the washboard kind that has you driving your ancient vehicle like one steers those flat-bottomed boats with airplane engines through the Florida Everglades. The jarring, rolling journey was mentally and physically challenging, the dust swirling around my sunglasses when I slowed in arroyos, and my ears ringing from that constant grinding noise of rubber upon stones.

No doubt the Chaco Culture National Historical Park hoodoos and rangers like it that way, because it holds down the numbers of free spirits making their way into this destination of great mythic past undertakings. The length of the invaders' stay is also limited by the bumpy, dusty, lengthy drive out, a thought that certainly has affected the decision-making of those, again, wishing to keep the numbers of beer-bellied trampers and their families to a low roar. There's not much time to steal artifacts when just a drive around the canyon paved road loop and a walk through some unearthed ancient realm will find you glancing at your watch in late afternoon. Not to mention that it's still close to a hundred miles to the nearest motel.

I didn't have a plan of exploration, and I was dressed in Bermuda shorts, a Giants T-shirt which had seen better days, and some moth-eaten Nike Mariahs I still had from years ago when I decided they were the next best thing to bedroom slippers. The reason I'm bringing this up, is that one of the first things you discover about the desert is that multiple perils await the unwary or ill-prepared. Sunburn, dehydration, rattler bites, and falls if you don't watch your foot plants, are just several of the more salient methods of changing a relaxed day into a distressing dilemma in a remote desert location.

When I went into the Visitor Center, I glanced at a few books, paid the fee that allows them to keep poor folk and ne'er-do-wells out, and then ambled into the theater to watch a video on the history of what they don't know so far. A video history of an oral history of a possible physical history is somewhat akin to knowing every nuance of what Marie Antoinette did in her bedchambers: speculation reigns supreme. It was apparent from the video that the inhabitants undeniably had a sophisticated knowledge of astronomy, enough to create those famous sun and moon daggers on Fajada Butte. And yet sitting among several families of yawners from Iowa or other vacationing sorts of unknown origin, made yours truly aware of just how little most of the population has progressed since these Native sorts came up with their own set of complex behavioral patterns and impressive cities more than a millennium earlier.

It was all good stuff, and the curiosity I've gained for sport easily translated into an infatuation with these archeological surroundings. The documentary, for all its shortcomings regarding what definitively did or did not happen up through at least the 13$^{th}$ Century, had me psyched not just over the quest for a Cross in myriad possible locations—nothing more than bait for a journo with too much time on his hands—but also for just getting out there and wandering aimlessly round these little-understood architectural phenomena.

First, however, I had to decide upon some late afternoon and morning reading material. Since the Visitor Center's treasure trove bookstore offers a cornucopia of items piquing the imagination, I was just examining a Steven Lekson book, entitled, *The Chaco Meridian*, when a nearby ranger ostensibly checking inventory began what was going to be a fruitful interaction, at least for me.

"That's a good one," he said as I was thumbing the pages of the book on a speculative axis of Anasazi power. "A controversial approach to what could be either an accurate or inaccurate portrayal of archeo-astronomical alignment, at least of the three sites of Chaco, Aztec and Paquime," he delivered with the confidence of someone who has paid a lot of investigative dues. "Of course, just slightly off that meridian are Culiacán, La Ventana and other noted sites which may or may not intentionally have been built with any sort of alignment in mind."

His rimless glasses and thin physique, coupled with those initial clues of vocabulary alerting a listener that the information being imparted is worthwhile rather than a load of crap from a blogger just guessing what he's talking about, gave him the look of a physically and mentally fit Westerner. I figured this guy is the real deal. And within minutes I had learned he was writing his doctorate on one of three groups of ancient peoples in the area, that he funded this academic project by working as a ranger at the Aztec Ruins, and that he had come down to check out what additions and deletions had been made to a bookstore cache he described as one of the best in the U.S. Parks system. There was no hesitation over any question I posed, again the sign of someone not just having completed his homework, but of one who has devoted much of a lifetime to the investigation of an obscure culture and its relation to better understanding contemporary insanity.

"You might try, *In Search of Chaco*, by David Grant Noble, as well, depending upon how much you want to know about the specifics of Chaco being more than a picnic area."

This itinerant ranger's best trait was his thirst for kindred souls with a similar enthusiasm for antiquities. He knew I was a neophyte but could also detect that I wasn't your average Winnebago wanderer.

"Let me ask you something which you probably get all the time, but which I find a growing curiosity. Have you heard of anything called a Mogollon Cross? And if so, do you think it exists?"

A smile crept across his face, and he glanced down at the hatband he was nervously tweaking between tanned thumb and forefinger. "Oh, yah, I've heard a great deal about it over the years. All with several variations on how it came about, where it was lost, who was carrying it, and a surfeit of other speculations on something of value from ancient times which fuels legends. It's like the Seven Cities of Cibola. Do I believe they existed? No. At least not as cities of treasure. But then more has been written about them, even if conjured up by Spaniards to further induce the funding of exploration of the Americas and the proselytizing of Native Americans into Christianity. There's probably been more written about them than about the gold reputedly thrown by the Aztecs into Lake Texcoco along the Tenotchitlán causeway and now covered by Mexico City. Or about the Treasure of the Sierra Madré. So, who am I to put a damper on such myths? The curiosity seekers, treasure hunters and related book sales pay part of my salary. And since I'm trying to secure an elusive doctorate from the University of New Mexico on a civilization from which there is no written history, I have to be careful not to throw stones at those who seek the Seven Cities, Mogollon Cross, or any other antiquity of value which may be nothing more than the hallucinogenic dream of an explorer having drunk too much port in the 16$^{th}$ Century."

The two of us went on like this long enough for our own shadows and sun daggers symbolically to form upon nearby books and pamphlets. His name didn't matter, somehow, though he was to give me a card so that I could contact him if I had any more questions regarding the assault upon my own private treasure windmill. Then just as abruptly, our conversation terminated when the mask-less Lone Ranger departed to listen to and compare how a Chaco counterpart delivers the sort of walking tour dialogue which engages those carrying a paper bag containing a Gargantua Burger and fries for lunch.

Somewhere along a six-mile paved oval negotiating both sides of the canyon, I beached the old Pontiac. There were so few people around, I decided to take a chance and leave the top down. I didn't plan on being more than a Peyton Manning long ball away, anyway, and you might say I almost relished the thought of any banditos thinking they could rip out the radio in broad daylight with me indiscreetly peering down from some crumbling wall of sandstone rubble.

I figured one of the things I could do to mitigate a still mild throbber in my brain from the previous evening's drinking-and-beating combo was to hike the trail up to Pueblo Alto on the mesa above. Hah!

I found the beginning of this rocky path behind Kin Kletso, a ruin. But what the guidebook doesn't specify is that it zigs and zags so quickly upward amongst boulders, you have to use your hands even before ascending behind a huge stone façade. Now that's a rule I employ even when I'm not hung over. No hands. No way. When you're just a little overweight and wearing shoes with not much more support than water moccasin skin, you don't try scaling a 'trail' flouting more vertical than horizontal footage. I climbed about 30 feet in elevation above the ruins and got chickenshit. It was embarrassing sliding on my shorts down certain bits as young hotshots fearlessly scampered up and by in the other direction. But hey, again, carrying well over 200 pounds in one's very late 40s, when your head feels like a watermelon run over by a buckboard, dictates caution supersede valor.

One thing I noticed in several pueblos is that clear air can't have been a major consideration. Many of the windowless rooms were connected by four-foot-high doors only a $21^{st}$ Century midget could walk erect through. And if you had a torch or fire in any of them to see what you were trying to cook, it can't have been the same as sitting outside on a veranda, or in their case, probably on a stone patio without a parasol. And they had a lot of these circular kiva areas, where they probably sat around like a locker room football team contemplating either how they were going to fend off wandering invaders from the south, or smoking their own stuff.

The place had the exotic feel of potential treasure. But I hadn't a clue where to look, and then there was the matter of the handout Guide requesting that you keep your sneakers on the marked trails. You probably have guessed that I am somewhat of a rebel when it comes to rules or normal comportment. While I do occasionally suffer from bouts of guilt over my jaundiced middle-aged behavior, I get over it quickly. That's because I find annoyances foisted upon me by fellow citizens and/or their rules cause moody behavior. But isn't that the way journalists are supposed to be? Half crazy, alcoholic, iconoclastic, and capable of taking a few facts and spinning them into a yarn about as accurate as any given citizen's tax return?

So, what I did is to leave the Kin Kletso ruins and continue farther west on a dirt road that headed toward Casa Chiquita and Peñasco Blanco. Once I got about a hundred meters the other side of the ruins, I was completely alone. You know the drill about most turnouts along the highway or parking lots of State Parks and National Monuments. They are the destinations beyond which most itinerant families can't be bothered with walking more than a quarter mile from their cars. This means if you can get your butt down the trail just a little bit farther on, you have it all to yourself. And that's what the road along Chaco Wash was like. Empty. No *touristas* save me.

Now there's a little curved area of the road to accommodate getting across Clys Canyon. And it was once I was out of sight of any possible canyon cruisers and Smokeys that I let my pundit's curiosity overcome the need to follow the rules. As I was ambling along, I kept looking upward at the monolithic façade bits falling away from above and noticing that the top of the mesa was getting lower and lower. And that there were ledges with some hardy, desperately thirsty vegetation, particularly as I stumbled along the first leg of the Clys turn-out.

With a certain élan that can only be attributed to my near spontaneous combustion, I was off the trail and scampering upward. And with a few short climbs over or between boulders I had scaled the mesa and was up on top. Very naughty, but I couldn't help it since the alternative would have been scraping my knees trying to get up the steep, rocky trail above Kin Kletso.

The problem with this whole outlaw approach wasn't that I was defying authority. It was my lack of planning and knowledge of just what Pueblo Alto and all the other pueblos meant in the grand scheme of Anasazi civilization. I hadn't done my homework, and now that I had taken the trouble to climb up upon the mesa and maybe get a glimpse of the Great North Road, I realized the futility of biting off more than you can archeologically and historically chew.

There was also the disappointing discovery that along the way I had seen not a single item of value, even off the beaten path. No quartz. No pottery shards. No Mogollon Cross. Well, of course I hadn't expected to find anything the magnitude of the Cross. But it would at least have been nice to spot a tiny turquoise bead or some artifact I could illegally put in my pocket. Nada. Serves me right for ignoring Park rules.

Then guilt overcame me. Sometimes, that happens when even a societal retard such as me admits he has gone too far. I knew my having climbed up out of bounds was no good. My descent wasn't pretty, but it got me down the traditional route to Kin Kletso. I ripped the seat of my Bermuda shorts due to not being able to bound down with youthful agility. But again, isn't that the way journalists are known? Sloppy dressers who always have at least one food stain somewhere on frayed-at-the-edges clothing and one untied shoe with a hole in the side? Anyway, when I got down I felt relieved. My head was starting to clear and my ribs weren't hurting as much.

The next unplanned move I made involved walking over to part of the wash now dryer than a mesquite bush in late August. There were several places below where you could see that water once flowed, but for April, there was just a trickle. After checking around to see that no one would notice my descent, I schussed down a crumbling embankment onto the wash floor and began scrutinizing the dirt for any *objet d'art* which might resemble a clue to the Anasazi ancient civilization.

Just ahead I saw a glint, the sort of fleeting reflection of the sun as caught by something unnatural to the surroundings. Then it was gone. But I had seen it. So I backed up and retraced my steps toward the yellow disc in the sky again. And there it was, causing me to stop in my tracks. Keeping both bleary eyes focused on the exact spot beside a piece of dead driftwood, I awkwardly angled toward it, then took the stick of flotsam and stirred the dirt. And there it was. A tin foil chewing gum wrapper. Served me right for defying authority again.

When I had climbed back out of this natural aqueduct, which arid evolution may have played into the departure of the Anasazi, there were invasive moments when I questioned my vestigial sanity. Out in the middle of the northwest New Mexican desert, with sore ribs and a throbbing head, and I was still trying to pretend that I was Coronado or a daffy geologist thirsting for that find that will make all the past empty-handed expeditions worthwhile. Maybe not the Mogollon Cross, but maybe a silver nugget encrusted in dirt, or a diamond ring someone had lost while swimming in the wash when it once flowed uncharacteristically with the West's most precious substance.

The sun was out, however, and that, I told myself, was far different than the dim abysmal light you often set out in on the East Coast during spring when it might be gloomy for days. I decided temporarily to put the quest on hold and rejoin the human race. I hiked back to the Pueblo Bonito, a massive ruin which activities in its heyday must have resembled those surrounding a Yankees game. I could tell I was starting to get sunburned, so I put on a battered baseball cap some friends had made up for me with the words Algonquin Hotel Round Table plastered across the front.

Out on the main courtyard sandwiched among enough kivas to entertain the Elks, Masons, Odd Fellows, and perhaps ten other philanthropic organizations and drinking associations simultaneously, I spotted my intellectual Smokey friend from Aztec. He was lecturing a pack of Midwestern and Southern amblers on the best speculations available on what $12^{th}$ Century Indians did while taking centuries to complete construction of this monolithic stone-and-mud palace. But what I hadn't yet discovered, is that another of this disparate band of quasi-investigators was to enable my own obsessive treasure hunt.

# Kaliber at Pueblo Alto

(KALIBER)

O.K., so that red-headed woman had more than caught my attention during her brief invasion of my secluded realm off Highway 9. A siren encountered, and a siren dispatched. I was alone again, and that's the way I like it. Maybe it's an atavistic behavioral trait from my Navajo and Welsh ancestors. Then again, maybe I've left mainstream civilization too far behind. Even the St. Vincent-Millay poem about the candle burning at both ends had failed to free my mind of that woman, even though I've considered myself retired from the search for a female companion for quite some time now. Either they're high maintenance—and I'm a low-maintenance kind of guy—or they're petulant and edgy or misanthropic toward the male gender. For me, it's much easier to pursue my simple habits in peace, and the meager amount of money I had set aside for a year's hibernation was going to ensure no one of my diurnal paths to be any more important than another. Particularly when I might finally actively pursue the Seven Cities of Cibola, or alternatively to read a contemporary James Bond knock-off while sipping some Cruzan dark, Bacardi Select—or Ron Barillito when I can get someone to bring me a bottle from Puerto Rico.

I hadn't had more than four or five shots of rum that night after the woman vanished as quickly as she had arrived in my space much like a Cuban original Bacardi distillery bat. Eventually the next morning I awoke with a relatively clear head and vaporized what little alcohol was still in my septic system with a couple of stiff cups of Allegro Blend. It was only then that I could entertain getting back to deciding upon an adventure for the day. The thing about living alone and not having a 'job' was that it's hard to get going. Every day, or at least most days for me, I need to include some sort of vicarious experience through my reading before interaction with the reality of my natural surroundings—usually satisfied by a long run—and then a reversion to the vicarious liquid spirits-fueled musings.

Years ago, I had first bought a copy of Don Francisco Vásquez de Coronado's Diary and read it in just several periods of repose in the wildly painted pine bed I had at the time. The translation from Spanish gives a pretty good idea of the colonial attitude of divine right, as well as necessity not only of subduing and converting the natives, but also of bringing back galleons chock full of gold and precious stones to the king and queen of Spain. Coronado unfortunately managed neither. He did manage to get himself shot full of arrows and many of his amigos killed while wreaking havoc upon the various Pueblo tribes he encountered in New Mexico. But he hadn't really found those Seven Cities, nor brought back much more than a lot of outrageous tales of elusive treasure.

Now many feel that Hawikuh and other Zuni villages were the Seven Cities, while others feel the Big Seven were merely myths dreamt up to entice funding from Spanish nobility for expeditions to the New World. But your former Californian and Coloradoan had read enough, heard even more, and watched enough documentaries to possess the same fever found overwhelming if one ever comes upon either gold bullion or a substantial nugget. Just go to the Denver Museum of Nature & Science and slip into the Gems and Minerals chambers historic gold room if you really want to see if you have the fever. Then if you can stare at all that gold leaf and other hunks of the glittering substance without conjuring thoughts of your own private discovery, you're a better citizen than me. When you have a look at Tom's Baby, an eight-pound nugget of crystallized gold found in Breckenridge, I think you'll get the drift.

As you can see, with just the slightest provocation I digress when it comes to gold. So then if your imagination can take you just that one step further toward treasures on a much more colossal scale, you arrive at my own private halcyon proclivity to believe in the Magnificent Seven. Cities, that is. Roll those dice for a Seven. Somewhere out there, laden with silver, turquoise, and yes, maybe even gold.

Repeatedly during my directionless days, I combine a long run with some sort of exploration or another. First the scouting for something unusual from Mother Earth; then a gallop over even more of the same terrain to see what you missed above ankle level. New Mexico isn't as good as Colorado for rock hunting, but the best part of sleuthing for gems and other precious substances parallels fly-fishing: if you catch or find anything, it's just a bonus. The real fun is the quest, the search, the investigation, the scouting, the planning, the fever. I've been on more protracted outdoor searches at the end of which my body weight and what I'm carrying is less than when I started. But I never get bored. Give me my prospector's belt, complete with scratched magnifying glass, magnet, tongs, trowel, and then sometimes hang a World War II yellow Geiger counter somewhere upon me, and I'm set for a day's misadventure. The Geiger counter's for radon, the gas that comes off uranium, and other radioactive delights that you don't want to spend a great deal of time fondling or even proceeding within their cancerous proximity.

And I'm completely happy on my own, thank you. Though I'd have to say having the woman in white scanning the ground for substances worth collecting intrigued me. She's probably a major pain in the ass to a pariah like me whom she undoubtedly would label a typical male chauvinist or burned-out drifter. Then again, the nice thing about having been to Nam is that you don't give a shit what anyone thinks. Actually, from time to time, I do wish I had a few of the old buddies around. Or I get to daydreaming about one of those afternoons when the remaining testosterone drive gets indulged by a few drinks and then a sweaty roll in the hay with a woman who gets off the same way you do. One who lives for the moment rather than for family, country, religion, or some other honorable diversion from finding one's own essence of existence.

Few men pack in a good salary in a big city and head out into desert surroundings to discover the meaning of life. They've already found plenty of meaning in the bars and restaurants and women they frequent. I'll probably be dead when they're still teeing up on the 18$^{th}$ hole somewhere where grass growing and golf are still permitted. But me, ah, well...Maybe I read too much Edward Abbey. Or maybe I'm destined to be hermetic since even a brief stint as a forest ranger proved to include too much supervision. Still, one thing I do know, and that is that I will have really been out there. Out there where there are still no franchises, nor many fences, yet where survive the unusual hearty flora and fauna of the desert high country.

It felt good to get rolling in the old Subaru wagon, on which at least one layer of paint had incinerated from solar torture, and much of the rubber trim crumbled from fluctuations in temperature. But being well into its third hundred thousand miles, it's still going, even after I let it sit for long periods behind a rock near my shack.

Taking the southern route into Chaco Canyon is not advised by almost any reference you consult. It's about 22 miles of rolling, rutted dirt road, complete with huge rocks which can explode a tire, and elevated cattle guards over which if you take them too fast your head thonks the ceiling to let you know you're still alive. I mean, it should be a 20-mph trip, but I usually take most of it at 45 and hope I don't bust an axle or pop a tire. And of course, none of that addresses what would happen if you get halfway up that vast arid valley and it starts to rain or snow. Fortunately, the Suby Dooby's a 4-wheel drive, but even so, the trip is only for days when the sun has dried those ruts solid.

There's also a certain self-congratulation when you arrive at pavement near the Fajada Butte. That means you've made it, and even though you are still a long drive from anywhere, there is a satisfaction gained from having completed an arduous journey. All you must do is open the door of your car and you will see all the accumulated dust that serves as a reminder that you have tempted Mother Nature again and survived.

Did I mention the mixed feelings I get upon arrival in the canyon? There was a brief period I worked for the Park Service at Chaco. They were all real nice folks, and I didn't get fired, even though my attitude deteriorated over time. I don't know if you've ever awakened one day when it's time to go to a job, a day which cumulatively is nothing more than a long progression of such days, and said, 'That's it.' Meaning, you intended to make that your very last day of mindlessly earning money through employment you find distasteful or boring. Chaco duties were neither boring nor distasteful. It was doing what I was told that got to me.

I liked the Park. I just hadn't liked putting on a uniform every day. I had had enough of that in Southeast Asia. And there was also the fact that even though the accommodations are reasonable for such a remote and dry location, everyone there is like on another planet. Miles from the nearest restaurant, bar, cinema, gymnasium, or just plain anywhere to make you feel you're still a part of occasional sophisticated Western life. There's a reason most folks live in cities. And contrasting reasons why others do not.

Now for me, the problem wasn't being out there away from the busy main street of Farmington, or the galleries of Canyon Road in Santa Fe. It was having a limited choice rather than no choice in the characters you interact with daily. That may sound strange, but when I quit my job maintaining those mythic surroundings, moving down to my shack gave me the inexplicable freedom of not having to deal with a handful of pleasant people among whom you cannot pick and choose. Many don't understand solitude, but reclusion was welcome, and still is. When I need company, I drive into Grants, Gallup or Santa Fe and then have the luxury of speaking to whom I please. Observation is my thing, whether it includes my surroundings or the characters in local hangouts.

The journey up to the Chaco heaven on that spring day was for a different reason. I wanted to scout around the different ruins and see if I could detect any sort of pattern. Could the cities of Chaco have been construed as the Seven reputedly from Cibola? Probably not. But that sort of unplanned sleuthing is just the kind of exploration I like best. Getting out on a nice day and just peering at old construction or rocks or unusual cacti. Not the sort of thing for most people. Then again, Nam did that for me. Got me to the point where even being directly accused of rural insanity would do nothing to dent my ego. Get me out there. Give me a clue. Or don't give me a clue. It's the quest.

My intent was to start at what is generally considered the center of the original cosmological world of the Anasazi, Pueblo Bonito. It is from there that the Anasazi world spread out as if ordained to defy understanding by future generations on what exactly they were up to. And it is there, just as in Egypt, Peru, and Mexico, that an ancient civilization evolved in relation to its perceived universe, and in so doing evidenced some knowledge of astronomy and the relationship of heavenly objects to their own singular terrestrial domain.

There's a certain feel to the place, I'll say that. You don't have to work there to notice the aura. The changing colors upon the canyon walls in late afternoon; the phantasmagoric feeling you get while driving west on the paved loop; the solitary Fajada Butte acting as a daytime beacon at the east end of the vast elevated northwest New Mexican expanse. There is much to be learned from that cosmological center, yet comparatively little understood from the limited amount of unearthed former civilization.

The alignments portend that the Anasazi knew something of astronomy, and the cardinal directions, specifically. Yet when nothing written ever existed, save petroglyphs and pictographs, the speculations pounding through anyone's brain as he or she walks among such ancient creations are mind-boggling.

Chaco is not really something you can do in a day. You can find any given set of touchstones, tests merely inspiring you to investigate further. But if you've come from Illinois or Connecticut or more traditional living arrangements and are towing two or three hungry and tired children, there is little likelihood you'll make that drive in and out more than once. And therein lies a spiritual as well as archeological protective barrier from most spontaneous investigators. Oh yah, the curiosity's there. But by the time they arrive and get moving for clues amongst the ancient rubble, it's near that time in the afternoon to depart to get back to Santa Fe, or that motel that temporarily has become their haven from the arid elements and the burning solar disc above.

It's probably the kivas which most create the spell of past behavior few from contemporary urban surroundings can begin to comprehend as social gathering places like perhaps churches in their suburban lives. Round and shallow, and for whatever purpose, the Great Kivas exude communality. No matter where any Native Americans sat walked, or bathed therein, they were never alone, at least compared to those now ensconced in contemporary corporate cubicles or rectangular offices with isolated corners.

And yet within the many hundreds of rock-lined rooms of the larger pueblos, it immediately occurs to most visitors that there would have been little light without fire. And fires meant interior smoke, even with vents high in the walls or through the ceilings and roofs.

But these are just a few of the desultory musings that initially occur to those quietly ambling through the ruins. It's almost as if you have stumbled upon a construction-and-usage conundrum about which you can do nothing. It's a mystery. It defies your most vivid imagination. And yet slowly but assuredly it invades your psyche very much like the sirens of ancient sea lore.

For me, going back to Chaco can be a bit awkward. All my former fellow rangers are more than friendly when I return. And yet, encountering them, complete with all the false assurances of how everything is fine in my remote life, makes me uncomfortable. Everything isn't really fine, though it sounds from what I've formerly told you that reclusive life is the one for me. Much of my obscure habits do make sense. And yet if you talk to any urban anthropologist, they will tell you that the complexity of overall civilization never regresses. While pockets may exist or spring up which are throwbacks to more simple times, the overall achievements and complexities of civilization keep advancing. In mid $20^{th}$ Century we developed jet travel, and in late century the internet and electronic mail. Progress doesn't take a pause, nor does anyone's longing for simpler times easily find answers. Often those wishing a simpler existence must relocate, as I did, to a rural or small-town area to cast off all the accoutrements of urban complexity.

I did relocate. But unfortunately, you do not forget all that you have learned and customarily enjoyed in one of those complex and varied urban existences that habitually test one's mental fortitude.

You miss some of it. And you miss the sophistication of big city minds with big city dreams of accomplishment. But only some of the time.

For April, the day was bright on the Kelvin scale, enough so that if you turned around when passing Fajada Butte, you might be able to see nearly to Mexico. I didn't want to stop into the Visitor Center just yet and must go through all the pleasantries of reencountering one or more of my former amigos. There are always the best intentions. But if you are to avoid the repetition of explaining just how your obscure pursuits are going, you try not to encounter those you know only slightly better than the surroundings you have come upon without adequate explanation.

I beached the old Subaru in a lot near Pueblo Bonito, with the thought that I must always start at the cosmological center of the Anasazi realm. I had convinced myself that whatever clues would present themselves to me more likely than not would evolve from the huge complex of late-first and early-second millennium life. Realistic is what I would call my approach, one which never expects anything—as in fishing or rock hunting—yet always promises the inevitable: that peculiar discovery of some obscure object or concept which gives your day the illusion of being rewarding.

When I reached the broad courtyard and the nearby Great Kiva, there was a motley group listening to a lecture by a ranger I knew did not work regularly at Chaco. I was pretty sure he was from Aztec, and from past conversations knew him to possess an encyclopedic knowledge regarding the history and archeology of a variety of Southwestern Native Americans. He was gaunt, with a slightly slouching posture making him appear an intellectual uncharacteristically wearing a neat and pressed uniform. I was careful not to get too close, because I didn't want him to recognize me. And yet I suffered an overwhelming curiosity as to just what his approach to informing these tourists would be for the occasion. It was easy to pretend I was observing other parts of the ruins while I remained within earshot.

His patter seemed informative without being condescending, and it was obvious he was tailoring his remarks to the disparate band of adults and somewhat inattentive teenagers shifting from one leg to the other in the morning sun. We've all been 13 or 14 once and can well remember how a survey of those of the opposite gender often precludes close attention being paid to the non-essential matters at hand. The problem with hitting 50 or 60 or 70, as the saying goes, is that you're invisible, but your eyes still work.

"The guy knows his stuff," came the voice of a guy who looked like an overweight character not really fitting the profile of your average tourist. His face was red and bruised in places, as if he had been in a recent bash-up, and I got the feeling that the red arms and calves dangling from Bermuda shorts meant he had spent more time in cities than out on the local ranges. After he made that comment, he glanced once or twice at the ranger's retinue, and avoided checking me out further. But there was no doubt his remark was intended for yours truly.

"He's one of those idiot-savants who doesn't get the girl," I replied, "but rather a Nobel Prize just when everyone thought he's a harmless nerd on a quest for knowledge few can begin to appreciate."

"It's approach-avoidance for me," the big guy answered. "I want to know what he's saying, without standing amongst my fellow citizens. Somehow, I always recoil at moving in a mob. Which made it difficult for me to cover football games as a hack journalist."

Self-deprecating remarks I always take with a grain of salt. Some of those who speak as if they can't write a squib on a car crash, pen some of the most eloquent sentences. "I know what you mean," I concurred. "I always keep my distance. Otherwise, I'm repeatedly tempted to interject my own jaded input into an already fact-filled lecture. It's easier to stay on the periphery or out of range."

"Unfortunately, I wasn't able to do that last night—as you can see from my face. A little altercation outside an off-reservation place called the Radon Bar. My problem is not staying out of range. Particularly if I've had a few medicinal beverages."

"Yah. Well, I've been there. But I stick to my own pursuits outside of places like that. I'm like you: if I get a few drinks in me, there is the probability of saying something someone else is going to cause me to regret."

The two of us went back and forth like this, intermittently trading jabs at the foibles of urban existence and comparing the destinies of two solitary figures with a moderate to heavy disdain for that still sometimes strangely alluring mainstream life. The big guy was from New York and had put sports journalism on hold while he took a few weeks or months to scout out the Southwest. He had a manner of getting right to the point, candor for which I've always misguidedly striven. Because if you do, you inevitably have very few friends and have annoyed them enough so that they quit trying. His size conveyed that he had probably been more active in hard-knock sports at one time but was now combining a gourmand's diet with the same serious intake of alcoholic beverages I manage.

Before I knew it the two of us were still blabbing and walking away from the lecture group intent upon a one-hour dose of ancient civilization. Neither of us apparently is suited toward the conformity involved in moving along like a herd of grazing buffalo, anyway, and I think each figured the other might know a few things worthwhile or clever without the accompanying tedium of suffering solely the listener's role.

"I figure I got money in the bank, and just enough time out here to do some damage to people's opinions on New Yorkers and at the same time combine treasure hunting and cocktailing without having to cover a sporting event."

I couldn't help but empathize with this fellow cast-off of urban insanity. Yet at the same time, when I hear the word 'treasure,' it has the same allure that it's always had since reading Hardy Boys books.

"You hunting for anything in particular? Or are you just kind of feeling your way as to what might be out there in these deserts?" I inquired as we continued to walk up some steps near some smaller kivas.

"Well, I know you might think I'm a little unbalanced, but I'm a sucker for a good story. And two guys in a New Orleans bar told me about something called the Mogollon Cross. It was probably an apocryphal tale, but it was just long enough to whet my curiosity. I figure I'm out here. What have I got to lose?"

"Couldn't agree with you more on the search for some obscure geological and man-made attraction. I've heard my share of stories about the Cross, and I alternate between keeping a jaundiced eye peeled for anything on it and thinking it's a load of crap. That's the way I am, though. One minute I'm thinking certain historically elusive treasures like the Seven Cities of Cibola are just over the next ridge or below our feet, and the next that they were dreamt up by a couple of Spanish guys like us who wanted the King and Queen to provide them with the ships and other adventurers to get them away from the humdrum of Sixteenth Century Madrid Catholicism."

He kicked a stone, more in agreement with the common perception of the futility of such exploits. "It's the kind of hollow bullshit I always find more engaging than reality. People used to ask me, 'What's there to write about in football? It's the same cast of characters and games, week in and week out.' And it was then that I would just pucker my lips as if talking to a neolithic man. To even begin to explore the minutiae and trivia I find interesting about a sporting event with someone possessing a mindset of a goose destined to become pâté seemed pointless. Those sorts of guys are doofays, who think the only relevance in modern day society is the litany of internationally popular Bush crowd decision-making—

the kind that incites flag and effigy burning. Sport often is misidentified as a pursuit for the idle. They don't get the bit about it's being a metaphor for life itself. That everything is the pursuit. And that sitting on one's haunches watching prime time sit-coms is no different than scoping out your local football team. What you get out of it is up to you. Viewing can be mindless or inspirational." He paused but was definitely on a roll about my sort of intolerance for a risk-free life and inability to conform. "Sorry, I do tend to go on. And it gets worse when I drink."

"This afternoon I'm going to drive down to La Ventana to scout around. It's near El Malpais lava beds, about which many tales have been written of buried treasure. If you want to meet me at the Chaco Visitors Center parking lot around two, you could follow me down there to check for the Cross or anything else that sparkles, for that matter. I've got to go for a run up on top of the mesa. Going to try and check out the Great North Road. But I'll be back by two, if you feel up to a drive and a survey of some unusual terrain."

"Sure, why not. It'll keep me from cocktailing for a few more hours, and what better place to root around than in the Badlands."

A half hour later I had changed into my running togs in the Visitor Center restrooms and had driven to the Kin Kletso parking lot to begin the scramble up to the top of the mesa as a walking warm-up. My intention was to again check out the Great North Road from Pueblo Alto during a run round the loop trail that circles various levels of the mesa tops. There were bound to be few tourists up there, and the trail and mesa-top pueblo were among the few places I hadn't revisited since my days as an NPS ranger.

No one knows exactly what the intent of the Great North Road really was. But they do know it travels 50 kilometers within a degree or so of due north, just one more indicator that the Anasazi had a relationship with the heavens and understood cardinal directions.

At one point in the parallel 30-foot-wide roads now basically covered with dirt and vegetation, the dual highways expand to four parallel roads. That remains a great mystery, as do the roadside *herradura* hut ruins occurring intermittently. The roads are particularly hard to fathom because the Anasazi reputedly lacked wheeled vehicles and domesticated livestock to pull them. Some feel the roads were built to lead the dead north to the spiritual afterlife, perhaps to where the Great North Road ends at the rocky outcroppings of Twin Angels and beyond which lies a descent into Kutz Canyon.

In my many explorations of natural phenomena both above and below ground, I have found there simply is no substitute for seeing something yourself. You can examine guidebooks and websites, listen to stories from miners, archeologists, anthropologists, geologists or all-ologist yarn spinners, and watch a cornucopia of video documentaries made by Anglos. But put yourself out there, keep walking in areas few have ever passed over or under, and you will be amazed at how your perceptions alter, and your consciousness is changed.

And I'm not talking about Native American rights or sacred grounds, though they often are reason enough to leave areas untouched. But rather the effect Mother Nature herself has upon you when you take the trouble to visit. They talk about auras. Yet time after time when you're out there somewhere along that creek bed, in some cave, or above the vestiges of some ancient civilization, goose bumps or hair standing on end are just two possible effects. Each natural phenomenon has its aura. Whether any such specific visitation alters your future depends upon what your senses take in during the pursuit.

Initially behind Kin Kletso you have to climb up perhaps 40 feet or so until you reach a passage between the mesa and a vertical piece of sandstone permitting a narrow rocky trail up to the mesa top. Once up there, hikers or risky runners can set off east along the mesa's edges to circle above the prehistoric Jackson stairway carved in the wall, or north up a series of levels to Pueblo Alto perhaps 300 feet of elevation higher than the 6100 feet of the canyon floor. I wanted to get to Pueblo Alto as quickly as possible so that I might gaze down across the rolling valley to the north.

After slowly ascending over sandstone outcroppings and jogging amidst the sparse sagebrush, cacti and other hardy survivors of the northwest New Mexican high desert, there it was, the mesa-top pueblo from which the Anasazi most certainly could view anyone coming from the north. Was it some kind of reservoir? Or merely a lookout station to provide advance warning of anyone approaching their canyon civilization?

While gazing out from either New Alto or Pueblo Alto the same questions always arose as to just what the Anasazi were up to by building the roads. I realized that the spectrometry employed to 'see' former roads and other invasions of natural terrain undoubtedly reveals a lot more than I was going to be able to scrutinize and digest while trotting. Yet my curiosity was still there. I wondered, for instance, if at one time the Great North Road was completely level? At least for the 50 kilometers until it reaches Kutz Canyon. Sure, there are now rolling ups and downs along the route, but close to a thousand years can do that to landscape beset by winds, rain, snow and running water, or to eliminate any grading efforts. You could probably distinguish topography as far as Pierre's Ruins, or about a third of the 50K to the stairway down into Kutz Canyon leading to Twin Angels. Archeological examinations have shown berms and stone walls lined at least parts of the road. What was the purpose of the berms? And when the rest of the world had the wheel, why had this invention gone undeveloped in the astronomically complex civilization of the Anasazi? Had they gone to all that trouble simply as a path for the dead? And those horseshoe-shaped *herraduras* that had once stood sentinel along the route. Were they way stations for those traveling north or south?

I was sweating profusely even though it wasn't that hot. The sun is so bright in New Mexico that 60° can sometimes seem like 80°F when you're running just a moderate pace and watching the ground below to avoid tripping on a prickly pear or piece of sandstone. Whenever I explored the loop, I felt like Lewis or Clark heading into unknown territory. What was it I was seeking? Or was it simply the run over sacred ground of one remote branch of my ancestors that was the answer?

Well, there was one other reason I was up there. Long ago I had jumped the rope surrounding the now out-of-bounds mound south of Pueblo Alto to violate the American Antiquities act by picking up several inch-long potsherds. I wanted to return them. Nothing to do with the *chindi* Navajos would say might haunt me in retribution. Call it more a regression to the spirit of the place I should have held sacred all along.

Meanwhile, the continuation of my run east had me scanning the ground for artifacts anyway. I saw nothing other than the guiding rock cairns to keep you on the trail and the eternal components of Mother Nature such as occasional crumbled sandstone indicating they had once perhaps been built into something useful. The rust-colored pipes interspersed along the mesa edges are perhaps the most colorful part of the journey. Theory has it that crawling sea life created tunnels that then filled later with iron-rich minerals making them look like spidery, rusty rebar planted here and there to stabilize the rock.

My intent was to run the five-mile loop. Yet occasionally I stopped to contemplate possible meanings of man-made contributions or to take in the sweeping panoramas south across the canyon and down the expansive valley beginning between the West and South Mesas. I had agreed to meet the big man at two, and that still gave me a half hour or so for stops and spontaneous investigations. There was stuff out there. I was sure of it. Artifacts, untold discoveries, and curiosities defying explanation. It's my type of thing. And somehow, I knew that eventually the whole cosmological world of the Anasazi was going to come into focus. It was just a matter of time and further explorations.

Many people might think, 'Hey, you're part Navajo, figure it out.' But I merely had a great-great grandmother who was a Navajo, and the rest of my ancestors were a bunch of drunken Welsh coal miners and coopers and their watchful wives. Besides, the whole spiritual approach of the Anasazi is Puebloan. Even if I wasn't a half-white guy who may have just enough color in his skin to qualify for Native American programs and assistance. I don't even want to try to take advantage of any such minimal bloodlines unless forced to avoid getting kicked out of my off-Reservation squatter's shack. Still, when you have some Indian blood, it's easy to think you have the wisdom of Sitting Bull and the adventuresome spirit of Geronimo.

It was on my return that I spotted a substantial pottery shard. The piece was like an iceberg. When I caught a glint of the chiaroscuro of faded black-and-gray paint upon clay under dust, only about 10 percent of the piece was visible. It took me a couple of minutes to dig out, and when I did, the zig-zag pattern remained nothing more than another mystery. Did the Anasazi attach any meaning to the patterns on their jars? What did they carry in them? And why would there be shards end up where they are away from Pueblo Alto or the other main pueblos below?

I thought about trying to carry the piece back with me the two miles I still had to run. Another violation of the Antiquities Act. But the temptation was always there. Yah, O.K. so there'd be the habitual ethical problem of taking artifacts from a sacred location. But have you ever checked out the British Museum in London? There are more sarcophagi and mummies in that haunting reliquary than probably all of Egypt. Not that that's a justification. It's more that if I wanted an excuse to steal sacred property I could fall back on the old 'everyone's doing it,' or 'I'm a Navajo and it's on our Reservation,' or any of the other quasi-justifications one can come up with for theft. But to paraphrase the character Houk from the Tony Hillerman book, *Thieves of Time*, those who steal potsherds are merely those who achieve the same result before archeologists can legally dig them up and steal them for museums.

It was heavy, anyway, so I covered it up and found a rock I placed approximately three feet east of it, so that if I wanted to come back and try and at least examine this exotic find, I could return whenever I wanted. I left this ancient artifact to the gods of Chaco.

Galloping the last mile or so back along the mesa front to the descent to Kin Kletso infused me with some strange energy. If I wasn't a cynic, I'd think that my having decided to leave the artifact had been rewarded by my ancestors. The globe was shining above, and I felt rejuvenated for a semi-alcoholic middle-aged Nam vet with a reality problem.

After I changed into some dry clothing in the Visitor Center restroom, the big guy was waiting by a huge vintage cobalt blue machine. I know, I should have showered, but, hey, field expediency, as they used to say in the military. I probably could have used the shower if I talked to one of my former Park Service co-conspirators. But like I said before, that would have required all the obligatory chit-chat that at my age and reclusion I no longer wished to endure.

Quivira Cantrell's old Pontiac was some campy 50s cruise vehicle. We came up with a plan for him to follow me to Grants, and then leave my truck and take his styling machine on down to La Ventana.

I could tell this was going to be an expedition I would like. The big man and I shared the same thirst, and I don't mean for medicinal spirits. I wanted the Seven Cities, and he wanted the Mogollon Cross. And something told me they were not Halona and the Zuni seven cities, but rather that both the cities and the cross were around somewhere within range of the San Juan Basin. All we had to do was find them.

# The Wizard at Acoma

(CHICHILTICALLI)

Hosteen Ketl Lizhiní-Shá is somewhat different than a traditional Diné. I mean, he's old, so he's supposed to be a bit eccentric. And serving as a Pullman waiter for years probably altered his mind-set from once dominant Navajo traditions. But sometimes I think he takes the whole Native American mystique thing too far. When I arrived at his hogan, he was back in the tipi burning sage. He was probably making an offering to the *wei*. It's one of the traditional things he still does on a regular basis, when he's not sneaking a smoke on the rocks up behind his place. He's not the stereotypical Native American who drinks enough to forget he lives in what has become a white man's country. He's the stereotype with periods of verbal lacunae and thoughts left unsaid. Even his hogan is a little unconventional. Traditional hogans are round or six- or eight-sided and don't usually have a porch, but his was a combination of the rectangular mud walls and pine log corners slanting inward at the tops, with a dilapidated wooden porch protruding off the front.

Ketl still believes in the resurgence from the south of the peasant hordes that will displace the white man conquerors and reacquire their native lands. Of course, all of that forgets that most of our tribes originally on the continent constantly warred with and took lands from one another. It's a convenient spiritual philosophy. And still, old man Ketl and those that think like him are right to dream of simpler times, when hunting and gathering was still a noble tradition of survival rather than what a bunch of overweight white hunters do from duck blinds.

I had come to his place in a philanthropic spirit. He doesn't like driving as much as he used to and spent the better part of an hour telling me about the two white females he drove into Cuba after they crossed paths at Pueblo Pintado. I told him I had sent them there. We both agreed there was something mysterious about the little girl.

I was going to drive him down to Acoma. He likes the history of the place and hiking round there. It is a spiritual center, even if Coronado in the sixteenth century didn't recognize the aura. But I knew I was in for a few lectures on how hard done by the Sky City world—the present USA's oldest continuously populated city—has become compared to its halcyon days of warring with the Spaniards.

Even though I arrived about 15 minutes late, I knew he wouldn't be ready. Almost like 'Indian time,' and the stereotypes built around the concept that minority peoples are slow moving and slow thinking and thus time has no meaning. In many Native American lives, the daily path of the sun and monthly path of the moon have more meaning than the concept of years.

In Ketl's case, he is just an old man who prefers a certain mystique about him. Occasionally it leads to a few tourist/guide dollars, during which exploits he probably hearkens back to his days as an authority on the Santa Fe Railroad. He has a good heart. And he has paid his dues. So occasionally I go up to his hogan and we might smoke something making us feel our Native American kinship—even though through our mothers I'm a Zuni and he's a Diné. And Hosteen Ketl also has a way, when it suits him, of divulging some scrap of gossip he picked up somewhere in his wanderings.

When you catch the odd glance at his charred pipe and sunburnt wrinkled visage, Ketl Lizhiní-Shá appears like what most white people associate with an Indian look. Wizened, long white-haired, and taciturn. The students of Oxford would love him if a journey that far for him were still possible. When you asked him something, he had a way of puffing his pipe a few times, or gazing down at some burning sage before answering, a whole studied approach to what he had discerned over the years works best with the palefaces he encounters. It also gives him a certain stature, without being a chief. Ketl's more of a raconteur for the tourists, a persona the modern-day Diné find amusing or pitiful. He's still part of the Navajo fabric, however, and he's also a cornucopia of historical information on northwest New Mexico, again, when the mood strikes him. Like many a Navajo, he can pass long periods without saying anything. Then suddenly, out of the blue, he'll make some profound statement about the state of Native American affairs, or upon the meaning of an artifact he came across while on one of his spiritual walkabouts that day. And "Yah-te-eh," was all we both said for quite some time after he returned from his tipi.

As we set off east from his desolate digs near Coyote Canyon along highway 9, the hair on my neck suddenly stood on end. It may seem I'm exaggerating, but taking any sort of journey with Ketl is an honor. While aging leaders in the Anglo world might misbehave and fail to set noble examples while working for huge corporations, tribal elders still command my respect. Many Diné and Zuni still harbor an atavistic notion of age being a requirement of wisdom. And I was just old enough to have been brought up more on the Anglo written and spoken word than on television and video games, a factor in my appreciation of knowledge acquired through both real and vicarious sources. I also like the traditions of story telling from tribal elders. There may be many things that Ketl doesn't know—written wisdom, for instance, acquired while reading at Magdalene

College in Oxford. But there is nothing to compare with the man who says little, yet occasionally speaks from a lifetime of experience. There was no forked tongue lingo from Ketl. Well, maybe a little for the tourists. But only harmless stuff, rather than outrageous fabrications that affect people's lives negatively. He wasted no words, an art form mistakenly confused with ignorance by those loquacious talk show types that equate garrulousness with intelligence.

"What do you think the Acoma first thought when they heard Vasquez de Coronado was coming? Do you think they went for the 'Gods on strange animals' routine? Or that they were beasts with hairy faces?"

Ketl stared straight ahead out the cracked windshield of my truck. His eyes squinted a bit as he followed a hawk circling over a passing mesa. "The Acoma were only partially fooled. They had never seen metal armor or horses. No men with beards...But as other pueblos along the Rio Grande later figured out, the best way to deal with the Spanish 'invaders' was to lure them northeast. Reaffirm the Seven Cities and gold...Greed is a powerful siren."

As I imagined what he was saying, I knew he was right. Coronado and his band were a long way from Spain and Mexico City. And in an unforgiving desert as big and seemingly empty as all of Spain and more. Had they been less myopic and courteous, who knows? But like many tormented souls and fomented fools in the West, they were driven by treasure hunting, and failed to pay attention to the most valuable treasure of the unexplored territories' resources:

Water.

That liquid common in much of the world yet extremely rare in others. But always far more precious than gold. The standing and flowing substance that sustains all life yet is only appreciated when it starts to disappear. You can feel the blood it creates flowing just under the skin through your arms right now, can't you?

I didn't initially respond to Ketl's remark. It was all part of our ritual. My distantly related uncle thought of me almost like a son, and I thought of him as an avuncular wizard, to whom I could posit candid remarks about either contemporary or historic periods. The time always passes quickly. Periods of cogitation amidst spectacular surroundings. During these episodic journeys I always imagine I'm passing a peace pipe to a Zuni Chief in a tipi. Or watching the Apaches attacking John Wayne and the other Anglos inside the Stagecoach in Monument Valley. You're never quite sure how your mental and physical passage will be, of what perils you will encounter or visual delights you will digest out in the wilds of New Mexico or Arizona. Before I knew it, we had said little more and had arrived at the junction of highway 40 in Thoreau.

"Coronado was no fool, either," Ketl suddenly said after lighting up a hand-made cheroot of homegrown stuff.

I waited for the ancient one to continue. But there was nothing.

We drove in verbal silence yet motor vehicle cacophony among the juggernauts heading east along the great interstate transporting much of what railroads used to carry.

"Why wasn't he?"

Ketl took a deep hit on his smoke. I could tell he would roll the matter round that ancient brain of his until he found the words to express his silent analysis.

"Well...He created the illusion of his group being more powerful than they really were...The Spanish were vastly outnumbered. But they had superior weapons...And realized that they had to move on before disease or local tribes figured out their weakness and that they weren't actually gods."

I nodded, unsure if I believed all his commentary.

"But the main thing was the expedition itself," he added before again drifting into silent contemplation. "Coronado could write whatever he wanted. Every day was more interesting than the

Catholic days of Madrid...And the Seven Cities of gold legend grew like a fish story."

"You know the part-Navajo guy who lives further up on highway 9 that still is poking around northwest New Mexico to find the magnificent seven. He thinks they really exist, and he mines just enough peridot to support a quest as well as his rock hounding habit. The guy is like a modern-day prospector. Except that his primary motivation isn't buried treasure. He hunts rocks and then drinks rum while he looks them over."

The old man drew deeply on his glowing paper magic cigarette. Without his even saying anything, I knew what he was thinking. That it was just another guy spun off from shallow *belagaana* urban complexity now trying to find the meaning in life near Ketl's Glittering World. *El Viejo's* lips twitched almost invisibly, always a sign that some verbal observation is about to be delivered.

"Treasure hunting is for those who don't see the treasures all around them," Ketl remarked before pointing out a jackrabbit scurrying into some roadside bushes.

I figured it best to let the whole subject of Kaliber Ristraverdé drop. More likely my Diné uncle preferred to be bothered by as few other humans as possible before the spirit departed his physical being. No *Yeibechai* Night Chant would save him ultimately, anyway. Solitude was probably his most comforting companion. Later I would learn the two had a strange monthly symbiotic relationship.

We turned off the Interstate and began the single lane drive alongside the black lava beds of *El Malpais*. If you've ever been to the south end of the Big Island of Hawaii, the New Mexican 'Badlands' lava is similar even though the road was built beside it long after activity ceased. On the island of Hawaii, a highway often ends where the flow has most recently crossed the road. *El Malpais* is inactive, yet it still evokes that eerie feeling you get during a close encounter of the first kind with the effects from one of Mother Nature's unpredictable forces, even if now dormant.

The thing about many a highway and byway in New Mexico is that the concrete and macadam have little relevance, while the journeys upon either offer unique opportunities for first-hand observation of their majestic surroundings. These causeways of the West provide visitors and residents phantasmagoric surveys of more wildly spectacular rock formations than they'd ever be able to see during a far more extensive series of hikes. The views don't have the calming effect equal to being on foot. But they do provide the average citizen with the opportunity of going beyond video experience to a live, changing diorama of life. *El Malpais* is part of that magic fabric. The broken black chunks appear like a giant obsidian comforter that has been placed upon a bed without smoothing it out.

As a contrast, La Ventana is a giant arch that Stephen Lekson might find almost conforming to the speculative linear north-south Anasazi axis projection he places upon Aztec-Chaco-Paquime. It would seem there were very few architectural accidents from the period. Scouts and astro-archeological visionaries determined the best geographic as well as optimal locations for establishing residency. Available water, rocky fortification, and spiritual views were all considered. To many of those taking the trouble to drive down to the giant arch, La Ventana may seem in the middle of nowhere. But those people must ask themselves, long after a former world of primarily rural survival rather than urban sophistication, just what exactly is the middle of nowhere?

Ketl no longer has much of a sense of time. We supposedly were heading for Acoma, the pueblo still existing on top of a mesa further east of La Ventana. The old man likes revisiting his favorite places. Apparently, it's the sort of thing you do when you know your remaining lunar periods are numbered. So, the 20-minute drive south off I-40 allowed him to revisit both the lava beds and the giant arch.

When we got there, I knew we wouldn't stay much longer than the time it takes him to walk the trail to where he could better gaze up under the arch. La Ventana is another of those sites that can cause the back of your neck to shiver. In fact, if you imagine the majesty of a giant arched sandstone spectacle in the sun, you may even feel the back of your neck tingle after reading this.

Anyway, it's impossible to tell what Ketl was dreaming when his rheumy eyes looked up at the natural phenomenon. When we arrived, there were no other cars in the isolated lot, though one with a young couple was just leaving. The visit was ephemeral, as expected. Ketl never said a word, nor did I. He can suddenly allow some personality to escape, like he apparently did for the old woman and her granddaughter he met at Pueblo Pintado. But his real persona reveals the diffidence of one who thinks more than he talks. We've known each other a long time, and just to see him looking up at La Ventana is an uplifting experience. Sort of a social experiment in perceiving how you will feel in perhaps 30 years, when the importance of close companionship may either strengthen or diminish. Somewhat unnerving, yet at the same time reassuring, in that aging merely means more exposure to the unforgettable views of nature as well as indelible memories of those treasures.

We didn't stay long, and as we were climbing back into my truck, I noticed a vintage 50s convertible that looked familiar now parked in the corner of the lot. Then it came to me. It was that guy Cantrell's cobalt Pontiac I had seen at the Radon Bar, and it still had New York plates. He was around somewhere, but I didn't want to deal with the old man's displeasure over having to spend time with someone whom he would consider unworthy of New Mexican citizenry due to being a new arrival. To Ketl, unless you were born in New Mexico, you were an unworthy invader never to be taken seriously. So, without any comment by me on what I had observed, or determining where Quivira Cantrell had wandered, we departed La Ventana.

In less than an hour we had reached Acoma, the view from the north of the valley below spectacular and redolent of just what most visitors picture when they think of a New Mexican landscape. A broad sweeping arid and mainly treeless valley, expansive table mesas, and sandstone walls illuminated in various shades of Southwest pastel colors by the sun.

"Coronado had no idea when it came to understanding Native American life," I said as the truck descended into the valley. "Yet with probably only fifty men he was able to threaten an entire pueblo on top of a mesa. Mind boggling."

"He brought white man's diseases and the Catholic religion. Two arrivals the Zunis and Acomas could have done without."

Ketl hates going into the trailers which house the Native Americans charging tourists for bus tours and camera privileges. He says it reminds him of how far down the great tribes have fallen, in that they now rely upon tourist and gambling revenues for unnatural subsistence. Both the Acomas and Navajos count heavily upon those visitor dollars. But that distasteful fact is still difficult to digest for the old one. He forgets that his economic survival for many years resulted primarily from serving white people on trains. That such dignity comes from the life each of us creates for ourselves, rather than from external analysis by non-Native American observers who too easily dismiss our cultural phenomena as primitive or childlike. Who's to say, for instance, that watching a bunch of 300-pound men pound away at one another in a Super Bowl is any more culturally valuable than Zuni or Diné tribal members dancing to drums? Or that playing the stock market and driving a Lexus bring greater happiness than chasing a deer with a bow and arrow while on horseback? The Germans have the word *weltschmerz*, or the burden of the world upon one's shoulders, to describe the difficulty in accepting the foibles and problems of one's fellow man. Ketl has seen a lifetime of such extremes of behavior, yet he is somewhat doomed to remain silent. The old one chooses not to interfere with progress, at least as the world outside of his Changing Woman's creation sees it. His time has passed. Or so he thinks. Many may argue that Ketl's solitary and simple existence fails to utilize a lifetime of acquired knowledge. Yet Hosteen Ketl to my thinking thrives upon that simplicity, even though he is trapped between the old and new, with no remedy. His life will end with little fanfare or acknowledgment of his contributions to those with whom he has come into contact. Maybe both of us would have felt better at the time if we had known that the trailers were just temporary, awaiting the Sky City and Haak'u Museum to be built.

Anyway, that's the sort of stuff I conjure up when I'm with him. He inspires me to maintain my own path. Right now I am what many would consider an overqualified National Park Service staff member. And yet I feel much like the old man: I am a citizen of neither the Indian nor white man's worlds, but rather caught between both. Particularly after reading at Oxford, I understand each to some degree. And yet I cannot decide if I were to abandon one or the other, if either chosen course would bring peace of mind. Maybe that explains why I call Haak'u and its inhabitants by the white man's names, Acoma, and Sky People. Because I am of both worlds. My New Mexican existence remains existential. I go to work. I read. Occasionally I interact with either Native Americans or pale-faced curiosities. It is my fate for now, which I choose to accept until divine guidance or perhaps a good woman leads me in one direction or the other.

Like Ketl, I have trouble accepting the nature of my surroundings when I enter the trailers the Acoma members use to corral the tourists. You can buy the usual fast food and curios inside, and yet the whole scenario somehow seems inappropriate to the majestic natural surroundings. Again, neither of us knew back then that the hospitable Acoma in their future Cultural Center would serve lamb stew, fry bread, pinto beans, and other more traditional Native American dishes.

I try to tell myself to take both Indians and white folks one at a time. That some lead superficial existences and or speak with forked tongues, while others maintain their ideals and tell the truth as much as possible with a touch of humor. Many of those that enter the trailers are like cattle or sheep. They arrive in those huge Winnebago's or on tour coaches and are quite docile while they wait upon a shuttle ride up to view what is the modern-day Acoma pueblo.

Ketl had me park at the end of the lot so he could smoke in peace, out of range of anyone who might take issue with even a local puffing on an illegal substance. Ketl is too old to care if he gets caught, anyway. What are they going to do? Put an old man in jail for smoking hallucinogenic substances?

When I got inside, I realized that I couldn't handle it. Just as quickly I returned to the lot, and informed Ketl that I had to go on a walk. And it was only minutes later in the middle of the valley that I felt a return to sanity amidst such venerable surroundings. Again, it's not easy to reconcile a white man's education with an atavistic Native American mentality desperately calling for a simpler existence. My life remains a quandary.

# Ketl's Vision

(KETL)

When I return to places held sacred by Native Americans it usually depresses me. Even though for years I worked on the great form of transportation that brought white men out here to shoot buffalo, I have learned both worlds. Each has value. Yet what many consider sophistication is only a reduction in the more important daily functions of life. Is a restaurant meal with continental cuisine any better than corn tortillas fresh off a hot stone slab? Or a diet of hamburgers and French fries more nutritious than our traditional corn, squash, and beans?

Some think me a bitter old man, whose time is gone. And they are right. Yet one of the great solaces of old age is the ability to suffer no fools. O.K. so your limbs aren't as limber, you have to take a piss more often during the night, and you have to give up many of life's food and drink pleasures. But the comfort of solitary habits late in life helps one prepare for the long walk north to the final destination of the *Aniné*.

Chichilticalli thinks sometimes I suffer from dementia or Alzheimer's. But really, I suffer only a few physical changes, some memory loss, and a broken heart. I'm not naïve enough to think our *Dineh* lands one day will blossom with affluence. Our territory is primarily desert, and that's as it always has been. Oh, sure, we tolerate the tourists for the coinage of their realm. It buys the corn and beans and an occasional morsel of junk food. But as an ancient Indian like me approaches the time when *Aniné* become more visible on the horizon, these mainly undeveloped lands still beckon. There is no call to urban life, but rather a haunting summons from Changing Woman for the final struggle before the spirit leaves and the physical body decomposes underfoot within *Diné Bikeyah* lands.

For instance, the arriving hordes in modern day coaches and RVs. They are much like humans peering at goldfish inside of an aquarium. Their attentions are held for one or two hours maximum, and then like Coronado they move on, hoping that something else will jumpstart their spiritually deadened souls. All the while natural salvation is right within their grasp. Yet the quote, 'first and second worlds,' aren't going to regress to my type of existence. The internet, television and jet travel are here to stay. Forget damask tablecloths, silver settings and unsurpassed views of passing desert terrain on the Santa Fe Chief. Unless you can afford the American Orient Express, that era is gone.

But it doesn't mean a lack of nostalgia. Many would argue that I have failed to enter the 21$^{st}$ Century and Third Millennium, and they are correct. I take great pride in a traditional approach to my desert environment without television or the internet. I am a living anachronism.

On many a day, I might spend well over an hour concocting a late breakfast of eggs with peppers. I never met a pepper I didn't like. You have to build up to the hotter ones, of course, and a lifetime of habaneros, serranos and jalapeños may cause eventual stomach problems. But what habits don't eventually cause problems to the elderly? Even if you're Pat Boone drinking milk, or Joe Weider pulling a boat with your teeth out to Alcatraz, you still end up with aches, pains, and maladies.

Indians often live to old age. That's because many spend more time outdoors than indoors. Moving rather than sitting. Your skin eventually becomes cracked and leathery. But since it is an honorable distinction to attain the wisdom of many moons, external appearance does not matter. It is the inner spirit which best creates value within a tribal member.

The reason I ride with my friend Chichilticalli to *Haak'u* is because, like Chaco Canyon, the Sky People's place holds great mysteries and has a sense of magic. There is no gold. No silver—other than what jewelers buy to practice their art. Yet the aura of Acoma, if you ignore the trailers and RVs below the pueblo, always mesmerizes me in a way like Chaco and Monument Valley do. From the north you look down from above and there is an immediate feeling of having come to a magic world, even if now in some places invaded by trailers, vehicles and discarded fast food containers.

I didn't say anything to Chichilticalli when he left to go into those white metal boxes. He has the stomach for modern day Indian life. I don't. Usually, I smoke some medicinal herbs and then walk off the road somewhere where it is still peaceful and one can find solitude. Meditation alone remains the best companion for any elder. Out in the Acoma valley I find a spot. Sometimes I find the same place I have been before, but more often I discover another place with a view. Maybe on a sandstone outcropping. Maybe under a mesquite tree. Or sometimes on the rim of an arroyo. My natural surroundings still seem inviting even though soon I will leave them behind. The *Haashch'ééh* have made it so that during the aging process, the simple things of life appear more and more appealing. Fresh air, sunsets, scampering lizards, and all the desert settings that many take for granted, come better into mental if not visual focus as one ages.

Whether I like it or not, for short periods I still occasionally think of the ancient ones and how they encountered the Spaniards. It shouldn't surprise white people from outside the Southwest that

Indians initially were fooled by men with facial hair and silver skins who rode in on magic animals. Native American ancestors had no idea what they were encountering. Even poor translations were enough to disillusion them about the pale-faced invaders. They wanted treasure. The same sort of treasure that still haunts many of the modern-day invaders who value money more than the intrinsic natural wonders around them. It's not just the gold and precious stones. It's the monetary value of those stones that fires their imaginations and obsesses them with their quests. Sometimes I try to imagine what it would be like to open a chest of Spanish doubloons. And then I realize that the coins, whether shiny or not, would have little meaning for someone like me who buys little more than food. I trade with tribal women: I tell their children stories and they make most of my clothes. I have an old truck with little value that I rarely drive. I was given a cell phone I rarely use because all the people I know complained they couldn't contact me. To me, not being able to be contacted has intrinsic value. It permits uninterrupted solitude during those times when you wish simply to pursue the simple habits that bring your life meaning.

In the valley below Acoma, I was sitting out in the mid-day March sun meditating. For me, it is nothing more than reconnecting with my natural surroundings. Sometimes I don't even close my eyes but allow them to go out of focus even more than they usually are. I have eyeglasses, but rarely wear them. I can see at a distance fairly well. And the importance of meditation for me is to envision what appears out of the ordinary. And it may be of this world or that of the spirits.

As I sat in the bright light of the sun my eyes slowly went out of focus from their gaze out at the *Haak'u* mesa below the pueblo. For some reason I began to concentrate on the white woman and Indian girl I drove into Cuba. I can't say why, but probably because the little girl looked like she had a lot of Pueblo blood and didn't say much, just like me. There was something about her. I could almost feel that even at her young age, she is capable of great visions. During a vision of my own while in the valley of the *Haak'u*, giant pine logs came in and out of my view, and I felt as if a river of water was flowing all around me. But it was dark. Nighttime. There were many stars in the New Mexican sky, the kind you sometimes see against a blue ceiling in some Santa Fe bathroom. Several of the stars were twinkling. Seven in particular. And then my senses reminded me again of the water and the sounds it makes when drifting slowly by. And I saw a large plant with red flowers...

"Hey, Ketl," a voice sounded from somewhere at the end of a long tunnel. I couldn't understand how I could hear anyone, particularly a male voice, in my dream beginning with an old squaw and a young visionary in the high New Mexican desert.

"Hey, Ketl."

Then I realized it was Chichilticalli. He had walked up the road and being a Zuni tracker himself, had found my footprints leading to where I was entranced in my strange vision. I kind of cleared my head and wondered just how I was to interpret what I had seen in the dream. I opened my eyes only a little bit at first, the bright high desert sun acting with the enormous power that sustains all life on our planet. I could see Chichilticalli with his hands on his hips and his head slightly cocked. But I didn't say anything.

"Ketl, sorry to interrupt your meditation, but you said you wanted to be back before sundown, and you said you could watch a video at the Visitor Center while I stop in to see if my schedule is changed at all this week because of arriving *touristas*."

My mind tossed remnants of my recent dream and what Chichilticalli had said back and forth several times like the changes passing clouds bring to daylight. I had no control over these fleeting images of two worlds. If only I could interpret what I had seen. No matter. Chichilticalli has been good to me. I think he knows I will not see many more days of sun and nights of stars or monthly white light from the moon. He drives me to the areas of northwest New Mexico I find hold the most magic.

Chichilticalli looks like the stereotype you see in Indian and cowboy movies. Slightly aquiline nose, pockmarked face, and maybe an appearance that makes him look as if he is a jewelry maker rather than a National Park Service employee with an Oxford education. The strange thing, though, is he is well liked by his fellow workers. Chichilticalli never lords his education over other Native Americans, Hispanics, or Anglos. He even treats obnoxious visiting *belagaana* with respect. And he helps out at the Zuni Pueblo whenever he has some spare time. But I think eventually he will write an alternative history of the tribes of the Four Corners and central New Mexico.

I only wish I could leave him with something. A token. An emblem of his kindness toward an old man. I could leave him my hogan, I suppose. The Zunis don't care as much about vacating places of death as the Diné. But Chichilticalli is caught between the modern and ancient worlds. And living up in my hogan would be too isolated from the complexities of urban life he needs at least some of the time. And even though his exterior is not the type you see on the cover of *Vanity Fair*, he has a good heart. Someday he will find a woman who can dance back and forth between the old and new worlds. One who can appreciate the great high desert as much as the great books.

"Ketl, I can come back if you want to spend some more time..."

"No, that's O.K. We need to get going."

Ten minutes later the two of us were crossing north over the broad valley and beginning the climb out which eventually would carry us back to Interstate 40, the highway of the huge metal beasts of the 21$^{st}$ rather than 16$^{th}$ Anglo century.

Again, I wish it were possible to tell the comfort I have

just knowing someone like Chichilticalli honors me. He makes no demands and is respectful of my needing extra time for the simple daily movements that younger people take for granted. He is as loyal as a favorite piece of turquoise. But few are aware of his efforts. He is reluctant to say much, not because of being the quintessential Indian, but rather just the opposite. His ability to talk like a white man confuses many people he encounters. So, most of the time, he keeps quiet when he's around Anglo strangers. It's too bad, really. Because some day Chichilticalli will be remembered as one of the truly wise Native American minds. And his day will come, a day when he will make formal contributions to both Native American and white history.

"So, Ketl, do you wish to say anything about any visions?"

His words merely re-invoked the same streams that passed through my mind on the Acoma Reservation. There was one perplexing part of the vision, one that rarely occurs. A number came toward me in a blinding light.

"There was one thing I didn't understand," I said while staring out at the winding road in front of us.

"What's that?"

"There was a number."

"Maybe someone's address or age."

"Nah. It was 1066."

# The Madwoman at Chaco

(KATARINA)
When you've got a precocious nine-year-old granddaughter set upon visiting some ancient ruins, your daily regimen is fixed in stone. We were driving down from some time-forgotten motel in Aztec to Chaco Canyon, and Kahlo was beginning to get that sort of nervous impatience that comes from a combination of youth and an insatiable curiosity. Given my preference, I would have driven back to Santa Fe and sat on an Inn at Loretto balcony with a vodka and the *New York Times*. Yet, as we all know, the maternal instinct, even when estrogen has all but disappeared, still mandates shepherding young grandchildren.

I think if she could have done so, Kahlo would have dressed in chaps. For an adopted young woman with primarily Indian blood, she was far more the cowgirl than Indian maiden on the open range. It wasn't that Kahlo could bust broncos or throw a lariat, but more that her boundless enthusiasm always inspired her to want to be Annie Oakley, Belle Starr, or some other woman with a piquant Western reputation.

Kahlo was a study in contrasts. Perhaps the longstanding speech pattern problems she suffered were counteracted by a zest for wide-ranging adventures, ones often bordering on what I would construe as dangerous for a young woman. However, Aurore has always encouraged her daughter to maintain both curiosity and a sense of adventure. Often it has been difficult to sit quietly and not interfere with risk taking many would consider unacceptable for someone under 10. But we all have been children at one point. And there is always the possible alternative of raising a bookish nerd, who if delving too far into the vicarious spectrum, has even greater adaptation problems with peer groups and adults alike.

It's a notion with which I'm familiar, because in my childhood I was very much the same. Read all the classics. Practiced the piano while my socially better adjusted friends were playing doctor in tree forts or arranging dolls in miniature houses. I was a bit of a tomboy, as well, and there was a time when playing the piano was given a backbench while I developed my own adventuresome persona. The problem with childhood, as with adulthood, is always one of balancing your own behavioral penchants with peer acceptance. Not many children wish to know a piano prodigy. But they do just fine with a cowgirl, or dollhouse surrogate mother.

Having Kahlo under my care is helpful in several ways. I drink less. My daughter gains some separation time from the offspring. And Kahlo's infectious adventurous spirit rekindles some of the youthful feelings one rarely feels when over 70 years of age.

At first Aurore was going to come with us, but then demurred because of wanting to drive to a Mining Museum as well as cyber café with free computer usage in Grants, during which she could privately examine the exotic flora of the area. It seems she has a fixation that her sister was poisoned, which certainly wouldn't be beyond possibility since my daughter Ashleigh was despised or tolerated by a wide variety of family and former friends. Aurore's sister had become more obstreperous before her death, my feeling being that she was snorting too much cocaine. But then with my drinking, I was always reluctant to criticize her, habitually hoping she would find salvation in the form of a man who really cared for her. None of the women of our family fares well with the male gender. We seem to attract offbeat types to whom we are nothing more than an exotic bit on the side or household novelty.

Anyway, Kahlo was squirming in her rent-a-car seat the entire drive down to Chaco. The last perhaps 20-mile segment was a dusty rolling passage through a desolate area making one wonder how the Anasazi ever even reached Chaco Canyon to locate there. But then if you are used to going to Safeway instead of shooting a buffalo for dinner, the whole concept of canyon living seems a bit primitive and remote. When you're my age you question how you ever found romping around such great outdoor expanses inviting. Oh, it's not that one has lost the ability to enjoy beautiful desert vistas and the odd darting lizard. It's more that the energy levels required for hiking amidst sage and cactus somehow dissolves into a faint memory.

Kahlo, on the other hand, habitually gets excited if a rabbit runs across the road and disappears behind a mesquite bush. Because interacting with other young sprouts often proves too daunting, she divides her time between the vicarious pursuits of internet surfing and book reading, with an ability to climb things, or run over them as fast as possible without falling and scraping her knees. She is androgynous in that sense. Not able to leap tall buildings in a single bound, but rather capable of covering and discovering massive amounts of Wild West territory in one energetic go.

To prepare for Chaco, she has been studying Park Service web sites, blurbs on archeology and astronomy, books she has taken out from the Santa Fe Library or purchased at the Santa Fe factory outlet bookstore, pamphlets from Aztec Ruins, and maps she has dug up in obscure book shops or obtained at parks we've visited. There's no telling what she has learned at this point. And little chance she'd tell me, anyway. Once in a blue moon Kahlo suddenly will blurt out a spew of information or conjectures, usually provoked by my having questioned something she finds obvious.

Like many children, her feelings toward relatives vary from adoration to ridicule. One minute she'll be beaming in thanks for some effort you've made, the next annoyed when you have misread some phenomenon she insists is caused by something entirely different. When she starts fiddling with one of her braids you know Kahlo has either been conjuring up some important analysis in her lexicon of obscure deductions, or is about to take exception with the statement she feels you have just erroneously made.

The best strategy is to make the occasional observation merely to watch her reactions. When you get to know this tiny prodigy, it is easier to decipher how she will react to almost anything. The trick is, almost everything. Meaning, often some remark you find seemingly innocuous, Kahlo determines to be ridiculous. Once I said something to the effect that living in rural desert areas must be boring. It was as if I had implied her personal pursuits were a waste of time. Kahlo shook her head and snorted, as if to say I had better get my head examined.

When we got to Chaco, my plan was to provoke her into providing the highlight of my day as to the real nature of what went on with the Anasazi besides the pounding of drums and making of pottery. When dealing with my granddaughter, you must be very ingenious to extract comment. As I've previously mentioned, at times her stutter disappears. But to rid herself of that impediment, Kahlo must feel extremely confident on her subject matter, and that there is some immediate necessity to reveal her discovery.

When we had paid our entry fees at the Chaco Visitor Center, Kahlo didn't even wish to spend time watching videos or perusing books. She wanted to get going to see the Great North Road. Kahlo once said that this apparent road to nowhere was one of the keys to understanding the knowledge of the Anasazi. But she wanted to see for herself at least part of this highway apparently traversing from below the Chaco mesa top more than 30 miles north to Twin Angels. And who am I to prevent a nine-year-old from scampering up a rocky path to implant some more obscure data in her brain?

Indeed, just the short walk from the end of the paved road loop to Kin Kletso was trying Kahlo's impatience. She would get a few paces ahead of me, then turn and shift back and forth from foot to foot because of having to wait for the aged one. Finally, when we got close to the ruins, I sent her off to make her ascent up to Pueblo Alto and the Great North Road. Well, not exactly the Great North Road since much of it and many others now apparently remain covered by centuries of accumulated soil and hardy desert plants. Kahlo tells me that aerial spectrography or some such reveals roads no longer visible.

Anyway, by the time I reached what appeared to me an insurmountable scaling of rocky zigzags leading up the canyon wall, Kahlo had disappeared. I made a gratuitous survey of Kin Kletso, since at my age, while I still enjoy learning a thing or two, my interests have largely evolved into vicarious accumulation of knowledge which does not tax my fleeting energies. Some say if I would get off vodka, my energy would increase. But I once went several months without alcohol, yet the only surge experienced was boredom. When you've spent seven decades and more on the planet, most of the efforts one can make to improve physical wellbeing are tempered by the inevitable.

So, I walked around a bit, examined a few rooms, kivas and other pueblo creations making me glad for my eventual return to modern-day hotel room life in Santa Fe. Yes, questions still arise to someone as jaded as I. It's more that their answers seem to be of little import when one begins the protracted process of ridding oneself of earthly possessions for the final journey, whether it be to Twin Angels or elsewhere.

Kahlo said she wasn't going to hike the entire trail loop above, but rather attempt to walk down and out along the Great North Road a bit to do some of her Sherlock Holmes routine. Of course, a grandmother doesn't want to be accused of being over-solicitous, but well into the second hour of Kahlo's absence my concern was growing. After all, should something happen to her, I, as well as my daughter Aurore, would never forgive any such oversight of Kahlo's survival abilities amidst Mother Nature.

Finally, when sitting in the car and stealing the occasional sip from a flask was doing nothing to allay my maternal fears, Kahlo came bounding down the dirt road from Kin Kletso.

"Was it worthwhile?" I inquired innocuously.

Kahlo nodded vigorously, without even so much as breaking stride. "I n-n-need to go to the Pueblo Bonito kiva," she threw over her shoulder, as if all I had to do was manage to get back to the car as fast as my still shapely legs would take me.

She was fidgeting a great deal beside the car, waiting for the aged one to catch up before she walked on to nearby Pueblo Bonito. Kahlo was onto something, there could be no doubt. Yet being her grandmother meant that I might never be privy to these startling revelations from the nine-year-old prodigy. Her eyes were darting back and forth, as if what loomed amidst her surroundings was not as important as what was now harbored within the window of her mind. Kahlo lives in her own world. It isn't easy for anyone not having such preoccupations to understand her wanderlust and insatiable curiosity. On the other hand, we've all had those moments in childhood when visiting an observatory or waterfall or some such kept up our excitement for weeks on end.

I remember one past incident that held me spellbound, even when I was well into my late 20s and studying and performing classical piano. I had become enchanted with the solo by Bill Evans in *All Blues* on a Miles Davis album. It felt more right than any other brief jazz piano interlude I had heard. My mother surprised me with a concert ticket, and although of adult age, much like Kahlo, my excitement over the actual encounter captivated me for almost a month. The actual performance was ethereal, a terrestrial heaven to an adult with a childlike curiosity much like modern day youth experiences with favorite rock, country, or hip-hop groups.

For Kahlo, Chaco Canyon had taken on a mystic quality. Now visiting it as well as having studied it in books and on the internet had fascinated her ever since we had arrived in Santa Fe. I could tell her research was merely fueling some sort of theories she would doubtless pursue relentlessly. It was as if Kahlo's world had become that of the ancient Anasazi, and her focal point, getting into the mindset facilitating the origins of their archeological achievements. She wouldn't yet reach 10 years of age for quite some time. Yet that was no handicap for someone of Kahlo's acute sensibilities and boundless curiosity. My only hope was that she would not progress too far into the ethers of intellectual pursuit. That may sound short-sighted, but my own childhood experience combined with maternal instincts warned me against any such ascent into obscure knowledge further distancing Kahlo from her peers. The deeper one proceeds into the accumulation of knowledge, the lonelier it gets, and the fewer others remain with whom to share your discoveries and accumulation of arcane knowledge. Most children are watching television sit-coms or at best, reading Harry Potter. Few are investigating ancient ruins with the thirst of an anthropologist. The challenge from a mother's or grandmother's standpoint, it seemed to me, was to balance encouraging her curiosity for knowledge with the social skills necessary to survive in modern day life.

When we got to Pueblo Bonito, Kahlo spent an inordinate amount of time peering into the Great Kiva. For someone like me there is difficulty in imagining exactly what those Indians were up to centuries ago. Yet judging by Kahlo's attentiveness to this same circular meeting place, she was seeing a great deal more than the average Midwesterner in Bermuda shorts peering into a ruin before driving to get his hamburgers. One minute she would sit down on the edge and begin kicking her legs out; the next stand just outside the upper outer wall, arms akimbo, much like she had done at Aztec. Suddenly she would fiddle with her braids, cover her eyes momentarily, and then slowly scan the entire open pit.

Several tourists nearby noticed this intense focus by a little girl, yet also sensed she was not to be interrupted. During these investigative periods I try to stay just enough distance away to appear detached, as if she is completely on her own. With crafty ingeniousness I duplicitously walk amidst this ruin or that to convey the implication that yours truly is far more interested in my surroundings than the reality of the matter. It's important for Kahlo to believe I at least share some of her same analytical skills, lest she become even more indignant over the sarcastic comments I occasionally make when the vodka is doing more of the talking.

This went on for perhaps another half hour. My legs were feeling like stumps, and I had gone a long time without any liquid elixir to dull the pain of pending finality. Yet for a period I even disappeared from Kahlo's view by walking round the back wall of the Pueblo. It seemed to me these Anasazi sorts lived in confined spaces, insofar as the paucity of windows. Of course, much of the upper stories had disintegrated, so perhaps I was selling their ingenuity short. Maybe they beat drums in the lower rooms and barbecued jackrabbits on the rooftops, I have no idea. I will admit that after wandering about even a few of these archeological mysteries, one does find the imagination adrift as to what their intentions truly were. A bunch of Indians in the middle of the desert, with limited water, no fast-food chains, no cable TV, no libraries, and they probably did just fine, thank you. Of course, they did depart like a John Ford stagecoach in maybe the Fourteenth Century. Were they attacked? Did the water run out? Or did they simply just move on to greener deserts? And then all those legends of treasure and the Seven Cities. What, if anything, did those tourist siren tales have to do with a bunch of Anasazi pueblo builders in Northwest New Mexico?

There could be no doubt Kahlo had already formulated answers to some of those same questions and would formulate more. But what? And would she make them known to anyone? For a girl of nine, with the social skills of perhaps someone six, would she ever reveal her discoveries? At that point, I didn't have a clue, but accepted the futility of trying to guess the future for such an *enfant terrible*. On the other hand, my overall premonition was that Kahlo was finally going to let loose on this one. I couldn't be sure how or when. But I sensed that the tiny investigator had already formed massive impressions on arcane speculations as to why these originally hearty desert survivors had chosen such monumental building projects in a spectacularly barren area.

The next nomadic phase of her quest involved a brief excursion up to the elevated kiva of Chetro Ketl. To Kahlo the adjacent ruins were just a short walk away. To me another bunch of masonry partially disintegrated seemed no more intriguing than watching reruns on TV, and a long walk for someone forestalling her normal dosage of mid-day liquid refreshment. Constantly I had to remind myself that my ward for the day must be encouraged to pursue her curiosities. Sometimes she would look up at the skies, as if they exhibited some sort of clues regarding the natures of these crumbling edifices. I, of course, was always lagging behind. Kahlo obviously felt a certain responsibility to her grandmother, yet on the other hand regularly found those protective urges supervened by a child's thirst for more information and the satisfaction of an enormous curiosity.

Again, she spent a great deal of clock time peering at this and that round the elevated kiva. There seemed to be some common thread she had discovered. Yet just as suddenly she would shake her braids back and forth as if in serious disagreement over her own observations. It had to be perplexing for the energetic investigator. Her relentlessness certainly proved taxing to her aged companion, I can tell you that. It's at such enervating times that I suffer from having agreed to relieve my daughter Aurore of the responsibility of such a precocious adventuress for an entire day.

Eventually Kahlo insisted we move on to Casa Rinconada. I insisted we take the car, even though she would have liked either to run, walk or migrate there on horseback should such transportation have been available. During the brief ride round a curve in the loop road, it was obvious her deductive powers already had been piqued enormously.

"Baths, b-baths," was the only thing she repeated intermittently.

"Kahlo, we're in the Wild West. You'll have plenty of time to bathe later. It might be better if you get all the scrutiny in you can, because just getting to this remote location is a major effort I'm not sure your mother or I is going to be willing to make on a recurrent basis."

The look Kahlo gave me was like many that Shirley MacLaine gave Jack Nicholson in Terms of Endearment. The glare power was off the charts. Her disgust with my myopia was palpable. Which I understand, but persistently feel powerless to change. There's little doubt that I've paid my dues on this planet, and the importunate fact that my granddaughter gets impatient with me or intolerant of my inability to see what she sees, makes me only minimally guilty. I'm not going to cave into a nine-year-old all the time. Occasionally, I am forced to stand my ground, as if perhaps there are other *raisons d'être* besides archeological phenomena. She was annoyed with me. But she'd also get over it. I had accompanied the impatient analyst on too many of these expeditions to try and placate her beyond just letting her carry on. There was little doubt that Kahlo continues to typecast me as a minor intellect, not realizing of course, that much of her innate abilities, as well as environmentally acquired talents, derive from genetic predisposition.

At Casa Rinconada she repeated the same attentions upon the large kiva. And yet something bothered her about it, particularly the apparent walkway leading up to the central circle from under a northern section of the wall. None of the other kivas I had seen had such a subterranean entrance. And judging by how Kahlo carefully examined this apparent kiva quirk from different angles, it was apparent she was a bit perplexed over its function. Then her braids rose and fell on her jacket, a sign that whatever purpose the strange ramp had served, Kahlo suddenly had a grasp upon her own theoretical possibility.

Suddenly with the same careening nature of someone her age, she bounded over to her senior accomplice.

"Are you h-h-hungry, Gram?"

"Not as much as you are, I'm sure. One doesn't cover several centuries of archeological phenomena without developing an appetite. I've brought some of your favorite peanut butter and banana sandwiches. Where would you like to eat lunch?"

Kahlo pointed much like an Indian scout might in denoting a rising smoke screen on the bluff.

"Do we need to take the car? Or is the distance something your grandmother can manage on foot?"

"C-c-car."

We drove east, to some sort of turnout along the south wall of the canyon.

"P-park here," she said, again pointing as if a spirit resided somewhere by the side of the road. "I w-w-w-want to think."

The last statement was nothing more than stating the obvious. My company was born more out of necessity rather than choice. Even though a sign said that cars were not to be left unattended, we spread a blanket, while I brought a portable folding chair from the car. Kahlo would have been happier with both of us sitting on the blanket, but I would have been happier with a vodka tonic and the latest *New Yorker*. Still, I again felt as if something momentous was going to issue forth from my unpredictable granddaughter. The sort of stuff that makes investigative type's hair stand on end, or suddenly convince them there are supernatural powers.

"Grammy," she suddenly said after devouring a PB&J sandwich, some Tostitos chips with a hint of lime she always insists upon, and nearly a full container of bottled water.

"Yes, dear. I suppose you have made some of your inventive deductions today, haven't you."

She nodded, looking down at the blanket in front of her.

"And I suppose you are going to tell me that the Anasazi held circuses or powwows in their big kivas."

I couldn't help myself. It was not the sort of time to try to be clever. There are so few moments between a pair so chronologically, if not educationally, disparate. Kahlo continued to look at the blanket. Then suddenly she looked up and was trying to dash tears from her eyes.

"What is it, dear?"

Kahlo refused an explanation, just shaking her head and wiping her eyes with a sleeve. Several awkward minutes went by, the same sort of lull I had experienced with her before. One that portended she knew some obscure revelation that might affect us both. Who could say?

"Gram,"

"Yes, dear."

"My friend J-j-joel should be here. He'd know if I should t-t-t-tell."

# The Great North Road

(KAHLO)
"Tell what, Kahlo? Inevitably you consider your Gram unable to fathom your deductions. I suppose today up at the Great North Road you have discovered it was some sort of horse-and-cart path for transporting silver or some such."

"Nooo," I answered, shaking my head. I couldn't tell her why I had started crying. That would just make me cry more. And I didn't want to talk about my friend Joel, who is ten, but who had to leave New York because of his asthma. I'm almost ten and Joel could understand me.

Most people my age think I'm stupid, because of my stutter. That only makes it worse. I know that sometimes when I get on a subject I'm familiar with, then my stutter goes away. I can't explain it, but I think it has to do with confidence. Even though Joel would sometimes make fun of my stutter, he reads as much as I do and wants to learn just as much, too. He was my only real friend because I'm never comfortable in groups of other kids. Joel and I would go exploring together. That's why I wish he could be here with me in Chaco Canyon. Grammy is too old to be able to climb steep trails and go on long walks. Then with what I know about her future…

Still, Gram annoys me sometimes with her sarcastic comments. She is just trying to be amusing, but then she'll say something so cynical about things I find important. I can never make up my mind if I should tell her anything I learn. I know Gram and my Mom want me to keep learning, but at the same time I know they think sometimes I go too far when it comes to my investigations. Because I'm nine, I have to trust my intuition when it comes to what I like to do, even if other kids or adults think I'm weird. And one thing I've noticed about Chaco Canyon. Almost everything I read about it is speculation. Since there was no written history, no one knows for sure why the Anasazi did things. Everything I've deduced so far is the same: speculation. But it's doing my detective stuff that makes me happiest.

To me, learning is much more fun than other people. I do like being with Gram, though. She really cares about me and knows much more than just about the piano. Mom says she's shrewd. But then Grammy'll say something like she said about the Great North Road.

"The Anasazi didn't have any such animals," I answered, surprised that it came out without stammering. "They didn't have horses; they didn't have cows. They didn't have the wheel. In all the books I've read, and on all the websites I've found, no one can tell what the Great North Road was for. Maybe they didn't use them to transport souls to Twin Angels. When I look at Google Earth or maps, or even when I was just up there looking down upon where the road starts, there's very little left to the naked eye. Many centuries have changed the terrain. Topography different. Elevations changed. Soil collected by wind and erosion. Very little left of original roads."

"So do you think you know what the Great North Road was used for?"

"Maybe the Great North Road was made up of a giant series of aqueducts," I answered, amazed that no mental feedback was re-introducing my stutter. "What if individual segments, each of which was graded ever so slightly to the south, utilized gravity? Research has already shown segments were made of non-porous material and they also have found berms on the edges in some places and cuts through geologic rises. Why would they add berms to the edges? What I envision were like giant gradual water slides. What if one reason the Anasazi built them was to collect water, and that's why at certain points pottery shards have been found? They carried the water in pots. If you look at the loops on the tops of some of the pots you can tell they used ropes to carry them, probably at opposite ends of shoulder poles."

"Interesting," Gram remarked as if my speculations were merely novel rather than possible.

"Then what if the *herraduras* were used for collecting water from the road segments? When it would rain, maybe they knew enough about gravity to slope the segments ever so slightly toward the herraduras. From there, by pottery they carried water—at least at first…I don't know about whether they had siphons…But whether they did or didn't, Pueblo Alto was probably their biggest reservoir."

I didn't want to tell Gram about how I think they got most of the water up to Pueblo Alto and what I discovered there. Hydraulics is a field of knowledge I'm still trying to digest, and Grammy would probably think I'm nuts, anyway.

"But what about the parallel parts of the road in the middle?"

"I can't explain the four parallel roads near Pierre's Complex. But maybe water was not the only reason they built the roads during times of drought when the Chaco Wash was not running well. What if another important purpose for the Great North Road might have been to transport the pine tree beams they used in their ceilings? They ran out of logs for more than 200,000 pueblo beams. The Anasazi had cut down all the trees they could to the east and west on the mesa tops and hillsides. And the ones from the west probably had to be towed upstream, up what they now call the Chaco Wash, or carried overland. They were still building, even though water was scarce.

"Each Great North Road segment was approximately 30 feet wide. Why? What if that's just wide enough for three or more men to roll the longest logs they used for roof beams perpendicularly down the slopes of the road segments to the next arroyo? The hardest part might have been hauling the logs up from Kutz Canyon after they floated them down the San Juan River and hundreds of men carried them up Kutz canyon rim. Maybe after they hauled them up the steps to the mesa top near Twin Angels, much of the rest of the way probably was just rolling new architectural beams down road segment ramps almost level but gradually sloping south.

"But isn't most of that terrain rolling, Kahlo?"

"It is now. But 600 years is a long time. Wouldn't the ridges and arroyos change quite a lot due to erosion, wind, snow, and rain? What if the streams coming east from the Continental Divide ran with more water back then before the great drought? If you look at the terrain on the National Atlas web site maps shaded for terrain, or at elevations on Google Earth after pinpointing the Pueblo Bonito and then proceeding straight north, you can see a lot of things. Like how over 158,400 feet, or the distance of 30 miles, the elevation of the terrain, even today, varies only about 200 feet from below the mesa top at Pueblo Alto almost to Twin Angels. It wouldn't have been very hard to make a series of road segments, even without level aqueduct constructions resembling those the Romans used to cross elevation changes, where after rolling logs down a long segment, 10 men merely carried it up a ramp to the downslope of the next long segment and so on. Meanwhile the *herraduras* probably captured the water from those slopes during rains and snow melts."

"Well, at least you have been using that active brain of yours, dear."

It was then that I realized Gram had only heard part of what

I said. First, she didn't have the same interest in the subject I do. Second, she has a short attention span unless it comes to reading, playing the piano, or listening to classical music and jazz. There were lots more I wanted to tell her once I got going, especially about Pueblo Alto, of course. But I know Gram. There's not much point. She was probably going to tell Mom that I've been hallucinating again. Especially if because of her questions, I was unable to continue without stuttering. If you were to ask her what I just said, she would only have retained bits and pieces. It's sort of like Sherlock Holmes having warned Watson about your brain being an attic with only so much room. And that eventually when you push a fact in one side, another falls out the other. It's not her fault. Gram's over 70 years old. She's more than seven times my age and has spent a lifetime accumulating knowledge and memories she now is getting rid of by drinking. I suppose when your body begins to break down and you want to discard a lot of things before you leave for good, you also want to throw out a lot of facts that aren't very important anymore. I have my whole life ahead of me, while Gram has hers behind her.

Sometimes she'll surprise me, though. She's a brilliant pianist, and although she scoffs at a lot of the stuff kids my age listen to, she can still dance and sing as if she were much younger. And underneath all her sarcasm, Gram is really nice. She tries to disguise it by being tough on me sometimes. But I can tell that she just doesn't want me to make the same mistakes she did as a young girl. It's about fitting in with other kids, and not getting too far removed from what normal kids my age do. She complains a lot about being outside too long, too. But really, I think she likes most of what we do when we walk around places like this. And she doesn't drink as much when she's outdoors like at Chaco Canyon, even though she sneaks sips of vodka sometimes from a silver flask she doesn't think

I know about. It's Gram's way of dealing with the pain of getting older, she always tells me.

Anyway, my mind somehow never stops. While I was eating my peanut butter and banana sandwich, I was thinking more and more about kivas, pottery, petroglyphs, Chaco roads, cardinal directions, and all kinds of unusual facts most people would find boring. After seeing Aztec and La Ventana and Chaco, I only wanted to see more.

You'd be surprised at all the cool stuff I've seen on internet sites. Maps, analysis of astronomy and archeology and how the Anasazi might have combined the two disciplines in their architecture. I can't help standing over a kiva and looking down and observing things. What I think I've learned is not something I want to tell anyone right now, even though in my mind those deductions are just as possible as all the things I've read. I thought about waiting until I'm older. People have trouble believing archeologists who speculate. Believing a nine-year-old girl's theories is probably like little kids believing in Santa Claus. Still, Chaco has its own aura and magic. Every minute I'm here, I'm excited. The sun constantly creates different impressions of the colors and ruins.

The sun and moon daggers on Fajada Butte seem to signify the Anasazi knew more about astronomy than meets the eye. My mind whirls much too fast. But I love it. I try to get Gram excited, too. But then I realize the accumulation of obscure knowledge is for people like me who prefer reading and learning to chatting with other kids or adults. I just keep up my investigations, even though all the kids I know back home wouldn't have much interest in hearing about ancient ruins.

Mom is about as inquisitive as I am. Right now, she's over in Grants using some coffee house computer to investigate plants. She could have used the computer in our hotel room, but she likes getting out. She thinks someone poisoned my aunt Ashleigh, and she could be right. Not many people who knew Auntie liked her. Or someone in the family might have been mad when she accidentally pushed Gram down the stairs.

Mom quit her job as a publishing firm book editor in New York. She said she got burned out, but I think it was because she broke up with another guy from the financial district she always seems to fall back on as boyfriends. Since she divorced her husband years ago before she adopted me, she's tried all kinds of relationships with poets, artists, but mostly businessmen. I think she's smarter than all of them and that's the problem. But also, Mom doesn't like a conventional life of the suburbs and kids. If she hadn't adopted me, I doubt if she would have ever had a child. She's like a child, herself. Sometimes I think I have more common sense than she has. My mother also has a short attention span. One minute she's discovered rock hunting, and the next exercising on a mountain bike. Then another day she might decide to read all the works of William Styron or Edith Wharton.

Her friends have trouble keeping up with her unpredictability. Sometimes she'll hibernate for days, and I'm the only one who sees her at meals. When she goes out at night, Mom might have on makeup that is almost kabuki level, then the following evening wear none at all with a hat so that she's hardly recognizable. She's not a chameleon. But one writer she knows calls her mercurial. She rarely repeats herself in long-term pursuits. But maybe rock hunting will prove to be a hobby she sticks with, I don't know.

I think if Mom took another conventional job, she wouldn't like it, but would like the opportunities to meet men not as strange as she is. She needs a boyfriend who is a little unconventional, but not too eccentric. Mom said she saw a guy living in a canyon south of Chaco that was totally off the wall. But I could tell by the way she described how they sort of encountered, that she was curious about him. Mom's like that. She forms love-hate relationships with lots of people, including her sister Ashleigh. Mom likes tension in a relationship. If things start going too well with a man, I always know the end is coming. Her passion for a man goes away if he's too attentive. I've heard Mom's friends say it's because she doesn't have enough self-esteem. I'm not sure about that. I think in the back of her mind is that no man is up to her level, unless for some reason she isn't up to his. It's like swordplay for her. She never likes the adoring types, like in the movies. It's not that treating her badly works. It's more keeping some mystery going as to how much a male really cares about her. Maybe it's her red hair, I don't know.

Anyway, I need to focus on my investigations, because when I get back to Santa Fe, Mom says I have to enroll in school at the end of spring break. Most kids like school, and I like parts of it. Particularly science. But sometimes I think I can learn more doing my own reading, like I do when I'm not at school. For instance, combining internet surfing and Chaco Canyon in real time are amazing. It's just too bad that it's so far from anywhere. Maybe that's why the Anasazi chose this high desert location. Not many visitors. Not many animals. And not many plants. You might almost think they were crazy. But then if they were to see all the people stacked in Manhattan high rises, what do you think they'd think?

Mom certainly got burned-out trying to keep up in New York. Living there for her was another form of love-hate or approach-avoidance. Manhattan may be the most exciting place on Earth. But it can also be the most stressful for both kids and adults. As they say in the West, there are only the quick and the dead.

"Any more expeditions for today, dear?" Gram said while calmly picking up some of the leftovers from lunch. She barely touched her sandwich, and that's another thing that worries me about Grammy. She gets too many calories from vodka and not enough from food with vitamins, minerals, and protein.

"N-n-no, thanks. I think I've s-s-seen enough for today." There it was again. My stutter. You have no idea how mad it sometimes makes me. But when I think about it, usually it only gets worse. It's strange, but Grammy's sarcastic observation on the Great North Road made me forget about my stutter. You saw how I was able to tell her a lot of my observations without faltering. That's what happens sometimes, even though none of several psychologists in New York could completely free me of stammering. They said it's too much awareness of self in everything I do. Who isn't aware of what they do? I've tried everything I know to get over it, but nothing seems to work permanently. That's why I do better on my own. Thinking is an uninterrupted joy, while talking often brings social agony. Kids laugh. Parents try to finish sentences for me. It's all weird when you're nine. I just hope it's gone by the time I'm 20.

"Kahlo, dear, are you finished with your can of Coke?"

I looked down on the can and the straw in it, and suddenly it came to me. I took a last sip through the paper straw and held it and the red can out from me. "Maybe I've d-d-discovered s-s-something else about the Anasazi,"

Gram looked at me like I'm from Mars. And according to what I've read, we're both probably from Venus.

As we were walking to the car, I had another one of those overwhelming feelings I get just like in my visions. It felt as if the stars were out even though it was the middle of the day. Suddenly I got goosebumps and I felt like Grammy had disappeared. It was as if I had traveled back in time for the moment, back into the 14$^{th}$ century. The Anasazi were in the canyon, even though I couldn't see any of them. I heard a distant coyote and the fleeting screech of an eagle overhead. Then silence and complete solitude. Vaguely I was aware of the importance of the number seven. That sounds stupid because everyone knows the Seven Cities are merely a legend. Yet I could feel them. They were near.

# Aurore Cyber Sleuth

(AURORE)

A day away from my mother and daughter is the only time I can relapse into the real Aurore Dupín. No nagging Katarina to cut back on the vodka; no worrying that Kahlo is going to fail to return from one of her expeditions. Ever since I left my New York publishing house, there has been an increasing quest in the rediscovery of who I truly am. It's not as if I will give up my wonderful vicarious pursuits which involve the printed word as much as possible. It's more an alternative return to all that a woman *d'une certain âge* does when unencumbered by the daily rigors of child-rearing or maternal solicitude. Everyone has habits they hold dear. One of mine is being on the road and not knowing exactly where I'm going to end up. I mean that rhetorically as well as specifically. One begins a diurnal adventure with a rough plan in mind. But more important are the twists and turns that occur spontaneously. No provocation necessary. Serendipitous encounters liven what could be far too predictable into an eventful day.

For instance, when I was out in the middle of nowhere in northwest New Mexico and suddenly there was some societal misfit having chosen a hermetic lifestyle he finds appealing. Strange? Maybe. But then who's to say what's behaviorally odd and what isn't? From his perspective, electronic tedium in a Manhattan high rise would most probably test his limits. On the other hand, living the way he chooses means he doesn't have to shave, doesn't have to do business lunches, and may attribute the wearing of a tie as some obscure regimen for those who value acquisition over nature. I'll probably never see him again. And yet I can and do thoroughly empathize with his peripheral life, even if his personal habits may be slightly more rustic and rough-hewn than I would choose.

I was in the Pontiac PT Cruiser faux-antique sedan I bought one day in a fit of needing to feel young again. I was on the road, El Sol was climbing above the desert highway, and for the day I was going to mimic my daughter with an investigation of my own. It's probably pointless. But then sometimes the most unnecessary activities provide the most satisfaction, and I am one of those pseudo-intellectual women who think just enough of their own mental acuity to attempt solving a mystery.

Certainly, when my sister died, the doctor's report listed 'cardiac failure.' But this pronouncement came in a small town in upstate New York where there was no coroner. It was almost as if the local GP who made the diagnosis wanted it behind him as fast as possible.

I think many things with Ashley had failed, and during this process she had developed a vitriolic approach to almost any interpersonal encounter. She had acquired the nasty habit of contentiousness over topics as limited as the purchase of groceries, or whether the accumulated detritus throughout her Manhattan condominium was affecting her moods. There was no telling Ashleigh anything, and by the time of her demise, a long list of souls had accumulated who were going to feel relieved not to have to skirmish verbally with her any longer. She was a shrew who could no longer be tamed.

My late sister may or may not have died of natural causes. The fact that her death was listed as unremarkable may be relevant. Then again, it may not. For me, even if someone had medically assisted her departure with some sort of undetected toxin, the point was not to try to exact retribution, but rather to satisfy a curiosity as to who would kill my sister and why? There are at least eight relatives or former friends I can think of who might have developed the requisite antipathy to relieve her from her misery, and with relish. That's not an insubstantial list. And have I mentioned the growing legions that had worked with her at one point or another and would gladly have expedited her departure or paid someone to do same? We've all known those rare birds society has chosen to find obnoxious because they follow their own whims as if no one else on the planet exists. My sister certainly fit into that category, caring not a whit whom she offended either by her behavior or through what some had typified as habitually vindictive verbal abuse.

Ashley was a few years older than I, and to say that she had long before her untimely death lost the common touch remains an understatement. Someone as unsuspecting as a delivery person might suddenly be enveloped by Ashleigh's venom and just as quickly discharged from her front door.

My sister was bitter for several reasons. The most obvious derived from the category of spurned suitors; one only slightly lesser so perhaps from her heavy diet of chocolates and other simple sugars, leaving her with the widest possible variety of mood swings one can obtain in any given short period. Ashleigh was choleric, impatient, omniscient, arthritic, intolerant and perhaps another couple dozen nasty adjectives from villainy school. She stayed up late and slept much of every day. A doctorate in mathematics from MIT placed her in a promising limited elite pantheon of living number crunchers. But at the same time, it left my incessantly irritable sibling devoid of the social skills one believes a person of genius should still possess.

We've all read the book or seen the movie, *A Beautiful Mind*. Well, one might easily argue that Ashleigh had a beautiful mind someone had poisoned with the hopelessness of another far less fortunate.

She fought with almost anyone she encountered. Everything and everyone annoyed her, and toward the end she had become far worse than unbearable. Nothing or no one could placate her. Ashleigh was pitiable, really.

When I say no one, there was, however, one person whom she treated with a minimum of disdain, and that was my daughter Kahlo. For some reason, and it may have been an identification with Kahlo's inability socially to fit in with her peers, Ashleigh confined her normal condescension to a mere torrent of advice to my adopted offspring. Kahlo and she would go on long walks in Central Park. There was little my daughter would have said on these walking lecture tours, anyway, due to her speech impediment. Yet the strolls proved symbiotic for the pair of them, in that Ashleigh could then lapse into her musings and ramblings without fear of interruption. Kahlo listened patiently, even sometimes reverentially, her heart plagued by the bitterness of her aunt. Ashleigh talked, pontificated, and ranted. It was an odd relationship. But perhaps no odder than the hundreds if not thousands of those eccentric souls struggling within a vibrant urban scenario like Gotham. Or, as Tennessee Williams and Harper Lee determined, just as often to occur out in the provinces.

At any rate, it was a challenge to try to discover if Ashleigh was killed or died of natural causes. This premise was nothing more than a starting point for a sleuthing adventure similar in scope to what my daughter enjoys while galloping round ruins of one sort or another. Whether the digging is actual or rhetorical doesn't matter. The hope of discovery fuels one onward.

You may wish to know why I was driving to Grants for the privilege of doing some internet investigative work. My decision was based upon the fact that traveling to Santa Fe and back to rendezvous with my mother and daughter would be, even to someone of my ability to fritter away time, a waste. Then I had been to Chaco and Aztec, and the prospect of remaining in the remote towns of Aztec or Farmington did little to inspire me while my daughter further explored northwest New Mexico or strayed into southern Colorado.

Another reason was the history of Grants and its Mining Museum. Originally it was the end of the railroad line heading west. Another peculiarity was that during the 50s uranium mining sprung up in the area, and this bizarre interruption to the natural surroundings fascinated me as well. Fortunately, the decline in both the building of nuclear warheads and nuclear power plants reduced the need for uranium and the entire industry waned. But the residual spell of uranium, and its discharge, radon gas, still hover like specters.

Radioactivity is something I have found intriguing ever since as a child I stuck my feet under an obscure shoe store's fluoroscope and watched the tarsal bones in my feet wiggle down below the viewfinder. No one seemed concerned at the time about the dangers of X-rays and radiation. Even in the 60s luminous watches were still being painted at Arizona factory desks with radioactive paint pots sitting at arm's length from unsuspecting workers.

Very few today would consider using a Geiger counter when rock hunting. The danger of radiation in most areas of the West is minimal, though unusual locales and certain of the thousands of abandoned mines, particularly in the Rockies, still emit hazardous emission levels of radon. Yet radioactivity has its own allure. It is invisible as well as highly dangerous and toxic, a combination gaining it a haunting mysteriousness. At one point below Jamestown, Colorado, mineral spas even featured exposure to radiation as rejuvenating and healthful.

On a previous encounter with Grants, I had been in this one coffee house right along the main street of town. It wasn't a Starbuck's, but more the brainchild of another of those cast-offs from some larger urban environment now trying to start a new life with a reduction in stress in a small town. It was destined to close within a year, but for the moment breathed cyber life.

The modern-day coffee house has somewhat supplanted the old greasy spoon, in which everyone knows one another. Except that instead of clogging your arteries, in the modern version of the gathering place you can torment your blood sugar and mood swings with legal stimulants and baked treats. Of course, to be *de rigueur*, such a den of bean distillates must be a cyber-café as well. Carrying a laptop and cell phone are all part of the image of someone who is *a la mode* and *au courant*. You rarely catch a young person perusing a daily newspaper. It simply isn't done. Instead, they can be seen hovering in front of laptop flat screens, mesmerized by the light and movements, the written word taking a back seat to video games, dancing imagery, and flashing short bursts of information.

Will their language skills be kept up? Doubtful. But then some sociologists argue that language was created to describe that which we cannot see. Now that we have photography, motion pictures through film, high- and low-definition video and DVDs, as well as the ubiquitous internet and its ability to transport anyone to the four corners of the Earth with videos and photos, who needs language? Reading this tract, for instance, is not for the faint of heart regarding vocabulary, abstract concepts, and imagination.

But then the last two decades of my life had been limited primarily to the arcane knowledge of those who read. Publishing house editing and production remain best conducted by those with the broadest vocabularies, irrespective of whether that extensive base is actively used in works they oversee. One conjures images of a nineteenth-century Bob Cratchit sitting high atop a stool with a croupier's visor scrutinizing obscure figures and texts that only a small select contingent of citizenry encountered. In current reality, the business of writing and publishing is dynamic, not the least marvel of which remains the meeting of occasionally social minds with a thirst for clever wit, memory expansion, and the pursuit of trivia.

I gave up all this artful pretension to intelligentsia in the best interests of both myself and my daughter. In any profession, on many a day one wakes up and questions his or her sanity. I was the same in Manhattan. It could just as well have been Lawrence Kansas, Boulder Colorado, or Lake Forest Illinois. As a head groggy from the previous evening's indulgences begins to clear and the eyes peer out into the overcast skies and smog, you wonder if the fight is worth continuing. And indeed, one day I no longer wished to continue the battle to be among the informed and infamous. It was time to go, and suddenly I knew it.

Part of that decision, of course, was prompted by wishing my daughter to be able to grow up in more natural surroundings. Kahlo loves climbing things, running, jumping, and examining all kinds of outdoor phenomena. These proclivities for someone more a Hardy Boy than dancing diva were difficult to pursue other than in Central Park, so the intrigue both of us had developed over the great open spaces of the West beckoned. Southwest architecture, furniture, and cuisine of Santa Fe, through magazines, documentaries, and the internet, had acquired a certain allure I could not easily dispatch from a brain normally overloaded by publishing trivia. We went West. And we brought the predictable, sometimes irascible, yet lovable Katarina with us.

Surprisingly, the whole approach-avoidance thing with the complexities of urban existence was easily overcome. Oh, sure, I did miss some of the *haute-chic* lunches and dinners with eccentric scribblers and artists. Yet the dry, sunny, wide-open areas of New Mexico became a part of my pleasure realm with amazing alacrity. I love New Mexico. Sometimes I even feel I have been born a Native American, though my ancestry is completely European. Kahlo, however, remains the adopted gem of my life. And she possesses certain what I believe to be atavistic traits of her Indian and Mexican heritage. I haven't derived this opinion lightly, but find her elliptical manner inherited partially from bloodlines rather than strictly resulting from her speech impediment. Sometimes things about the great outdoors are best left unsaid.

Why all this was pinballing round my mind on the way over to Grants merely proved that I have yet fully to divest of the complex examinations endured daily during urban life, and which are best cast off when amidst natural surroundings too spectacular to ignore. Cruising into Grants brought me back to reality. It was a throwback to its past railroad depot and Route 66 era, and on that Southwestern day, I was going to see if any of its aura would pervade my enjoyment of solitary investigations.

The coffee house was sparsely populated, a sign that most in Grants were working nine-to-fives for a living rather than contemplating their existences or writing the Great American Exposé. I got a sugar-laden scone and skim-milk latté and settled in at one of four computers on a table against a wall. I wasn't sure what I was after, or if I even wanted to discover untold possibilities of what may have killed my sister. But I didn't care. It was the search itself, within a medium relatively new in a life of nearly half a century, which intrigued me. No mother or daughter to divert my limited attention span. No office waiting with a million phone calls and e-mails. No deadlines. It was just going to be the internet and me for a couple of hours, the sort of relationship I can entertain without painful misunderstandings.

The first thing I noticed in my quest was that many houseplants are poisonous. The good news is that they filter our interior air of carbon dioxide and certain pollutants. Other bad news is that many of them have toxins that are dangerous. How dangerous? Not much in most instances, unless you make them part of lunch or dinner. However, aloe vera, chrysanthemums, crotons, poinsettia, and rhododendrons are just a few of the common decorative household flora that can be perilous.

In reading over their characteristics, it seemed highly unlikely that any of them were toxic enough to kill Ashleigh even if they had by some nefarious tactic been ingested. We all know that cyanide and arsenic, for instance, are very effective in dispatching someone. Yet they are too obvious and would be discovered as lethal sources.

For some reason I still felt as if there had been a missing element in my sister's demise. She didn't overdo drugs nor consistently abuse alcohol, and notwithstanding her irritable demeanor, seemed as physically fit as almost anyone I know. Which isn't to say that heart failure wasn't a possibility. She was in her mid-50 and had engaged in the usual indulgences earlier in a strife-ridden life, those destructive habits that can negatively return to affect one's health when their influence is least suspected.

My mother felt she was using a lot of cocaine, but I happen to know Ashleigh rarely indulged in the white powder. Neither had she ever complained of chest pains or shortness of breath. So, if one were to hazard a guess regarding her untimely death, it might be a relatively undetectable substance that had triggered the stoppage of her ticker.

There is something to be said for looking at plants such as Röhrs Dieffenbachia Superbae, which is also called 'dumb cane,' and which takes away the speech of anyone foolish enough to snack upon it. The imagination goes wild with the possibilities of Miss Marple's adversaries trying to come up with the perfect toxic substance to eliminate someone standing in the way of inheritance or requited love, yet subsequently to disappear without a trace.

It was amazing what a surprisingly calming effect the whole sleuthing process was having upon my day. I hadn't felt this good in years, and I owe it all to an innovative medium in which literally, there are no boundaries. It was if I had discovered my own enchanted garden, one in which I could delve without moving any more than a mouse and my eyes. The screen represented the world's largest library, and I had a library card. Site after site illuminated me further, the thought of some common household item relieving my sister of a heartbeat seeming more and more probable.

Many people have read the book or seen the film, *White Oleander*, and are aware of the flowering plant's poisonous qualities. However, further perusals apprised that the Red Oleander is more toxic than its fairer cousin. According to the web site from which I was digesting this noxious information, cardiac glycosides inhibit a cellular membrane pump from properly maintaining the balance of intracellular and serum potassium. This interferes with the heart's electrical conductivity, and wham! Arrythmia or a rapid and weak pulse can suddenly lead to weakness, collapse, or even death. Dogbane and foxglove are two more beauties. Ingesting Dogbane can cause arrythmias and possible heart stoppages; swallowing Foxglove can induce first- and second-degree heart block and ventricular tachycardia, also possibly leading to sudden extinction.

My pulse was certainly quickening. Maybe I was reading too much into my sister's reputed heart attack. Maybe no one hated Ashleigh enough to slip her some exotic plant bits in her salad or a drink. And yet the whole vast survey of obtainable plants did indeed make the mind conjure up strange deeds by someone permanently infuriated with my sister's latest insult.

My indulgent scone continued to heighten the pleasurable synaptic activities involved in dissecting the anatomy of a possible homicide. Then again, maybe it was just wishful thinking on my part. I too had experienced a love-hate relationship with the ever-exacerbating Ashleigh. One day she would treat me with the respect of a peer and the admiration of an adoring sibling; the next spew forth venom and unleash a vindictive attack difficult to comprehend. Many had felt Ashleigh schizophrenic. Yet I merely considered her ongoing inability to find suitable companionship at her own levels of genius unpredictably erupted with some mild provocation into a torrent of verbal abuse. It was beyond her control much of the time. That was a cert. Because she was my sister I tolerated those exasperating moments, knowing full well that an hour later she might well forget the entire contretemps.

Still, someone may have killed her. And sitting in front of a computer screen in Grants gave me some of the deductive powers of Miss Marple, Sherlock Holmes, or Joe Leaphorn.

Two hours passed in sheer vicarious bliss. Not over the fact that someone might have murdered my sister. But rather because of the delight in this singular academic pursuit without being on the clock of a publishing house or some other demanding institution. The trick of life itself suddenly became apparent: successfully balance the real with the vicarious and your education as well as enjoyment will transport you unexpectedly to spiritual nirvana. No one of the opposite gender need be involved. Just you, combining in compressed but relaxed fashion the desert, a book, and imaginative internet sites.

An hour later I had checked into an off-Route 66 motel, one of those rare gems distinguished by a rusting billboard a block away from the original highway and now main street of this former uranium and railroad town. It had the same name as a now defunct Las Vegas hotel, the kind of one-story kitschy-50s-style remnant that is clean and now run by an immigrant couple from Mumbai or Karachi. I didn't plan on spending much time there. Already I found my reverie from the cyber-café evaporating quickly in the desert motel air with a hint of bathroom disinfectant.

My plan was next to drift over to the Grants Mining Museum. But before I did, I wanted in the manner of an erstwhile New York book editor to cogitate upon what I had learned. I wasn't sure if my sister had been assisted by poison to terminate her pulse. Yet my list of suspects still loomed like a gang of Wild West marauders capable of anything from train robbery to murder. None of them was evil, per se. It was more that after years of abuse and methodical torment from Ashleigh, any one of them could have artfully helped to discharge her from her miserable existence.

And of all the possibilities pervading the mind of an itinerant quasi-aesthete, no one loomed more suspicious than my former husband. Permanently afflicted with the wild streak of a college sophomore and the ability to become increasingly candid with an evening's measure of cocktails, my free-spirited ex had on many an occasion entangled nearly in death grips with my sister. Sometimes they would shout at each other until hoarse, and I wondered if any of these explosive encounters was going to come to blows. None did. Yet neither would cede a point, nor back down from in-the-other's-face tactics. Verbal brutality reigned, and although I hadn't seen my former spouse in years, he certainly would have been capable of dispatching our mutual nemesis, a trait acquired before marriage to one of the Dupín family of indomitable women.

I've painted a sordid picture of the man with whom I spent a good bit of time in Gotham. Yet he had an unusually clever wit, was quite kind when he so chose to be, and made an intriguing conversational companion for many years. He did have a weakness for other women, though, certainly assisted by a life-long proclivity for hard drinking and partying.

Right now he is little more than a series of memories. During a Santa Fe phone conversation with a journalist back East I know, however, I was informed that my former partner was reputed to be out West on an extended sabbatical cum-treasure hunt. And it was after this cell phone conversation that I suddenly found him leaping to the top of my list of possible suspects. If anyone might have killed Ashleigh, it could well have been my unrestrained former husband, Quivira Cantrell.

# Into the Mine's Eye

(CHICHILTICALLI)

Working at the Northwest New Mexico Visitor Center may seem a little limited for someone with an Oxford education. Yet I felt the more Anglos I could talk to in the Center, the more they would realize that their stereotyping of Indians remains *reductio ad absurdum*. It was a perfect scenario for someone divided between the typecast of the elliptical Zuni or Diné who speaks infrequently, and the European-educated Indian who can startle tourists by speaking with an English fluency commanding their reluctant respect. It was all a game, but an important one in informing a white world distilling all Native Americans into simpletons. I'm not sure why I still feel this inter-racial mission to be part of my ranger work at the Visitor Center. Maybe it's the look upon some of those tourist faces when the words coming out of my mouth don't match their preconception of how I should talk.

At the same time, I do like getting out of the Center from time to time. Meeting that treasure hunter from New York in the Radon Bar and the head-knocking afterwards was just one of the novelties of such expeditions. Today, for instance, I was to drop off some flyers at the Mining Museum back in town. These periodic junkets mean that for an hour or so, or sometimes longer, I don't have to deal with the cavalcade of visitors whose questions often gravitate to where to get a good feed rather than the complex history of the area.

I grew up in the Southwest, so the fact that the downtown area of Grants is only a little more recent than when the stagecoach was replaced by the railroad no longer registers. The Mining Museum may be one of the town's more modern edifices. It sits just off old Route 66, and beyond the parameters of summer remains a repository forgotten by time. My favorite is the display case just inside the door. There, can be discovered minerals indigenous to this part of New Mexico, and I always find myself reexamining its contents as if suddenly a huge South African diamond will have been added to the collection.

"Hey, Ed," I said to the geriatric chap tending the front desk. Ed will probably finish out his days volunteering at that information and entry charge kiosk, and part of our routine is to argue about the north road into the Chaco ruins.

"Driven the road into Chaco from 550?" he rhetorically asked with just the hint of a wry grin.

"Nope. But you know, at least the first three miles are paved."

"But the other 18 aren't."

"To me, hard-packed dirt or gravel is the same as paved."

"To you, the Santa Fe Trail was paved."

And so it went each time the two of us encountered. A little repartee between middle- and old-aged chaps. Ed was the type of guy who would take issue with almost anything someone younger might say. And I was the perfect foil to rise to the bait. For a moment he silently shuffled a few things on the desk in front of him, while I placed several stacks of our informative regional attraction pamphlets alongside the others.

During this impasse when the two of us were contemplating what sort of verbal jab to come up with next, in through the door came a striking woman in her late 40s or early 50s with hair the same orange color popular on adobe walls in Santa Fe. She had a certain panache, the kind that quickly had her gravitating to the front desk like a tumbleweed blowing up against a fence. She wasn't from around here because she had walked in with too much confidence. A sort of urban sophistication disguised by jeans, an old pair of Reebok white aerobic shoes, and a soft-rimmed canvas hat.

She looked vaguely familiar, but I just as quickly deduced that impression to be impossible. All her facial movements seemed abrupt as the striking woman quickly glanced about the room and at the pamphlets available within reach. Her face had that sort of drawn beauty of a gracefully aging former high-fashion model you sometimes see in the magazines. Her elbows suddenly landed on the circular desktop, and she leaned in toward Ed.

"How much is it?" she asked.

I couldn't help staring at her, trying to figure out how I knew her. She allowed my eyes to catch hers just for a moment, but soon she was off over to the rock case. "Oh, wow!" she said upon arriving at this cabinet of exotic minerals.

Ed and I resumed the sort of banal chatter two locals come up with when a magnetic meteor is hovering nearby, and they want to pretend she hasn't attracted their attention. Whew! For an older white woman, she was something. Even Ed was trying to avoid scoping out that slender rear end normally featured among college coeds.

The way she was scrutinizing the minerals in the case, leaning in for better looks from time to time, meant she had more than a perfunctory interest. Maybe she had property somewhere in the West and was seeing if anything in there matched what she had seen out on the back 40. Or maybe she was a rock hunter. The museum gets a lot of those sorts, but usually their backpacks are faded, hiking boots scuffed, and their faces have taken a lot more sun than this magnetic woman's pale skin. She possessed a big city style.

I had just told Ed that in March we don't get that many yet coming through the Center and was asking him how his numbers had been, when I glanced back over at the mineral case. She was gone. Probably had taken the mineshaft elevator downstairs into the mock mine, I guess.

"She ain't your average tourist," Ed commented, shaking his head. "The problem with being as old as I am, is my eyes still work."

"Come on, Ed, you don't have any problem a little Viagra won't cure."

"You may be right, but my last opportunity just left on the evening stage."

I figured it was close enough to lunch that I could head down into the mine for a few minutes. It was a trip I had made many times with school kids and others on mini-tours, but this time I wanted to satisfy a curiosity that hadn't come from a doobie-induced reminiscence. There was something very familiar about the carrot-topped lady, and although I wasn't sure I would figure it out, I wanted at least one more chance to look her over carefully.

Down in the mine it didn't surprise me to find no one in sight. The memorabilia, photographs, old mining equipment and rock walls were my only companions. That's the way it is in this part of New Mexico. While Santa Fe and its plaza are busy much of the year, you have to try to drive over to our arid mid-point in crossing to Arizona. If it weren't for Acoma, *El Malpais*, and a few other points of interest, we might just have our tiny former mining and railroad town to ourselves. The Northwest New Mexico Visitor Center, for instance, isn't in town. It gazes out over the edge of the previously molten *El Malpais*, just off the interstate. But it is set back from the highway enough that a lot of tourists never make the effort. Sort of like a shopping mall, where if you're located on the second level, you get only half the traffic of the first.

The Mining Museum's a bit like that. Most of the year you have the run of it to yourself. If you are down below alone, you can pretend you're going to do some drilling or hammer and chisel work. It felt kind of weird looking for the mysterious woman amidst such subterranean surroundings. I opened a door that led into a small room designed to simulate a rest area for miners. She was standing on one leg with her back to me, scrutinizing an old mining photograph on the far wall.

"You don't remember me, do you?" she said without turning around. I couldn't figure out how she knew who had come through the door.

"You look familiar, but I can't figure out..."

She turned around to face me, and when she did it reminded me of unexplained sensations I had only felt when coming into the presence of certain venerated elder Indians. It wasn't just someone in her late 40s possessing such an aura, there was also the sound of her voice making me feel we had recently had a conversation.

"It was in Oxford more than 20 years ago. Actually, it was in Cambridge, where circumstances had the two of us both showing up to rent a punt. I was over for the day from Oxford and so were you. It must have been chemistry, but suddenly we were sharing a punt on the Cam. You were reading astronomy, I believe, and I was spending the summer romping through the Trout, Turf Tavern, and other points of interest around Oxford. You almost fell out of the boat getting the pole stuck in the mud repeatedly, and I made the sort of smart-assed remarks I generally dispense in the company of an attractive male. It was a very romantic overcast day destined to transmute into future futility. But for the moment, it was right out of Thomas Hardy. I had a bottle of Pouilly Fuissé, and you had brought Wheat Thins and cheddar, a combination perfect for a day under threatening skies."

With her recalling our unexpected initial encounter, it all gradually came back in a truncated stream of consciousness. Somewhere along the Cam we had tied the boat up beside a meadow, and halfway through the wine had found ourselves entwined under an oak. It was simply a couple of Americans finding romance in an ancient setting.

"Your name was the same as the famous French writer—if I'm not mistaken. Aurore Dupín, wasn't it? Even though you were dressed like a woman, if I remember correctly. Pleated white skirt, white-on-white linen blouse and navy-blue espadrilles? It was one of those brief encounters when two strangers ignore protocol and simply get on with responding to unexpected chemistry."

"Mm. We most certainly did get on with it, didn't we? Two Americans from opposite ends of the country reading and screwing in Oxford."

"Well, I don't know if I'd put it that way, but—"

She paused to glance down at the table. "You had to force my hand, though, and because of your wanting more from a slightly older woman, lost my favors."

"It's the sort of thing a Zuni does when he finds a kindred spirit."

She looked at me and shook her head. Her arms were crossed in front of her, and we stood at opposite ends of a table that may have hosted miners 75 years earlier. I had no idea where Aurore Dupín had been the last 20-some years, but she still had the same magnetic appeal as that halcyon summer in England. Yet because of the two us having moved on to contrasting realms during those elapsed years, our Mining Museum *deja vu* dissolved into an awkward situation from which there was no escape.

"Well, I suppose you're still living by the stars in an area of the country dark enough at night to observe Ursa Major or whatever one discerns from a stretch of the imagination."

"Sometimes."

It had been a long time since I had sharpened my wits, yet in the company of women such as Aurore, even an American Indian had to remain aware of verbal thrusts and parries.

"It's inherited. Most of the Pueblo tribes in this area have Anasazi blood, and the Anasazi probably knew more about cardinal directions than most modern surveyors who have Google Earth to zoom into trouble."

"And I suppose that outfit means you ride on horseback throughout the Navajo Reservation capturing cannabis desperados and alcohol smugglers."

"Actually, I'd have a difficult time arresting anyone sharing my habits. The only arrests I make involve stopping myself from returning insults with overweight tourists who ask questions about Geronimo or the Milagro bean fields."

She turned back to pretend to examine a few more of the antique photos on the walls. "You're a ranger, are you?"

"In a manner of speaking. I don't get out on the range too often. Spend most of my time in the Northwest New Mexico Visitor Center."

"An Oxford-educated park ranger, eh."

"Mm."

"The stars haven't become your calling?"

"No. I'm afraid I've lapsed into the stereotype of the Indian who doesn't say much and lives either the simple life or the life of a simpleton."

The red locks spun and she smiled. "Aldebaran, wasn't it? Chichilticalli Aldebaran, the Native American Rhodes scholar. I'm sure you've remained a bit of a Columbo type, the kind of shrewd observer who never quite lets on that he knows a great deal more than he says. That could be witty but prefers the elliptical manner of his Zuni ancestors and reaffirming to white folks that he's a simple Indian."

"Mm."

"Well, inexplicably I still find the trait involving lacunae intriguing. But then intrigue has been my *modus operandi* for this little excursion from Santa Fe. I've moved there from New York, you see, as perhaps a rebirth from a life of too many cocktails and other tales. The intrigue is something I've conjured up myself. Everyone loves a mystery, and I think my sister Ashleigh's death falls into that category. She may have died of her own abusive mindset. Then again, someone might have assisted that process with some sort of strange substance. Whatever the case, she had spent some time out here in New Mexico just before returning to a demise in upstate New York, so I figured I'd have a look round some of the high desert delights she had visited before departing the planet."

Ms. Dupín's explanation of both her move to Santa Fe and her investigations into her sister's death triggered a flood of desultory invasions recollecting how it used to be during our enthusiastic torment of minds and bodies. Aurore wasn't your average American coed loose in Europe. She was more the post-collegiate undercover intellectual, who could cut you to bits with a volley of verbal darts, or just as soon rock and roll until the two of you were covered in sweat and overheated with exhaustion from the aftermath of spontaneous combustion.

It all came back as if it was just a month or two ago. The candles, the cold rooms, and the stooping for the ancient door at the Turf Tavern. While in Oxford, neither of us could be bothered about the future. It was rather a time when youthful drives overwhelm all else, an unrestrained period of indulgence before the delayed responsibilities of adulthood.

Ashleigh had no idea that not only was I aware who her sister was, but that I had spent time with her. Aurore was on a quest and for the moment, I thought it best to let that possibly volatile information lie. The two sisters back then had very little to do with one another, so I was reasonably assured that the late elder sister never informed her sibling of what had occurred at Aztec and on the rafting trip. I wanted to keep away from that topic.

"Santa Fe, mm? Isn't that a little too low-key after life in the urban skyscraper fast lane?"

"Most certainly. And that, my dear Mr. C-man, may save my life if not at least imbuing me with a taste for Southwestern architecture, furnishings, and cuisine. Who knows, I may even take to cowgirl boots."

And then she turned and disappeared through the type of rough-hewn door still found in many a mine where men pick and shovel their dreams into wheelbarrows. Because I didn't want the stream of reminiscences to stop, there was no effort on my part to follow her into the mine. There was no going back to that Oxonian era, yet the mind could return even if the bodies could not.

I was fairly certain the woman in white would be trouble, and I had just enough ancestral blood in me always to find the wait as appealing as any action. Aurore Dupín was the sort of female you couldn't actively pursue anyway. She preferred the unobtainable, probably the likes of Kaliber Ristraverdé and those who would prefer sitting out behind a shack with a book of St-Vincent Millay poetry rather than a dinner in Santa Fe at Geronimo or *al fresco* on the Coyote Café patio.

Another peculiarity I remembered should be attributed to women like the carrot-topped peril was that you couldn't let her go too far with her verbal parries nor ask too many questions of her. It was all about the finesse of conversational interplay, really, very much like the pub blather and trading of insults one encounters daily in British life. Aurore was hopelessly enamored with approach-avoidance. Get too close, and a male with an attitude might be incinerated by unpleasant repercussions. Make no attempt at verbal skirmishing and the same adventurer might be dismissed like a choirboy.

Growing up in a pueblo did not give me the skills to deal with someone like Aurore Dupín. Those could only be assimilated through being literate and quick witted, with plenty of practice in the white man's world of concrete, electronic software, and nocturnal noisy group encounters. Still, I knew that as the memories slowly disappeared into the mine's vapors, I would ineluctably be drawn to another round of verbal masquerading with this amazing woman of urban sophistication. She knew little about astronomy, Native Americans, or the West. But she had the sort of formidable mind that ticked over like an IBM mainframe. And just to bask a few more minutes in that light, might mean some verbal skirmishing even a Zuni living in two worlds would endure.

After following a large tunnel-like area mocked up to resemble perhaps a gold or silver mine, I saw nothing more of the woman in white suddenly having materialized in the Wild West. The image of her initial swaying through the museum front door was still rattling around my ranger brain with the intensity of an eagle atop a rattlesnake. Maybe she had taken the elevator back upstairs to the display room.

"What are you doing here in Grants, Aldebaran?" suddenly came from behind. It was Dupín, with her arms still crossed but her mind fully engaged.

"'It's a mystery,' as they would say in *Shakespeare in Love*. I suppose I feel an allegiance to my heritage and so stay in the area. Some might depict my job as menial, but I characterize it as instrumental in defying the stereotypes palefaces have of all Indians. That, of course, is an oversimplification. The real reason probably has something to do with pursuing research in the white man's world and what that would entail. I'm not a coat-and-tie kind of bloke. And where better can I survey the heavens than right here in New Mexico. It probably has one of the smallest populations per square mile of all the States, almost like Alaska and Wyoming. Light interference at night in the northwest part of the State is no worse than the middle of Nevada. I can study the constellations above if not the heavenly bodies within the Visitor Center in peace. Nobody hassles me at work, except with occasional inane questions. And I still have time to contemplate my existence, a pursuit I'm sure you'd typify as one of under-achievement."

"We all underachieve. It takes far more courage to achieve anything worth reading. I'm certainly no exception, having recently opted out of scrutinizing others' written work rather than risking writing something noteworthy of my own. But then I come from a family of drinkers, and I can blame the inherited trait of life through the bottom of a glass as both an entertaining truth serum as well as determinant of my fate. Besides, in having reared one of the oddest prodigies around these 50 disparate States, I feel as if my contribution to the planet may end up being more significant than anything I could conjure up actively doing."

Aurore was pacing back and forth during this strange exposition, while I shuffled from one foot to the other, unsure how to respond to her self-abnegation. It was a mystery. But just listening to her made me hearken back to those days of fusion in Oxford when a bottle of wine and an afternoon of secret bonding were the only two pursuits that mattered.

"Anyway, that last convoluted rambling dissertation upon the meaning of life by yours truly is enough for today. My inclination would be to tempt fate by picking up where we left off. But oddly at my age, an afternoon nap without having to worry about closed or open entry ports and an elevated temperature currently seem more appealing. But it has been novel running into you once again. It's just as well I probably won't be back to Grants, though. I've always found that trying to recreate the past is nothing more than the wish that a finite romance become infinite.

"Which reminds me," she added. "I need to get on with my day of exploration and investigation. You never know what sort of discoveries the reality of the desert or the vicariousness of the internet will reveal."

"Like the fact that Ashleigh and I were thrown together on a rafting trip down the Colorado River during her time out here?" I gave my remark just a moment to sink in, enjoying the quizzical look upon Dupín's face. "She didn't like me much. I don't think it was the fact that I was an Indian, or the discovery that I had known her sister intimately which annoyed her. Ashleigh, to me, was just desperately unhappy with everything and everyone. And when I wouldn't jump her on a sandbar halfway down the river and under the Big Dipper, it was just one more disappointment for someone destined to find her fellow rafters more shallow than certain parts of the River of No Return."

"She never told me she knew you."

"She didn't tell you a lot of things."

# Guadalupe's Tequila

(KALIBER)
If you've spent a substantially decadent part of your life in urban areas, they still haunt you when you leave them behind. West L.A. and Boulder may seem disparate destinations in terms of complexity, but you can get drunk with interesting and well-educated sorts in either. Even though I had pitched it all to live in a shack in a canyon south of Chaco, I still get almost a libidinal response for a restaurant, bar, or coffee house in one of those conglomerations of adobe or wooden buildings where folks talk about nothing and everything.

You realize that it isn't the setting or the people in the setting that matter. It's what is said and what inexplicably careens round your brain like a pinball. Who cares about sports, politics, show business, the environment, global warming and a hundred other novelties? Under sober circumstances I could give a rat's ass. But give me a rum and tonic, a Corona, or a shot of tequila and suddenly I'm your peripatetic philosopher with an answer for everything.

Sometimes you just want to be left alone. But fueled by a couple of spirits, I find that conversationally engaging my fellow citizens becomes ever more appealing. A good verbal skirmish, particularly with someone who has stereotyped me as some numb-nut transient who was lucky to come up with the five dollars to buy a drink. They always look at me when I first respond with other than the guttural or monosyllabic sort of shit that they're expecting. I love the power of unanticipated disruption. One minute some overweight businessman with a lot more money than me has deigned to engage me in a brief chat about the weather or how to get to Tesuque. It is an innocuous start to what will be an entertaining conflict.

Of course, I'm always of the mind that to temper the vices, exercise is paramount. Maybe that's what kept me alive in Nam. When you're mentally stretched to a dried-up rubber band with a nick in the edge, physical fitness may be the only thing keeping you alive. My own salvation is running. But it's not for everyone. Most people find it boring, and too hard to do even a mile. I find it cathartic, purgative, and the best antidote available for toxic liquid intake. If you can run 10 miles, there's more than an even chance your ticker is going to keep from clogging and most of the nasty stuff from bottles is going to be flushed out of your skin and lungs like the water from laundry on a line. You think I'm kidding? Just knock back a maxed-out trio of margaritas at the Rio Grande in Boulder before staggering blissfully back to your motel a mile to the east, or to the Boulderado or St. Julien Hotel if you've got some bucks. Wake up the next morning and run the creek bike path up and down for an hour or more. It ain't going to be easy, but by the end of that run, you're going to need about a half-gallon of water. And guess what that's going to do? Purge all that remaining tequila that your liver is squawking about removing from your overloaded system.

I needed to spend some time in a bar like the Rio, so I drove to Santa Fe. I got one of those antique motel rooms along Cerrillos that are just as clean as the other monsters in town but a lot cheaper. My favorite is the King's Castle, which if you get a room at the back, you don't hear the four-wheel drives and low riders blasting by until late hours. The showers used to have those antique metal saloon doors that only cover between the knees and shoulders. They're gone, of course, because everything in this modern civilization always needs to be updated or changed—just one more reason I've moved out to where a book and a glass of liquid refreshment are the two most complex things I deal with.

I checked in, the chap from New Delhi or Calcutta who slides the window open to take your money thinly disguising he was on the verge of telling me there was nothing available—even though I scoped there were no cars in the courtyard or built-in porticos. I can't blame him. I needed a shave, and the loose Hawaiian shirt I was wearing didn't inspire much confidence that the credit card would go through. But it did, and I departed the small motel atrium without grabbing any of the hundreds of tourist brochures and without inhaling deeply the fleeting scent of lamb vindaloo.

Twenty minutes later in running togs, I cut over to the spur of the old Santa Fe Southern tracks coming up from Lamy and now used for nothing more than a tourist train slowly transporting out-of-towners through the desert countryside with no fear of getting attacked by outlaws on horseback. To get out of town as an overland harrier, you see a lot of the backs of some of those homes with tall broken wooden fences and huge metal parts in the back yards and jump across some arroyos which last saw water around the turn of the century. But it's worth it after a couple of miles. First you get on the concrete of Los Chamisos bike path for a short bit and before you know it, you're back running along the Santa Fe Southern tracks, a rutted, red rock-strewn dirt trail southeast for as long as you keep breathing and the hawks don't get you as carrion. There are some serious short ups and downs that throw people off mountain bikes, but gradually it levels out and you pass by the sorts of places discreetly hidden among the black cholla and scrub oaks and owned as second or third homes by wealthy sorts from Grosse Pointe Woods, Lake Forest, or Dallas. That's a bit of an oversimplification, of course. But then when you've taken to living in a bare cabin, it's the sort of drivel and pontifications mélange, even without alcohol, you come up with while pounding pavement or red soil underfoot.

Anyway, I dehydrated myself enough to get rid of the Myers's dark stuff from the previous evening's reading. A ten miler, or five out and five back, did amazing things for my jaded mindset. Maybe it was the endorphins kicking in, or maybe it was the last ounce of rum departing through my skin, but I got back to the old King's Castle a few pounds lighter. After a shower and shave, and a different Hawaiian shirt to go with my red Converse low tops, I was ready. Not ready to meet some Wild Western woman wearing a fertility necklace and cowgirl boots, but with my left hand resting around a Guadalupé's margarita, ready to survey as many of those women I couldn't afford as well as those who ooze sexuality without surgical assistance.

Part of my departure from the perils of mainstream meant doing without a lot of what I had before in terms of amenities and companionship. But then, the risk and mystery attached to whatever was coming next still held a quasi-romantic such as myself captive. I say quasi, because I had no intention of trying to meet any woman, no matter how sophisticated, sexy, or eager. When you have no money, no property, an old car, and attitude, it's not even enough to attract the bite of a rattlesnake, much less one of the sirens of Santa Fe.

The reason I go to Guadalupe's Cantina, just off St. Francis, is because its parking lot is packed with local license plates, always a good sign that the spirit of a place appeals to the indigenous. It also has an unusual small bar with about 200 types of margaritas and whatever tequila you want, caramelized, 100 percent agave, Reposada, silver or gold, you name it. There are only about six seats at the bar in the back to try and discourage tourists from discovery. A disparate cast of characters deposit themselves in front of a spectacular array of Mexico's finest spirits.

It was a weeknight and it was early, the sun having not yet gone behind the other side of the valley when I drove in and beached the Suby. Reaching the destination where one can deflect pain for an hour or two, there was only one seat left, and as I oozed into it, I had a brief sensation that this woman in white sipping a margarita while leaning on one elbow looked vaguely familiar. But not wanting trouble, I took care in staring straight ahead rather than greeting her like you do when you're young enough to hope to score the same evening you meet someone.

I just needed the proximity to other people. No chitchat with strangers. Just being able to scrutinize whatever I wanted with impunity. And there's nothing better for doing that than a bowl of corn chips, a hot sauce made from scratch capable of firing the tonsils, and a liquid concoction from agave or sugar cane to put you in the mood for daydreams of yesteryear and limited future adventures. Like the uncle Chichilticalli Aldebaran told me about, I never met a pepper I didn't like. And it's not hot enough unless you sweat below the eyes.

"You're the one who lives in a canyon south of Chaco, aren't you?"

She kind of caught me off guard. When her face turned in my direction and that fresh rust-colored hair created a halo around it, the woman in white presented an enigmatic appeal. As she was probably close to my same age, she still seemed a little bit too old for my tastes, yet I still found the tired kohl-rimmed eyes and lipstick inexplicably attractive. She had those eyes that convey an intelligence that mystifies. Her posture exuded confidence, the kind one gets from many battles fought in deep urban trenches. I had seen it in L.A. with female studio execs. They could carve you into beef medallions before you knew the type of knife they were using. Insult you worse that you thought possible, and yet smile as if daring you to come up with a better retort. It was all a big-city game, only to be played with enough practice that spontaneity gave you the rapier-like ability to come back at someone with just the right verbal dart. But if you exercised those sharpened wits, there was always the risk of barking something inevitably leading to trouble and causing you unreasonable regret when you awoke with a hangover in Westwood.

Then it all came back to me. The woman with the rock hunter's determination to make her adventure in the Southwest pay off. She was the one who had vanished from my canyon space more quickly than she appeared.

"Yah. And you're the rock hunter, right?" I responded with no inflection revealing any predisposition.

She looked at me with those eyes. I could tell she was deciding just what retort appropriate to some smart-assed cave dweller.

"Mm. Didn't know I'd stumble upon anyone sipping a drink in an arroyo. Thought I'd just have a look round at some of the geology. Not expecting to find someone combining poetry by Edna St. Vincent Millay—yes, I have good eyes—and cocktails. But then New Mexico does strange things to people, doesn't it?"

Now it was my turn. I deliberately delayed my response to hold her in suspense. She was feeling me out, no doubt about it. Trying to decide whether I was a fish to be reeled in and then thrown overboard as too small to keep, or a fellow predator capable of my own cunning devices.

"When you leave the city for quieter times and have chosen some remote location not exactly on the Gray Line route, you don't expect to find a woman in Doc Martens with an attitude browsing nearby on an outcropping."

The tip of her lip hinted a smirk. "True, true," she began wryly. "I guess the unexpected pleasure escaped both of us. I did my best to disappear. You never know if someone out there is making letter bombs because of the post office job they left. Anyway, I hope my invasion was fleeting enough. Didn't mean to interrupt your escape from rabid urban reality."

This was getting good. I took a long pull on my Don Julio 100-percent agave marg and slowly turned toward her. I could tell that soon the pair of us would either be spouting real nasty stuff or placating one another because of some bizarre mating dance. What are bars for, anyway, if you don't engage some unwitting soul to your right or left in a rousing polemical round of specious or spurious blather? She was tough, beautiful, and not about to relinquish the upper hand. Ah, but neither was I. And therein lies the start—as they would say in Casablanca—of a beautiful friendship. She just didn't know it yet.

"Oh, you didn't. Occasionally someone from Omaha drifts up from their RV parked by the side of the road and has a look round the canyon. It's one of the hazards of reclusion just like co-habitation amidst urban sophistication. You can't always choose those with whom you come into contact. There might be a poet. Then again, there might be an arrogant trust funder with an attitude and the delusion of enlightening any population with his or her presence. Or maybe they're just wanting to find that nugget or piece of turquoise that will wow them back in Poughkeepsie."

Amidst all this, a top-shelf Robbie R Margarita she had ordered arrived, she took a good slug of it to take the edge off and was ready for the next round. The art of a good argument requires delaying tactics as well as confrontation. There was no doubt: the woman new to the West was just getting warmed up.

"Is everyone in New Mexico on the loose from some former corporate confinement or other interpersonal disaster? In just three days my mother and daughter met an elderly Navajo who sits out amidst the ruins and contemplates eagles or whatever one does under the desert sun; I ran into a Zuni Indian former acquaintance-cum-park ranger who has a degree from Oxford and is confining himself to lecturing tourists on where the nearest rest facilities and curiosities are best found; and now I again encounter someone who apparently seems to find alluring the combination of desolate drinking and looking like a reject from being an extra in Gidget goes to Hawaii. There must be a bar somewhere in Santa Fe where most of the patrons either work or have other more predictable pursuits."

I thought it best not to divulge the Zuni she mentioned had to be the same dude I knew. But I could point her in the direction of a few more predictable sorts. "Oh, there are, there definitely are. If the riffraff here doesn't appeal, you could always try the Inn at the Anasazi, the Coyote Café or Geronimo. There's an up- or down-market place for everyone here on the Altar. You just have to know where they are and who frequents them. Not everyone is a cast off from Hollywood, New York, Texas, or Boulder."

"Touché." She pursed her lips after another sip of the agave and lemon juice—Guadalupe's insists upon using lemons rather than limes due to more consistent availability. Her eyes were more like sapphires to be used much like those neon light rods they duel with in Star Wars. "That's the first refreshing notion I've heard in New Mexico," she added. "I'm the sort who vacillates back and forth between a magnetic attraction to things that are bad for me and things that will keep me alive without trouble. The first is exciting and the second boring. The trick is to find a precarious balance that makes you glad to be up and around in the Great Southwest. You give up the subway, Nathan's hot dogs, the Rainbow Room, the Algonquin cocktail lounge and all the other elements of Gotham singularity, and you wonder if sanity will ever be included as part of life in New Mexico. Or if all its citizens are either Native Americans detesting the invading hordes, or the hordes themselves, having brought parts of Iowa, Texas, and California with them."

"No one seems to arrive here knowing their true thirst. Desert life is an acquired taste unless you were born here. But you're here, and so something in the *Sunday Times* or a National Geographic documentary must have attracted you."

"I think it was a chance to dumb down. To get back to the basics, even if it does involve interacting with those who don't wear Brooks Brothers or horned-rimmed glasses and drink Cosmo's. One never knows what the high desert may bring, except perhaps the occasional enigmatic resident who has stared into the sun too long or smokes too many medicinal cheroots without having to face a job at a Wall Street investment bank or insurance company."

It was unclear whether the two of us were ever going to get beyond the sparring we had first initiated south of Chaco. But as her glance panned the tequila bottles in front of her, I could feel we were going to cut through all the bullshit.

"I'm sure exactly why I have gravitated to this former Spanish depot of the desert is of no import to you. But just so you won't think I was interested in poaching your cabin or am an internal revenue investigator looking for wayward taxes, I should mention that I wanted to try out the Southwest to see if spectacular surroundings could somewhat remedy a precocious daughter's speech impediment. And I also wished to see some of the last places my sister frequented before an untimely demise. Someone might have poisoned her. Then again, I can think of a whole list of eager assassins who might have come up with just the sort of undetectable noxious substance one needs for permanent relief from someone without a congenial clue."

"Death near the Rio Grande, instead of Death on the Nile?"

"Death in upstate New York of reputed natural circumstances. But what's natural about death in your 50s?"

"Sometimes I'm not sure. About whether I'm dead or still alive," I added after clearing my mouth of chip bits. "It's a symptom beyond the age of 45 one can never quite be sure of."

"The only experiences beyond 45 one can be assured of are the aches and pains of increasing age. One can talk vitamins, antioxidants, and a low-fat diet, but that merely delays the inevitable. So, the two of us sit here in a place called Guadalupé's Cantina with our own self-prescribed anesthesia. Life does indeed look better through the bottom of a glass, to paraphrase an essential ingredient of the Three Musketeers."

I pursed my lips and further examined the yellowish liquid in my glass. She was right, of course. Still, there is nothing worse than concurrence for putting the kibosh on a good conflict. "Your sister was popular, was she?"

"Oh, yah. As much as someone who never had a kind word to say about anyone can be. Ashleigh had the mind, temperament, and money to disdain everyone. If she deigned to speak to someone, whether acquaintance or relative, it was all about Ashleigh, or all about the listener's shortcomings. Nothing really did seem right or rewarding to my sister. None of us is exactly sure why. She didn't do drugs or alcohol with the same alacrity of her nearest kin. She just had a nasty disposition, perhaps because of being jilted by some cad who became the straw that breaks—"

"She wouldn't per chance have had a jet-black page-boy haircut, skin the color of a cadaver, and a penchant for the color black?"

The woman in white looked at me as if suddenly I had acquired visionary tendencies.

"Ashleigh never wore anything but black or red. On her best days she remained in mourning for herself and an exhausting inability to relate to her fellow man."

"She was out here about two years ago?"

"Mm. And there is only one way you could know that. You undoubtedly must have had the displeasure of her company."

I smirked just like I used to do in Nam when someone in a clean uniform arrived in the jungle and started asking questions about things that still wouldn't save them from the horrors of combat. Sort of like a *schadenfreude* you develop perhaps as a way of coping. Someone is worse off than you, and that makes you feel better. As the two of us drifted into agave nirvana there was no going back now. There was no way I could deny having encountered the terrifying Ashleigh.

"She was muttering in the Tesuque Market. Something about recovering from a raft trip, decanted while she was examining an array of pastries in a glass case. Yours truly not only was able to take in these ramblings from this woman in tight black jeans, black cowboy boots, and a black tailored cowgirl shirt with black pearl buttons, but also could not avoid speaking up when she turned that impertinent gaze upon me. 'You must live in the area,' she began. 'Would you recommend having sugar or protein if one is to entertain some sort of high-elevation breakfast?'

"How do you respond to a stranger who seems drunk without having had any alcohol? No matter what reply given, trouble had to be the inevitable outcome. I think I responded something like, 'It depends upon whether you like blood sugar levels slow and steady, or dissolute enough to include an afternoon nap.'"

"That's Ashleigh, alright. Give her just a breath or two and she's on you like a vulture on carrion."

"I've been called worse. But carrion might be apt in describing my current desiccated carcass."

"Fortunately, we are availing ourselves of a substance better than formaldehyde for pickling and preserving," offered the woman in white. "And yet we are still here, and she isn't. Perhaps a lesson in tolerance which I often find outside acceptable parameters."

"Tolerance is for those either genuinely sympathetic or afraid of confrontation. Personally, I'm better at complaining than doing anything about it."

"That was quite Wildean. It's too bad you and Oscar couldn't have spent more time with Ashleigh. She might have benefited from a good dose of returned disdain."

"You must be Aurore, I assume. Although I spent just enough time with Ashleigh to refuse her idea of rocking the Tesuque and Santa Fe areas together, your name did come up several times. It's a moniker hard to forget."

"To make an impression can never be good or bad. It can only be remarkable, as Mr. Wilde might remark. I'd rather someone of consequence remember an encounter, even if their reflections are unpleasant."

She was stirring the pot again.

"I won't forget," I replied summarily, perhaps to imply duly noting a backhanded compliment from my Gualalupé's encounter. "I never did see Ashleigh again. I had the feeling that if I wouldn't do her in my Subaru in the parking lot, that there was little point in continuing. She was just dangerous enough I did consider it. But then I've come to an age where a good night's sleep and lots of liquid refreshments have found increased value compared to a quick exchange of fluids for that brief electrical charge one immediately regrets thereafter. Ashleigh did have a unique allure. It's just that I was able to ignore it primarily because I could tell she was used to getting what she wanted. We went to market, so to speak, rolled around a bit and then parted company as if it had all been a big mistake."

"So, Ashleigh was unable to use her enchanting persona and physical attributes upon you?"

"I came up short. At my age I'm no longer good at the highly visible games one can get up to in the carpeted area of a station wagon in a crowded parking lot.

"The last thing I remember is her ranting something about never being able to forgive her sister."

# Dupin Poison

(AURORE)

This post-hippy character was annoying, but at least he had a way with words. If I was younger, and not intent upon finding my sister's terminator, nor upon protecting my daughter from an onslaught of those who merely aggravate her stutter, I might either have told this guy to fuck off or taken him back the Inn at Loretto and found out if his libido could overcome a lifetime of alcohol. I was in that kind of mood. Maybe it was examining poisonous plants in Grants, or maybe it was again encountering Chichilticalli Aldebaran in the Mining Museum, but latent urges I was doing my best to suppress were acting up. I couldn't work it out: whether I was going to chop this guy up into minced jalapeños, or trade verbal arrows until we had had enough tequila to supervene any inhibitions that two strangers over 50 might let get in the way before jumping one another.

Suddenly I was tired. Tired of too many dances or prances with men, tired of shepherding my mother and daughter around Santa Fe, and tired from a shot of Hornitos I had just downed along with my Robbie R silver margarita. Did I really care if someone killed my sister? Probably not. The long drive from Grants had given me freeway-lag and the sort of attitude that finds everyone within range annoying.

What kind of a name is Kaliber, anyway? When he told me that, I immediately started hearkening back to the old Western, Have Gun Will Travel. Kaliber Ristraverdé wasn't the sort of name you found at an art opening in Manhattan. The point that he obviously was better read than his Hawaiian shirt and red Converse low-tops made him appear, connoted a contrast scoring points, however. And his interjections had a way of insidiously demanding we proceed further conversationally. Even though I was tired and beginning to think that returning to the room at the Inn empty of my two relatives still up somewhere around Chaco Canyon was the best idea I had had since exiting the Mining Museum without arranging anything with Chichilticalli.

But then I'm a sucker for an inquisition. And his last remark did make me wonder just what sort of scathing splutterings my sister uttered when they last discarded one another.

"I'm sure Ashleigh told you the usual sort of dronings about how hard done by she was in terms of her nearest relatives."

"Actually, no," the reclusive off-highwayman replied. "I remember it was something about she'd like to kill you for what you said about some guy back in New York and her. Maybe it had to do with their using each other, and you enlightened her it was just another excuse to continue her self-pitying lament. She was rambling, and I was only taking in part of it. By then I was certain she was missing a screw or two—both literally and figuratively—and I was wondering why the two of us were leaning on my car fender in a remote part of a full parking lot. I haven't a clue how we got into the back of my wagon and under a tarp. All I had had was a cup of French Roast and an apple fritter. Both of us began firing on all cylinders and were stupid enough to think our selves invisible in broad daylight.

"Strange things happen, though, even to the likes of a couple totaling more than a century between them. My temperature had only gone up maybe two degrees and suddenly I threw off the tarp and climbed out. Your sister appeared like the Ghost of Christmas Present. Her face was contorted as if I was turning down the greatest piece of ass since Marilyn Monroe. I can't even remember all the vicious shit she unleashed about my lack of Valentino-esque abilities, but by then I was immune. It was time to trade a few more insults and then to disappear individually back over into Santa Fe."

What came out of his mouth was provocative, I'll give him that. Yet I had consumed just enough tequila to be missing bits of what he was saying. Not really important, I told myself. What was important was the light glistening off the rows of tequila bottles behind the bar. They told their own story of man's inability to cope with mundane reality. You had to have some magic potions for this and that. Tequila took away the pain of realizing each of us isn't necessarily destined to lead a charmed life. And there are still those dark alleys where one reaches the depths of distasteful experiences no matter what. The depression over the loss of eternal youth, or the inability far earlier to cope with the hormonal urges that cannot find the right conduits at the very moments you most desire them. I was drunk. But I had that wonderful narcotic feeling one gets after the third or fourth cocktail. The point where none of the other desperate souls around you matters, nor does the life you have momentarily escaped. A pleasant melancholy achieved through liquid spirits. You are removed from daughters and mothers and past boyfriends and the constant battle to prove yourself worthy. Worthy of what? Who knows? I took another unladylike gulp of the silver liquid and allowed myself an indiscreet bleary scrutiny of this Hollywood reject to my left. He needed a shave and a haircut. Yet he wasn't about to get one, nor change his attitude. And that was O.K. Two juiced souls in a Mexican bar with a New Mexican attitude. The rest of the world outside could continue its madcap ways, while we were comfortably ensconced in our own private den of euphoria.

"So, your mother and daughter are cruising the Chaco ruins?"

My reverie was broken by this tumbleweed-blown character with the mind of a Gothamite and the escape act of an inmate of Alcatraz. His question slowly filtered through the agave haze, and it was time for a reply. How to summarize a lifetime shared with two of your same gender so totally different from, and yet so undeniably alike yourself?

"Kahlo never cruises. She has the mind of a 30-year-old and the energy and body of a kinetic person twenty-one years younger. Katarina, before it gets too late in the afternoon and she's inhaled too much vodka, is the leash. She tries as best she can to restrain Kahlo's enthusiasm, enough so that my daughter doesn't break her neck mimicking Annie Oakley or the subject of whatever biography she has recently digested."

"A miniature Wonder Woman. Maybe she takes after her mother."

"She has my enthusiasm; I'll grant you that. But she could never hold still this long without careering off to climb some rock or look for a jackrabbit. Kahlo, if she is fortunate enough to reach adulthood after the age of 13 or 14—and her grateful progenitors are lucky—may lose her hyperactive tendencies. Then again, here in the Wild West we will be relieved if she survives the next four to five years without broken bones or shattered dreams."

"And your mother prefers vodka to tequila."

"One might assume a certain message in that remark. On the other hand, you're here, you're imbibing as much tequila as you can into that dissolute frame, and perhaps are none the wiser nor better off for it."

The remark obviously found its mark. Mr. Kaliber put the glass to his lips, then tried to take just a moderate sip. The intent was to appear nonchalant, as if taking the verbal jab in stride just as one ignores any *faux pas* and pretends it a mere bagatelle.

"I drink with a lack of responsibility for myself, but that is my prerogative," he replied with raised eyebrows. "As a contrast, some might argue that you are drinking for three for whom you are responsible—though you may depend upon them as much as they upon you."

I had had just about enough of this character having misconstrued shack living as a romanticized Walden Pond. He was up for an agave-fueled clash of high desert proportions, there could be no doubt about that. But sadly, he was right. I had to think of Kahlo and Katarina, even if a good verbal knee to the nuts is just what this desperado needed.

The moment was probably one of the few times when I have consumed enough spirits to begin mentally preparing for just the right thrust while deferring doing so. Just the right remark to send this incubus packing. Yet somehow, I still found him dangerously interesting. Perhaps the one trait I find most attractive in those of either gender is indifference. Not caring about what someone else thinks has always had its appeal. Even when some of the most arrogant authors in my jaded urban world had scoffed at some notion I expressed or contradicted an opinion belaboring the obvious, still I came back for more. It was my nature, I suppose, and that is probably why I am single and shall remain so. Men and their testosterone must have the upper hand. Women and their estrogen learn to suppress intolerance over this penchant by the more aggressive gender. Except for me. I'm a slow learner.

But it was time for a nap and a return to the reality for which I would need to recover sufficiently to deal with a precocious daughter and undoubtedly inebriated mother. Certainly, Kahlo would be brimming with stuttering factoids about her latest expedition into Chaco Canyon. And I would be the captive audience my mother had failed to be on the long ride home.

"I assume it wasn't arsenic or rat poison. Otherwise, an autopsy would have discovered the cause of your sister's demise."

"There was no autopsy, though that would certainly have

discovered a body perhaps destroyed by untold synaptic surges from an inability to cope with mere casual encounters. To me, Ashleigh was too young to die from heart failure. And after all, she had a heart of cast iron derived out of extensive broken promises from a long list of men she engaged with her vicious, black-humored ways.

"No, what I learned in Grants while perusing the internet, was that the typical household has an entire garden of common plants which one should not entertain snacking upon. Crotons, Chrysanthemums, Aloe Vera, Azalea, Poinsettia, English Ivy, and Philodendra are just a few novel decorative numbers that can cause problems if you should choose to include them in a salad or mince pie."

"My favorite is Dieffenbachia," added Ristraverdé. "The stuff grows huge yellow-and-green leaves until it tips over. And if you happen to have a guest with a propensity to go on and on over something exceptionally boring, you can always add bits of the leaves in *hors d'oeuvres*. It is also called 'Dumb Cane,' and fortunately if it passes down an obnoxious guest or relative's gullet, his or her voice is silenced."

"Still, Dieffenbachia won't kill you, while white oleander or hemlock might. On the other hand, red oleander can prove ideally lethal for someone wishing to make a death appear a heart attack."

"What are the attractive symptoms?"

"Well, it has cardiac glycosides which fool with your intercellular and serum and potassium levels. Those levels screw up your electrolyte balance and cause arrythmias in the old ticker. Eventually enough of it can cause the inability of the heart to function, leading initially to difficulty in breathing, then to weakness, collapse and possibly death."

"Charming."

"Mm, and just the sort of mysterious substance to give the appearance of a heart attack or heart failure from natural causes. Since there was no autopsy upon the remains of Ashleigh, 'heart failure' is what the local GP ruled."

"The perfect murder."

"Well, if she was indeed murdered. Ashleigh had never had a heart condition before. Of course, dogbane and foxglove, I learned today, will achieve the same result if either can be imaginatively included in someone's diet. Somehow her death by heart failure was all too convenient for any number of people with grudges against Ashleigh. She was a princess with a cast iron scepter doubling as a mace."

"It sounds as if the women in your family are a hard-assed bunch with no weak spirit."

"None, unless for the elder members drinking weak spirits is considered. Oddly, however, Ashleigh's habits, other than her inability to cope with anyone differing in opinion, were far better than either Katarina's or my own. She wouldn't be nearly as polite to you, however. As you learned in Tesuque, one of you undoubtedly was destined to leave, while the other licked his or her wounds."

Cabin man leaned back in his chair, and his eyes were those of an animal having seen it all in the steamy thick vegetation of Southeast Asia. There was a depth I hadn't seen before, as if to say that nothing anyone could do or say back in the lower 48 could have even a shred of the horror he'd experienced in jungle combat. His eyes conveyed that conventional domestic verbal skirmishing was like kid's play, even though his wits and vocabulary weren't sharpened nearly enough to fence successfully with far more literate and arrogant Oxbridge or Harvard types.

I could just see Ashleigh and this Hollywood outcast each seeking the other's most vulnerable spot—certainly not the heart, as Claude Rains might point out—while at the same time inexplicably attracted to the dangers of close contact. A submission to sexual desire combined with a competitive drive to avoid cerebral submission. It was then I decided my only strategy, at least temporary for victory, was to decline further sparring and make an unexpected departure.

"I really must get back to the Inn," I said with a conviction that rang hollow. "Kahlo and Katarina will be arriving soon, and I'll need just a half hour or so to wind down from the tequila before the onslaught of my daughter's latest discoveries."

"And just when things were progressing toward a polemic crescendo over someone few, if any, will ever miss after her untimely demise."

"I have a bothersome feeling," I said before draining my margarita glass and pursing my lips, "we are destined to encounter one another again."

"I should hope so. Just think of the many remaining intriguing elements regarding your sister's death that undoubtedly haven't been explored. Like how you will eventually explain the cross she had tattooed on her left glute."

# Hogan's Hero

(QUIVIRA)

God, almighty, my head hurt. I had to get a grip on myself if I was ever going to have a Southwestern day without the benefit of a hangover. Who knows how I found that Gallup bar with the *piñatas* glaring down at me as I powered through a series of margaritas with a taste not much better than diesel fuel. Money wasn't a problem, my attitude was. Let's be honest. Most journalists drink because they are forced to endure consciences tortured by a lifetime of critiquing the foibles of others. It was nasty work telling the truth. Most people either didn't want to hear it or relished the same paragraphs you labor so hard to extract from a disparate bunch of factoids your investigations and interviews discovered. Writing about football was no different. You called it how you saw it and that meant a bunch of big guys wanting to meet you late at night in Harlem or Brooklyn and make sure you left the area with some serious internal damage. What quarterback liked to read he had lost a step? What linebacker wanted to hear a running back mowed him down like a wilted cornstalk? It didn't matter if you wrote about sports or politics or religion or society. A good percentage of your readers were going to end up feeling you're a smart-ass who thinks he's omniscient. They were right about the smart-ass part, but wrong about my being an all-ologist. But that's what you got paid for: taking risk in everything you critiqued, whether right, wrong, or just plain outrageous.

Being more than 2000 miles from New York was doing wonders for my mind but playing havoc with my liver and kidneys. Of course, when you first go on vacation you tell yourself you've earned a few nights of indulgence. And you have. But the problem is that once you get into sugar, alcohol, or junk food, you find you crave them at almost every opportunity. So far, I had had about a million hamburgers, pizzas, and alcoholic bevvies. It was catching up to me, and if I was ever going to do any constructive investigations in the line of treasure hunting, I was going to have to get going before eleven o'clock in the morning.

You know you are a bit beyond it when you keep tripping on flat carpeting, that off-color stuff underfoot in those non-descript motels that are financially inexpensive but unexpectedly costly because of how you ended up there. Still, it's far easier to drive up to your own door in some faded concrete line of rooms like the Bates Motel, than to stagger through a deserted hotel lobby pretending that it's not 2:30 a.m. There's no one in the hotel to notice you but the night manager. But even having anyone share in your misfortunate lack of ability to remember what floor you're on can prove embarrassing. Far easier to stumble through that motel's hollow plywood door into a room smelling of disinfectant but empty of any snickering gargoyles.

At least I had read quite a bit about treasure during the afternoons when I had had enough New Mexican sun and decided a nap to be the best benefit of not being on assignment to some newspaper or magazine. On several afternoons before I went to Chaco and La Ventana, I digested a whole stack of tourist brochures and cheap books I had purchased from those beat-up bookstores where the owner is more interested in possession of tomes than selling them.

Take peridot, for instance. What a gem. Even Cleopatra reputedly wore the precious stones many thought were emeralds. And if the Mogollon Cross legend was to be properly fueled, what better trivia bit than where most of the precious olivine minerals come from. Not from Myanmar, as many would suspect, nor from China or Pakistan. Nope. Three of the biggest source locations were in Arizona and New Mexico. Oddly, two of them were called Buell Park, one in the Cactus State and one in the Land of Enchantment. Yet the producer of 80-90% of the world's peridot was right where it should be for legendary purposes: the San Carlos Apache Indian Reservation on the Peridot Mesa—not far south from the Mogollon Rim.

Native Americans were the only ones mining the precious green rocks, and quite often they sold them by the barrel or other container full rather than sorting them for quality purposes like De Beers or some other international company might do. Could the cross have originated from the Hopis or Apaches? Or could it have been crafted in Spain only to have its stones replaced en route by Vasquez de Coronado?

It was enough to drive a man to drink. That and the many lost treasure stories you can read about or listen to a fellow tippler disgorge late at night in some forgettable establishment for pickling an overwrought brain. Since in the early 1900s it was illegal to possess gold, and before that many people didn't trust Wild West banks which could come and go from bad management or be robbed at gunpoint anyway, the possibilities for exotic tales were boundless.

And that doesn't even address the Spanish explorers, gold, silver, and turquoise miners, as well as Indian and cowboy robbers who emptied stagecoaches, banks, and trains whenever they could. Robbers, thieves, and blackguards from the period hid huge stashes of cash and gold in all kinds of places. Lost gold and silver mines, including Prospector Adams' entire hill of gold near Pinos Altos, were just the sorts of legends of hidden caches creating endless speculation driving men to head out into the middle of nowhere with picks, shovels, and burros.

Tales of treasure were endless. The missing $100,000 from the train robbery reputedly buried somewhere out on *El Malpais* southeast of Grants; the stagecoach robbery strongbox supposedly underground in the vicinity of Stein's Peak in Hidalgo County; the Spanish gold bars allegedly deposited in the Caballo Mountains 35 miles from Las Cruces; the $40,000 of missing gold coins from the wagon train possibly hidden 25 miles east of Springer; The Santa Fe Cimarron robbery's 25 bags of gold coins or the two pioneers' $40,000 in gold coins, both reputed to be underfoot somewhere near Ute Park; the exotic Gran Quivira treasure comprised of 1,600 burro loads of gold and silver supposedly in the vicinity of the Four Corners' Hell's Canyon in the Manzano Mountains; the lost Hoskannini Silver mine of Monument Valley, Arizona; The Red Jack Gang proceeds from the Wells Fargo robbery near Riverside, Arizona; Ben Sublett's Lost Sublett Mine in the Guadalupe Mountains of Texas.

I mean, all I needed was one glimpse of the Wells Fargo & Co strongbox photo at LegendsofAmerica.com and I was a goner. For instance, the Lost Padre Mine of the Organ Mountains, important historically because of La Quinta, or 'the Fifth.' The Fifth meant the percentage of any found treasure mandated to go to Spanish royalty. The Spanish explorers went home from the Organ Mountains empty handed, but who knows whether unique rich veins still exist somewhere near Las Cruces?

Then what about the alleged U.S. Army payroll robbed from a stage regularly traveling between Forts Wingate and Whipple? The bandits rode north from the point of robbery near Albuquerque, and to this day the cache allegedly is buried under a hidden rock arch near Blanco, south of Aztec, New Mexico.

Undoubtedly the most bizarre treasure legend concerns the Victorio Peak treasure. In 1937 Milton Ernest 'Doc' Noss was exploring an area of the Hebrillo Basin in a desert known as *Jornado del Muerto* in southern New Mexico. Noss discovered an abandoned mineshaft. Proceeding further inside, the prospector reached a cave-like room in which he reputedly discovered a gold statue of the Virgin Mary, gold coins, jewels, and letters dated 1880. On a return trip to this hidden cache Noss was supposed to have found a crown with an incredible 243 diamonds and a ruby. But even more provocatively, the intrepid explorer supposedly discovered hundreds of gold bars. Were they part of the eventually assassinated Emperor Maximillian's treasure moved north from Mexico to be hidden in the 1860s? Or was it the *Casa del Cueva de Oro*, or Spanish House of the Golden Cave, with treasure deposited by Don Juan de Onate in 1598?

Meanwhile, Noss reputedly kept hiding gold bars—illegal to possess by U.S. law—throughout the New Mexican desert. The story became ever more convoluted with accidental mineshaft collapses; the U.S. military taking over the area for White Sands Missile testing; a rediscovery by two airmen; intentional further tunnel collapses to re-secret the treasure; and possible shipment of more discovered gold bars to Fort Knox. What happened to all the gold bars Noss pulled out? Are some still buried in Victorio Peak, or elsewhere? Who knows, but just reading about all these stories in one source or another had me going, I'll say that.

I'm a sucker for this sort of thing. The hair on my arms sometimes stands up as shivers ooze to my fingertips. Sometimes I think it's about the only thing short of a former bullet pass from John Elway that'll still get me going. And the wonderful thing about treasure hunting, is that although there are no guarantees, there is also little to stop you from those thousands of seemingly empty arid or mountainous areas that may or may not contain that shiny stuff you're seeking. Kind of like fishing, where the catch isn't important.

It's rather the images of that 25-inch bass or six-foot yellowfin tuna that antagonize your imagination. It's all dreamlike stuff, but once you've been a journalist, your fodder is the stuff of dreams. You can't wait to follow up on the next good yarn, even if it is apocryphal.

I thought I'd have a wander round the lava beds of *El Malpais*. The broad expanse of burnt black disgorgings from down under that dare you to try and discover anything amidst its once fiery emanations. I could always return to Grants or some other depot with liquid refreshment samplers. There was no hurry, either. I had money accessible through the old plastic Visa debit card, and the time on my hands to walk or dig or stumble upon something novel.

I was tempted to drive all the way down to White Sands. But then what's the point of trying to search for Emperor Max's or old man Noss' ersatz treasure on lands that the government declines to let you explore and that may well still be radioactive in places from atomic testing. I quickly overruled any such foolhardiness and decided that walking—well at least for the most part—in legal areas would do me just fine, particularly since I'm the sort who may well stray off the path just slightly if I get the feeling that ignoring out-of-bounds signs will be to my advantage. You only live twice, as Ian Fleming says, and I certainly spent my first chronicling the outlandish acts and deeds of those who dare to try the impossible or attain the unthinkable.

And now it was time to make vicarious pursuits real. I simply love doing something no one else has. Or bringing it to life through a good written yarn. Think of your favorite columnist and how you look forward to hanging on their every word. I'm not that good, but I'm provocative. And if I ever find some of these bizarre caches said to be buried here and there under cacti or juniper trees or turquoise veins, I will do my best further to inspire those quests which to the risk-free appear ludicrous.

The top was down on the cobalt Pontiac, and it was another

day in the Land of Enchantment. The beauty of having no job or assignment was the gratification of those whims that every man dreams of indulging. *Travels With Charley*, for instance, in which John Steinbeck asserts that the one thing he found everywhere is that people wished they could make the journey with him. I'm doing it now, and the spirits are with me both day and night. America is a vast cornucopia of possibilities, and I was going to have my day in quixotic field exploration.

The plan, however, was first to head to up to see an ancient wizard Chichilticalli had advised had a wealth of information on the legends of the area. The Indian that had helped me out with a few good right crosses outside the Radon Bar suggested that this Ketl antiquity of the Navajos might provide valuable clues as to where one might begin to poke his nose into this vast expanse of sand and rock.

Set back from the highway were a hogan and attached teepee that fit right in with the stereotype of the Native American caught between two worlds. There was no satellite dish or phone line, but this Ketl character probably still had to buy his provisions amidst some sort of urban sophistication. Yet the whole ramshackle place smacked of a pariah who could care less about tract housing or his neighborhood cybercafé. I personally had fought purchasing a cell phone, aware that each of us at some point draws a line between our familiar comfort levels and progressing technologically into the new age.

It was obvious *Hosteen* Ketl had maintained his antediluvian ways without having to bow to all the gadgetry of modern times. There was a rocking chair under a portico propped up on slightly curved pine poles, and it was readily apparent that from alongside the road his view over the valley, with its sunrises, was an important part of the old man's daily habits.

Ketl was nowhere in sight as I braked the Pontiac in a cloud of dust, but it was early, and at his age he might well watch the sunrise and then take a nap. My friend from the Visitors Center, Aldebaran, had told me of his history of working the Pullman cars and a uranium mine near Shiprock. To me, it was a wonder he was still capable of witnessing more moons and suns.

After I knocked on a doorframe alongside of which a hanging ristra looked as if it were more than decorative, I heard someone yell that he would soon be there. When he came to the open door, I felt as if I were stepping back into time. The old man didn't have a headdress of eagle feathers, but he did have the long straight white hair and the tanned, wizened skin of a sage who knew far more than he generally chose to reveal. He had the aura of a visionary; I'll give him that. Few men have that kind of presence anymore, the kind which clarions an entire world of knowledge and wisdom.

"The name's Quivira Cantrell. Chichilticalli said I should look you up regarding something I'm interested in."

"Come in," he replied, gesturing for me to step back in time.

The front room had a lot of the stuff white folks associate with Indians. I mean, the walls had eagle feather sprays, bundles of sage, and black and white photos of the Santa Fe Pullman cars, men coming out of what appeared to be a mine, but none of any ceremonial congregations. A candle was burning on a rough pine table, as if the light was important to some sort of daily ritual. An animal hide hung barring the door to what I supposed led to the teepee.

The thing is, I didn't know if this ancient one would be responsive to some journalist on holiday arriving at this front door to discuss treasure. Many Native Americans didn't take kindly to palefaces snooping around ceremonial grounds and sacred sites. Then again, I was here, I was a journalist at heart, and I love a good story. There was no doubt this Indian taking a seat on a high-backed plain pine chair—far simpler than you would find in an urban abode—

had an extensive memory of tales. It was whether he would divulge any of them to me, and for what purpose?

"What brings you through the Diné Reservation?" he asked after a pause while my gaze finished circling the room.

It wasn't a trick question. But I felt it was. His introductory remark made me aware of entering a potential minefield of racial tension. It didn't have to be that way, but my next remarks probably would determine just how the two of us proceeded on his turf.

"Well, I came out here to get away from all the turmoil of the East Coast. But along the way in New Orleans, I ran into a couple of deep-sea treasure hunters in a bar who told me a good yarn about something called the Mogollon Cross. At first, probably like anyone hearing such an outlandish tale, I listened with the jaundiced perspective of a guy who left all that kind of stuff behind at about age 14 or 16. But then once I left my sister's place in Durango and headed south, the terrain of New Mexico did something to me. It wasn't an epiphany or anything, it was more like I felt like I was arriving at a place where I could let my imagination go. Discover a different type of existence than the one I had had in bars and reporting on NFL games.

"Then I decided I might just see what I could learn about one of the local legends of lost treasure. You may not believe it, but I don't care about the notion of how much money it might bring. Oh sure, I might buy a few things including a place to live. But an actual hands-on experience with treasure intrigues me far more. I want to touch something magic and extremely valuable."

As I had deposed my intentions, I could see little upon a face impassive from probably having heard this sort of drivel from a hundred if not a thousand tourists or train passengers. The stereotypical Indian face had just stared at me while listening attentively, and I had no idea whether he'd like to cut my throat or offer me a cup of some boiled potion one drinks on a reservation with no legal alcohol.

The Navajo elder waited in silence, as if I hadn't yet finished.

"You already have," he replied.

"You mean minerals and soil all around us, I suppose," I replied before suddenly realizing no reply would have been better. But I had his attention. And I couldn't be assured I would have it much longer. "I'm sure Chichilticalli told you about the Radon Bar incident and how he rescued me from a good hiding. I guess he was a boxer back in his college days." Now I was fumbling for some key that would signal me he was an ally, hedging for time, because I couldn't read the old man's reactions. I hadn't been able to go through the ice-breaking dance two white people go through to lessen the tension of discussing anything of worth with a total stranger.

His eyes drifted, rather than out through the front windows, to a vast panorama of meaningful surroundings, pinching a little as he allowed his orbs to look into my soul. It was another awkward moment, perhaps like Custer might feel just when he has seen Sitting Bull look over his shoulder at several thousand fellow tribesmen. I had no experience of talking with this sort of character. It wasn't like in the movies, where if things went bad, you called in the cavalry. I was another of the endless hordes who tramp through his lands, hoping to find something of value other than a good view that they could take back to show their friends in Savannah or Grosse Pointe Woods.

"What would you do if you found such a cross?"

He had me there. Usually, I'm pretty good at an impromptu answer, even to an impertinent question. But what would I do if I found the Mogollon Cross or one of old man Noss' gold bars? Probably try and trade it for cash, even though I had told the old Navajo I wouldn't care about the money. What was I going to do with discovered ancient treasure? Rebury it? Hand it over to the authorities to put in a museum? He had me and I wasn't sure what to say.

"I don't honestly know. Probably examine it wistfully for a day or two and then decide to sell it to some big-time collector. When you're a journalist, it's the quest and story that interest you most. But I've gotta say that if gold, diamonds, old bundles of currency or the Mogollon Cross ever came into my hands, I might prove to lack the conscience an occasional treasure hunter does to leave it be."

About halfway through my musings aloud, his eyes had moved back from the horizon to my orbs. Waiting for this ancient one to judge what I had said was nerve-wracking. Suddenly it was if I had importuned all of Native America with my greed to find something of worth they valued far more if left alone.

"That's the first direct answer I've ever heard from a white visitor," he said with that penetrating gaze of a thousand years. "At least you're honest enough to admit the thirst that accompanies most who enter these lands. Chichilticalli said he thought you had some character. He also said he didn't know if the search for the Mogollon Cross would overcome an honest nature. Treasure legends have a way of doing that even to men of the highest callings."

I nodded, not knowing where this was leading.

"If you weren't on the *Diné Bikéyah*, I still would be inclined to keep what I know to myself. I like protecting what's out there." He then lapsed back into contemplation for what seemed an eternity. "Let's step outside," he finally uttered portentously.

And with that he was up, apparently quite nimble for someone of his advanced years. It appeared he didn't eat much, and Chichilticalli had told me the old man smokes both the legal and illegal stuff. When we got outside, he walked right off the dilapidated wood porch onto the red dirt, the sun illuminating a mesa bordering the valley to the north. His boot kicked a rock toward a bedraggled prickly pear cactus and a black beetle scampered to safety. His arm came up and a dark, veined hand swept in an extended panorama.

"These are the lands that once contained only Pueblo, Diné, Apache, Ute, or what your people call Indians," he said as if a ruler peering out over lost territory. "They tried to live in harmony with the gods of the heavens and Earth, taking only what they needed for survival. And that is the difference today. The white man comes, takes away, and returns little to the land."

I stood transfixed, staring out at nothing. Guilty. What could I say?

"Come over here," he said setting off slowly toward the teepee attached to the side of his hogan. Then he stopped short, and slowly turned around to arrest me in my tracks.

"I have something for you inside which may alter your journey."

He then coughed before gesturing to his conical room. "This tipi is my connection to the past. I know both ancient and current worlds, yet for me, this small chamber is from the past. When I am inside these animal hides on poles not normally associated with the Diné, it is as if I am returning to my ancestry. If you choose to enter, I ask you to do so with the spirit of a man sharing destinies with others of a different calling." And with that he held up a flap so that I might enter this private den of contemplation and spiritual endeavors.

We stooped down and walked inside. A desert quiet came up as he moved something on a rock mostly out of my site. It was odd, but I suddenly felt some sort of transformation. Not something you could immediately identify, but more as if the aura of the past was pervading my jaded urban brain. There were no furnishings save a large piece of red sandstone that served as a table. Upon it were several books with faded covers, a candle, eagle feathers, a porcelain pipe and what looked to be a giant piece of rose quartz. There was also an earthen dish containing the remnants of a burned bundle of sage. I was sure that somewhere more discreet Ketl kept his tobacco and other aromatic smoking substances.

He sat down cross-legged and signaled me to do the same. At my current weight, this is a request normally I would decline. But under the circumstances, as Claude Rains might say in Casablanca, I did so. With difficulty I assumed the same sitting position as my host. Now, intermittently I suffer from tinnitus, and suddenly as if arriving like the Santa Fe Chief from a distance, I became aware of the normal vestigial ringing in my ears becoming louder. It was sort of like the Last Supper in the original M.A.S.H. film, the whole scenario reminiscent of some metaphysical ceremony of greater import than one's initial impression.

"Do you smoke?" he asked, pulling out a baggie from a cigar box that had been out of sight behind the rock table.

"Not too much anymore. However, we are on Navajo land, and I would feel uncomfortable declining any hospitality offered."

He nodded as if he understood far more than my response intended. There could be no doubt about it, old Ketl was dancing the tightrope between two worlds, and had carved out his own existence while ignoring the worst of crowded, toxic urbanity in favor of a healthier dose of a life of outdoor spirituality. He took a leisurely approach in lighting up the magic pipe, and while he puffed on this spiritual device to get it up to value, the aromatic teepee slowly became a secret chamber for male bonding in which the citified paleface journalist was going to experience something he normally wouldn't amidst the scribblers at Rosie O'Grady's or the gourmands of his favorite Gotham nosheries.

When he passed me the pipe, I shivered with a moment's apprehension that I was traveling into an unknown world. Nothing was going to change physically, yet the two of us undoubtedly were going to do some time traveling to unspecified destinations. It's the nature of smoking things that affect one's perspective.

Who knows how much time elapsed as we both sat there amidst our own thoughts? I was aware it was getting warmer, but I didn't know where this sharing of the pipe was leading.

It was at some unexpected point in this cerebral journey that I noticed he had something in his lap that he then held out toward me. I took it and placed it in my lap without even a glance at its contents.

"I am old, and will not enjoy many more sunrises," he said. "They say I am too old to change. I have a cell phone I rarely use, and do not want a computer or daily newspaper. Yet I have been abrupt with many white people, perhaps because of what they did to my people on the long march to the Bosque or in the uranium mines. They did not tell us of roentgens and radon, or such things. Still, I have survived and have lived to see no two colors of light exactly the same upon the mesa.

"I have also learned that the white man will keep coming until perhaps the water runs out. Then they will leave much like the Anasazi. But I must mend my fences. I must do so soon. That is why I agreed to let Chichilticalli direct you to me. Because I know you will search no matter what. It is your great adventure. When white men can no longer shoot the buffalo or Indians."

His whole dialogue was resonating in my ears, but I was having difficulty taking all of it in. I didn't know if he was intentionally speaking that way, or I had smoked enough he was starting to sound like a traditional Indian from Anglo movies. I was in the haze of one who hasn't smoked magic substance in a long time. Then I became aware that what Ketl had passed me was a map.

"What is this a map of?"

He took another inhale from the great white pipe.

"It is a map leading to the immediate future."

"What will I find?"

He reached over, turned the pipe upside down and tapped out the ashes in the sage remains. Then he turned back to me, his eyes conveying a wisdom I had not yet witnessed in life.

"You may find nothing. Or you may discover everything."

# The Uranium Man

(KETL)

I watched the big white man leave my tipi and listened for the sound of the engine of his ancient blue machine.

His perception of the *Diné Bikéyah* and the surrounding lands of what they have named New Mexico may not change. He has come for treasure. But does he recognize treasure when he sees it?

Every man at some point must go on such a quest. It is unfortunate that modern civilization makes such pursuits 'entertaining' instead of necessary for survival. The white man's adventures, short of war, do not permit the rites of passage so familiar to many southwestern Native American tribes. For the *belagaana*, to shoot an animal or to catch a fish is mainly for trophy purposes or stories, not for survival.

But then when I look back on how as a young man I valued my heritage, escaped it, and then found it again, maybe I have been no different than those Anglos who work in the tall glass buildings.

In the early 1940s I was fortunate to be among a second batch of Navajos to be selected to join the U.S. Marine Corps in Camp Pendleton, California. Somehow the marines discovered the largely unwritten Navajo language was ideal for coded messages. With its difficult vocabulary and tonal inflections, our language to most remains indecipherable. They found a young Diné could translate a message in less than a minute that took 30 minutes for an encoding machine. We were shipped to a series of islands in the South Pacific, and all acquitted ourselves with honor and dignity. We received commendations for our work in World War II.

Yet I was still very young when the war ended. I remained impetuous and wanted to prove myself in the vast and complex western world of America. I knew that the Diné were different from the Anglos of European descent who came in great wagons to the Southwest. They built the trains I worked on.

The great iron horses took me far from the *Dinetah* of Changing Woman. Back then I had become ashamed of my dark skin color, hairless face, and lack of English language talk. On three occasions I was beaten by white men without ever having said a word. I learned that prejudice is worse than any *chindi* haunting a dead man's hogan. I was afraid of the white man's world, but scornful of my own world's poverty. I was determined not to be the victim many of the Diné accept as their fate.

You may not understand the dignity of the Pullman car conductor or Santa Fe Chief restaurant waiter. But I did my job with great pride, and most of the white people onboard treated me well. I ate well, slept well, and saw the *belagaana*'s adopted country through large glass windows. It was one of the happiest times of my life, even though I had abandoned my heritage. The happiness different from our *hozro* came because I had done something totally on my own. I was at peace with myself for having taken unusual initiative.

When I met white people, they didn't care about the clan name of my mother, nor could they tell if I was a Navajo or a member of the Mesa Flower Clan. Others asked me if I was an Apache or Cherokee and said I should be in the movies. Now, more than 50 years later and after having lived through most of the 20$^{th}$ Century, the whole experience seems like a dream. A journey among two worlds in which I wished to be recognized, for what I do not know.

Still, I do not regret serving the white man. It did not make me understand their culture. But the years on the Chief let me see much beauty beyond *Dinetah* and to meet many *belagaana* who prefer the indoors to being under the hot southwestern high-desert sun.

Like all attempts by Navajos to integrate into the white man's world, eventually you realize you will never be totally accepted as one of them. They will not invite you to their homes, unless to display a novelty. Many pale-skinned ones think all Indians are childlike and simple. They think elliptical speaking or failure to speak means a lack of intelligence. They don't understand the Diné way of leaving much unsaid among surroundings of the Glittering World that say what is necessary. And ultimately, often without meaning to be so, they are insulting or condescending. Sometimes they talk about Native Americans as if you are not even present. Others looked right through me as if I wasn't even there. Toward the end of my iron-horse travels the patronizing smiles of pity rather than genuine friendship made me leave the trains. I felt humiliated I had not been able to converse adequately in their tongue, nor to convey the Diné way of life. Not able to make them realize the true value of the great open spaces of the Diné *Bikéyah* and the *hozro* it can bring to those who can accept Changing Woman's Glittering World offerings.

But I had not yet seen 30 standing suns when a truly evil trip into the bowels of the white man's world insidiously began. When I arrived back from the Pacific and release from the military in California, I had been fortunate to find a job on the Santa Fe Chief. Many Navajos were not so lucky. Quite a few of them took jobs in mining a substance from what the Diné would now say comes from the Black World. It was called uranium and it was supposed to be necessary to develop weapons to fight communism. The mining of uranium then was considered patriotic. It was mysterious like the coyote of the Yellow World. No one was told anything about roentgens, radiation, radon, or any other warnings regarding the extreme dangers involved in exposure to this radioactive destroyer of the lungs and other parts of our bodies and souls.

When I left the railroad, friends helped me get a job at a mine at Cove near Shiprock. Over time more and more got sick. I was lucky and in the late 50s realized something wasn't right about entering the Black World to dig up Changing Woman's secrets best left untouched. I had a persistent cough but thought it nothing more than a viral *chindi* that eventually would be sent away.

By 1970, however, of the 150 Navajos who had worked the uranium mines, 133 were dead.

Some were from my clan, and many were friends. I cannot tell you the tears that were shed at the many ceremonies held to prepare them for separate four-day journeys to the underworld, ones that would free them of any *chindi* and permit them eternal peace underground. Eventually I received $100,000 from the government for what they identified as the lung cancer that troubled me. A *Yataalii* performed a Blessing Way and gave me many herbs and roots to boil up as a potion, and over a year my lungs got better, and I survived. I gave most of the $100,000 to the Tribal Council to help the families of the many who gave their lives to the invisibly harmful substance.

Yet I try not to dwell on that Black World past. I have reached an age where a Diné must prepare himself for the afterlife. I haven't really done much so far. This is probably because I tell myself I have been able to defy the white man's rules for cancer and survive without chemotherapy or radiation. Maybe my time will come soon. Then again, I may see many more sunrises from the porch of my hogan.

Encountering the big white man brought back many memories of the past when I learned by working on the edge of their world. It is not just the color of one's skin that is different, but the climate and culture from which he comes. Quivira Cantrell knows the world of cities. I know the world of the desert. He is not the first *belagaana* to ask me about treasure. To me treasure is a word associated with the great natural phenomena of the sky-water-Earth world. What is the value of the sun on the sandstone at dusk? Or a jackrabbit hurrying to safety without encountering a coyote? Or the sudden desert cactus flowers after a heavy rainstorm? Yet to someone spending his whole life in cities, only shiny minerals are considered treasure.

That is why I have sent the big man on his quest. What he finds and how he reacts will tell much about him.

# Loretto Piano Music

(KATARINA)

When one is used to the reassuring surroundings of certain amenities and a lifetime of acquired mementos, returning to a sophisticated Santa Fe hotel room compared to endless dust and rock can be as if reaching an oasis. There is no doubt anyone can appreciate the grandeur of the canyons and rock formations of northwest New Mexico. Yet when the biggest part of your day formerly was reading the *Times* in a stuffed chair high above Central Park on the Upper East Side, or strolling down to the deli, finding oneself back amidst all the comforts of urban civilization can be a welcome relief.

Not that Kahlo feels the same way, mind you. Right now, my granddaughter has her headphones on at the computer while I am wearing another pair as I try and pretend I have again regained my piano playing abilities, even if I must endure a rented electronic instrument instead of a Steinway. Still, I feel much better when Kahlo is doing her exploring vicariously. I don't have to worry about her being attacked by a wandering predator, nor of her falling to some sort of calamitous injury. She seems just as content to investigate Chaco Canyon with Google Earth, as to be bounding here and there amongst the actual crumbling ruins. If anyone were in our room without headphones, he or she would hear little more than the tapping of plastic keys by two generations of Dupíns.

I was using some sheet music to attempt a Beethoven concerto, and I must admit, playing far worse than flawlessly. It's much like learning to walk again after an injury, I suppose, when one tries to use one's fingers much like they performed several decades earlier. It simply is astonishing how little the aging rheumatic digits cooperate after having been far less active in creating melodies and now forced to stretch where once they danced effortlessly.

The nice thing about playing electronically to headphones, however, is that because of performing only for oneself, there is ample time to reflect upon notions such as the explanations my granddaughter was babbling about on the south side of Chaco Canyon. The little phenom said so many things so quickly during our picnic lunch, I could barely take them all in. Often, to Kahlo, a concept or theory or analysis of an occurrence is blatantly obvious, while opaque to someone like me lacking the same zeal for the particulars of endless natural and man-made phenomena. For instance, I know the little mite was trying to tell me the Great North Road was used as a series of aqueducts and highways for hauling logs or some such. But where does she come up with this stuff? It isn't like she's had any formal engineering or archeological training. She is more the Agatha Christie of the internet and ancient sites, her powers of observation apparently far more acute than most scientists six or seven times her age.

Aurore doesn't know a thing about these discoveries, and I don't know whether Kahlo will choose to tell her much or not. I didn't want to get into any of these speculations last night and put my precocious grandchild on the spot. That's the sort of thing she detests. Everything must come from within when you're her age, particularly when any divulgences are inhibited by a stutter. I doubt if she's said anything to anyone but me, and that was perfunctory, I'm sure, compared to the extent of the discoveries she's made in Chaco and other remote destinations.

I hope my saying something to the bartender in the La Fonda last night didn't do my granddaughter a disservice. One never knows if one should let such observations by a nine-year-old remain secret or not. Then I was lonely, Kahlo had gone to bed, and Aurore obviously was in no mood for conversation after several hours of tequila in some local establishment. I didn't tell the bartender much, of course. But with pride, suddenly I found myself almost bragging about my granddaughter's powers. Just a garrulous old woman, I guess.

"Hello, all," was the greeting Aurore gave after returning from the Aztec Coffee House. Kahlo merely glanced up briefly, nearly oblivious due to far more important things on the screen in front of her.

"Has Kahlo said anything to you about her Chaco speculations?" I asked my daughter, confident that the music coming through Kahlo's headphones would prevent her from hearing our conversation.

"She stuttered something about how excited she was about what she had discovered, and that she wanted to go back there again. But other than that, she has been as inscrutable as ever. And since I'm the one who must instill discipline, normally I do not also wish to become her hated questioner."

"I never know whether we should encourage her in such pursuits or not. You can't be certain if her nearly perpetual solitary investigations are as valuable as the camaraderie most kids her age enjoy with each other. I just wish she had a friend or two her own age. But I suppose that will come with time when she is back in school here in Santa Fe."

"I'm not sure," my daughter quietly replied, dropping into a chair nearby my piano and musing aloud. "Not sure if we should encourage her as much as we do, and not sure just how important peer acceptance is at this point in her life. She is a prodigy, there is little to deny that. The question is, in the long run, how do we, as family, try to gain a balance in her mental pursuits with normal activities among kids her own age who like video games and the Simpsons more than trolling the internet."

My daughter loves that child as if she were her own flesh and blood, and so do I. It's odd, because at times I find I do have my own prejudices about people from certain backgrounds. Aurore is far more open-minded when it comes to such things, enough so that she adopted Kahlo more than eight years ago.

The adoption process was long and convoluted, but Aurore felt there are already too many people on the planet, so why not take on one already here. Why she chose a Native American adoption agency is probably more a philosophical choice from having a collective white guilt of centuries. Anyway, agencies do not reveal the exact parents, but did tell her Kahlo was the product of a Mexican mother and Zuni Indian father. Yet since her arrival in New York back then, the only non-white elements about the little sprite remain the color of her skin and certain atavistic visionary tendencies that may or may not derive from her Indian or Mexican blood.

"So, what in particular got her so excited on her latest Chaco expedition?" Aurore inquired to break my reverie.

"I let her go for a hike up on top of the north Mesa. I wasn't sure if it would be safe. Then again, I couldn't make any difficult climb at my age, and Kahlo was insistent that she had to see some things up at Pueblo Alto and gaze out at the Great North Road. On the electronic camera she carries in her backpack she showed me some photos she took facing north up at Pueblo Alto, but to me it looked like any other rolling valley with a wash or two in the distance. But Kahlo was certain she had discovered at least some of what the Anasazi were up to with the Great North Road. Something about using them to haul logs for the overhead beams in their pueblo constructions and to use as aqueducts for collecting and transporting water. I'm sure she'll tell you when she's ready. Right now, I think she's using the internet to firm up some of her potential discoveries. The real question, I guess, is how seriously do we take her?"

"I don't know," Aurore replied, getting up from her chair and walking to look out the window. After she spoke, it was as if we became a couple of Navajos, waiting for the other to say something. "What are your plans for today? Are you and Kahlo going to go anywhere?"

"She did mention she wanted to go to the Southwest Reading Room of the Santa Fe Library. She seems to love that room. At least she tries to go there as much as possible while we are here in the city. I wonder if a grade school library will be any kind of temptation at all for a prodigy like Kahlo. I hope she doesn't find going back to school nothing more than frustrating."

"I know. I know," Aurore responded pensively. "A duality constantly affects me: do I continue to let her act three or four times her age mentally during her investigations; or encourage her to become more like her peers and watch television and play on swing sets."

"I think we both know the answer to that one. But tolerating her tangents of spinning off from kids her own age forces all of us to enter unknown territory. Sure, Kahlo is very much like both of us were, I with my piano playing and you with your incessant reading. But she is also way beyond either of us. At her age, I think we should give her free rein, short of dangerous exploits. Hopefully, over time, she will make some new friends at school. After all, this is a city of great breadth when it comes to who lives here and where they've come from. We'll just have to hope there are other little geniuses bored with home economics and Dick and Jane reading."

"I'm sure you're right. We've got to let Kahlo delve where she may, and hope that what she discovers while stimulating an already overwhelming curiosity will provoke her mind, even if she finds herself missing out on video games. Sometimes I think she would rather know the genetic traits of a lizard than catch it."

"I've caught a few with a little bit more body temperature and the same swiveling eyes in my day," I added. "Unethical men and lizards are two species best left to their own devices."

"Mm. The trouble is, those devices somehow always end up ensnaring Dupín women. And although Kahlo right now is too young to attract those attentions, what will we do when some fourteen-year-old shows up to take her to the mall."

"Wish them good luck. After all, both of us were once young and impressionable and we survived. Maybe we're underestimating Kahlo. Perhaps you should concentrate more on your other mystery."

"You mean, regarding the infamous Ashleigh?"

"I do. And what have you learned in your latest internet surfing of nefarious plants or other investigations?"

"Well, I discovered some interesting side effects of household plants, should anyone suddenly not notice the odd leaves, stems, or flowers in their latest designer salad or smoothie. Lots of seemingly innocuous things like Dieffenbachia or Crotons can really give you a bad day or end all the bad days you've endured."

"But even if someone did assist Ashleigh to the next spiritual world, who might have done so and why?"

"Ah, that is a question probably for Shakespeare. However, I can think of at least four to seven conniving or even philanthropic sorts who may have reached their limits before providing mortal assistance."

"And those might be?"

"Well, my ex-husband for one, used to thrive on near-violent verbal contretemps with my sister, and I can think of no one she knew better equipped to relieve her of her misery. Then there's Kaliber Ristraverdé, the hermetic post-hippie somewhere south of Chaco. Over margaritas at Guadalupé's he told me that when she was out here, he suffered moderate verbal abuse just for turning her down after some hanky-panky in a Tesuque parking lot.

"Or there's you, for instance, whom she pushed down the stairs. Probably not enough slight to take your own daughter's life, but you have to admit Poirot would at least give you consideration. Then there's me, someone dear old Ashleigh loved to provoke with lashing, loathsome, vindictive barrages. Maybe I was pushed a little too far. Or what about Chichilticalli Aldebaran, whom I first encountered at Cambridge two decades ago? It seems he was on a rafting trip with Ashleigh, and things didn't go all that swimmingly."

"Or maybe she died of a heart infected with self-inflicted mental trauma."

"Quite possible. Though I would think a stroke from the stress of surviving in a world of all those whom she constantly found annoying more likely."

One could always attempt to scrutinize the pattern of behavior in either my surviving daughter's or her daughter's life and find nothing more specifically identifiable than the predictable. It's the sort of thing that drives a woman of my age to vodka. Once I get a couple of stiff belts in me, I can better handle the unpredictability of my bloodline. I love both dearly, but one always questions whether some advisory or disciplinary corner could have been turned differently. Or whether a mother or grandmother has failed as a role model and shepherd. The main thing I've learned about Kahlo, however, is that the little dervish is the wizard of contemporary knowledge investigations. Nothing stops her. Well, at least nothing in the conventional world of children. Her attention can be held for hours on end in front of that encyclopedic computer, just as easily as most children are held spellbound by cartoons on TV. Yet every day I wonder if we haven't allowed her to open Pandora's box. Has she indeed discovered something that will bring her even more speech impediment-inducing stress? Or will she further distance herself from all peers as a social pariah? I'm only glad that primary care falls upon my daughter, Aurore, a risky situation perhaps a bit like putting the fox in charge of the hen house.

Like all youthful spirits, however, Kahlo remains only nine when it comes to energetic explosiveness and/or changes in direction. Suddenly she had stripped off her headphones and was over to me in bounds far longer than one would think a young girl could manage.

"Grammy?"

"Yes, dear?"

"Do you want to w-w-walk over to the l-library with me?"

Now the idea of strolling over to the library this early in the morning, with or without this young prodigy I find so endearing, is not usually the sort of exercise high on my list. First, I must always assess Kahlo's reasoning for such adventures.

"What are you going to look into there, Kahlo?"

"Probably the Will and Ariel Durant series," Aurore muttered as she picked up the *New York Times*.

"Hy-hy-draulics."

"Hydraulics?"

Those braids moved up and down on a white sleeveless T-shirt with a logo of Chaco Culture upon it. With Kahlo, you need know how to balance certain questions with the inevitable result that her stutter will only get worse and answers even more incomprehensible.

Within five minutes the two of us were moving towards the square and the center of Santa Fe's universe. It is not a city that never sleeps like New York. Yet even though at a soporific elevation of more than 7,000 feet, the city magnetically attracts people from all parts of the globe to scrutinize its architecture, furniture, art, jewelry, and mix of white folks, Hispanics, and Indians. As we drew nearer to this unique cultural center, Kahlo alternated young girl-like walking with skipping, all the while lost in thought and oblivious to her historic surroundings. Our usual pattern is that I let her get only so far ahead before wanting to protest, yet at the same time unwilling to dampen her unbridled enthusiasm.

Inside the library, she gravitated to the Southwest Reading Room much like a sleuth threading a maze, the paths of which are already known. I trailed at a modest distance, fully aware that young people need to feel independent of aging caregivers.

It is not difficult to understand Kahlo's being drawn to a room of special antiquarian knowledge with the sort of décor and treasures so inviting. The sea of sturdy pine tables and warm lamps, the arcane Western books hidden behind locked glass-windowed bookcases, and the huge leather-and-pine easy chairs along the wall evoke the true spirit of the pursuit of knowledge. Nothing but total silence, with the slight exception of the rustling of papers or pages, only the diffused light coming through the tall eastern windows down onto the easy chairs and readers hovered over tomes of great exploits and amazing accomplishments. All contribute to a remarkable aura of Western wisdom.

In the stacks elevated by one stair at the north end, a young Indian, whose face and ponytail I felt quite sure that I had seen, fleetingly appeared before replacing a book on a shelf and disappearing into another aisle. He looked like the ranger from the Visitor's Center near Grants. But then what would a ranger be doing all the way over in Santa Fe?

"Sh-sh-shall I meet you in an—in an—hour?" Kahlo whispered as she placed her backpack upon a table near the windows.

"In the lobby, dear. Have fun."

As I was leaving, Kahlo began to unload some papers and a book or two from her backpack the front desk allows her to bring in without checking it there. Just as she was sitting down, however, it was as if she had been apprehended in mid-air. Her gaze became fixed upon something at the north end of the room. It was only then that I realized she was staring at the Indian ranger who had once given us sound advice about Pueblo Pintado.

# Kahlo Reveals

(KAHLO)

Usually, I go right to work when I get to the Southwest Reading Room. It feels the same way my bedroom did in New York City. I imagine myself in familiar surroundings with friends there. It also seems like the Wild West and has creaky floors and the scent of books. I can't explain it, but I feel as if I am closer to Annie Oakley and Calamity Jane when I sit down at one of the huge wood desks. And what's great is, if I'm quiet I can use the room and books just like adults can.

Today I hoped to get one of the librarians to unlock a window case that hide some of my favorite Western books. But I also wanted to look at photographs of hydraulic machinery from books in the main stacks. My latest speculations on Chaco are probably so unrealistic that I'm sure I'll never tell anyone but Gram about them. The trouble is, when I was up at Pueblo Alto, I saw what I saw. I don't have X-ray vision or anything. Ideas just come as if they're right in front of me. And then there was the Coke can while talking to Grammy. No one would believe me, anyway, though.

I hadn't even sat down when I noticed someone I had met before up among the stacks of books. The man looked like that ranger we talked to at the New Mexico Visitor Center near Grants. I couldn't quit staring at him, even though he didn't see me. He seemed to be doing a search of his own just as I was unloading my backpack. Then I thought to myself that even if it were the ranger, he wouldn't remember me. Most people don't remember a quiet little girl with braids. I probably wouldn't.

Soon he left the room and I tried not to look up as he went out. He might have seen me, and I knew that if he had said anything to me, I might not have been able to answer properly. That's why I like the Southwest Reading Room. Even if an opportunity for some conversation or another comes up, silence is necessary because of people reading. It's the perfect world for me. And sometimes when the cumulus clouds cover the morning sun and then drift farther across the sky, the lighting on my desk changes in such a way that is almost like a miracle. I get more goosebumps on my arms when I'm reading about the Anasazi, the Diné, or how badly the Navajos were treated by white people in the nineteenth century.

This time a woman with the kind of glasses on a string around her neck—I think Mom called it a lorgnette—was real nice to me and agreed to let me have some books on hydraulics as well as from behind glass a couple of my favorites with photographs of the West by Edward Curtis and Alfred Stieglitz. Sometimes I have a problem because I can't get a library card until we get a fixed address. But on other days when I tell them my mom's buying a house and we're staying at the Inn at Loretto, they say it will be OK for a couple of hours. When they let me look at rare books, the librarians even give me white cotton gloves so that oil from my fingers doesn't get on the pages.

Maybe I had spent about an hour looking at photographs of hydraulic machinery when it was as if something I envisioned came true. After the ranger, whose name I remembered as Chichilticalli, had left the reading room, I wished he would come back. I can't say why, but a vision had him walking right past me again.

And suddenly, that's what he did. I had put a book on hydraulics aside, and with the sun beaming down over my shoulder I was just staring at a Curtis photograph of Chief Joseph I often return to for inspiration, when Chichilticalli walked right by with two books under his arm and took a seat at a desk at the other end of the room. He didn't see me. His coming back was both good and bad. I'm glad he did. But I wasn't sure I could even say hello to him without stuttering. I tried to concentrate on the book of photos in front of me.

"Hello there," a voice from behind my shoulder quietly whispered to pull me from distant thoughts of Pueblos on the high plains. It was the ranger from Grants.

"Hi," I answered softly, afraid to try to say anything else.

"Curtis is one of my favorites. Which reminds me, we're trying to decide upon a series of lectures for kids connecting astronomy with the archeology of some of the ancient Native American civilizations, and I was wondering if you would mind giving me some of your thoughts out in the lobby?"

I was very nervous, but just nodded and closed my photography book. Most kids would be pleased to be asked their opinions. But when you're not sure what will come out of your mouth and how it will sound, sometimes it can be scary.

"Would you rather sit on a bench outside?" ranger Chichilticalli asked when the two of us were standing out in the lobby.

"S-s-sure."

I can't explain it, but just as the two of us took a seat on a bench across from the Palace of the Governors, I felt reassured. I think it had to do with a vision I had as we walked out. I'm adopted. But suddenly I could see my real mother out upon a grassy field in *El Malpais*. I was being born, and—

"My name is Chichilticalli, as you've probably seen on my nametag. It's a long name, and it comes from the lost ruins below the Mogollon Rim some 200 miles from my Zuni birthplace. It's even longer than my last name, Aldebaran—the name of a first-magnitude star. What's your name?"

"Kahlo," I answered without any problem. I was amazed. But I felt relaxed while Chichilticalli was sitting there with me.

"Like the Mexican painter."

"Mmm-huh. Mom loves her work. She says Frida Kahlo exposed the truth of a lifetime of pain from her streetcar accident." That was the first long sentence I had been able to say without interruption in a long time. My confidence began to soar, and now I knew I could answer his questions without stumbling.

To me, Chichilticalli looked like the classic Native American you see in one of those Tony Hillerman episodes on PBS Mysteries. He was staring across at the Palace of the Governors, the profile of his face sort of like one of the Pueblos in the photographs I had just been examining.

Then he turned to me. "Kahlo, what a NASA educator and the Park Service are trying to do is decide what sort of programs for kids to introduce at some of our Visitor Centers like Chaco Canyon, El Morro, El Malpais, and Northwest New Mexico. We tried a pilot program with the NASA woman that seemed to go over well with kids. But it's not often I get to talk to someone who might give me some input more relevant than responses from adults. Do you think kids would have an interest in listening to someone talk on the connection between astronomy and archeology?"

I tried to nod enthusiastically. "Most of the web sites I've looked at connect the two in some way. I don't know about books, though. Because most of the kids I know don't use them much anymore. Almost all of them have laptops and either spend their time playing video games or surfing web sites more for the visuals than the text."

"I think most young people are familiar with the sun daggers on Fajada Butte. I think it would be good just to use that as a launching pad for other connections between the heavens and what ancient civilizations built."

I nodded in agreement.

"Maybe they'd be interested in the Super Nova, which first appeared in the constellation Taurus in July of 1054 and later became the Crab Nebula. There's even a pictograph in Chaco Canyon near Peñasco Blanco thought to portray that occurrence. The Super Nova was said to be four to ten times brighter than Venus, and at least for 23 days was visible in morning daylight...Anyway, that's the sort of thing I'd like to talk about, but maybe it would be too boring for kids."

"Unh-uh," I shook my head in disagreement. "Some kids wouldn't be paying attention. But I think a lot would. Maybe the Anasazi began to build certain cities because of the phenomena. There was CM Tauri, you mentioned, in 1054, an annular solar eclipse in 1065, and the brighter-than-usual passing of Halley's Comet in 1066. Is it a coincidence that Casa Rinconada and Pueblo del Arroyo began to be built in 1070? Or Casa Chiquita, New Alto and Kin Kletso in 1100?"

I didn't want to get into what I felt to be even more important than when those cities began to be built in Chaco Canyon. Mom says men don't like to think women brighter or better informed than they are. I certainly don't know as much as Chichilticalli, and I probably already had said too much. But it felt so good to talk without stuttering.

"I think you could be onto something there, Kahlo. And maybe that's enough reason that kids should be given more of an opportunity to make connections just like those. The links between astronomy and archeology may not have been thoroughly proven, but the way the Anasazi built their structures used alignment with the cardinal directions. As you may know, they arranged windows to let in moonlight to certain points or sunlight through others at solstice dates, and many other indications all lead in the direction that they were aware of their relationship to many phenomena above and below the Earth."

He sure seemed to know a lot of the stuff I had read about. "Do you like astronomy? I do."

Chichilticalli smiled. "All of the Native American tribes in the Southwest have a cosmological relationship with the sun, moon, and stars. The variations between what the Zunis and other Pueblo tribes, such as the Anasazi and Hopi, as well as the Diné, Apaches, Comanches, Utes, and many others, believe, mainly differs according to the emphasis they place on either the sun or the moon. Most of their planting and ceremonial activities still relate to the seasons as determined by astronomy. Yet because particularly the Anasazi had no written history, what is known is primarily derived from archeological digs, geology, and tree ring dating, storytelling passed on, or speculation based upon visual evidence from the remains of ancient cities and from pictographs or petroglyphs.

"Anyway, all of that is my heritage. When I was lucky enough to attend Oxford, I decided to read astronomy because I was already involved through my ancestry."

"Why aren't you an astronomer?"

"I'm not sure, really. Probably because I think it's more important to me to interact with Anglos and help diffuse the attitude that all Native Americans are predictable souls lost in the past."

"I'm in between. My Mom has fair skin, but I don't."

"You are much like me. I was born of a Zuni mother and Navajo father, but a lot of my education came in the white world, so my thinking process is somewhat divided. You look to have Native American blood. But according to what I learned from my uncle Ketl, and what you just told me, you are being raised by *belagaana* women. So. like me, you are fortunate to be a part of two worlds."

Chichilticalli had no idea how true that was. But I was curious whether another vision just coming through was correct. It might explain why I didn't stutter in front of him.

"Did you ever have a wife and children?"

My favorite ranger stared across at the Palace of the Governors for a long time. I didn't know if he was going to answer or not. But I felt I had to know.

"Once I had a beautiful wife. She was from Mexico. Her name was Magdalena, and she came from Guaymas, on the Sea of Cortez. But I met her in Gallup, we eventually married, and together, we had a child. It was an unusual birth. With Magdalena more than eight months pregnant, one day we decided to take a short walk along the Zuni-Acoma Trail on *El Malpais*. Suddenly the time for my daughter's arrival could not wait. A woman passing just happened to be a nurse and helped Magdalena deliver my daughter on the seat of our truck in the trailhead parking lot. We drove to the hospital, and everything was fine.

"So, you daughter was born on *El Malpais*?"

"She was. Argentacruz had the same coal eyes as her mother—sort of like yours. It was a stressful time. I had come back from Oxford to New Mexico and was still taking odd jobs while deciding what to do with my life. My wife was a very artistic weaver. But selling blankets was not enough money to live on.

"Then one day Magdalena said she didn't feel good. That day turned into a week, then a month. Several purifying ceremonies with a *Hataalii*, or Diné medicine man, didn't seem to cure her. We sent her to a *belagaana* doctor, who discovered too many cancerous tumors in different locations to operate. She died within several months."

I could tell it was an emotional moment for him. I had several more important questions, but I thought I should wait until another time—maybe back at the Northwest New Mexico Visitor's Center. It looked like he was trembling.

"Anyway, that was years ago, and this is the present. I have my work, and you have your investigations. Speaking of which, I thought I would ask you what you think the main purpose of the Chaco Canyon cities were for the Anasazi?"

This is the question about which I had spent hours and hours deliberating. I was pretty sure what I thought. But I was also scared that people would think I'm just an eccentric kid. If I weren't sitting on a bench with someone I trusted, at my favorite library, on a beautiful day, I probably would have stuttered something about not knowing. But it was Chichilticalli, and I felt confident the time had finally come to tell someone a little about my visions.

"Ceremonial baths."

"Baths?"

I nodded. "Did you ever read about the Baths of Caracalla in Rome?" I waited for just a moment, very pleased that another whole sentence had come out without interruption. "The baths were a public gathering place." I hesitated then because adults sometimes make faces when I tell them my ideas. "What if that's what many of the Grand Kivas in Chaco, Aztec, Chimney Rock, and other Anasazi sites were primarily created for? What if they were like wading ponds for parts or all each year, where residents could immerse themselves in the most valuable substance in the West both then and now? Water."

"What about the rectangular boxes on the Great Kiva floors?"

"From what I've read, archeologists already believe they have evidence that the small square rock containers were used as fireboxes. What if the larger rectangular masonry containers, usually on either side of the smaller box, contained rocks which had been heated in the firebox and through their stone walls could heat all the surrounding water—at least in the spring and fall, when the run-off from the Chaco wash and from off the mesas above was too cold for comfortable bathing?"

"So, you think they carried water in pots to fill them?"

"Maybe at first, because you can see by the three loopholes on the taller pots that ropes were used to carry them, probably dangling from each end of a shoulder pole. But some of the Great Kivas might have been spring-fed or filled from mesa run-off collected in the troughs already identified by archeologists behind places like Pueblo Bonito. If you looked at the photo on page 29 of *Chaco, A Cultural Legacy*, what would you see?"

Chichilticalli just shook his head as if he couldn't guess. I took the book from my backpack, opened it to that page, and handed it to him.

"What you see growing on the now much deeper dirt floor of a Great Kiva are green plants. Yet very little else is still that green in the canyons except along the washes. Why? What if the plants in the kivas mean rainwater collects if the floor under the dirt is mortared solid, or maybe that pipes feed water from the troughs below the mesas to the kivas, or that spring water sometimes still seeps up through the kiva floor?"

"Interesting," he said as if lost in thought.

"The floor of the re-created Great Kiva at Aztec is low enough to make it possibly spring-fed, at least for part of the year. And if you look at the central smaller cylindrical kiva nearby it appears to have benches at two different levels. What if that was to accommodate sitting at different spring water levels during high and low run-off seasons."

Chichilticalli smiled and slowly nodded his head in agreement. Then he looked away and I could tell my speculations were simply increasing his curiosity about others. "Another thing that has always puzzled archeologists is the purpose of the little alcoves in the wall surrounding the Great Kivas," he said, turning back to see my reaction. "Any ideas?"

"Did you ever go to a rec center where before swimming you put your clothes in a basket or locker? What if that's what the alcoves were for: putting clothing and jewelry before bathing. As you have probably read, a very long turquoise necklace was found in one alcove at Pueblo Bonito."

And then it was time to stop. I can't say why, but I wasn't sure I could maintain my confidence. Probably because Chichilticalli looked like he was thinking over each of the things I said. I had already revealed enough of my speculations. Besides, my theories on hydraulics and the walkway from underground on the north end of Casa Rinconada were still formulating. They were coming to me sometimes as a mixture of visions and deductions from what I've observed as well as read in books and on internet sites. And what I had revealed so far to Chichilticalli were just some distillations of impressions and visions I felt more confident about. They could be wrong. But at least he listened with a serious look on his face and didn't dismiss everything because I'm just a kid.

"Kahlo, thank you for sharing your impressions with me. I have a feeling much of what you've learned from observations or seen in your visions may well be correct. But the important thing is to keep investigating. You don't have to be 75 years old to make archeological discoveries. You just need a healthy curiosity and a keen eye. You have both.

"I sense you have revealed as much as you can share right now, and that's O.K. I understand. It's always risky to venture explanations of phenomena well-educated people have spent centuries trying to unravel. I'm honored that you've chosen me to reveal your special observations. They really are quite remarkable."

Of course, my telling all this to Chichilticalli was no accident, no more so than much of the designs and locations of the Anasazi constructions in Chaco Canyon and elsewhere are. I was pretty sure about why I felt so comfortable with him, but I wanted him to answer the one question that might reveal whether a vision I had was correct.

"What happened to your daughter?"

"Several of my wife's family and friends offered to take Argentacruz in and raise her. With my having to work, it would have been difficult for me to spend enough time with her. Yet I did what I now look back upon as a selfish thing, even though at the time I felt I had my reasons. Because I had received part of my education in the white man's world, I thought it would be good if my daughter could receive some of the same opportunities. It went against all my Zuni upbringing, but I decided to place her with a Santa Fe adoption agency. I've deeply regretted it many times, but because I was alone, unhappy, and jobless, that was my decision at the time."

"And do you know what happened to her?"

"Only that she was adopted by a family back East. I only wish I could see her again?"

"I think you will."

"Why is that, Kahlo?"

"I think I know what happened to her."

"Do you think one of your visions has told you of her whereabouts?"

"It has. And you will s-s-see her again."

For the first time Chichilticalli looked at me with the saddest eyes I have seen, as if I had suggested the impossible. But I hadn't.

"I-I-I," I began before mental feedback prevented me from saying more. Then the vision of *El Malpais* returned of Magdalena on the car seat and then dying in a hospital, and I told myself I had to try again. I closed my eyes and hoped I could say that one word. But I couldn't get beyond the 'D.'

# Quivira's Quest

(QUIVIRA)
When I left old Ketl's teepee, my attitude was somewhat like a cat burglar who has just received a list of Parisian mansions and the itemized jewelry at each location. I was quite keen to get out there with my newly purchased kit and dig up the largest treasure cache ever found in the Southwest. That's the kind of mindless daydreaming journalists come up with when let loose from the normal parameters of sports writing, when a lot of what you'd like to say gets toned down. You'd like to say stuff like certain quarterbacks with leg braces should check into retirement living homes, or that so-and-so running back hasn't just lost a step, he's lost the use of both legs.

But you can't, you don't, and you won't. Because you can always throw a few stones, but they better be accurate and within the realm of possibility. Otherwise, you're gone. And another young punk who has just graduated from Princeton or Stanford or somewhere else where one learns an artful turn of phrase is right behind you waiting for his opportunity to eclipse your incisively clever screed. And I did say 'his' opportunity, because while plenty of female writers are good and some even write or speak knowledgeably about football, it is a man's game. A game where you fight until you have nothing left in you.

And that's sort of what I felt about treasure hunting. If I was going to do it, I was going to bust my ass searching, and any rules that may get in the way be damned. You just had to be careful, that's all. Watch out not to be on private land, and then to avoid the crafty Homeland Security Agency wayfarers, Bureau of Land Management marauders, Navajo Nation Police sleuths, New Mexican State Police surveyors, County Sheriff observers, National Park Service rangers, FBI delvers, CIA trackers, and a hundred other legal beagles, to make sure they don't catch you off limits doing something untoward. No risk, no gain. You had to get out there, sneak around carefully, and then later cover your tracks and diggings should you find anything.

The thing about treasure of any kind is that no one tells the complete truth. And why should they? I mean, after all, if you disclosed the amazing chest of gold coins or pegmatite of emeralds you've discovered and where you've found it, you'd have to be as brilliant as the lifeboat seating capacity on the Titanic. So, people make stuff up. The way rock hunter Ristraverdé tells it, they say they found it 100 miles this side of Mt. Taylor near a creek, or five miles up an arroyo in the Chuska Mountains, or in a cave just off a remote location somewhere in Kutz Canyon. No one is going to say exactly *what* they've found, nor exactly *where* they found it. Otherwise, there'd be a million other grubstakers heading off with floored SUVs to see if they could carve out their own portion of those shiny little objects worth so much moolah. Finders' keepers. If you're smart and keep your mouth shut until they're fenced or legally sold to some collector, museum, or government department.

Old man Ketl's quest intrigued me, though. There was something fishy about it. But at the same time, I think he kind of took to my candor, so I had to believe his map was not completely bogus. And like most other quests in life, it is the search that fuels the imagination, anyway, not the ultimate discovery.

I was no more ill-equipped than half the other scraggly characters who over the centuries had wandered round the mountains and deserts looking for the Arc of the Covenant, lost bullion, moss-covered nuggets, and other items that infect the in-most-cases deluded treasure seeker. And what I had learned so far in the Southwest was that the sunny high-elevation days made the ever-changing dramatic surroundings far more inviting than any of the more lush and green forests or mountains I had seen back East.

What you contrastingly notice about a great deal of northwest New Mexico is that quite a few commercial concerns as well as the Indian tribes themselves have figured out a way to remove both oil and the world's largest natural gas deposits from such pristine surroundings. You do see the odd oil-drilling rig slowly revolving like a praying mantis dipping for food, or those painted but partially rusted cylindrical oil storage containers here and there seemingly in the middle of nowhere. How much revenue the Jicarilla Apaches and others ever saw or still see after the skimming of their profits from government trusts remains accurately to be determined.

When I turned off highway 550 to the Angel Peak lookout point, I faced nothing more than a dirt road and a long open-topped truck with its bed in the air as if someone had forgotten it out on a prickly pear patch of land. Not a lot of trees, considering the meager level of annual precipitation making it tough on even yucca plants.

The parking lot at the overlook fortunately was empty, and without even beaching the blue monster I could see the giant colorfully striated valley gouged out by La Plata and San Juan Rivers' confluence below.

I climbed out and had a peer out over the canyon. From the angle I had, Twin Angels in the distance somewhat resembled a line of four molars with the second one from the left missing. The gigantic water-excavated terrain looked majestic enough like you'd expect the Grand Canyon to appear, but also revealed some type of mining or similar activities invading the river valley floor in the distance to the northwest. It's funny, but with all that beauty spread out before me, after about five minutes I couldn't wait to get back in my car and examine the map. Then again, I've always craved watching people far more than taking in any spectacular surroundings.

The first point referred to in the upper left quadrant of the tattered and wrinkled document in hand was Kutz Canyon below Twin Angels. Trying to read something with Navajo, Spanish, and English notations next to partially faded drawings of mountains, valleys and other geographic novelties is not easy, even with the reading glasses I was forced to use sometime after the age of 40. But one thing was clear: a dotted line from the westernmost Twin Peak to a stunted juniper tree near the center of the ledge adjacent to what is now a parking lot had a 90° arc drawn between it and another dotted line proceeding in a southeasterly direction. Along that line was simply '200m' and an 'X' at the end.

I headed south across the lot, trying to maintain the integrity of a 90° angle, and began to wander through some sagebrush growing in sandy soil. I kept looking back to try and estimate when I had walked 200 meters—a distance I should well be able to estimate, having been on 100-yard-long football fields so many times.

When I paced off what I thought to be the distance, nothing immediately jumped out at me except more sagebrush and the occasional suffering cactus. Then I saw a small weather-beaten wooden cross with some long-ago wilted flowers tossed beneath it as if someone had buried a pet there. Looking further in the area revealed nothing else unusual, so I concluded that the cross must be the sign upon the map. It didn't look old enough, but then maybe it had replaced some original marker to mislead amateur seekers such as myself.

Now just to put myself in the right frame of mind a day earlier, I had bought a whole bunch of rock hounding equipment in Farmington. I had a canvas web belt tricked out with a mining hammer having a point at one end, a magnifying glass, a magnet, tweezers, a small rake, and a trowel. I had also purchased a spade should I really need to get my back into some digging.

Since the faded white cross marker was small, I chose the trowel for the task at hand. I took a long look around in every direction to make sure none of those uniformed maintenance and surveillance sorts or tourists were in the area, then quickly pulled out the cross and began to dig. Whoever had created this misleading scenario, if my observation was correct, could well have something of value concealed below, because most people assume coming upon a white cross and flowers simply means a burial site of a former loved one. Not this former denizen of Manhattan, however. Raising the dead means no more to me than raising a pint in the Hungry Toad pub.

Within no more than a couple of minutes under the sun heating up to its solar self for nearly April in Northwest New Mexico, I found something. It didn't have a rolling lock where the discoverer must align all the letters to spell 'Apple' or anything cryptic, but it was a metal cylinder of some sort resembling an extended Budweiser can, or maybe a can for three tennis balls. Any paint it might have once had was gone just like the Anasazi.

A metal cap was designed to come off quite easily, so I took one more quick 360-degree survey above the scattered sagebrush and odd juniper bush, then opened the magic container. Another scroll like my original was inside, but rather than read it, I threw it on the ground, and after replacing the container back in the small pit, concentrated on recreating the burial scene. It didn't take long, and after smoothing it out and putting the cross and flower remnants back, I was up and occasionally roughly raking here and there to cover my footprints back to the parking lot.

I felt smug as I got back to the old cobalt beast without spying another single soul. This was ideal, I told myself. The whole process could have been so much more difficult had any family from Kansas been tramping about with a digital camera, or Bureau of Land Management type emptying the trash or checking for any spray-paint marking by teenagers.

While sitting in the car I had my first peer at the creased scroll. Someone had painted a large rock outcropping with a small pond barely visible in the center below several monoliths or a high wall of rock. Under the painting were the words, *CIBOLA SALTA.*

My mind was racing as I mindlessly gazed out at the Twin Angel Peaks and the tops of the strata of Kutz Canyon. Were the words Spanish, or salt misspelled? There were a million Cibolas on the map of New Mexico. A County, a town, a National Forest, not to mention the famous Seven Cities. A salty city? What could that possibly mean? But then I told myself to apply all that journalistic acumen. Where would I find rocks such as those in the painting? And perhaps a near one of the geographic Cibolas?

Nothing came to mind. The trouble with hurling oneself into the middle of a treasure hunt with just a little web site exploration and the reading of a smattering of historical or journalistic tracts is that you are extremely ill-informed regarding all the natural as well as unnatural phenomena in New Mexico. I was no Joe Leaphorn, even though at least retired for the moment. But Navajo Leaphorn, even if fictional, had grown up in the area and spent years on the Navajo Tribal Police force. I had spent days in motel rooms or at libraries scoping out just enough to give myself delusions that I could still end up discovering something of untold value. Just what it would be, however, remained a mystery.

The only thing that came to mind regarding the rock formation on the map was Shiprock, a giant natural monolithic formation most people have seen in photographs that comes up out of the desert northwest from where I was located. I needed to talk to a local or two, anyway, and so I decided to drive up to the town of

Shiprock and see if I could get any closer to decoding the meaning of the scroll—without revealing much to anyone about my purpose.

When I got to the town of Shiprock, I realized why Native Americans need casino income and government royalties on mineral extraction from their lands. The place looked like one of the world's largest trailer parks with a few fast food and gasoline emporia on the main drag. It had the feel of low-level subsistence about it, the kind where the natives no longer can shoot buffalo and grow maize and beans to survive, and now need to come up with the money for Ford truck payments rather than bartering or stealing horses and cattle. Everyone on the street and in front of shops looked like real Navajos, and here was this big gringo driving into town in a garish 50s tank.

But, hey, I was on a mission. And just as whites shouldn't stereotype those of darker complexions, the reverse might be said, as well. You had to take people one at a time. I had done it for years in covering sport, and what you realize is that saints and scoundrels alike come in dark as well as fair skins. I told myself I had to keep an open mind, even if I did look like I had just blown in, with attitude, from L.A.

"Are you able to drive right up to the actual Shiprock?" I asked an Indian woman in a convenience store after buying a bottle of water.

She looked at me like she had heard it all before, but from worse white folks who just wanted information without buying anything. Still, she remained polite. "You can get almost as close as you like. Some say Shiprock looks the same from a distance as it does up close. I suppose it depends on how many times you've seen it."

I had already scoped out an atlas map to see how to get there, but I didn't see highway 666 going through town. "Is highway 491 the old highway 666?"

She nodded, and I waited for her to add something about the different number. She didn't.

"Why'd they change the number?"

"Some think the number 666 is unlucky."

"How come?"

She pulled a piece of tape off the cash register. "Maybe drunken-driving deaths on the road," she then added without looking up.

Well, stranger things had happened in my world, so I left it at that. Who's to say that Navajo superstition is any different than the number 13 in the white world? Or the number 7? If the pale-faced city dwellers can leave out floor 13 in a lot of buildings, it made sense that the Navajos should be able to change an unlucky highway number to one with which they feel more comfortable.

There was the feeling of being a gringo space invader, though, so I took off down 491 to see about scoping out the Shiprock cathedral rocks shooting up into the western sky.

I never even got close enough to check for anything to do with anything called Cibola. Even from a distance, the rock formations were too different from the painting on the scroll. I figured I would just continue down highway 491. At least the drive south was scenic, some of the passing mesas resembling miniature Monument Valley outcroppings and small mesa tops upon which in a TV ad a new four-wheel drive sometimes sits. My altered plan was to get to Gallup and after grabbing a cheap motel to see what I could learn there.

Rather than anyone galloping through Gallup, most were ambling or cruising the old Route 66, the former great highway still harboring a huge number of those dilapidated motels, eateries and curio shops that once were the highlight of passing through on the famous concrete ribbon. Now they appear little more than slightly off-kilter attractions from the much faster Interstate 40. Gallup, of course, is even mentioned in the famous song.

I got a motel for something like $26. It was a price lost in time, and I suppose I should have been suspicious. It was clean, but only later did I realize the nocturnal delights of Burlington Santa Fe and other mile-long freight trains tooting and rumbling by right behind the entire row of old motels about once an hour all night long.

Not far down Route 66 was a place called El Rancho, one of those ancient rustic lodges you associate with the bygone Wild West halcyon era of cowboys, Indians, and stagecoaches. Inside all the pine beams were nearly black from the many tar, stain, and varnish coats applied over more than half a century. Big stuffed chairs for perusing the morning newspaper or sitting by the huge hearth, as well as colorful Navajo rugs, soft tungsten-lit lamps, and a painting-lined, burnt pine-railed balcony above all helped create the ornate lobby's atmosphere of warmth from a different era.

A quick perusal of a desk handout conveyed a whole 'A' list of recognizable stars like Alan Ladd, Paulette Goddard and Kirk Douglas having stayed in this palace built by D.W. Griffith's brother back in the late 30s. They had all worked on the many Westerns like New Mexico, Fort Massacre, The Bad Man, and Desert Song, filmed in the area.

The bar at the other end of a side hall was dark, and only a few couples hovered quietly in booths. I planned on devouring some of their restaurant's famous barbecue, but first I figured I'd have a margarita to calm myself from treasure hunting sensory overload. There were only about three or four stools along the bar at one end, while an elevated stage to one side faced away from the den of spirits to a non-descript banquet room with tables. On that stage a guy was tuning a guitar while waitresses were putting out party favors and place settings. I thought it had to be for some sort of Gallup wedding reception.

I focused on sipping the customized marg I had talked the

bartender into making, feeling myself again musing over what the rock painting could be. Trying to figure a way to find out where the formation was, without showing anyone the actual scroll.

An elderly chap attired in a pearl-buttoned shirt, a white Stetson, and jeans cinched by one of those large hand-tooled silver buckles, sat down on a stool at the other end and ordered a quick cocktail. He seemed preoccupied, and occasionally glanced over at the stage. The old man looked the part of an Indian from the area, and with a weathered face fit the stereotype of minding his own business.

"He's the one who..." the middle-aged woman tending bar was told by the waitress before I could hear the rest of what was said.

"Let me shake your hand," she said to the late arrival in front of her.

Just like Jim Chee might do in a Tony Hillerman novel, I waited for him to turn my way or to say anything. He didn't. The old gent just kept his eyes straight ahead, as if lost in thought and not wishing to be disturbed.

"Your daughter getting married?" I suddenly blurted, my journalistic past rearing its persistently inquisitive head. For a moment I didn't think he was going to respond. But he took a long look at his drink.

"No," he responded impassively. "It's a fund raiser."

"A fund raiser?" I nonsensically repeated to keep things going.

Another pause by the old Indian. "She's running for president of the Navajo Nation."

In the local newspaper I had seen his daughter's name and asked him if he was familiar with the British television series with the same title as his daughter's and his surname. He answered that he wasn't. But that was all that was said. Nothing more. And I decided to mimic his elliptical manner.

Soon the old Navajo finished his drink and walked over to check out the booming thunderstorm and rain pouring down outside. It didn't necessarily augur well for his daughter's fundraiser. But maybe in times of drought, a downpour was a good omen.

The old man disappeared, and I resumed my demented mental process of how deviously to extract the information I needed. When I ordered a second margarita, an opportunity presented itself.

"A friend showed me a photo of some famous rock formation in New Mexico, and it had a small pond underneath dead center. I told him I wanted to visit the location but had forgotten the name. Does that description mean anything to you?"

She was wiping a tumbler dry with a white towel, and never interrupted part of every bartender's work to contemplate my question. The woman walked to the other end of the bar to put the glass on the back shelf, then returned and placed her hands on the bar right in front of me.

"You know," she said, "There are a lot of famous rock outcroppings in these parts, but the only place I can think of that might match that description is El Morro."

"El Morro?"

"Yah, it's been designated a National Monument and means 'Inscription Rock.' Back beginning in the 1600s when they stopped for water from the pond, many Spanish explorers and then later others engraved their names on the rock facings."

"Is it far from here?"

"Probably a little more than an hour from here if you head down toward Zuni and then over through Ramah."

When I cruised down into the Zuni Pueblo, I could tell I was getting anxious. The point-of-interest marker mentioned that this was where the reputed Seven Cities of Cibola once stood. But you could have fooled me. Yah, it had some prominent red rocks and mesas in a canyon area much like Chaco, but it sure seemed to have morphed into the adobe version of Shiprock. It was hard to envision as a once-great civilization. But on a Sunday, the streets were deserted and even the jewelry trading posts and visitor center for seniors seemed to be locked up as if the Zuni had fled their living accommodations just like the Anasazi had. I'm sure folks were just sleeping in, of course, since there was a lot of relatively new iron in many of the driveways. But my preoccupation with the search had me leaving as fast as I had arrived.

On the way across I was amazed at how many times the surroundings change from arid and colorful to lush and green, like in the town of Ramah. And it all obviously was connected to the availability of water. How people still managed to grow things in such sandy, rocky, soil probably containing as many nutrients as Death Valley remained unsolved. But I didn't want to stop, as the quest was still like a siren tied to the mast of the good ship Discovery Pontiac. Except the search was more like in *Cadillac Desert*. When I had passed through the Visitor Center of El Morro National Monument and looked up from a paved path, the rock escarpment clearly resembled the painting on the scroll. But there was no mention of any Cibola.

I decided to do the big loop that circles the front of the rock and traverses the ridge from which the Anasazi once could look down from their pueblo. I would check out all the inscriptions when I completed the loop.

After a switchback ascent from the back of the north side, the passing above a box canyon's walls soon became a little hairy. Someone had used a concrete cutter to make a couple of indentations outlining a makeshift trail where adventuresome types could bound from white rock to rock with a 200-foot drop below. And there were only a couple of iron pipe railings where the possibilities for falling were the most precipitous. It was the sort of journey you wouldn't want to attempt after a few beers. But I made it, stopping briefly here and there to see if there was anything signaling something to do with any Cibola location.

After viewing the former cities of Chaco Canyon, the Anasazi ruins on top of El Morro ridge seemed small potatoes, even if a lot of the former pueblo rooms had not been excavated. While I was crossing the rock ridge, however, a ranger had walked by in the other direction, which immediately made me suspicious that I had been profiled as one who might desecrate the monument by carving my initials or gouging *Kilroy Was Here*. He was polite enough in saying hello, but certainly those single males who pay their admission must become suspects time has shown might try to leave their marks. It's the sort of thing I would have done in my 20s, probably, just to say I had gotten away with it. It's funny how in journalism, you find many of us who would make few compromises on reporting our trade, yet make others when it comes to personal behavior. However, carving my initials in a giant rock so that I could be immortalized is not my thing. Treasure hunting for the moment, is.

When I hiked down through the rock wall to a trail among a scrub oak and piñon forest, I turned left for the smaller loop guiding oglers below the inscriptions. Following the beaten-up plastic guide I received as a reference, I quickly came upon the moss-filled pond into which water was dripping from above. It didn't look clean enough to drink, but I guess in 1600-something when you've ridden horses for a whole day, it's the sort of compromise you had to risk after straining it through a handkerchief.

Some of the inscriptions had enough filigree to look as if a Tiffany's jeweler had helped some Spaniard make his mark. You'd think the time involved alone would have precluded such explorers from leaving their autographs in the seventeenth century. But vanity lives in every era.

I had ploughed through maybe about half of the inscription

points of interest protected behind a log fence to keep contemporary miscreants from abusing existing signatures or surreptitiously adding their own, when I came to a halt. A recent lightning strike had closed part of the path, and examiners were instructed to go all the way around the other way to conclude their scrutinies of how it was OK in 1628 or so to leave your mark, but not so in the third millennium.

Yah, I made the effort to amble all the way around to just below the point where I had left off, hoping to find the words *Cibola salta* inscribed somewhere, or some other clue of what in the hell the scroll was depicting. I mean on both sides of the rock you had every Tom, Dick, and Harry, having used even stepladders, or having stood on a friend's shoulders, having gashed away at this once unmarred site. Now their names are protected, and you've got to believe a few drunken sorts in the middle of early third millennium winters will have a few pops in a bar in Grants and then decide to drive out to try their luck without getting nabbed.

But there was nothing. Nothing to do with Cibola. OK, so certain Spaniard's elaborate inscriptions had been very formal to acknowledge just in whose behalf they were acting while terrifying the local Indian tribes by riding through in armor plate or shooting the odd remote scout with an arquebus. But you didn't see Billy the Kid's name there, or Val Kilmer's who lives somewhere east of Santa Fe, or Julia Roberts' who is reputed to reside in Taos. I mean if some of the signatures weren't so arty and old, other more contemporary ones might be sandblasted away.

Anyway, after I read through a phone book of names high and low all the way around to the north side, I decided to pack it in. Before I did, I looked carefully round the pond and gazed out over the valley like an explorer might do to see if there were any sign of one or more of anything resembling the Seven Cities of Cibola or the Cibola River or Cibola something or other. Nada.

I also had a peer round the center, watched the video, looked at the memorabilia behind glass, and engaged in all the other impromptu investigations I could think of before completely giving up.

"Is there anything named Cibola around here?" I asked a studious looking ranger behind the counter.

"This is Cibola County, and that's the Cibola National Forest in the distance across the road to the north. Then south of here quite a ways is more Cibola National Forest. No real Cibolas, though, unless you consider some of the tourists."

I smiled a thanks, even though at my current weight I was approaching a facsimile of the same tourists he was talking about. He sounded as if Cibolas were something besides a name.

After they lent me a railroad spike to try my luck unsuccessfully to insert my own moniker on a sample rock outside or gouge something for folks to remember me by, and I saw no clues there either, I headed for my car.

When I got in, I went over everything I had done and considered whether there was some sandstone unturned, the same sort of mental procedure I sometimes went through after talking one on one with an NFL running back. Did I forget anything?

Nah. I went over every place named Cibola on the map and everything I had done since the old Navajo's teepee, and nothing overlooked so far came to mind. It was time to start the car and move on.

I was just going over the original scroll from Twin Peaks again, when I noticed an animated family, speaking in Spanish, walking by the back of the car. My mind didn't tick over until they had arrived at their own truck. But then it came to me. Translation.

"Excuse me, but do you speak Spanish?" I asked, hoping they also spoke English.

"*Sí, Señor.*" He smiled as his kids and wife gazed up at the imposing stranger. "I was wondering if you could tell me what the words 'Cibola Salto' mean.

He screwed his face up in thought for a moment, then crossed his arms over a Denver Broncos T-shirt. "Mm, Cibola is the word for a female buffalo," he replied before turning to his wife. "*Como se lo dice en Inglés, salto?*" he asked his wife.

"Leap or jump," an attractive woman in jeans and camisole answered.

"Yah, 'buffalo jump,' or 'buffalo leap,'" he smiled, pleased they had been able to help.

"*Muchas graçias,*" I said with a grin. "Thanks very much."

Back in my car, I thought it over. Where in the hell was I going to find a leaping buffalo. The Twin Peaks scroll had a painting ostensibly of El Morro rock formation, the words *CIBOLA SALTO*, and just below it, the very small letters OFP I had missed before because the letters had been faded enough that only the bright sunlight now streaming through my car window onto the paper enabled it to become visible. But where would I go next? I decided another look at the original scroll, which also had a rising sun in the second quadrant and what looked like a volcano and only the word 'caldera' in the third quadrant left to right, top before bottom. The fourth had a drawing of what appeared a lava bed, a cave below it, and a nearby pine tree with partially orange bark and an 'X' on it.

So, what do I do next, I asked myself? Head off to a sunrise? Find a volcano and jump in it? Or is there simply something up in the tree? I was stymied, and for a journalist, again told myself to put on my thinking cap, no matter how many memory cells I might have lost through alcohol overindulgence.

Why had the map's illustrator gone to so much trouble over El Morro, the pond, the inscriptions, and the words *CIBOLA SALTO*? Maybe I had missed something amidst the inscriptions? But what?

And how would I know if I found it? And what did the letters OFP mean?

OK, so when in doubt a good journalist always rereads his notes and tract or retraces his steps to ensure not having missed something. Feeling a bit dehydrated, tired, and cranky, I climbed out of my car, determined to at least walk back to the rock face once again.

But when I got there, I quickly became more dispirited. I couldn't bring myself to go over the entire War and Peace of inscriptions again.

Well, yes, I could. So I did.

What you realize is how desperate people are to make a name for themselves, or more accurately, to carve their way into posterity. A second scrutiny revealed nothing to me. Maybe I was dense and looking right at something that was a clue. Then again, maybe this whole quest was an exercise in futility.

My mind was exploding in a million frustrated directions as I walked the winding path back to the Visitor Center. But something made me stop. Call it a Navajo Notion, or a New Mexican Mental Flash Flood, but suddenly I came to a stop and looked back at El Morro. My eyes slowly began from the bottom and surveyed upwards upon the escarpment.

And there it was.

A giant leaping buffalo on a tall monolith. The mark on the huge rock resembling the painting had probably arisen due to some iron in the mineral accreted in just that one spot. But the mineral stain did look like a bucking buffalo, much like a bucking bronco.

I whipped out the old scroll painting again and felt a warm sensation as I gazed back and forth from the rock face and the painting on the paper in my hands. Below the words *CIBOLA SALTO* was an arrow pointing down and the letters OFP. What the hell could that be? Not 'One for All,'—close but no cigar. 'Over Fallen Pine?' perhaps?

Soon I had wandered back to standing just below the tall monolith, close enough that I could no longer see the buffalo high above. I was staring at inscriptions and a wooden fence. Then I really began to suffer. It was getting warm in the sun, I was losing more non-alcoholic fluids, I was tired from the two-mile hike round the mesa-top loop and back, and my attitude was disintegrating into apathy and the thirst for an air-conditioned motel room.

But I told myself to hang on. The Spanish explorers did. The Indians still do. That it was still a long way to Grants and then I might just have to come back again.

Inscriptions and a fence.

The inscriptions were mainly just names and dates. The fence was just poles and rough-sawed crossbeams to keep pocketknife-wielding *touristas* from attempting their own messages for immortality.

Wait a minute. Fence and Pole: FP. Then OFP finally came to me. 'ON FENCE POLE.' I walked a step forward to the pole and carefully began to go over it. There was nothing carved on the front.

But as I leaned over a cross bar, the reverse side made the hair on my arms and the back of my neck stand up. Carved about one foot up from the bottom of the back of the fencepost was '*PonderIceX2LSteeplePlus50m.*'

I pulled the original scroll out of my canvas shoulder bag and went over it again. The fourth quadrant appeared to have lava, a cave, and a tall pine tree with an 'X.' That had to be the next step. The sunrise in quadrant two probably meant to head east. But what did the Caldera mean? Were there any volcanos in the area? Maybe I could weasel some more information out of one of those rangers, I told myself.

"There isn't any kind of volcano near a cave around here?" I asked the same ranger behind the Visitor Center counter.

He pursed his lips and reached below the counter to pull out a pamphlet.

"That's got to be the Ice Cave and Caldera about 15 miles east of here. They're both on private land and there is a fee to get in. But if you're looking for a cave and a caldera together, the Ice Cave has got to be the place."

# Kahlo Sees at Rinconada

(KATARINA)

When you are into your eighth decade, sometimes if feels odd to be acting as guardian for someone one-eighth your age and with 10 times your energy. Yet as any grandmother knows, there is a certain delight in being needed by someone so young and exuberant. Maybe it's like reliving one's childhood.

Anyway, Kahlo at various points seemed suddenly to have enough of surfing the internet for further explorations of arcane knowledge, and to wish to return to more natural surroundings. She wanted to go back to Chaco Canyon.

"It's a long drive, Kahlo. And I'm not certain Aurore will approve. In another two weeks the Santa Fe school system will be starting up again after Spring break, and you've already been away from school for a month."

Kahlo gave me one of those looks. The kind that an aging pianist/grandmother is becoming boring and officious. Not exactly a pout, mind you, but more like the conveyance from an angelic face that you are bringing an early monsoon to a perfectly good day for archeological investigations. I knew eventually I would cave, and I wouldn't really need to discuss the matter with my daughter. She was still asleep, I had had my coffee, and departing to Chaco Canyon would mean nothing more than quickly preparing some luncheon items before leaving a cryptic note that Kahlo and I had gone off on one of her daily quests.

"O.K., Kahlo. But remember my agreeing to this against my better judgment the next time I want you to accompany me to a classical music concert at St. John's College or on a walk too slow for your inevitably impetuous pace."

I bore up well on the long, dusty drive into Chaco, tempered somewhat by an overcast day. When we got to the Visitor Center, we were informed that a lecture would be starting in 10 minutes at the Casa Rinconada. With just that seemingly routine announcement, Kahlo's eyes lit up much like Christmas tree bulbs, a reaction I attributed to nothing more than the serendipitous fortunes of repeated trips to one locale. Still, my granddaughter put a book she had planned to purchase back on the shelf and encouraged the aging one to move a little quicker, else we miss the beginning of another talk on the arcane civilization to which Kahlo has taken as if it were her own.

When we drove round the loop to the ruins on the south side of the canyon, a growing group of 10 or so was listening to a Smokey Bear ranger just beside the parking lot. Kahlo leapt from the car before I even had a chance to turn off the engine. It was as if a prophet were speaking, and not a morsel of his gospel could be missed.

Ranger Plentyhorn, as his nametag announced, was going through all the introductory remarks Kahlo hates. The ones for the uninitiated from Iowa or South Carolina, who haven't a clue of what they are about to learn. My granddaughter always wants to get right to the heart of the matter, and I could tell by her pacing behind the taller adults that she was impatient to proceed both with more profound exposition as well as the walk up to the actual ruins.

"Some contemporary theorists feel that based on the alignment of elements of Casa Rinconada to the cardinal directions that the alcoves in the walls of the Grand Kiva may be attuned to the number of days in the moon's trajectory around the earth," the ranger explained to a several people edging toward or with their hands and elbows leaning upon on the upper ledge of a reconstructed Grand Kiva wall. "And by the way, we try not to touch anything while viewing, because of further deterioration through contact," he said while glancing over at two young kids leaning on their hands upon the stone to peer down into the oval.

As the ranger continued his elaborate explanation, much of which slipped through my mind like the statistics one inevitably hears on any such historical lecture tour, it was apparent that he had spent a great deal of his life concerned with these ancient cities. Living in the National Park Service housing near the Visitor Center certainly has its limitations. No fast-food emporia, no convenience stores, and only one soft drinks and water dispensing machine in the Visitors Center discouraged all but the intrepid from staying more than several hours or camping at this remote location in the high desert. What you bring is what you get. Yet some made the effort more because they had to tell their friends and neighbors they had completed the pilgrimage. Made the effort to see just what the documentaries and books conveyed regarding this mythical locale.

Kahlo, on the other hand, with her unique powers of observation and adventuresome spirit with internet research, was miles ahead of most of those typically uninformed listeners incapable of digesting all the elements of such a technical talk. It's a good bet she could match a significant percentage of the speculations ranger Plentyhorn and other lifelong students of the Anasazi bandied about.

Through much of his remarks my granddaughter paced, peered, or looked up at the heavens. It was always a serious challenge to try and second-guess what that little whirling wonder's mind was cogitating upon. She fiddled with her braids as the ranger moved the disparate pack to the northern underground passageway entrance to the kiva, stared at the big oval below as if it were the Lost

Continent of Atlantis, then listened intently as the lecture turned to the alcoves again.

"I don't know what they think," he answered a question regarding what contemporary Pueblos and Navajos thought of an Anglo dispensing information regarding one of their sacred sites. I noticed two women probably from one of the Indian tribes in the area walk away and leave shortly thereafter. It was as if they had heard enough from the Great White Father concentrating more on archeological and astronomical detail than on the deep spiritual significance they had hoped would be explored further.

None too soon for me the lecture tour was over. The crowd began to break up and amble back down to the parking lot. Except Kahlo. The little investigator was hovering over the open stone room leading down to the underground entrance to the Grand Kiva. Something was puzzling her. At least her leaning upon two fists as she surveyed the reconstruction below made it appear she was unsure of some notion or other. I knew better than to try to entice an early departure. My granddaughter was far from through with the area south of Chaco Wash.

"If they do pave the road in, I'm gone," I overheard Ranger Plentyhorn telling a female scientist from NASA scheduled to give a kid's lecture that evening on the relation of Chaco archeology to the stars. Apparently, paradise for anyone is always under attack, what with the internet, jet travel, SUVs, and the relentless migration west of folks like us from the more traditional urbanity of the East. Ranger Plentyhorn had devoted much of his life to scholarship, no matter the color of his skin. The presence of white people in an ancient Indian site of special meaning is an ethical consideration varying extremely, yet perhaps partially deriving from those same skin colors or lack of same. Just who lives in any area varies quite a bit from century to century. Yet I'd just as soon leave key descriptions to the relatives of those having built the cities a millennium or so earlier. I don't think I'd want a Navajo from Arizona lecturing in Times Square on the history of Manhattan and why New Yorkers have chosen to construct tall buildings of steel and concrete.

As I was watching the ranger and a last-few worshippers walking back down to the parking lot, I turned to see Kahlo skipping off down a trail paralleling the mesa and road below. The little dervish knew I could choose either to follow or to wait in the car where my reliable secret flask awaited. I looked at my watch and it wasn't yet high noon in the desert. I would be good. I would take a walk instead of a drink.

In the distance down the trail, just beyond a big boulder on the right, Kahlo was standing, arms akimbo. It was obvious she was onto something provocative.

Several minutes later she bounded back to walk alongside me. "Th-th-there should be a ci-ci-city here," she said of having apparently scrutinized more crumbling areas of stone or a mound which might signify another of those lost civilizations archeologists are always digging up all over the Four Corners.

"Why is that, Kahlo?"

Her lips pursed, and I knew a conflict was going on between further cogitations and whether to interrupt her mental analysis for the aging one's always intrusive question. She toyed with a braid. She bit her lip. She rubbed her hip. Whatever it was, it was a good bet Kahlo had solved one of her quandaries.

"They need to ex-ex-excavate."

And that was it. She asked if she could walk up to Tsin Kletsin above on the south Mesa, but this time I turned her down for another potentially dangerous solo journey. I thought there were going to be tears. But I could see just standing in one place in Chaco Canyon had somehow made her day. Nothing was going to dampen my granddaughter's exhilaration from whatever her latest deductions had told her. Tsin Kletsin could wait.

Yet on the way back to the car, she did painfully stutter through a request to find someone at the Pueblo del Arroyo parking lot walking down to survey the pictographs and petroglyphs. So that she could make the surveying stroll with them. I agreed and told her I would watch documentaries or read in the Visitor Center and then return in two hours to pick her up. She wanted more time, but I warned that 120 minutes of walking and gazing would have to do it. I was not going to begin the long journey back to Santa Fe too late in the afternoon.

Undoubtedly Kahlo would endure the family of three she joined for her pictorial viewings. She's not good with strangers. But I had a quiet word with the two middle-aged sorts from Michigan regarding her taciturnity. I conveyed that it isn't rudeness, but rather a speech impediment. They assured me they would not question her unless she spoke first.

Meanwhile I contented myself with browsing through various books I pulled from the Visitor Center shelves, the sort of glossy coffee table tomes with as many photographs, drawings, and maps, as paragraphs of text. It isn't that I am not a voracious reader. It's more that at my age, even with reading glasses that magnify text into the size of newspaper headlines, to save my eyes I choose to read selective passages on subjects I find more absorbing than endless speculations on dead people's rock constructions. I'm also better at viewing videos more like travelogues than plowing through academic treatises. Fortunately, the three documentaries I watched on Chaco Canyon, *El Malpais*, and El Morro, each blended a plethora of facts with a broad array of cinematic wizardry. I had no choice, anyway, because you know how grandmothers worry when their charges are off on Annie Oakley-like adventures. I needed to fill the time to avoid preoccupation with my granddaughter's sanity and safety.

But she came back unscathed, and visibly excited. There's no telling what the ancient visual recreations on the mesa walls had conveyed to her. She was pensive, fidgety, and impatient to resolve certain mental conflicts only the introverted can spend hours upon. Her speech impediment served Kahlo well, since with the inability to speak without stumbling came the parallel universe of deep mental evaluations of everything with which her special investigative world came into contact.

Kahlo obviously did not wish to reveal anything to the aging one driving her back to Santa Fe. I know the drill and accept my fate. She is mysterious for a nine-year-old. But then I suppose I was too, particularly when seated at a grand piano far bigger than I was. I only wish it were possible to climb inside that mind often resembling a meteor in flames. My daughter and I could only hope that one day, Kahlo's time would come.

"There sh-sh-should be a c-city," was the only utterance she repeated, somewhere beyond Cuba.

# Quivira's Cross to Bear

(QUIVIRA)

Finding the leaping buffalo on El Morro had been a minor triumph. Not enough to get drunk over, especially since the quest wasn't over yet. But important enough in a good story later to be told to find enthusiasm surface I thought long ago had vanished in a football locker room or Manhattan mid-town bar. I felt a renewed energy and wondered whether it was the sort of peace with one's surroundings old Ketl had mentioned.

Still, there was more to be done before that afternoon beer or cocktail in Grants, and I hadn't done any homework on the Ice Cave. The very moniker seemed somehow apocryphal in 70° air, but then stranger phenomena existed on the planet, some of them like gravity right under one's nose. Ketl was right on that score. The old Navajo had chosen his natural surroundings over the acquisition of possessions, a watershed moment at some point I also made with the selection of a profession from which few acquire much more than a lifetime of good stories.

Before I turned off highway 53 it was already apparent that the huge lava beds of El Malpais National Monument had spread farther west than appear on a road map. Within areas of forest alongside cleared to complete the highway were wide swatches of the formerly molten material always reminiscent of a botched sod-and-turf application.

The road into the reputed cave was through a mixed forest of tall as well as stunted trees, conveying more a feel of a Chuska Mountains forest than an expanse of lava volcanoes and caves. In a small house I paid my fee and was given a map.

"We'd appreciate it if you'd leave your web belt of tools in your car," the young dude behind the counter said as if telling one to leave his backpack at the front of a convenience store. "There is no digging permitted on the property," he added while placing something back on a shelf behind him. "However, we do have the treasure hunt sluice out in front at which you can buy a pack of dirt with a guaranteed precious stone of some sort in it and then practice sluicing and panning to find it."

I nodded to agree with the instructions, although really the last thing I wanted to do was leave my tools behind when I might have to do some serious digging. Nor did I have any intention of playing the sluicing 'finders, keepers.' But getting caught still wearing the belt would be worse. He might have someone checking for tickets down the path to whom he could easily make a cell phone call. I compromised by leaving the belt in the metallic monster's trunk, and by stuffing a trowel blade in my back pocket.

Since the walk to the Caldera was longer, I thought I would make that effort first, before undertaking the ten-minute stroll to the cave. Yah, so the spin on the Caldera might be construed as a bit misleading. The guy behind the counter had said you could see down 800 feet. But the viewing point was on the southeast side where part of the cone had collapsed, so you were only halfway to the top. That meant the view was of 400 feet of crumbled rock above and the same distance tapering below, all dotted by the occasional stunted pine with the temerity to try and find a purchase on such a surface. It reminded me of examining an open-faced coal quarry.

Yet I could feel my pulse begin to quicken as I walked back down to the old house doubling as a curio shop and gatekeeper's residence. I could almost feel that Mogollon Cross. It was near. My journalist's curiosity told me that.

The trail began to thread through real lava beds broken by rock formations and tall pine trees. My mind was racing to the carving on the back of that El Morro fencepost. Another apparent conundrum that just a year ago in Manhattan I would have tried to comprehend with the creative aid of at least three Bombay martinis. How would I even begin to find the fence post demarcations? And what if I did find the bloody cross and several tourists were munching granola bars while passing by in plain view?

Fortunately, there weren't many takers in late March, one of the things I liked best about my trip so far. The density of the species that jeopardizes the environment most was at some points almost as rare as they might be in the outback of Alaska. If you came upon one person on a trail, or one car on a scenic road through an amazing combination of canyons and forests, such a New Mexican high-country encounter almost seemed intrusive to both parties. You had much of the huge space between Mexico and Colorado to yourself. Maybe not in July or August, but for most of the year urban families had to deal with schools and jobs and soccer leagues instead of simply rising to greet the sun rising over a mesa.

I'll have to admit to a raging skepticism on whether there could be any legitimate ice in a cave with the temperature above ground having climbed to around 70°F. I mean there are ice skating rinks maintained through coiled refrigeration below. Maybe someone had figured out a way to charge $9 a head to view a cave rink without a Zamboni.

While descending several levels of wooden stairs leading down to the mouth of the cave perhaps 60 feet wide, I could feel the temperature begin to drop. It was an eerie feeling. That sort of cold and clammy shiver you get if you have ever entered a walk-in freezer with a lot of carved up livestock in it. With each step the air palpably got more and more like winter until below a platform there it was: a poorly illuminated area of slightly discolored ice, maybe 50 feet across. Yet above it on a back wall of rock was a wave of frozen white drippings you sometimes see in Midwestern winters when a gutter consistently overflows because of sagging.

My whole attitude changed. It was as if some strange Freon-like gas behind the walls was expanding or contracting enough to cool down this chamber to its preternatural state. I took an electronic photo or two and was done. I couldn't see anything remarkable enough to explain either the temperature or how the pond remained frozen solid. But at 32° Fahrenheit or so, not only did the phenomenon below look like naturally formed ice, but the surrounding cold vapors made it all seem realistic rather than contrived. The Ice Cave was as mysterious as the disappearance of the Anasazi.

Yet during the entire time my mind began to drift back to the cryptic message upon the fencepost and how I would possibly determine what to look for next above this peculiar anomaly of nature. Two young chattering kids joined me to break the spell, and I found myself climbing back up the stairs not knowing what my next move was to be.

Peering down into the open lava pit above the entrance to the cave revealed nothing substantive in terms of my quest. Nor did a perusal of the short path leading up to the volcanic beds and forest above.

Approaching a pine tree, I was amazed at the mixture of normal brownish bark and the orange color interspersed throughout.

Wait a minute.

'*PonderIceX2LSteeplePlus50m.*' Ice had to refer to the Ice Cave. Yet

I had 'pondered' the subterranean chamber and discovered no obvious clue. However, when I got closer to a pine tree intruding upon the edge of the path, I spotted a small 'X' carved upon it.

Then it came to me.

Deciphering the message wasn't about pondering the Ice Cave: it rather referred to a *Ponderosa* pine and the 'X' upon it somewhere near the cave. Suddenly the verbal and numerical jumble all made sense much as if I had been a cryptographer all my life.

Find the 'X on an Ice Cave Ponderosa pine; walk to (2) a steeple of rock to the left (L); proceed another 50m in the same direction.

After making sure no one was trundling along the trail in either direction, I scrutinized the mixture of vegetation and rocks to the west side, or to my left. Then again, this assumed that you had to be able to see the 'X' before heading off in the same direction, rather than quite the opposite of departing away from the 'X,' resulting in a different search altogether. But I told myself to remain patient. This may take a few false trails like runners use in 'Hares and Hounds.'

I saw one of nature's accidental cairns to the left and began stepping off toward it. It sat atop a small boulder, beyond which continued in what I carefully stepped off to be 50m straight line.

Yet when I painstakingly had proceeded off limits to a small area I felt sure was about the correct distance beyond the steeple, there was nothing of note in sight. No cross. No marking. No National Monument warning or unique sign of nature.

I zigged and zagged back to the Ponderosa with the sinking feeling that such a code could be extremely ambivalent. But that was the fun of treasure hunting, wasn't it? I mean if it were easy, there'd be no magic substances left out there. I again stood at the 'X' on the tree; pondered; looked in the other direction; pondered again.

Then another notion hit me. Maybe the 'L' didn't mean left. Maybe it meant '*Lava beds*,' the sprawling black jumble of encrusted material off more to the right or east of the trail. Soon I spotted an array of lava pushed up in such a way as to resemble a steeple. I mean for all I knew any of a hundred lava or rock formations could resemble a church spire. *Calm down,* I told myself. *Literally take it one step at a time.*

This journey was harder. Not only did I have to wait for another family to pass by, and to feign burying my nose in an Ice Cave brochure as they did so, but then I had to negotiate walking over uneven lava probably every bit as sharp in places as coral.

But I reached the simulacrum of a steeple, then continued in a straight line, fortunately out of site from any passers-by on the trail.

And I could now feel it.

The Mogollon Cross was near.

No one around. Time to get out the old trowel and at least use it to try to pry up some of the charred black stuff.

I soon realized that the small digging tool would be of little use. Big hunks of lava made it apparent that little short of a long pine lever or tire iron was going to be of any real advantage. Then where exactly should I dig? Again, I saw nothing portentous after following directions without the use of a string or some other method of determining a straight line.

A gradual slow survey around my position gave me some good news: I was out of sight from the trail, and there were at least two pieces of lava vaguely forming a cross. Amidst the black rock also sat one reddish piece of sandstone. Just the fact that it was there, with none other like it in the vicinity, I took as a sign.

It was heavy, maybe the weight of a 50-pound sack of potting soil. But, hey, when the possibility of that peridot and silver loomed somewhere below, I felt like the Boys Town kid whose brother 'ain't heavy' as I began to lift one side. Oddly, after I pushed this red harbinger aside, a mix of dirt and powdered lava sat invitingly below. I took one more look around to reassure myself no one else was witnessing this clandestine effort. Not a soul.

My trowel made a clinking noise when striking something that had to be one of three things: rock, metal, or more lava. Need I say that my pulse had risen to well over a hundred?

Digging and scraping in an increasingly haphazard manner, I uncovered nothing more than a piece of granite.

*Keep digging*, I told myself. Then my trowel suddenly struck something with a different hollow sound. Scraping away some soil revealed what looked to be an ancient piece of rusted armor. Maybe it was an arm or shin plate. Maybe it was just a buried piece of more modern oxidized pipe. I scratched and scraped until finally I was able to extract the rounded metal artifact from its burial.

Underneath was what appeared to be a nearly disintegrated sack of hemp. Its drawstrings looked like they once had been sealed by stamped wax now almost completely gone. Just a hint of red remained on a crumbling string.

When I lifted the bag, I knew my quest had reached its conclusion. I could feel the shape assuredly had to be a cross inside. It was heavy for its size, and I felt strangely its magic contents were about to intrude into a life that to this point had known only the treasures of sporting events and interviews with great men.

It had to be the Mogollon Cross.

# Kahlo's City

(KAHLO)

When I walked just north on the trail from Casa Rinconada to a point beyond the big rock on the right where I knew there should be a city in Chaco Canyon, the funny thing is, I thought of being in school. Grammy and Mom would never understand how much more you learn from your own observations, books, and the internet. They came from a generation that believed reading, writing and arithmetic were the most important knowledge to be passed on to all kids. They didn't have the internet, e-mail, Google.com, Google Earth, and the world's biggest open library for the reading and writing part. And they didn't grow up with the evidence of ancient civilizations like those of the Anasazi available electronically in upstate New York.

Grammy would do anything for me, but her attention span for research of any kind must have vanished before vodka became her best friend. She is always so kind to me, even though she did put her foot down when I wanted to hike up to Tsin Kletsin. She has no idea why I choose to do what I do on my learning expeditions. But she almost always encourages me if she feels someone my age won't get in trouble.

Every time I go to Chaco Canyon, I get goosebumps. I don't know if adults get the same feeling, but the canyon and its former citizens have become my best friends. Since I left New York, of course, I haven't met any new kids who might become friends, even though I still have Mom and Grammy. But I never had many, anyway. Just Joel, who moved away, and Luz, my Puerto Rican friend who didn't care about skin colors at all.

Luz and I would read things aloud to one another. I can't say why I liked it better than electronic games or television sitcoms and animated shows for kids. But I did. Luz and I told ourselves that one day we both would make an impact on our world. It was a sort of pact. It wasn't easy for her being Puerto Rican in New York. But she never complained, even though her parents sometimes did. Luz always said she had to take responsibility for learning all she could, and just being around her made me want to work harder on all my investigations.

Grammy can tell when I'm impatient at talks like Ranger Plentyhorn gave at Casa Rinconada. It's as if you're studying trigonometry and suddenly a teacher starts teaching addition and subtraction. Or an adult says something to you, like, 'When you get older, you'll be able to understand.' Why do they always say that? Just because I'm nine doesn't mean I can't understand most things. About the only real hard thing for me to understand is prejudice. I've seen the way Luz and I were treated sometimes by kids in school. Not a lot, but little things like not getting invited to sit at certain lunch tables. I never cared that much if I wasn't included because I had books and the internet as friends. It hurt Luz a lot, though, and sometimes she would cry until I reassured her. I worried more about whether she could hold up until she got recognized for her brain rather than her skin color or ethnic background. For me those moments were OK, though, because Mom always says my day will come.

But it doesn't really matter, anyway. My day has already come, many times over. Every time my visions or deductions tell me something about Chaco, even if they're wrong, it's like a best friend complimenting you by sharing a secret.

For instance, during the Casa Rinconada lecture, I kept thinking about the entrance ramp from the north. My perception was that it was for baptisms of some sort, where maybe priests or other adults dropped down underwater in the exterior kiva chamber, and then seeing the sunlight or moonlight streaming down through the water to the south, walked up the ramp until their whole upper torsos were above water in the main kiva bath. But I didn't get the usual strong electric signals I usually get during that vision. I wasn't sure. And like I've said before, most people aren't going to pay much attention to a nine-year-old kid's theories, anyway.

I felt far more certain about the city that should be several hundred meters west of Casa Rinconada. A missing part of the overall Chaco puzzle that fit into the vision kept returning again and again. When Don Pedro de Tovar probably visited Chaco in 1541 or 1542, he couldn't deduce what had been thriving several hundred years earlier.

All the way back to Santa Fe I was preoccupied with the south side of Chaco Wash. The city was the only thing I felt real clear on, and because I didn't get to go up to Tsin Kletsin, I couldn't examine another possibility for my hydraulics idea.

I think I was a little bit scared. I know that sometimes I get too involved with investigating stuff, when I should be spending time with kids my own age. It's so easy for me to bury myself in books, the internet and thinking about Chaco mysteries. I admit I'm addicted to the whole process. But sometimes I suddenly feel this shiver pass over me. It has to do with worrying about learning too much and not being able to talk about it with anyone. Not just my stutter, because I could also write something. It's more to do with being in a Neverland without any others to talk to. Grammy loves me dearly, and most of the time would do anything for me. But she'd pretty much be happy spending the rest of her days on a patio, with the *Atlantic Monthly* or *Vanity Fair* and one of her favorite drinks in her hand. Gram encourages me all she can, but what I learn about ancient civilizations, particularly if it's technical at all, doesn't interest her very much.

Then Mom is too busy with her own investigation of my Aunt Ashleigh's murder. Because of what I know about Ashleigh's death, I'm sure Mom's on a misguided search. But Mom calls her investigation a 'catharsis.' I think it's more something to keep her mind occupied because she has gone so long without ever remarrying. I think she'd be happier if she could find a man who is her equal, but that she can respect and from whom she can accept kindness. But it will probably be hard for her to find the sophisticated urbane sort she likes in the West. Mom does best with approach-avoidance. She tends to scare off men who pay too much attention or buy her things or call her all the time.

She will listen to me when I tell her things from my visions and explorations. But she is more interested in form rather than content. While Mom might be skeptical about some of my theories, she always encourages my continuation of learning.

My mother was probably going to be annoyed that Grammy and I went to Chaco again. She thinks I've become obsessed with the ancient civilizations there. Maybe I have. But every time I go, I learn something new, or experience visions of what might have happened a millennium earlier. I feel something like a magnetic field around me.

Right now, the mesas, the crumbling stone walls, the sunlight, the books and watching videos in the Visitor Center theater are more exciting than anything. When I wake up and know I am going to Chaco, I feel like maybe I was once an Anasazi priestess. From what I've read, they only had priests, but maybe I would have convinced them of my worthiness. I can't wait 'til I'm older. Part of being listened to with seriousness is being tall enough that people don't look down on you. Well, at least that's what it feels like when you have a moment or two without a stutter and you can see someone's mind drifting off. You can tell they think a little kid doesn't know anything important.

Santa Fe is like a 20th Century Chaco in a way. It's doesn't have that many Native Americans. But I like the buildings, food, furniture, and art. Whenever I walk around the Plaza, I imagine all the Native Americans sitting under the portico of the Palace of the Governors like it was eight or nine centuries ago. Many of their faces still look the same. And many of the colors they wear are still the same. I pretend some of them are Anasazi, even though I know they're modern-day Pueblos, Diné, and Apaches. They still have the silver and turquoise traditions of their ancestors, and I like that, too. Grammy let me buy one of their necklaces, and sometimes I pretend it's got magic powers.

Anyway, Mom was in a good mood when we got back to the hotel. She had spent the day looking at homes, and said that though they were expensive, they weren't as bad as in Manhattan. Mom liked a three-bedroom adobe condo she looked at in a gated community above Bishop's Lodge Road. She loves expeditions like that, where she can poke around a lot of interiors for ideas. Mom pretends that she's sophisticated and isn't very domestic. But she loves interior decoration and cooking, even though she would probably say they're not that important. She's always preparing for a nest and a husband even though there may not ever be another one.

"How did everything go, then, today, Kahlo?" Mom inquired as she browsed the classifieds in the *New Mexican*. "Any special visions this time?"

I knew she wouldn't really pay attention to my answer. Once Mom has her own explorations going, she usually keeps preoccupied.

Plus, she told us she had been to a place called Guadalupé's, where she met the strange man from the canyon again and drank some margaritas. I didn't really feel like talking, anyway. But I knew I had to say something, or she would think I'm too weird.

"Wh-wh-we listened to a ranger about Casa R-r-rinconada."

"Oh, yes."

"And-and-and I found where a city sh-sh-should be."

"Really. And where should it be, then, Kahlo?" Mom asked as she turned another page of the newspaper.

"L-l-lower left."

"Lower *left*?" Mom looked up from her newspaper and I saw Grammy drop the mail on the table and look over at me, too.

"Mm-huh. Lower l-l-left."

# Quivira's Quandary

(KETL)

Just like Geronimo, you could always hope for the best. That didn't mean *hozro*. It meant a chance. There was a chance that big man Cantrell would undergo his own rite of passage. I figured the chance of that was probably about the same as steady rain for a week in the Glittering World.

My day began just like it always does. I arose from my bed, made a cup of coffee, and went out to view the arrival of the God of Sun. It matters little that my hogan and tipi are more traditional than many of my fellow Diné choose for homes. Some of them live in trailers and some in the same rectangular houses the white people have. But I feel better in front of my hogan when I know that I have held to the traditions of my ancestors.

It's not like I only live in the past. I do read some Anglo books, newspapers, and magazines. I drink coffee. It's more an attitude of respect for the time-honored surroundings within which I am fortunate enough to live. The winds sometimes whistle. The sun warms my soul much like a lizard warms itself on a rock.

Sometimes Chichilticalli comes to talk. He is very proud and refuses to impose his white world education on any Native American. Often, we say very little, just sit on my porch gazing out at the great valley and distant mesas or the sacred mountain *Tsoodzil*, the white people call Mt. Taylor, to the east.

Other times Estibalíz stops by to bring me some of her chili sauce or a *ristra*. For years nothing has changed. Estibalíz leaves her truck by the side of the highway and waits as any Diné out of politeness would do to allow me to make ready for a visitor. Soon she is at my door with a smile I always attribute to her Apache and Mexican heritage. We have done a dance of life for a long, long time. Once she kissed me on the cheek during the spring solstice. But I think both of us are too old for bodily contact. Well, maybe not. But such things are awkward when you have known each other as long as we have without any of the type of thing much younger people find natural. Estibalíz always seems to arrive just when her company is needed. She may have a *Hataali*'s sixth sense of when I want to see her.

On that day, I was thinking of her when a car pulled up alongside the road below. It was the big blue car of the journalist Quivira I sent on the quest. He had a bag with him and that wasn't good.

"Hello," the big man said as he walked up toward me.

"Yah-té-éh."

I gestured toward the other chair on my porch. He seemed nervous, maybe because he could see I noticed he had not arrived empty-handed. It was what I expected. A lot of *belagaana* come to the high country in search of something. Mr. Cantrell was no different. He was just a little more honest than most. Still, it's always good if the visitor undergoes a test. A test that may alter his consciousness.

"So, I'm back. I followed the maps and wonder what the meaning of all of this is. I have to say I got completely caught up in the Cross. But I'm not sure that once you've found what you were seeking, there isn't a huge letdown. I found what I figure may be the Mogollon Cross. My blood pressure was higher than the elevation when I was getting close. Every stop—Twin Peaks, Shiprock, El Morro, and the Ice Cave—each had a strange intangible allure. It was as if a siren had me within her powers, and there was nothing I could do about it. Beckoning, bating me on to finding something I might be better off failing to discover.

"Then I found it. It was almost like a scorpion in my hands. It would have been a good thing if I had put it back in its subterranean hideout. But I figured if I did, someone else would find and remove it. A sort of modern-day quandary over one of life's ancient mysterious objects.

"I waited until I got to my car to take it out of my backpack and out of a tattered burlap sack. Just for a moment I felt like I was rich. But almost immediately I got this bad taste in my mouth that I was defiling the magic expanse around me. *El Malpais* was as if Mother Nature had had an upset stomach and getting rid of all that liquid stone had put her right again. Up came lots of rare things, and the badlands became a last dyspeptic respite for most creatures. A perfect place to hide the Mogollon Cross.

"But it's no good. I should have put it back. I didn't because I didn't think it belonged under a pile of lava either, that and the more obvious that someone else would eventually unearth it and hide the Cross somewhere else."

And with that he handed the bag to me.

"Aren't you going to check it out?"

I set it down on my lap and gazed out at the morning sun. Mr. Cantrell was uncomfortable in his chair, unaware that his quest was no more than a mirror of any visitor's search for taking some of the *hozro* back with them. Hoping to capture physical treasure to possess rather than taking in the essence of the great high desert and its mesas and mountains.

"I figured I'd be better off giving it to you, that you'd know where it should be. You would have a sense of what is right for something 400 to 500 years old of strange value. My mind was in a fever driving all the way here. It was as if the badlands had infected my brain with an irremediable guilt and an unfamiliar burden of lack of character."

"You have failed your test," I said with the deliberation of one having knowledge of what is best. "But there is hope."

The early sun was streaming through the door, and I gave my last remark a chance to settle. I stood up and motioned for Mr. Cantrell to walk ahead of me. He stood on the porch, then moved out onto the red dirt, a silhouette against the light from the source of life. I came up alongside him and we looked out at the New Mexican desert for a long time. Then as the two of us continued taking in the Glittering World morning, he began to speak.

"You don't know this, but I'm the type of guy who always puts adventure ahead of everything. Give me an assignment to cover a great contest and I was up for it. Set me off on a road trip to the middle of nowhere and I'm the sort who can always find the adventuresome silver lining."

Then we walked back and settled into the rocking chairs. The two of us looked further at the red and orange illuminations upon the rocks. It is the Diné manner to wait. So I did.

Mr. Cantrell ran his hand through his hair.

Maybe five minutes went by. Then I handed the bag back to him.

"Examine the contents again," I instructed the visitor.

His large, bruised hands pulled the silver-and-peridot Mogollon Cross from the bag and turned it over several times in his hands.

"It feels heavier," he said as he turned it so the light would reflect from one of the green stones. Then he put the cross back in the bag and handed it back to me.

"It is no more than metal and colored stone," I stated, placing the bag and its contents on the table beside me. "I said there is hope. Like many *belagaana* who come here, you came with an ulterior motive. You wished to find treasure. You hoped to find riches that would make you grow in the estimation of others. Along the way, beauty was all around you. It is the true wealth of the Glittering World.

"But you took very little notice. Your mind was clouded by thoughts of glittering metal instead of the warmth of sunrises and sunsets. Light shining off silver and gems instead of reflections off pieces of quartz sent up by Changing Woman. The thought of how much the found objects would bring in currency, instead of how memories of beauty could be had for those possessing their own *hozro*."

Mr. Cantrell's hands were steepled in front of his chin. He was not used to anyone revealing a truth different from his own experience of reality. He was puckering his lips, lost in thought and oblivious to the marvels right in front of us.

"But," I continued, while much like a Diné, he said nothing, "there is hope."

Again, I waited, in the manner of my ancestors. In my experience on the Santa Fe dining cars, *belagaana* always have something to say. Often, they do so without any meaning. To them it is a bridge to keep conversation going or to extend talking. For a Navajo, there is no need of such contrivances. More often we share without speaking.

"I know I should not have taken the cross from its bed. But I did, and after all, it made for a fabulous two days of adventure. There is a certain frustration in deciphering clues, finding nothing where something's supposed to be, and following misleading before rewarding paths. Yet I felt alive when I was on the quest. And when I'm alone with a drink in my hand, the alcohol may be the only thing keeping me from self-pity."

There was no need of telling him that, with Chichilticalli's help, I send at least one pale-faced visitor a year on a similar quest. All have come to ask about treasure. Each one remains oblivious to the real treasures of our world.

Only one has succeeded in our test. She was a fiction writer from the mountains of Colorado who had renounced all formal religion yet loved her natural surroundings. She followed the maps and paths and arrived at the destination. In this case the site of the buried treasure was near the Santa Fe Southern tracks between Santa Fe and Lamy. The location made her quest more difficult because an outsider could easily argue any discovery made there was not on sacred ground. For her quest we had hidden a Zuni signet ring, of silver and turquoise. The turquoise was mere plastic, but she found it, examined it, and put it back.

Others we have never seen again. Sometimes we hear they have gone to Indian trading posts to try and sell their discoveries. But no matter. They have failed and the Glittering World finds ways of returning them to urban destinies with fewer natural rewards.

"You have done no differently than others on a similar search," I explained while still looking out across a valley of more value and beauty than any jewelry, gems, or coins of the realm. "They suffer from the illusion that happiness can be purchased or owned. It cannot. They believe taking something rare back with them must have financial value. They are wrong. The most valuable things they can return home are memories of the natural beauty they have enjoyed due to listening to their senses. Bright days. Cool nights. Mesas lit by changing light. Prickly pear cactus surviving on little water. Paths lined with black *chollo* or *chamisa*. All of these create impressions with which they are unfamiliar. These natural phenomena are the Glittering World."

Out of the corner of my eye I could see the visitor having returned from his quest was searching for what to say. It was our good fortune he said nothing.

"I did say there was hope," I repeated after another pause in a setting with nothing more than the occasional sound of the wind or a crow announcing an arrival from the top of a rock. "You have brought the Cross to me, thinking I would know where to return it. You did this rather than keeping it or trying to sell it as many others might do. This shows you are a *belagaana* with a potential spirit of understanding *hozro*. When you returned the cross to someone from whose domain much has been taken or excavated, it was a sign. A sign that you may still achieve what the English language calls harmony with your surroundings. But you must continue your journey through our lands to see whether the attraction of metallic or mineral treasures remains greater than an appreciation of the true Glittering World."

Big man Quivira had the look of someone caught between two destinies. He was lost in thought, and his battles were far from over.

"Yah, I did bring it back. But I could just as easily have tried to fence it through some shady characters back in Brooklyn.

"I have to say, though, that when I looked up at that leaping buffalo at El Morro or when I heard the old man in the El Rancho bar before his daughter's fund-raiser, that each encounter did set me to thinking about just what in the hell I was really trying to achieve with my trip out West. I mean, you're looking at a guy who over the years has found a few drinks, bets and female companions his *raison d'être*. I couldn't wait to get out and look for rare gold coins, rare gems, Mogollon Crosses, or whatever else lured me through the desert while nearly completely oblivious to my surroundings. I've barely noticed any Glittering World. Barely gave a thought to the cactus and mesas. My imagination precluded any notice of any natural phenomena. I mean, I only took two or three minutes to gaze out at the Angel Peak and Kutz Canyon. Too much in a hurry to follow a map to something magic. Yah, and I'm not sure whether any intrinsic values will triumph in the end. There's still a good chance someone brought up and having spent his whole life in big cities will fail to be converted."

The big man had spoken the truth as he sees it. From years of writing about what others do, he has a better sense than most about other people and lands different than he knows. Of accepting that not everyone wishes a life of living in crowded conditions. That the variety of the great *Diné Bikéyah* provides a diversity missed by many visitors.

I took the cross from its burlap sack.

"Tin over iron and cut glass."

"No!"

"Yes. Mineral wealth is merely an illusion. This Cross was made by a friend of mine in his hogan last year. Treasure hunters seek material wealth with history. They look for silver and peridot or turquoise or gold.

"We hold our quests for a certain few with the potential to learn our Glittering World's treasures. It is a little game I play to contribute to *belagaana* progress. It is no different from Chichilticalli's devoting himself to their instruction at the Northwest New Mexico Visitor Center.

"The Diné will survive. But the Glittering World must be understood better if our survival is to become free of outsider manipulation. It has always been the case with the Navajo and all the tribes you call Native American. The battle never ends. It merely now is fought between tourists, new resident arrivals, and the descendants of the *Bikéyah*'s centuries-old inhabitants as if they are partners in a dance of life."

# Kaliber Bar None

(KALIBER)

The thing that came to me on the way back to my shack is that I've got to stay away from women like Aurore Dupín. It's too bad, because she has an interest in rock hunting like my own. She's not evil. She's just a typical woman out of Manhattan with a bit too much *savoir-faire* and education for someone a little rough around the edges like me. It's in her nature as it sometimes is in mine to engage in polemics. And then big city wit plays its part, as well. You need to sharpen your wits to duel with someone like Ms. Dupín. Our second encounter in Guadalupé's verified that. Otherwise, you will be eviscerated before you know it. And that's why I need to keep my distance and just go about my solitary habits. It's much easier to read Edna St. Vincent Millay than it would be to deal with her daily.

Something about the upper hand always insinuates itself between the genders. The Mars and Venus thing really is true to some extent. I always attribute it to hormones. Testosterone makes men aggressive and estrogen most women nurturing. But big city life and myriad other factors can change all that one way or the other. Dupín can be as aggressive as her sister Ashleigh was, but she put a lid on it at Guadalupé's. I don't know what I would have done if our little approach-avoidance dance had mandated to the Gotham *femme fatale* that we go back to her place and get up to some serious physical instead of mineral exploration. I always tell myself I'm retired from such behavior. But, hey, if something fell in my lap, I'm sure I could come up with enough testosterone to mix it up into the late hours.

Yet it's so much more relaxing just to get out the old rock hunting belt and go to it. With those tools dangling from my waist and my imagination of glistening hardened carbon stones, I have all the relaxation I need for this stage in a life not amounting to much in the estimation of others. I never push it. I just go slowly, ambling here and there, looking for outcroppings that may signify something other than sedimentary rock. The adage of the search being more important than finding anything always remains true.

There is no finish line for rock hunting. It's a needle in a haystack you seek, but choosing the right haystack is a very important part of the game. Probably akin to selecting a spot for fly-fishing. You have to know the waters or terrain.

I had a little of the Allegro bean distillate jet fuel and piled in the Suby beater. A Bureau of Land Management survey map hopefully would keep me off private property during the day's hunting. My plan was to climb up part of Mt. Taylor and just see if any formations or pegmatites jumped out at me as potentially having disgorged precious stones or glistening metal.

The glistening myth is quite the exaggeration for most rock hunters. Other than strip mining, where huge shovels gouge out many tons of rock in one go, most gold mining, for instance, is considered productive if there is three-quarters of an ounce per ton or better. Since a ton of granite is perhaps a three-foot-high cone, you can probably get the drift of just how laborious finding any substantial amount of the shiny stuff can be without using heavy equipment or a sluice box.

Not that there's a lot of gold in New Mexico, anyway, other than that hidden by white men over the past couple of centuries. Then again, one never knows what may be discovered when you least expect it. If by some whimsical chance you find yourself in an old mine that has had some partial collapses inside, those slides might have uncovered new walls of rock never encountered by human explorers. Suddenly in front of you could be veins of precious metal all leading to one of the mysterious mythical sources known as a Mother Lode. When the shiny stuff increasingly appears amidst quartz or other mineral content, enough so that you unexpectedly feel the hair on the back of your neck or arms tingle.

Of course, in New Mexico, silver or turquoise are among your best shots. Most of the property along the Turquoise Trail between Santa Fe and Albuquerque is now private land. Rockhounds are better off finding their own virtually unexplored areas, the magic kind where suddenly your senses tell you that you are very near. That preternatural feeling that some of those dirty and disguised offbeat minerals other than clear or colored carborundum may polish up to peridot, moonstones, turquoise, agate, jasper, or chert.

I've never studied geology formally and know just enough to be dangerous in terms of stumbling upon something I shouldn't in a place that I oughtn't. Bad karma. For me such spiritual maxims or barriers have rarely impeded a day's sleuthing on property that may or may not be legal. I suppose it depends upon my mood, really. Usually, I'm a law-abiding citizen. It's just that formal property rules often become annoying if you don't own any. Just like those in Hollywood who audition for parts for which they are ill suited: sometimes if you persist you get the part or find something unique. You need to take a few risks if you're going to find an unusual mineral. And unusual to me is anything that catches the light or looks interesting under a magnifying glass. Sometimes even picking up a rock with a lot of iron ore or lead in it is a trip because of how dense and heavy it is. The whole rock-hunting phenomenon is like anything else: the farther into unexplored territory you go, the more excited you get. Go fish. Treasure awaits.

I figure I'd have a meander up La Mosca Canyon on the back side of Mt. Taylor. The 11,000-foot-plus extinct volcanic peak is known as the Turquoise Mountain, but who knows?

The thing about luck is it only occurs when you put yourself in its path. No one ever found a moss-covered gold nugget while sitting in front of a TV. Nor unearthed a 20-carat emerald in their rose garden. You have to get out there. Have to breathe in that early morning fog when the sun first burns through, and you know it's going to be a halcyon day. The kind of feeling you get on La Mina Trail in Puerto Rico's El Yunque, where water is dripping and rushing and thundering all around you and the plants and trees and coqui frogs and orchids are all in harmony with the wet elements. The magic makes itself known when you find the right settings.

On my New Mexican expeditions, often I will walk for more than an hour, oblivious to any rattlers, mountain lions, scorpions, or crafty other living hazards one can come upon out in the middle of a day's destiny. With my rock hunting belt on, the glass is always half full, my mind fulminating with hallucinations on those glittering natural phenomena that may be lurking just under that decomposed log or somewhere in the vicinity of an array of quartz exploded from a pegmatite millennia earlier. Modern marvels to me are not man made. No, they sit waiting, unadulterated, unchanged, and untouched for thousands if not millions of years. Until that one imaginative adventurer finds his trowel, fork, or hammer gravitating downward to some obscure location that suddenly enchants like your favorite musical melody.

A little clairvoyance is necessary, I suppose. Enough so that you get to share the magic of the confluence of heat and mineral content that produces those rare dirt-covered gems or moss-obscured nuggets capable of dizzying even the most placid minds. A willingness to be wrong most of the time, but right just occasionally. Some strange telepathic phenomenon tells you that you are very close. Oh, so close. Oh, so near to exultation without human contact. It's in the air. But it's almost always underfoot. The planet's treasures. The remarkable hidden wealth right among the other living and dead organic and non-organic wonders all around. They are always there. You are not.

Even though at that time of year Mt. Taylor's Trail 77 approaching from the south might be devoid of humans, a few souls or a Cibola National Forest ranger might be wandering along. My idea of La Mosca Canyon vicinity was to circumvent any such encounters.

From my topo map I found a trail and began to gain elevation. When I had gone about a mile, I noticed an outcropping that looked different from most of the sandstone formations you see prominently nearly everywhere in New Mexico. It was disguised by pine trees, but I figured I'd get through the aspen, scrub oaks and juniper until I could have a better look. I was pretty sure I was on Cibola National Forest land, but to that point the tools in my belt had done nothing more than jangle as I walked, and those tools rely upon no such delineations.

When I got close to the outcropping, it was evident there was more than sedimentary rock in the area. Yet that could mean either nothing, or everything. There might be rare gems invisible for a variety of reasons, or nothing more than some granite, quartz, or other dense minerals one overlooks as common, although each plays its own part in the striking panoply of Mother Nature.

I began to dig near some scattered quartz that looked like it might have erupted from a small pegmatite. I found a round piece of rock that looked like it could be a geode, a hollow sphere in which crystals such as purple amethyst sometimes form. When I finally unearthed it, I hammered on the metamorphic rock globe, but it didn't sound hollow. I hit it harder and merely chipped the surface before tossing it back down. Nada.

That's kind of the way my morning went. No great discoveries, but a lot of anticipation that can get the pulse going. Scrape off a piece of rose quartz here. Discover a little mica or fool's gold there. Or be taunted by a glittering piece of green, only to find it's broken glass—meaning someone has been there before you.

Suddenly it was getting colder. A dark bank of clouds was approaching, and I warned myself that lightning might be the biggest peril anyone can encounter on a mountainside. Uncommon sense told me to get the hell down the mountain, even though it would terminate my rock hunting for the day. That amazing cache hidden in the nineteenth century would have to wait. And what if you found a hoard of gold bars, anyway? How in the hell would you get them down the mountain? A wheelbarrow wouldn't work. Or maybe it would if you took a few at a time and covered them with some sort of stones that made it look like you were just acquiring decorations for your garden. But with a barrow full of bullion, you definitely wouldn't want to come upon a ranger.

That's the sort of drivel that always goes through my brain when the mountain air gets to me. A loud thunderclap brought me back to my senses, and it was only then while hurrying downhill that I noticed the opening to a cave. Now most of you would probably encourage me to get in there until the storm passed. But without a flashlight, I'm kind of wary of such places as being havens for other critters such as rattlers or four-legged predators.

It started to pour hard enough I ignored any such apprehensions and ducked into the opening partially obscured by a scrub oak. Once inside, the cave appeared to be an old mine shaft of some sort, but the light was so poor that I didn't want to wander back very far, especially as there was water standing underfoot.

There I was, probably in some mineshaft hombres had blasted out in search of just the sort of stuff I was looking to find with a trowel and miniature spade. The noise of the cloudburst was echoing all around me. I should have brought a jacket.

Yet within minutes the heavens had ceased their interruption to my day's adventure. Slowly the sun again popped through the passing cumulus, and I had a quick glance around this seemingly empty tomb. There didn't seem to be anything of note. Wait a minute. What's that over against that wall?

After quickly beavering over to where I had glimpsed metal, I found nothing more than a partially buried tin can. The light had caught part of the bit that was still un-rusted, and I had momentarily been gulled. But it's just that sort of serendipitous discovery that sometimes unnerves even the most placid prospector.

I still felt pretty good when I got down and decided to drive over to the Zuni-Acoma Trail to attempt a run. My feeling is, if you're going to drink, you need to temper such an indulgence with a purgative trot as often as possible. It looked like the thunderheads were passing, so I piloted the old Suby back through Grants and out along the extensive *El Malpais* carpet.

The badlands are a strange area. When you first head south from Grants you pass a few respectable if modest homes off to the sides of the road. But then as the desiccated lava flow to your left gets more serious, and the water in the area undoubtedly less prevalent, it's as if you are gliding along the edge of a moonscape. Who knows how many millennia it will take to turn that into soil? Or how many prospectors and banditos have buried stuff out somewhere in that desolate terrain?

The Zuni-Acoma trailhead has a parking lot, toilet facilities and a posted map and warnings of just how much your typical hiker or runner best be prepared if they head southeast from there. Some wire netting gets you across a stream of lava and soon you're down in a green and tan field with chunks of lava here and there. It's not the sort of trail to mess around on. There're large briquettes of lava on the trail itself, so that if you don't watch your footing, you can rip open a knee, shin, or elbow like you've stumbled on coral.

I didn't get very far, maybe a mile or so, and I had to take a pee. There were a few scattered scraggly pines in the area, and I diverted off the trail to duck behind one. It was probably an exercise in futility since there had been no other car in the parking lot and there was little chance a Zuni would come jogging by in Native American apparel and barefoot, or a paleface running by outfitted in Nikes or Reeboks.

After relieving myself I slowly peered around the vicinity, at the same time trying to imagine what Acoma or Zuni might have conjured up several centuries earlier on the same trail. New Mexico, for the most part, is like that. You suddenly find yourself mentally drifting back into time, imagining things that are no more contemporary than Vasquez de Coronado and his lot traipsing through. I may have some Indian blood, but it's vestigial. I have no right to daydream of warrior exploits. Yet in a life like mine, which admittedly is an eccentric one of reclusion and solitude, you have the luxury of contemplating your existence at just such unorthodox times. Thoughts of gems and valuable buried metals often intruded into my days. Reruns of poems and lyric passages slipped into my nights.

Off on a small promontory I saw a glint. Probably nothing more than a piece of quartz I told myself. But I had to check it out. When your day is nothing more than a series of such explorations, any clue or hint of something unusual can make your day.

I jogged over and whatever it was lost the reflection to the point where your errant prospector no longer knew where the illusion had come from. I moved back and forth to try and place myself in the same proximity to the now re-emerged late-afternoon sun. *There it is*, I told myself. The sun's light could again be seen bouncing off something not 25 feet away. I apprehensively drew closer, the scent of bullion creeping back in like a virus returning.

A corner of something unnervingly shiny was half buried in soil and submerged below a hunk of lava. My hand was shaking as I pulled out my trusty trowel. Maybe the buried bars from a train robbery? A gold brooch taken from a Spanish dignitary's wife back in the seventeenth century?

Well, hey, a somewhat tarnished gold tube of lipstick may not be from Fort Knox, but digging for it sure beats the hell out of watching TV.

I got on with my run. Galloping over *El Malpais* for a mile out and a mile back would do it. My legs were more tired from Mt. Taylor than I thought. I'd use them for the endless search another day. Rock hunting is mostly like that. Maybe like life itself. Much of the ongoing quest results in discovering nothing more than remarkable natural surroundings all too often taken for granted. But if you keep after it, the journey itself is the reward.

# Apache Country

(CHICHILTICALLI)

It was early morning. I was just staring out at *El Malpais* through the panoramic windows of the Northwest New Mexico Visitor Center. It's a modern place, but they've done a really nice job with the feel of the main room overlooking maybe 50 miles of badlands to the south and the mesas and mountains in the distance. I needed to come back to reality. Working at the Center could be construed as a waste of time for someone having read at Oxford. But as I've made known to a select few like Ketl, I have my own agenda here. My destiny may change at some point, but I kind of liked the uniform, responsibilities of broadening knowledge of the area, and chatting with those whose impression of Native Americans is derived from cinematic stereotypes.

Yet while staring through the windows because it was early enough that only a couple of tourists and their kids were watching a video of El Morro in our theater, I was preoccupied with Aurore Dupín. Just seeing her in the Mining Museum had been enough to inflame old passions. I knew it was no good. I had been down that road, not just in Oxford, but in New Mexico, as well. It was kind of like the same fate as Jim Chee in Hillerman's books. Native Americans can't get rid of their skins and traditions to become white. Nor do they want to.

There had been several white women over the years, always well educated, always strong-willed, Ms. Dupín being one of those rare specimens. When you grow up with women most of whom accept their domestic roles with equanimity, that atavistic inbreeding in your soul always rears its ugly head about the first time your interracial girlfriend says she doesn't cook, do windows, and finds disagreement with the male gender to be good sport. But then an Oxonian education somewhat altered that. The polar dual approaches to life end up being a conflict I haven't been able to resolve.

I knew I had to forget I had ever seen Aurore Dupín again. She had a brilliant mind and magnetic body to make you sweat at first contact. But over time she always ended up chewing you verbally to bits or keeping you at arm's length. She was a vamp with a deserved attitude. She didn't need a man, really, and that lack remains a hurdle just a bit too high to glide over.

Fortunately for me, a familiar face came through the door, and his size was significant enough that out of the corner of my eye I caught this arrival as he ambled toward the central desk where we keep the maps and other materials to try and assist visitors to experience our great domain.

"*Yah-te.*"

"Hey," was all he said as he came to a halt and turned away to face out towards the morning light over *El Malpais*. I figured he had come to the Center for a reason, but in Native American non-parlance, that meant waiting for him to reveal his intentions.

"What are you doing tomorrow?" he asked without taking his gaze from the horizon.

"Need to go up to the Jicarilla Apache Reservation to drop off some tourist pamphlets and check out a restaurant."

"What say we make the Great Train Ride."

"You mean from Antonito to Chama?"

"You got it. I figure we get up to Chama for the 8:00 bus to Antonito and the 10 o'clock train. You could drop your stuff off along the way if we started early enough. How long do you reckon it would take if I stay over at a motel in Grants, and pick you up early the next morning?"

I wasn't sure how to respond. Quivira Cantrell is the sort of Anglo who, once he gets an idea in mind, there is little stopping him from an adventure. He has a certain bravado and bluster about him. Yet he is an engaging character, with a wide base of general knowledge from which to draw anecdotes or experience applicable to almost any pursuit. Q man is a little loud, but he counteracts that by making anyone accompanying him seem a valuable adjunct to his next excursion. A certain male-bonding had occurred both inside and outside the Radon. From his journalism background he certainly could spin a good yarn. Yet he is also a devoted listener. It was almost as if his huge body makes him osmotic to stories, images, language, and anything else with which he has come into contact since his arrival in the high desert.

Taking the Cumbres & Toltec Scenic Railroad trip with him would probably preclude both boredom and relaxation. At the same time, the potential of accompanying Quivira Cantrell on almost any journey might make almost anyone apprehensive. You sensed the big man could be far more trouble than he had run into outside the Radon bar. And yet once anyone became involved with the journalist, there were no halfway measures. There was almost an intrinsic demand for companionship and loyalty.

"It might work because you could drop me off at Chaco fairly early the following day. I have to listen to a proposal by a NASA scientist there, and I'll be getting a ride back from Chaco with one of my fellow rangers to our Center in Grants. So, the trip might fit in with my going up to that area, anyway."

"Why not?" he responded while looking down through the counter glass at a map. "The way I see it is we make it up to Antonito for that 10:00 a.m. departure and then just let either the narrow gauge keep us amused through aspen and cottonwood groves, or other high-country attractions hold us captive. How much time do you need on the reservation?"

"Not much once we get there. Having breakfast in the Eagle Feather and securing a menu would probably do it. They don't do dinners except during the summer, and a fellow Park Service worker with a critical palate already gave me a pretty good report on what to expect.

"Leaving tomorrow morning might be dicey, though. As the crow flies, the distances to Chama and Antonito are far less than actual travel and highway time. We'd never make it to Chama by eight o'clock if we started tomorrow, no matter how early we leave. Our best shot would be to leave late this afternoon and camp at a place a friend tipped me to on the Jicarilla reservation. I have a tent. We'd still have a two-hour drive tomorrow morning plus the stop in Dulce for an Apache breakfast. And since the westward trip leaves the best for last, you're right: we should probably travel Antonito to Chama. That would save us an hour of driving each way."

Quivira insisted we take his Pontiac convertible, and I wasn't going to argue since my truck was at an age where just about anything from the windshield wipers to the alternator could act up worse than a Zuni with a Styrofoam chest of beer and a fishing rod. The two of us made an odd couple, but again, there was something about the big man that facilitated an insinuation into a life of someone like me with only a fourth the animation of the opinionated journalist. Both of us were wearing baseball caps backwards, mine a U.S. Park Service forest-green job, and Q man a NY Yankees faded navy-blue one resting upon his Easy Rider shades. Maybe we thought we were two young Navajos strutting in a football homecoming parade in Chinle.

We set off in the late afternoon sun with a Santa Fe diesel horn blasting somewhere not far away. Rather than going all the way over to Albuquerque and up 550 from Bernalillo, we set off on the 605 and 59 through Ambrosia Lake and Hospah. You could still make pretty good time on New Mexico's two-lane highways because often there were fewer other cars than jackrabbits in the middle of the Chaco Mesa area. Quivira had on a tape of Sheryl Crow and was crooning along as the mists began to burn off.

When we hit highway 9, I immediately began to wonder if Kaliber Ristraverdé would be up at his shack page-turning through some classic or examining an obscure piece of quartz under a scratched magnifying glass.

I had first encountered the Viet Nam vet during his brief period as a Park Service ranger at Chaco, then again in the Northwest New Mexico Visitor Center when he had come in with a dark-haired siren maybe a year or two ago. Later I would learn that the woman with him was Ashleigh Dupín, the same sister to Aurore I encountered on the long-ago rafting trip.

Anyone meeting Kaliber got a sense of a loner with the need to spend most of his quixotic time reading. It didn't really matter so much what he was reading. He just had to do it, or rock hunting, and alone. Ristraverdé was one of the few Anglos in the area who stuck to himself and rarely made it to any of the local bars, restaurants, or celebrations. Just a few words with him and you knew his appearance belied a well-educated man from an urban background. Yet Kaliber could interrupt an elaborate explanation just as quickly as he could wax articulately *ad infinitum*. It was almost like the gift of gab suddenly erupting from a normally taciturn fellow. As far as I knew he had no phone, nor electricity for wireless internet, and for anyone to get in contact with him remained a challenge.

He reminded me of *Hosteen* Ketl, my uncle who only partially had entered the third millennium.

I was one to talk, however. I wasn't as solitary, yet neither was I willing to go out of my way to rekindle former relationships with my own kin and expanded family members still living back in Zuni. Or to initiate new friendships with Hispanics or Anglos in the area, no matter how well educated they were. That sort of quiet life would be hard to explain to someone like Quivira Cantrell used to big city lights, sounds and conversations. You had to decelerate into the pace of northwest New Mexico almost like a step back in time. Sunsets, sagebrush, creosote bushes and hawks all began to reintroduce themselves into a life having jettisoned such curiosities for more literate pastures throughout more than a decade.

"Every day is a winding road," Q-man sang along to Sheryl Crow's song the lyrics of which unintentionally explain much about life in New Mexico. The big man was driving 70 mph in a 55 and the top was down, even though it was probably only about 60 degrees. We were speeding up highway 9, and I knew we were just about to where Kaliber Ristraverdé kept to himself in a sandstone canyon, when there he was sitting on a giant outcropping. I nudged Q-man's jacket sleeve flapping in the wind, and the big blue beast came to a grinding halt in a cloud of dust on the road's shoulder.

"Yo, Kaliber," he yelled. I saw the eccentric dude set down what looked to be a porcelain cup and tattered book so that he could use his hands to get down off the rock. He disappeared, probably having to retrace his steps to descend to canyon floor level. Then suddenly he was walking toward us, a thin man in a black T-shirt and black jeans offset by his faded red Converse low-tops with white-rimmed soles.

"What's up, man?" Quivira said when Ristraverdé had almost reached the blue convertible.

"Yah, well, just a little French roast with a shot of Myers and

William Styron to close out the afternoon," he said, only glancing up from the ground at the two of us when the sentence was finished. "What are you two doing up in these parts? On the way to harassing the Chaco rangers after dark?"

"Nah," answered the big man. "We're taking the Chama train tomorrow. And I'll bet you don't have shit planned up here in no man's land. Why don't you come along?"

Ristraverdé ran his hand through straggly hair that might not have seen soap for a week or more. I'm sure he jumped in the stream once in a while or maybe even had an overhead barrel of water with a hand-pull for showering when the mood struck him. But the former ranger somehow always maintained a wild look that foretold the necessity of keeping his distance from most other people. That behavioral quirk had made it difficult during his brief stint as a Chaco ranger. He slipped his left hand into a back pocket and checked out the Pontiac from front to back.

"Yah," he answered as if too much contemplation screws up a good impromptu road trip. "Why not."

We listened to some more Crow crooning and watched a hawk circling while Kaliber went back up to his shack to get a few things. In perhaps a testament to some facet of a past urban life, he returned wearing a beat-up Reebok hat and carrying a faded red Nike *Athletics West* bag. Soon this motley trio set off for Apache land and the Great Train Ride.

It was too noisy to say much. But we did hear how Kaliber had run into Aurore Dupín in Guadalupé's in Santa Fe. I couldn't tell if Quivira knew her or not, since he seemed more intent upon the surroundings and music rather than listening to Kaliber. Navajos are used to company with little conversation, but from my days at Oxford where the spoken word was raised to the deification of Oscar Wilde, I still felt Quivira would do his best to query Ristraverdé both between and during Crow flying songs. But he didn't.

We had turned off 550 and were heading up one of my favorite concrete roads, the mysterious highway 537. It stays that way because the Jicarilla Apache are generally quiet people who have never tried to solicit tourism much. They didn't really want me to leave any flyers about the Northwest New Mexico Visitor Center anyplace in Dulce. But they also needed the money of anyone passing through seeking gasoline or food, as life in the largely private Apache capital was difficult financially for many of them. Ever since their 90s claims of being underpaid for natural gas royalties by huge oil conglomerates and related statute of limitations problems, the Jicarilla Apaches have been even more resistant to outsider manipulation and visitors. Yet a certain mistrust seems to keep their reservation underdeveloped and quiet. You don't see all the franchise signs of places like Chinle and Kayenta on Navajo Nation lands, signage not seen in Zuni or near the gated communities of Anglo centers like Santa Fe.

For the first few miles, terrain alongside highway 537 appears much like the area the Great North Road once covered from the Chaco Mesa to Twin Peaks. You only see scrub vegetation and the occasional small oil pumping and storage station set back from the road along an arroyo. It was somewhat like a desert passage before reaching the Emerald Forest. Less than halfway up the highway, with probably a human density perhaps only slightly greater than much of Alaska, trees start to find enough water to develop entire stands. Then the rolling ribbon of concrete begins to include more and more coniferous growth and less arid, sandy soil. That's the way a lot of New Mexico and particularly the Native American reservations are. Most of their lands are arid, making water the most valuable commodity, even though oil, natural gas and sometimes even gambling pay the bills.

An Apache friend of mine had told me of a place in the forest at the north end of the highway before the turnoff to Dulce, and when we found it, it was even better than the Emerald Forest. If we didn't build an illegal fire to give away our illegal camping, my Apache connection said they never bother checking. It's the sort of area that tourists are warned away from or generally avoid, what with the stereotype of Apaches historically being warlike.

The two Anglo cast-offs quickly were into a bottle of Puerto Rican Ron Del Barrilito rum Q-man had brought along. I had a smoke and probably one shot of the golden sugar cane product for every three they had. The night was diffusing the wonderful scent of pine sap, and an owl hovered way up on a branch in the moonlight, hoping from his perch to spy a scampering rodent or small rabbit.

"I'm sorry, man, I didn't think you knew her," Kaliber suddenly said while refilling Q-man's shot glass the journalist had brought along in a camera bag.

"I never really did," said Quivira Cantrell while shaking his head. "I was just married to her for four years."

It was then I realized that the reclusive former ranger had finally figured out that the woman he had been talking about from his encounter at Guadalupé's, Aurore Dupín, had been married to Cantrell. There was almost a Native American lacuna then until the alcohol enabled the two of them to continue their conversation as if both had known of their commonality all along. You could tell Q-man hadn't seen her in many years. And it was also probable Ristraverdé was unaware of my encounter with the New York siren in the Grants mining museum. I kept my mouth shut because I figured I'd learn more about this enigmatic woman I had once known in Cambridge and Oxford, and again encountered recently. There was also a good chance that the subject of the late Ashleigh Dupín might also come up. It was the sort of situation where a Zuni upbringing gave me the power of listening many Anglos lack.

"One thing's for sure," Q-man added in the dim light of the half moon. "Had Ashleigh Dupín not abruptly died of heart failure, there are any numbers of people who would have been happy to strangle or shoot the shrew."

# The Great Train Ride

(QUIVIRA)

I awoke with my face in some red dirt. The last thing I remember from the previous evening in some Apache forest is that that crazy ex-ranger Ristraverdé had told me my former wife not only had moved to Santa Fe, but that he had met her. Then I wasn't sure, given the Ron del Barrilito I had downed, if my mind was playing tricks on me. For the millionth time I told myself that I could no longer blame journalism and the faux mystique of those who write for my drinking. Doctors had warned me to knock off the alcohol or sclerosis would eventually take over my undoubtedly perforated liver. But it was so much fun taking each excursion induced by those colored liquids referred to as the devil's curse. If white people think Indians have a problem, though, they should check out guys like Kaliber and myself. Aldebaran, on the other hand, is a Zuni Indian and doesn't drink much. Forget the stereotype of the drunken Indian. How about the stereotypical two white guys who blame former high-velocity lives for their guzzling and eccentric behavior?

Anyway, I was still alive and the thought of trippin' on the Toltec narrow gauge got me thinking we needed to get going into Dulce. I wasn't sure from what Chichilticalli had said whether the Indians there would even serve coffee, or if they did, if it would come anywhere near the level of Starbuck's French roast. But I didn't care.

My head felt like a squished cantaloupe and the last thing I wanted to do is get in the old blue beast and start zephyring up to the heart of Apacheland. But we needed to get going if we were going to get to Chama in time to catch that 8:30 a.m. bus.

I brushed some reddish soil off my face and looked over at Chichilticalli's yellow nylon tent. Part of one corner had collapsed, and it was obvious since the Zuni was still unconscious on his sleeping bag outside the tent that Ristraverdé had been the only one smart enough to take cover from the critters that probably crawled all over me during the Apache night.

"There are two things you need to know about breakfast here," Chichilticalli said as I nosed the Pontiac into a Dulce restaurant parking lot with weeds as prominent visitors. "Take off your baseball caps before we enter, and don't look any Apache in the eye. It's considered hostile and aggressive."

The Eagle Feather Restaurant wasn't open yet, though, which didn't give us much choice. To get to Chama on time, we needed to haul ass over the continental divide and leave the Jicarillas behind. Aldebaran wrote a brief note and wrapped it around some Visitor Center brochures he left on the restaurant porch.

I felt a sense of relief as we gunned it out of town. There were few people up and about, so I could ignore the 35mph speed limit on the highway threading between trailer homes, boarded up places, and houses with barking dogs and flatbed trucks parked in their dirt driveways. Not having to breakfast in Dulce was a relief, because I'm the type of guy who inevitably would say or do the wrong thing. I'd probably ask for something in an abrasive way, or talk too loud, or do some sort of Apache country no-no. It's my nature to be a social fuck-up and that's probably why Aurore found her own eccentricities were far easier to live with than my own. We needed to get the hell out of Jicarillaland and get to Chama.

We made the bus with plenty of time to spare. Chama's at something like 7900 feet of elevation, so even in early April you could see your breath in the thin air. A few of the blue rinse crowd came out of the Cumbres & Toltec Scenic Railway station below a line of the town's small hotels, restaurants, and curio shops. It was then that I again realized the tautology of how there is no fending off the inevitable. We all get older and don't look the same as we did when nature intended breeding to be foremost in mind. Lots of folks had canes or hearing aids, and I caught one or two surveying Kaliber, the Indian and me from head to foot. Granted, we didn't look like we were quite ready for AARP, but after a night of rum and a hard forest floor we probably appeared close to needing Medicare and a bath.

Even the highway drive from Chama over the pass and the long, winding ride along the Conejos River into Antonito got the old imagination whirring. There's a lot of spectacular territory through there, almost resembling what you think the high country of Oregon or Washington might look like. Occasionally we crossed over rusty narrow-gauge tracks, and you could see that the train along certain ledges provided spectacular views not available to those bound to motor coaches and the highway.

For some reason, maybe because I was sitting alone and Kaliber and Chichilticalli were talking across the aisle, I began to think of the Dupín family. Katarina, the intermittently cranky septuagenarian pianist; Aurore, who could metamorphose within seconds from New York book editor to irate wife; the perspicacious *enfant terrible*, who arrived after I was sent off, capable of the most astonishing revelations; and then the unpredictable late Ashleigh. The three survivors were better off ignoring any possibility of foul play. Could Ashleigh have been murdered? You bet. There were times when the two of us shouted so loudly at one another, I could have whacked her myself. But I didn't, as believe it or not, I generally only like organized violence like football and James Bond. The whole Radon Bar thing had been uncharacteristic for me, even though it might not have been for Aldebaran. I'm big enough that most people give me a wide berth.

Call it a premonition, but I had a feeling there was something strange coming about Ashleigh. It would probably be my luck if Aurore and her mother and daughter showed up on the train, as well. Then we'd probably have to do a dance of political correctness in front of Kahlo, the little wonder she adopted after we parted company. Still, they were on my mind, maybe since Ristraverdé brought up his tête-a-tête over margaritas in Santa Fe. The canyon man had been fortunate to avoid physical contact. Oh yah, Aurore had a way with men when she wanted, there was little doubt about that. It was easy to become enamored with my former wife. She wasn't exactly a siren, but far more compelling and dangerous. Often, after the wild carrot-haired look initially ensnared someone, her monstrous intellect and amazing perceptiveness osmotically and gradually overcame the prey.

Yet when we arrived at the Antonito station, I didn't see anyone standing alongside the train or in the station.

The whole scenario was like a step back into time. The station itself looked like it might have a hundred years earlier. The deteriorated brick edifice was set out on a wind-blown plain southwest of town, nearby a couple of obligatory shops selling the curios and keepsakes that help pay to keep such an antiquarian mode of transport alive. Since only scattered cumulus clouds drifted in the distance, there would be a good chance we could make the entire six-hour journey without rain or snow. But that's the sort of risk I like. Not knowing if the train was going to encounter any unexpected perils. No Indian attacks, of course, but who knew at the slow rate of speed we were going to travel in order that the old steam engine could chug away at a gradual enough grade to avoid slippages or derailments, if we'd be attacked by banditos on horseback?

Most of the geriatric crowd waiting to board looked like they had come a long way. You didn't see all the huge silver belt buckles, pearl-buttoned cowboy shirts and pointed boots associated with the West, but rather lots of gold-rimmed eyeglasses, checked Bermuda shorts, nylon jackets, and loafers with tassels. The only universal clothing item was faded jeans. Even some of the heavier folks had managed to squeeze a pair over wide-bodied hips.

The inside of the cars also conveyed you back a century or so. The walls and ceiling appeared as if having survived previous stove fires. Whole areas needed painting, or chipped wainscoting a little stain and sealer. The bench seats, since we hadn't bothered to pay the extra for the first-class car, were kind of like the dilapidated bus you always see rolling through safari country in movies. There was just enough cushioning to keep you from whining, but not enough to make you feel you were in the beginning of a new millennium. Our shared conductor had on the appropriate navy-blue hat and vest, but not the full uniform, and his initial spiel let us all know he was more an historian than a permanent employee of the railroad.

The steam-driven, six-car train began to roll west on a broad plain with not much more than chamisa, sage and cacti scattered throughout the sandy soil. To our left was the giant extinct volcanic Antonito mound, a sentinel for many driving south on highway 285 signaling the arrival of the Land of Enchantment.

There was also as much jouncing as on an old bus. You could feel why they had switched to 4-foot-8-1/2-inch-wide tracks and got rid of the old 3-foot narrow gauge iron rails. To accommodate a car wide enough to seat two on each side and still have an aisle in the middle, meant cars much wider than the wheels below them. This guaranteed the sort of tipping, squeaking, and jerking resulting from uneven or curving parts of the journey, as well as a speed of not much more than 10 mph to avoid derailment. The winding journey must be taken to understand how going off the tracks is not only possible, but has happened, although under unusual circumstances. In 1999 during snow clearing operations, engine 484 tried to plow through some ice and jumped off the rails.

Lifting a 176,000-pound locomotive back on the tracks presented quite a problem. To get the appropriate crane into position, an old road had to be modified. Although further derailments are unlikely, the hazardous possibility of coal sparks fires remains. At one point, the Forest Service in deference to such potential hazards shut down this fantastic wobbling transportation and scenery gem. But the CTSR responded. Now normally trailing each train at a discreet distance is a yellow flatbed motorized handcar with a canvas tent roof. The man riding in it has a fire extinguisher to put out any grass fires that may start from errant hot cinders escaping through the locomotive's screen-topped smokestack.

"I supposed it's too early to break the alcoholic beverages rule," Ristraverdé muttered as the train turned a long curve to climb up onto a plateau.

"I only drink when I can," I responded, "and this is one of those times I think it would be better to suffer magic elixir withdrawal."

When the Indian and Kaliber had gone out on the car-end platform to stretch their legs, someone had taken one of their seats. The Zuni now sat next to an elderly woman across the aisle, and you could see he was already suffering from an earful on Wisconsin home life or some such from a Marplean dowager out of an Agatha Christie mystery. Hearing often weakens in the aging, and her voice carried even above the din of the clacking of the wheels and squeaking of the ancient passenger car.

The name Cumbres & Toltec Scenic Railroad undoubtedly derives from the remote views of rock escarpments, mountainous forests, and the spectacular dizzying Rio de Los Pinos down below. Far above, the train winds round precariously narrow ridges and ledges or carves through sandstone and granite monolithic walls.

When we reached the old clapboard houses at Sublette where the locomotive takes on more water, the three of us made our way out onto the flatbed open-air car to peer at both the ancient buildings and the top of the canyon angling up from the river now perhaps 800 feet below.

The flatbed car was crowded, much like a section of the stands at a Giants game. The Indian and I were leaning on the ledge atop the car's half wall, while Kaliber was trying to leverage his way through an elderly couple to reach us.

"Normally this place is all boarded up, but one of the houses has had its shutters opened," said Chichilticalli.

"Maybe they're going to put in a Dairy Queen," remarked Kaliber just as he reached the rail.

"Queens may be on hand this evening," the Zuni answered as if predicting something momentous. "But I have a little surprise for you. A friend of mine, Tumahka Inoote, is holding a costume party here tonight by special invitation."

"Are we special enough?" I asked. "Or do you have to be an Indian chief?"

"Friends of mine are friends of Tumahka's. They've laid on a special car coming the other way from Chama, and it's going to have a whole lot of costumes aboard. When we get to Osier for lunch, if you want, the three of us can switch trains, and come back to the party here in Sublette. They're sending a late locomotive and second car full of party goers up from Antonito, and that train at midnight will take us all back down to Chama."

"How in the hell did this Inoote get the railroad to agree to opening up the old house, putting on the extra engine and cars, and the special late train ride back?" I asked.

"Lots of money," the Indian answered with a smile. "Although Tumahka is a Zuni from his mother's side, his late father was a Jicarilla Apache who left him huge stakes in oil and natural gas holdings. When Tumahka donated $1 million to the railroad, the Cumbres & Toltec people discovered that trading the party he had in mind for a few friends in return for his substantial donation was an offer they couldn't refuse."

"Free drinks?" asked Ristraverdé.

The Zuni took a long look out at the pine and aspen stands surrounding the ridge. "Think of it as your lucky day. You won't get the *hozro* feeling Diné like Ketl seek to put themselves in harmony with their surroundings. But Anglo as well as Native American bliss will still be attainable. Even though you'll wonder how it all comes together, there'll be plenty to drink and eat, as well as an array of beautiful ladies in costumes. If there's one thing Tumahka Inoote doesn't mind doing, it's spending money to have a good time."

After the water tanks were refilled, we set off toward the Mud Tunnel and Phantom Curve. By the time the train passed through the Rock Tunnel and by Garfield Monument high above the Toltec Gorge, we were still outside in the kind of spring air city dwellers seldom experience. It wasn't far to Osier and lunch, and I had built up a powerful appetite just bouncing along as if the three amigos were on a Robert Mitchum-like railroad river of no return.

Ristraverdé was beside the partially open window, peering out as if he were riding to the penitentiary south of Santa Fe. The old woman across the aisle could be heard in the middle of another rambling dissertation on Midwestern family life or similar perilous journeys she has made unscathed, while Aldebaran's face remained just as blank as the Native American tribal stereotype could be. The Miss Marple simulacrum was suffused with the self-importance of those no longer able to hold sway in the world of the young and restless. Chichilticalli was playing the dumb Indian simply because responding to anything the ancient one was shouting merely meant more of the same sonorous monologue.

The Osier dining hall was rustically reminiscent of the Estes Park hotel Jack Nicholson might be caretaking in the Shining. Except that it was sunny and lunchtime. I got in the turkey rather than roast beef or salad line, which led through a cafeteria-style serving area where I got a huge tray of turkey, stuffing, and all the trimmings. The room behind the obligatory curio shop was cavernous, with maybe forty picnic tables filled with passengers gaining enough sustenance to sit out the afternoon ride down into Chama.

Chichilticalli was right. The added car to the eastbound train was like a moving cocktail party on rails. At one end were some jury-rigged velvet curtains through the middle of which anyone lacking a costume could go and try on duds for the evening or wash up in the rear restroom. I decided upon General Custer, or whatever one becomes when wearing a fringed tan leather jacket with matching gloves and a pair of mock six-shooters. Kaliber got all duded out like Cochise, or whoever finds a headband and facial paint just the ticket for the high country. The best way to describe Chichilticalli was maybe the Cisco Kid or Hopalong Cassidy. He had on a double-breasted black shirt with chrome silver buttons down each side and sported a pair of pearl-handled revolvers I should have nabbed as Custer. The rule about no alcohol had also flown with the sparrows, a mini bar at the back offering anything from wine and cerveza to Jack on the rocks.

It wasn't much more than an hour and our car was shunted onto a parallel track and high ridge in Sublette. Inside the old house was decorated with red and green strands of chili pepper lights and both a real Wurlitzer and illuminated faux Coors juke boxes. Above the main room hung a revolving mirrored ball to catch the light from small spotlights as well as sconce candle lighting appropriate to the whole antique feeling of what the place probably had once been before being closed more than 40 years ago.

Apparently, some other folks, including Inoote, had ridden the special one-car train up from Antonito. The host was accompanied by an entourage of prosperous dudes and those kitted out as if going to the chateau party in To Catch A Thief. Normally the costumes alone would not reveal such munificence, but many of the older and younger sets were sporting expensive fertility necklaces, tiaras, and diamond brooches or stickpins. Then the Indian was correct about the babes. Many of these ladies of the evening had made décolletage into an art form. Pocahontas had nothing on any of stunners ranging from naughtily dressed schoolgirls to maybe well-endowed Hispanic, Native American, and European royalty in their early 40s.

The evening unfolded much like a Super Bowl day. The game began with plenty of hoopla and a welcome by Mr. Tumahka Inoote, Soon, however, the juke box music was pumping out hits varying from country, to rock, Motown and hip-hop, while medicinal beverages and canapés ensured that everyone got into the requisite lunacy ideal for such occasions. Diamonds caught the light, dancers caught their breath, adventuresome sorts caught one another in the upstairs bedrooms, and I even caught Kaliber dancing by himself to the song Afternoon Delight. What are tripping the light fantastic and spilling a few drinks amongst new and old friends, anyway? It was the kind of night when the smell of pine resin and scent of Jungle Gardenia intermingled with the same intensity as the terpsichorean efforts of the costumed revelers.

Yours truly had just had a spin round with a woman named Candace, dressed as someone you might expect usually performs as a hostess in Rose's Saloon. I was feeling no pain, having consumed enough shots of Jack and Don Julio to find Candace more than enchanting. It was probably going on about 9:30 p.m., and the music and lights and perfume and drinks and whirling colors had all enabled the entire soirée to reach a point of semi-levitation.

Then there she was. Best described as a curvaceous middle-aged siren dressed in all black. You could tell she had an attitude because of her cocked hip with one arm akimbo. Very little of her pale face was showing under a Lone Ranger mask and bolero hat. A tapered black silk cowboy shirt revealed white hemispheres partially escaping from a black lace bra, the sort of invitation a spider displays to passing insects. That's O.K., though. When you've had enough tequila, and the silver concho shells on a mysterious woman's hat and sequins on her jet-black cowboy boots are catching the light just so, the desired effect takes over. She reminded me of a slightly older version of Ashleigh, who always wore black, and always meant trouble.

What was even less timely was that Candace recognized someone she knew from Abiquiu, and before I knew it, I was standing alone next to a tall black *chollo* growing out of a pot. I then decided stepping outside for a little of the Colorado-New Mexico border mountain air might be wise.

Just off the front porch were the Cumbres tracks, and even though a couple of revelers were chasing each other round the water tower off to the west, I was alone in the cool night with the Big Dipper as an overhead companion.

"I believe it's Mr. Quivira Cantrell," suddenly came a voice from behind me. There was also something decidedly nasty poking me in the back I hoped was a finger and not a 38.

The voice was strangely familiar. It was almost as if my former wife's sister, Ashleigh, had come back from the dead and was now here to taunt me. I didn't turn around, waiting for this woman of the night to reveal herself. Yet we both stood there in silence. Maybe she hoped the gravity of the impending situation would set in. I had no idea whether this strange female behind me had anything in mind other than the same thing I did: a bit of fresh air.

"I'll trouble you for that Cortez Ruby Scepter sticking up from inside your boot—and you may wish to know that I'm not just glad to see you, that's a gun in your back."

I exhaled a cloud of breath forming a mist quickly evaporating in the hazy light from the house windows. I could hear "It's close to midnight..." of Michael Jackson's Thriller vibrating from within, but the song merely served as a counterpoint to the potential seriousness of the lady's last statement. How could she have known that when I unearthed the larger Mogollon Cross, I had also found a silver scepter inlaid with rubies, reputedly having found its way north from Cortés' Mexican adventures, that I had intentionally failed to reveal to old man Ketl? Who was this mysterious woman sounding like my former sister-in-law with a contralto instead of the deeper throaty voice of a smoker? I had an inclination it was the woman in black. But that was just a hunch, and I have learned from previous such hunches that perceptions after copious quantities of alcohol can be deceiving.

Then whatever it was in my back was pushing me sideways. Apparently, she wanted to get me away from the front of the house and round the back. But she kept nudging me, and I had had just enough to drink that I wasn't quite sure if the whole thing were a party prank or an amusingly daring railroad robbery. We began to move down among some aspen trees, and still she kept prodding me along. By then I figured maybe this was all a ploy for some slinky businesswoman to get laid. Somehow, she had found out about the ruby scepter and was feigning a robbery to enable getting her knickers off somewhere down amongst the aspens.

"Just keep moving," the voice said.

"Sit down against that tree and wrap your arms around it behind you," she soon commanded. Again, the resonance of the voice sounded very similar to what I remembered Ashleigh's to be from 15 years ago. *Nah*, I told myself. *Impossible. She died two years ago.* Besides, the voice was higher than I remembered, and that made it more likely a coincidence.

It felt good to sit down against the tree. The illumination from the party house windows could still vaguely be seen maybe a hundred yards away.

"Who are you? And I hope this is Kaliber or Chichilticalli's April Fool's idea of a female bandito stirring up faux male jeopardy."

"Unfortunately for you, I'm no April Fool, nor desperate to get you out here for a quick one amidst the aspens."

I felt my wrists handcuffed behind me around the tree.

"Sorry I have to do this," she said with about as much conviction as a female black widow before devouring her husband. She also put a piece of duct tape over my mouth and taped it to my cheeks. Only then did she step back in front of me, a dark silhouette blocking my view to any possible rescue from above.

"I'm going to leave you now, but don't worry. You'll be rescued in less than two hours. I took the trouble of taking two cell phones out of coat pockets. I noted the number of one and put it back. The other is in my pocket, and both have carriers capable of transmitting or receiving signals this remote from anywhere. When I am far enough away to be on a highway again, I will make the call, and someone from the party will come and get you. Until then, adieu..."

The woman in black disappeared in a vaporous trail down into the darkness of the Rio de Los Pinos canyon below. Undoubtedly, she had left some sort of vehicle on the supply road from Antonito to Osier, and by the time she made the call, would be on her way to Alamosa, Santa Fe or Chama.

Two things still made me think it had been Ashleigh, and that my late shrew of a sister-in-law was still alive. Ashleigh was the only woman I have ever known to wear an oddly pungent Black Queen perfume. And she always left the scene of an interpersonal crime with the word, 'Adieu.'

# Kokopelli's Flute

(KATARINA)

The last thing I needed was another trip to Chaco Canyon. Desert excursions for someone in her eighth decade are as appealing as a lack of liquid anesthesia for eliminating the aches and pains attendant with one's ancient state. I told Kahlo before we went to bed in some rustic motel in Farmington, that this would be our last trip for a long time. She would be reentering school in Santa Fe soon, and I would be reentering the world of non-chauffeur and largely sedentary elder stateswoman. She's a clever and enchanting little dervish, but after you've seen one pile of sandstone rubble and then another and another, eventually you realize that the reason the Anasazi probably left these arid surroundings and desert dwellings behind meant they had had enough, as well.

Still Kahlo was intent upon some sort of investigation regarding Kokopelli, the flute-playing icon from the early second millennium. I acquiesced to her entreaty to return to Chaco solely because I knew what disappointment lay in store for the diminutive, braided wonder when she reentered the more predictable elementary school. It's the sort of thing grandmothers do, anyway, and as I've convinced myself many times in the past, shepherding Kahlo remains a partial guarantee that I limit my vodka intake for the day.

The miniature adventuress gained the same exhilaration from her desert investigations I once derived from childhood piano concerts when what I was capable of playing was considered prodigious. She was a little Annie Oakley without the six shooters. Cut her loose amidst some cactus and crumbling ruins and her excitement paralleled what most children exude while watching cartoons. She loved the serendipitous discovery, and her speech impediment ensured that she spent a great deal more time cogitating upon such delights than being able to share them with others.

But what was all this leading to? What if the little wonder was onto astro-archeological revelations that had some real impact on the powers that be? And if her findings were of true value, would it bring the sort of public attention that makes a child's speech pattern even worse?

Still, a long time ago my daughter Aurore and I reached the conclusion that encouragement was far better than discouragement when it comes to the foibles of precocious daughters. I know. I was one once, and so once was my daughter a *wünderkind* of the publishing industry. Certainly, many could argue that my drinking is a result of my inability to fit in with most of my fellow citizens. But I would counter that this terminal habit has more to do with an inability to turn the clock back to one's previous youthful beauty, energy, and boundless enthusiasm.

I have to say that each time I made the dusty, bumpy journey over those 23 miles or so into Chaco from highway 550, it got easier. Even though the speed limit is 35, over time 45 felt more appropriate for most sections lacking judder ridges, and I could lose myself in thought just as Kahlo did while gazing out the window and dreaming of past civilizations. I took certain sustenance from the reality that I would not be making this dusty journey again for a long time. At least that's what I thought.

After we paid our entry fee and drove down the loop road, I

didn't like the looks of what was approaching from the west. A bank of purplish black clouds appeared like a hostile army about to overwhelm under-prepared forces. Yet when I inquired at the desk in the Visitor Center, a ranger assured that rain rarely came to Chaco Canyon. Maybe the odds were only a little stronger than getting hit by lightning. Yet in a life the length of mine, when you have seen almost every hazard and calamity come and go, one tends to be skeptical of pending nasty weather.

Anyway, it turned out I was wrong about Kokopelli—at least in terms of Kahlo's wishing to see any more pictographs on canyon walls. Apparently, she had seen what she needed on the previous trip while hiking with her Midwestern chaperones to the western edge of Chaco and Peñasco Blanco. With the skies appearing like the late summer and fall monsoons were coming early, my granddaughter's intent was to hike the perhaps five-mile loop up to Tsin Kletsin and back. Something about what she had learned about Kokopelli when she was drinking a Coke while last here with me.

I told her she couldn't go alone, but Kahlo got one of those looks that dissuade guardians from any necessary measure of restraint. I knew I was in for a long day if I insisted the nine-year-old adventuress wait to be accompanied by one or several adult visitors intent upon privacy in explorations. So I relented. I did insist that she take a hooded plastic raincoat along with her water bottle and energy bars in her backpack. Yet foolishly in one of those moments when one deludes oneself that youthful adventures can still be shared by the elderly, I decided I would accompany her. After all, if it did start to rain, I would worry that my granddaughter then would be all alone on an extensive South Mesa upon which lightning could strike or unexpected perils could sneak up from unknown haunts.

After she had filled out another of those trailhead forms which I suppose alert Chaco rangers as to who might have left a car for a hike and then never returned, off we went. Kahlo gamboled on ahead up the path from Casa Rinconada. The trip promised to be long and arduous for yours truly, and as we set off, I had the premonition my choice hovered between circumspection and quixotic septuagenarian madness.

I had planned to go for a walk round Chetro Ketl, which Kahlo says was once called Kettle, to delay the liquid pain relief I always fall back upon while sitting in the car. In coffee book photos the giant kivas to me all looked the same: round and Masonic, with the question lingering as to what any group, Anasazi or other, could have spent so much time constructing to enable sitting in a circle. It did help me better to understand Kahlo's curiosity, however. I mean, what were these sunburned souls doing out in the middle of these high desert plains and canyons for seven hundred years? Naturally, everyone tries to figure out why they just up and left. My own guess is that there were no fast-food emporia or coffee houses available during protracted droughts. No caffeine, bottled water, or junk food. That's probably why Kahlo and I make such an ideal odd couple: I put just enough restraint upon the child to prevent drastic mistakes in judgment; she makes discoveries with such enthusiasm, her excitement infects my perennial skepticism as well as mitigates the accompanying sarcastic attitude. Besides, just what was up at Tsin Kletsin did arouse even my jaded curiosity.

After an initial climb getting us up about a hundred feet above the canyon, the path fortunately leveled off. It wasn't really a path, but rather a vague continuance over flat rocky outcroppings marked by little cairns denoting the direction in which hikers were to proceed up to mesa top. At least the dark clouds to the west seemed to be log-jammed at the Arizona-New Mexico border. It was exasperating enough for Kahlo to have to wait at each new level until I caught up. All she needed is my usual critical demeanor to return if a downpour started.

But we made it up to the sprawling, desolate mesa top, and at first nothing of note was visible to the south but more sagebrush, tiny desert flowers, and a winding path through the sandy soil. Yet as we climbed just slightly higher in elevation, the Tsin Kletsin ruins gradually appeared on the southern horizon. Kahlo was getting excited, and I was stopping every hundred feet or so to rest my weary bones. The little investigator was probably covering double the distance by darting back and forth to make sure I hadn't tripped on a prickly pear cactus or sat down on a cairn to expire.

During the whole ascent we had seen no one, which was both bad and good. Bad in the sense that should we come upon several coyotes or fall and break a bone, there would be no other humans to come to assistance. Good because one got the feeling the two of us were back in the eleventh or twelfth centuries scouting locations for ideal new mesa-top dwellings.

When I finally skirted round to where I could walk up to the actual Tsin Kletsin ruins, Kahlo was already zigging and zagging here and there like a child looking for Easter eggs. She sat on the edge of a small kiva and kicked her legs out, then galloped down to peer round the remains of a rectangular courtyard below the north side.

It is said that Tsin Kletsin nearly aligns with Casa Rinconada and Pueblo Alto above the other side of Chaco Canyon. Kahlo says the three are aligned within one degree of due north. I could vaguely see Pueblo Alto in the distance and wondered if the Anasazi had figured out that the entire sky revolved around the North Star. I wasn't yet aware that the North Star due to its precession hadn't been as close to due north at the turn of the first millennium. But Kahlo was soon to correct that oversight.

As we began our descent, I wondered how in the world the pair of us were to get down to the South Gap without jumping off a cliff. Once we had reached the edge of the mesa, the trail became indistinct as it threaded amongst various magenta and dull mustard rock formations and outcroppings. Bounding from boulder to boulder is not the sort of thing a grandmother attempts lightly. Kahlo held my hand to help me down one particularly abrupt drop to another small sandstone plateau. Yet with the clouds to the west increasingly darkening, I again questioned my sanity in having undertaken an expedition under threat of a storm. Even though that Visitor Center ranger had assured us that it rarely rains in Chaco in spring, weather in the West often defies prediction, and so I accepted that while the skies might threaten to unleash a torrent, the likelihood of any such daunting prospect remained minimal. Factual material of the same worth corresponds to that of alcohol in moderation being harmless.

Still, here the disparate pair of interlopers from the East were, descending off a remote mesa into an L-shaped box canyon with the gods of Chaco about to exact revenge. I could only hope in what Kahlo has described as the cosmology of the Pueblo culture, that these gods would hold off on casting lightning bolts and thunderclaps down upon us.

Once reaching the box canyon floor, however, we at least began a rolling continuation of a discernible trail with little more decline. Off to the right was what appeared to be a long black snake weaving its way within the canyon wall. The dark indentation appeared an extended volcanic basalt tunnel ideal as a landmark pointing to buried treasure.

We were still making progress out to the South Gap hopefully leading back to the main canyon valley, when the heavens opened up. The deluge quickly created a variety of channeled rivulets of water streaming down perpendicular arroyos toward the canyon floor. Kahlo helped me put on a plastic parka like the one she had donned, then held my hand as the two of us continued our journey on a trail rapidly becoming soggier underfoot from the downpour. It little mattered that the spring squall was an anomaly. We still had more than a mile to get back to Casa Rinconada and the car, and I wasn't sure if my weary legs could get me there.

Over the top of the box canyon west wall flashes could be seen from distant lightning. Kahlo's Reebok hiking boots gave her the appearance of Minnie Mouse, their once grey-blue nylon and rubber having accumulated extra width from the wet dun-colored sandy soil accreted on her soles. My Nike trainers were doing a lot better, even though with exposed ankles the risk of rattlesnake bites had made me nervous before the weather undoubtedly drove all such critters undercover.

My granddaughter and I slipped and slid over narrow portions of the gradually descending trail, finally reaching what I felt confident was the South Gap leading back to our point of origin and a potentially dry rent-a-car interior. Yet as if we had again offended the spirits of our ancient Pueblo hosts, the rains became heavier. Kahlo gripped my hand tighter, and I could only hope we would eventually survive the wrath of these Chaco gods for having invaded their cosmological demesne.

# Quivira's Folly

(KALIBER)

All I knew was some woman named Candace and I had downed a cup of Jack Daniels each and were up to no good. We had used the ruse that with the music loud and Candace pretending like one of her breasts had accidentally dislodged from a red satin sheath dress, I was able to steal the Jack bottle while the bartender was blankly staring and thinking he needed to try and get a phone number.

Upstairs, Candace or Anisette or whatever her name was, and I somehow got into a bedroom closet that had one of those old iron keys, and locked ourselves in. It was a tight fit, and anybody coming into that bedroom must have heard us bashing around inside the closet. And yet there's something about being totally inebriated that makes you indifferent to any such discovery. The closet had that musty smell probably deriving from mouse droppings. Yet after a half quart of Jack Daniels and a couple of Patron margaritas thrown in to get warmed up, the confined space of the closet seemed a little bit of paradise.

We had finally got Candace out of her dress and were trying to relieve ourselves of any more garments encumbering further explorations, when someone shouted: "Hey, does anyone know a QUIVIRA CANTRELL?"

My first inclination was to ignore this importunate question.

I mean there wasn't just the interruption to what decidedly was progressing toward untold delights, but also the challenge, should we respond, of reappearing from the closet fully clothed. I ignored the call.

But the person kept shouting in all the upstairs rooms, loudly enough over the music that I figured maybe the entreaty was really about some distressing event that needed to be answered, even if it were an awkward pain in the ass and downer considering the true spirit of the evening.

When the two of us reemerged from our potentially exotic entanglement most associate with the back seat of a car at a drive-in movie, neither of us had a clue as to whether we had got on all of what we had taken off, nor whether we had put these various partially torn items back where they belonged. Neither of us cared. Luckily, few others we observed on the way out of the bedroom and stumble down the hall could discern such anomalies, anyway. I still felt good from the agave plant distillate and Jack, and I convinced myself that whatever trouble we might have gotten up to had merely been delayed. We would take care of the Cantrell problem, then find the closet or a stand of aspens to continue where we had left off.

"What has our friend Cantrell got himself up to then?" I asked a woman dressed as maybe Alice in Wonderland.

"Do you know him?" she yelled, dropping a Corona bottle over the balustrade. "Somehow some woman got my cell phone number and is asking for someone who knows this guy named Quantrill or Cantrell, or something like that. She didn't say who she is. She just said he's in trouble, and that one of the two friends he came with better rescue him."

"Yah, well, I don't know how the Q-man could have cocked up at a party off in the boonies like this, but I'll take the call." She handed me her cell, then used the banister to steady herself on the way back downstairs to a first floor full of whirling dancers and other frivolous nightcrawlers.

"Yo, this is Kaliber Ristraverdé. What kind of trouble has Cantrell got himself into, then?"

"He's in deep shit out...and...rescued." That's all I heard as some Four Tops Mo-town song was blasting up the stairwell and Blandace or Candace was kissing my ear as if the two of us were alone.

"Yah, could you say that again?" I shouted. "I've got a banana in my ear."

"He's—tied—to—a—tree!" the woman shouted. "About—a hundred—yards southwest of—Sublette Party Central!"

"Who is this?" I yelled as Candace slumped to the floor and I helped her back up to grasp the railing. "I can't hear a thing, even though I thought what you just said is that CANTRELL IS TIED TO A TREE!"

"I did!" I heard her garbled voice snarl just as the music temporarily stopped below. "Never mind who this is. If you don't want him to be eaten by coyotes or to expire from alcohol withdrawal, UNTIE HIS ASS FROM THE ASPEN TREE!"

We got him loose with the key she had said would be in his front shirt pocket and tore half his face off removing the duct tape. But there wasn't much more than his ego in tatters, and he seemed to take it with just a few loud curses and the breaking of an aspen branch over a nearby tree trunk. I guess I would have been furious, myself. Neither the Indian nor I immediately tried to pry anything out of him about what had happened. We figured in good time on the train ride back we'd find out. Then I wasn't in any condition to hear a long-winded story right then, anyway. And by the time we got him moving, it was 10 minutes after midnight. The train had blown its whistle with enough emphasis that if you wanted to get back to Chama, you'd better be on board with or without Candace, further liquid refreshments, or any clothing possibly left behind in odd places.

None of us needed the jostling of the antique Pullman car on the long ride back. Most fell asleep leaning on one another. Yet encumbered by the jaded but inquisitive mind I have for good stories, I had to find out from Q-man what the hell had happened to get him tied to a tree. I mean, how does a huge man like that get into a predicament in the middle of nowhere?

"Yah, well, she kind of caught me off guard," he said, slumping down on the Naugahyde-upholstered bench and jostling my shoulder as the old steamer went round a bend. "And there are two things I can't figure out. The first is, could this woman in black and a Lone Ranger mask have actually been my late former sister-in-law, Ashleigh, or was I just hallucinating on the tequila? And the second would be how she knew I had the Cortez Ruby Scepter? She had on the same perfume Ashleigh once wore, she was the same height and weight. But her voice was slightly higher, and she had that same sort of nasty-assed attitude that eventually made people want to kill her. And as far as we all know, she left the planet in a timely manner!"

"How did you ever get tied to a tree," I asked, Chichilticalli having fallen asleep against a window across the aisle.

"Good question. I had just stepped outside the party house to get some air, when a woman came up behind me and stuck what I assumed was a pistol in my back. She told me to give her the Scepter, and it was the kind of demand that conveys your ass is going to get shot if you don't produce it. Besides, at the time I still figured one of you guys had put her up to it, and that it was all a ridiculous party spoof. In my well-oiled state, I was just deluded enough to think there was also the lurid possibility that someone had dared her to see if the two of us could get up to something naughty out in the sticks. I handed over the miniature Scepter I had stuck in my boot, figuring I would get it back after the whole contrived incident was revealed to be a party scam. By the time I found myself handcuffed around an aspen tree far enough from the house that no one would ever find me, I finally began to feel some demented concern. There was something wrong with the scenario: I had neither a drink in my hand nor a view of a woman undressing in the wild."

All the while Cantrell was recounting this bizarre incident, I was having trouble staying awake. His voice was going in and out of my consciousness as the old tooter continued to wind through head-lit tunnels, along ridges or across the edges of valleys only partially illuminated by a full moon and the engine's beacon. I don't remember much more until in the middle of the night, with a light rain now falling, we found ourselves at a standstill in Chama station. As sleepy party survivors stumbled by me, I wondered who in our wildest imagination had been the woman in black? And would we ever see her or Q-man's lost Scepter again? Of course, I knew both answers.

# Kahlo Washed Up

(KAHLO)

Grammy and I were soaked through and through when we finally climbed out of the car and walked to the Visitor Center. Gram said we could sit in the car and use the heater, but that that would just waste gas, and besides, it would be warmer inside and we could walk around to let our clothes dry a little. She was in a bad mood, and I diverted off to the separate restrooms beside the parking lot. There was a good chance if I left Grammy alone, she'd have time to swallow some of the clear liquid she considers her pain medicine. When you're Gram's age, it's hard for anyone to tell you what to do, anyway. And besides, Gram always says that we self-prescribe the drugs we each think we need. I never did understand what she meant by that, but Gram reminded me when I questioned her that I would find out all about that later in a long life before me.

It was still raining, though not as hard, almost as if the *Kachinas* of Chaco couldn't decide just how much they should discourage all of us visitors having invaded their ancient realm. So much for monsoons only in the summer.

My cowgirl shirt was only slightly damp since I had put my hooded plastic jacket on fast. But my jeans and socks inside my hiking boots were soaked. I didn't know what we were going to do about getting back to Farmington.

It was probably about 4:30 and the skies still looked as dark as storms used to look over the Atlantic Ocean. There wasn't much light coming in the Visitor Center's tall windows when Gram finally told me that since the only food available was tomato juice from a machine in the center, we needed to get going. Our clothes were still wet. But since we planned on driving back to our motel in Farmington, we hadn't brought any other stuff to put on, and I had eaten the last energy bar I brought in my backpack.

Even on the paved part of the road out, it was hard for Grammy to see. The windshield wipers were taking care of the rain, but it was misty everywhere, kind of like it is near a pond early on a spring morning. We were just passing the road sign facing the other way that announces the Chaco Culture National Historical Park, when a ranger standing next to a big four-wheel drive truck waved us to a stop.

"The wash is running pretty high," said the ranger with braids and water dripping off his cap. "You might want to take a look at it before trying to get across." The tone of his voice and how he said it was the way I thought Pueblos and Navajos talked. I had read lots about them, including a bunch of the Hillerman mysteries, but Chichilticalli was the only one with whom I had spoken much. A vision said we're related, and I wondered if I could ever sound like him. Anyway, to me, what the ranger had just said seemed to be a thinly disguised warning.

Grammy just shook her head, and then tapped her forehead down lightly on the steering wheel. "How far is it to the wash?"

"Maybe three or four miles," he answered before climbing back into his truck and winding down the window. "It's pretty muddy going out. You might want to think about the campground."

Gram's face looked the worst I had seen it since one of her last arguments with Auntie Ashleigh. We had two sleeping bags and a tarp still in the trunk from when Mom and I camped out near Los Alamos. But the campground we had just passed by near an east mesa wall wasn't the sort of place Grammy approved of. She liked beds and showers. And I knew she would be worried sick about getting me some food, even though I wasn't that hungry. But I could tell Gram resigned herself to our turning back to the campground. The road out would probably be really muddy in places anyway, and it seemed like we had no choice.

Before Gram went into the Visitor Center to pay the camping fee, she took a big swallow from a silver flask she normally doesn't like me to see. Then after we drove to the campground, most of those already camping had put up tents along the edge of the mesa. There were lots of camping spots along the muddy road in and a large white RV where you were supposed to check in.

"Nasty weather, eh?" said a kind man inside of the RV. His volunteer co-host wearing a large turquoise fertility necklace over a blue blouse with jeans and snakeskin cowboy boots just nodded sympathetically.

"We came unprepared for this," Grammy mumbled with her eyes downcast. "We just have two sleeping bags and no food,"

The man disappeared into the back of the RV. But soon he returned with a yellow tent in his hand. "You can borrow this if you want. You might want to find a high spot to put it. Even though it's waterproof, if you don't, you might wake up with water coming in over the door flap. This storm is only supposed to be followed by another one."

"And I'm sorry we can't offer you more," said his wife as she handed us some Wheat Thins, a bar of cheese and a plastic knife, "but the park policy of having no food available holds down usage." I knew I would be hungry enough later that her offerings were better than a Christmas stocking.

The night was bad. Gram had to climb out of the car into the rain and lightning flashes several times to walk to the restrooms. I let her have the air mattress for under her sleeping bag, but while sleeping for a couple hours at a time in the tent by myself I still was able to dream about something to do with the Zuni-Acoma Trail.

In the morning there was running water in the Gallo Wash below the campground and some of the other tents had water around them. After returning the tent to the hosts, we drove to the Visitor Center, where one of the nice rangers arriving at the same time said she would lend me some jeans and a sweatshirt she had on hand for when her daughter visited. She was about Grammy's size, so she also said Gram could borrow a pair of jeans and a blouse while our clothes dried in her dryer. As we drove to her nearby house under the mesa wall, she told us the Center wasn't open yet, and that they were having a meeting in the theater.

"We're trying to collaborate with an educator from NASA to develop a children's program for astro-archeological explanations of Anasazi architecture," the lady ranger told Gram and me while she was loading our clothes in the dryer. "We can pinpoint their archeological alignments with the cardinal directions as well as knowledge they had of the solstices and equinoxes. But beyond that we're trying to develop more facts fun for kids."

"I have some ideas," came out of my mouth without any interruption. The sound of my own voice kind of surprised me. But then maybe her kindness toward Grammy and me by lending us the clothing helped.

"You do?"

I nodded.

"We'd sure love to hear them. Right now, several of us are meeting with Katalyn Morgen of NASA in the auditorium, and it would be great if you could share any of your ideas with us. We need input, and your ideas would be really helpful."

I nodded, and before I knew it, we had returned to the Visitor

Center and were walking toward the theater. Gram didn't come with us. She was tired and just wanted to sit on a couch by the window off to one side from the ranger desk with the huge topographic map behind it.

I was getting real nervous. It was one thing to talk to someone I felt confident with, but even Grammy often makes me stutter. Maybe it's because I feel like my own relatives are always judging my behavior, and that everything I do isn't good enough. It's not because they don't always encourage me, because they do. But I always feel like they wish I was more normal and did things like play with other kids and watch TV. Mom says I'm too sensitive.

There were three more in ranger uniforms and four other people who looked like scientists or administrators sitting in the front row in the theater, and a woman was talking from a chair and desk in front of them. She was using an overhead projector, but even though the lights were still dimmed, I could see the people from the Center as well as a photograph she had up of Pueblo Bonito. It was from a low angle and there were stars above it.

She smiled at me with a very warm look. "Everyone, this is Kahlo, and she might have some ideas about our program for kids," said the NASA educator with the nametag of Katalyn Morgen. She didn't introduce me to each one, which was good, because I don't do well with too many new people all at once. "If you need me to project any drawings you may have, just let me know," she added, glancing down at my backpack. And then she sat down beside me.

I'm going to have a hard time explaining what happened next. It had to do with looking at Rangers Luminita Lopez and Plentyhorn as well as six other faces I didn't know at all. The same thing has happened all my life. Mom or Grammy or someone else tries to give me an opportunity to express myself, and it's all like a bad dream. I tell myself not to worry, that they're just people. But then when I go to say something and see these adults all looking at me with anticipation, I choke up. Sometimes I even get dizzy while looking into their eyes. I start playing with my braids, praying that I will be able to tell them something that will make them realize I'm not just a stupid little kid with a speech impediment. But the pattern almost always repeats. I know what I want to say and think I can impress them that I'm normal if only I can get the words out smoothly. But then I stutter. And once I hear myself stutter, it only makes it worse. It's almost like a *chindi* evil spirit is keeping my mouth moving but nothing is coming out coherently.

"I-I-I m-m-may have it all wrong," I tried to begin, "b-b-but..."

Then nothing more came out.

I told myself that Gram would be disappointed, and Mom would be disappointed, and all of them would think I'm stuttering because I don't really have anything interesting to say. I just sat there next to the NASA lady, who was smiling at me to be reassuring, and I just froze. She was as encouraging and patient as she could be, but when I looked back at the eight in a row staring, I got these prickly points all over my arms and neck and felt the same dizzy spells I always get.

"I-I-I c-c-can't..." came out as the pinpoints of shock went up and down from my arms into my shoulders and neck.

Then I couldn't help it. I started crying.

Katalyn Morgen put her hand on my shoulder and told me "Don't worry, Kahlo." But I knew I had done it again, and I just couldn't stop my speechlessness and tears. It's times like these that the humiliation and disappointment make me want to jump off a cliff. I just wanted to get in the car and ride anywhere... Never see anyone again...Give up all my Anasazi speculations.

I was still looking down at the floor and wiping my eyes with the sleeve of my cowgirl shirt and hoping that it was all a bad dream when Katalyn helped walk me out of the theater. I stopped crying as best I could on the way. I know you think I should be able to stop, but sometimes I can't. The tears keep coming like I'm insane. You wouldn't understand how painful it is. Not to be able to say anything, especially when you want people to know that even if you're no good at speaking, you're still working as hard as you can to learn everything around you.

On the way through the lobby, I was going to go over to check on Gram, but she was asleep on the couch with her head tilting back against the window. Katalyn Morgen took me back into an office and sat me down. She reassured me that it was O.K., not to worry, that young kids often have trouble talking to a group of adults, and that is another reason the Cultural Centers need to develop separate programs for kids. "Building confidence takes time," she told me before further reassuring me that whenever I felt like it, she would always be available to hear my ideas by phone or e-mail.

I still felt the same humiliation I always get at times like those. But at least I stopped crying. I just wished Gram and me could go back to Farmington. I never wanted to see Chaco Canyon again.

Then I got one of the biggest surprises in my life. Chichilticalli walked into the office. I didn't know if I should, but I gave him a big hug. He seemed embarrassed, but gave me a big grin and took off his cap.

"I'm just on the way back from the Cumbres & Toltec Scenic Railway and two friends just dropped me off. Am I late for the meeting?" he then asked while looking over at Katalyn.

"We've started, and Kahlo was going to give us some input. But she's been up much of the night in the campground due to the storm, and we've agreed she might want to help us out when she's more rested."

I could tell even Chichilticalli knew that it was a lie. That I had tried, but then couldn't explain anything due to my stutter.

"I'll bet you wanted to tell them your ideas about the baths," he smiled at me. The funny thing is, just after he said it, he put his hand on my shoulder. I can't explain it, but maybe because I believe he's probably my real dad and I've never had one, just that gesture suddenly relaxed me. It's like you don't have an ounce of confidence and suddenly someone you admire helps you gain an ability usually completely missing. I knew I was in this magic room, and I could talk properly.

I nodded about the baths. "But I couldn't."

"Katalyn?" a voice abruptly came through an intercom. "Could you come back in the auditorium, please? Please extend to Kahlo our apologies, but we've stopped for coffee and in about 10 minutes or so would like to continue."

Katalyn looked down at the intercom, put on her reading glasses, and then flicked a switch. "I'll be back in just a couple of minutes," she said.

"Do you think you could tell Katalyn about what you told me on your bath theories?" asked Chichilticalli.

It was mystifying how I was able to tell. I went through everything I had speculated upon with Grammy about the Great North Road, and then to Chichilticalli about my baths ideas. I said it all without stuttering. The more I explained the visions, the more confident I felt. For some reason, their paying attention to me made me relaxed like a person used to talking easily with others feels. I could tell neither of them was judging me, and more and more of my visions and impressions came back to me like motion pictures as I continued. "When I was up at Casa Rinconada, and looked down into the Great Kiva, I envisioned it filled with water, and a priest dropping into the water of the small room on the north end and then following the light at the other end of the underwater ramp until he appeared to walk out into the kiva full of shallow water. Even when Gram and I went up to Tsin Kletsin, I thought, 'What if the lower rectangular walled courtyard below the north side was a bath in which they could sit and look north to Pueblo Alto?'"

"I guess they carried the water up there in pots..." Katalyn encouraged me as if she were imagining how they filled a bath on top of a mesa.

I nodded. Yet what she said reminded me of what had happened with the Coke can and Gram. I didn't know if I should bring it up or not. But I decided if I was ever going to, right then I might do it without stuttering. "Originally I think they did use springs, collect rainwater in cisterns, or carry their water in pots," I said before pausing to get more courage. "But what if around the $12^{th}$ century they began to use hydraulics?"

"You mean for the water?" Katalyn asked.

"Mm-huh." I started fiddling with a braid because I wasn't sure if they'd think my theory was crazy. But then I looked over at Chichilticalli and a strange power from his eyes gave me confidence.

"The last time I was here with Grammy we were having a picnic. I started drinking out of a Coke can with a straw when I suddenly realized that the liquid coming from the can to my mouth was defying gravity. From my readings at the Santa Fe library, I realized the Coke moving upwards through the straw was illustrating Pascal's law of hydraulics, which says that pressure exerted at any point upon an enclosed liquid is transmitted undiminished in all directions. According to what I saw on the History Channel, Li Bing used the principles in China as far back as the third century, B.C."

Both nodded, but I could tell they were unsure where I was going with my Coke can example.

"Then I remembered the pictographs of Kokopelli I had seen in books and beyond Peñasco Blanco. In every drawing dating back to the first millennium he is playing a flute. And from his flute playing it would seem the Anasazi knew about hollowing out reeds or other pieces of wood. So I thought, "what if they figured out how to use a hollow reed just like I used my straw, but on a much larger scale?"

"You mean, so they could drink out of pottery jars?" asked

Chichilticalli before putting his hands behind his head as if trying to understand.

"Maybe. But what if they could use the principle of hydraulics Pascal would only write about centuries later to convey water to kiva baths? Maybe when the nearby Chaco Wash or springs were running too low. It was because I remembered what I saw when I went on my hike up to Pueblo Alto. While I was up there, I looked very closely at some of the remaining masonry. I could see what seemed to be a narrow rock wall barely above ground which could have contained a hollow sealed tunnel leading off the northeast corner to a mound, and another similar rock wall and possible tunnel off the southern side to a bigger mound south of the ruins.

"I started thinking that the Roman Emperor Marcus Aurelius Antoninus created the Baths of Caracalla between 212 and 219. The Aqua Marcia aqueduct brought water from springs 90 kilometers away. Boilers created hot baths and the Romans used hollow terracotta pipes within the southwest wall of the Calidarium to capture solar energy to heat up the air. What if the Spanish explorers knew all this, told it to Native Americans in Mexico and eventually that knowledge traveled north with Native American traders or the explorers themselves? Or had traveled north centuries earlier from African explorers through the Mayans?

"I was thinking about all that sort of stuff when I was up at Pueblo Alto, and I saw what could be tunnels extending out from the main walls. Then I had one of my visions where I see something, and I can't explain…

"What did you see, Kahlo?" asked Katalyn.

"I don't know if I should say, because nothing in any of the books on the Anasazi reveal they used anything like my ideas."

"That's what we're here for, Kahlo. To develop programs for kids like you to develop their curiosities about the Chacoan and other civilizations. What you've said already shows a lot of important investigation, and we'd sure like to hear what any of your visions or ideas are. They're important, whether right or wrong."

I let go of my braid and looked down. When you're nine years old and about to speculate on how a great past civilization was, supposedly without the wheel and transportation animals, but might have used a part of science officially discovered in the Western world centuries later, suddenly your lack of formal training and age lower your confidence levels. "I-I-I..."

Then a magic electrical current shot through me. Chichilticalli again put his hand on my shoulder and nodded ever so slightly. It probably seems like I'm making it up, but just his hand on my shoulder and the look on his face that he believed in me helped me regain my confidence.

"Well," I said, not sure where to begin. "In my vision, first I saw water coming down the Great North and two other roads that converge to the north below Pueblo Alto. Then I saw water coming up through a masonry tunnel all the way up to the mound east of the pueblo. Standing on top of the mound was a man alternately pulling up and down on a rope at one end of a long pine log balanced on what looked like a wooden modern-day swing set. The log was balanced by a stone hanging from another rope on the other end. At the end of the rope the man was pulling I could see a wood-stone-and-leather disc moving up and down in a vertical pipe. The pipeline was like a hydraulic siphon pulling water up from way down below up to the reservoir. Another man on the south mound was doing the same thing on that mound, pumping water there, that would then travel by gravity through a long trough all the way down to Pueblo Bonito and the rock troughs below the mesa top from which a tunnel carried water into the Great Kiva and other circular cisterns."

Katalyn crossed her arms and leaned back in her chair. She

seemed to be thinking about my ideas. Chichilticalli put his cap back on backwards and smiled at me.

"It's just a vision," I said. "I mean, it could be completely wrong."

Katalyn rubbed her chin. "You know, Kahlo, I think what you've just told us is *very* interesting. Your ideas are just the sort of visions we need. Too many times those who study past civilizations get locked inside a box of linear thinking that only reaffirms existing theories."

"And so, you think that at some point the Anasazi quit carrying most of their water in jars and used a hydraulic system," Chichilticalli nodded while he thought about my ideas at the same time.

I nodded to agree. "And if you look at the photos of the pottery in books, they might have signified what the jars were used for by their painted zig-zag designs. One pattern might have been for carrying grains, another for drinking or cooking water, another for waste products, that sort of thing."

"You mean the patterns told them the purpose of the jars without using written language?"

I again nodded. "If you look at the three pots on page 17 of the book, Chaco, A Cultural Legacy, the irregular pattern, and slightly larger size of the pot on the left could signify it as being used for the deposit and transportation of human waste. Maybe the two jagged patterns above and below on the pot in the middle signify it was used for carrying maize first to be ground up and then to be baked and chewed. And the even, sloping pattern of white and black on the pot on the right could mean it was used to carry water up to any cistern in a pueblo or onto a mesa top."

"You know, this is great stuff, Kahlo. We really appreciate your taking the time to tell us your theories. Unfortunately, Ranger Aldebaran and I need to get back to the meeting. But I hope if you are going back to Farmington today, that you will be able to return to tell us more about what you think the Anasazi were up to. I think it's very likely you may be on to something."

And with that Katalyn Morgen stood up. She had to get going. I hoped she wasn't just polite to me because she didn't want to hurt my feelings. Chichilticalli put his hand on the top of my head before the two of them walked me out to the lobby to join Gram.

The ranger at the front desk said we could go over to ranger Lopez's house and get our dry clothes out of her dryer if we wanted, so Grammy and I went and changed back into our own stuff. We still had the problem of trying to leave if the wash was running over the road. But Gram had talked to someone from the campground with a big four-wheel-drive truck, that he said he had driven out to the wash crossing the road and found concrete less than eight inches below the sand and running water. He said he was going to try crossing and that if we wanted, we could follow him and he could pull us out with a winch if we got stuck.

Gram and I just sat there on the couch and waited while the man with the truck was over collecting all his gear from the campgrounds. Gram was a little cranky because of being afraid of fording the wash, and both of us were tired.

The Visitor Center was just about to open for the day when all the people from the meeting began to come out of the theater.

Before I knew it an elderly man with a neatly trimmed beard and wearing a suit suddenly was looking down at me through wire-rimmed glasses. His nametag said: Dr. Ranulph Benchley, Department of Interior.

"I shouldn't worry if I were you," he smiled while shaking my hand. "I was never very good at speaking to adults when I was young, either. Yet your ideas on the baths are *remarkable*. I hope we shall have an opportunity to talk in the future," he added before turning to go over to the front desk.

Then another man appeared in front of me. He looked like a

dignified Pueblo elder. His nametag read Dr. Robert Begay, Bureau of Indian Affairs. He, too, reached out to shake my hand.

"Thank you, Kahlo. I know it was difficult for you, but I liked your ideas about hydraulics. Keep up your important investigations." And he, too, turned back to talk with another man and woman who had come out of the theater.

It was all very confusing. Several of them were chatting and trying discreetly to peek over at me. How did they know I had said anything about baths and hydraulics?

"Good job, Kahlo," said Ranger Plentyhorn with a huge smile, as he, too, nodded in front of me.

Again, I wondered why all these people who deal with the Chaco Culture National Historical Park Center were being so nice to me. I had screwed up in front of them, and yet they didn't seem to mind at all. All of them but Katalyn soon disappeared into an office behind the front desk, and I felt a little foolish.

Anyway, the man with the truck arrived and Gram said we needed to get going. Katalyn walked over and we thanked her and told her to again thank the kind Ranger Lopez who had lent us the dry clothes.

"Well, your secrets are out now, Kahlo," she smiled. "Apparently when I answered the call to resume the meeting from the theater, I betrayed a confidence of yours."

Gram and I must have had questioning looks, because Katalyn Morgen just gave the biggest smile that made me think my failure in the theater was unimportant.

"When I answered them on the office intercom about returning to the meeting," said Katalyn, "I inadvertently forgot to turn off the 'talk' switch. They heard and recorded everything you said in the office. I apologize that I inadvertently let out your investigations and deductions, Kahlo. But according to Ranger Plentyhorn, you should have seen their faces: several of them used terms like 'provocative' and 'We've found a new committee member...' and the buzz among them was *amazing*!"

# The Late Ashleigh

(AURORE)

It felt good to have several days to myself. I dearly love my mother and daughter, but when you've a lot of time on your hands until you find permanent housing and your wandering cowgirl gets back into school, the constant proximity of two peculiar relatives can be wearing. Not that I'm not self-possessed in my own way, as well. I'm aware of that. Yet even though I abandoned a high-velocity lifestyle in Manhattan to move out to these bizarre desert surroundings, I still need my personal space.

I did a lot of things that one does when lacking focus and wishing to delay the inevitable struggle of condominium hunting. I was pretty sure I was going to take an almost new three-bedroom adobe number up above Bishop's Lodge Road, anyway. But in the meantime, I had indulged myself in such things as mindless shopping, the reading of *Cadillac Desert*, long walks around the delightful downtown areas of Santa Fe, and a variety of boozy lunches and dinners at which my intake of martinis, Bordeaux and Pinot Noirs necessitated napping at the Loretto. I even got chatted up a few times but begged off with the always repellant excuse that I would be rejoining my daughter and mother back at the hotel soon.

There was a lot of thinking to be done about the future. Oh, it may be chic to be on one's own when one has started to color one's hair as a last-gasp effort in a half century of big city survival. Yet I always missed the close companionship of a good male, even if within my soul lurks a secret series of cold-hearted demands for a prospective partner that can never be met. Good looks are always an attribute anyone can find magnetic, but a man with an off-beat sense of humor who has an equal drive for responsibilities and imaginative leisure time is hard to capture.

Then there was my drinking. Sometimes I could go a few days without any liquid crutch; then during other periods could come within a nearly empty 750 milliliter bottle of being a total alchie. Men who don't drink always tell you they don't mind. But you knew they would over time when they discovered what a clever friend the escape mechanism you employ to color the reality of getting older and less physically captivating truly remains.

The two other females in the bloodline were off somewhere in the northwest corner of this vast State, one probably dancing down obscure paths and the other moaning about the things one must do for a grandchild. Still, I missed them both now that they had been gone a couple of days.

Had I been 10 years younger I probably would have taken Mr. Kaliber Ristraverdé back to the Loretto to see if the two of us were still alive. To me he was safe because there was no chance I could ever fall for him. Obviously, the two of us developed the approach-avoidance syndrome in our brief encounters, a restrictive mechanism during which a Viet Nam vet with an attitude and reclusive ways exchanges verbal darts with a woman blessed with cantaloupe-colored hair, an even more off-putting attitude, and the pleasure of *schadenfreude* derived in skirmishing with adventuresome males. Kaliber would have been good fun, and the best part about it was that he would go back to his shack in the middle of that windblown canyon and get right back to rock hunting and all the other things an urban drop-out does to avoid feeling any serious emotions. My escape would be just as predictable, ensuring an ongoing life among women without lesbianism.

When I got back to the hotel, I had three messages. Two were envelopes at the front desk, and the other—since I had left my cell phone in the room—a telephone message from Katarina that the intrepid explorers were coming back to Santa Fe.

My first inclination was wondering how I could possibly have not one, but two written messages separately dropped off at a hotel in a town in which I knew virtually no one. Who could have written me? Maybe an admirer like Chichilticalli Aldebaran? The possibilities, I felt, were limited.

I sat down on one of those sofas that look like pine meets a gigantic, upholstered Navajo rug, and retrieved my reading glasses from off the distressed pine coffee table. The next thing that came to mind, judging by the excitement overwhelming my jaded self, was how truly emotionally destitute I had become. The first note from someone might make my day, and the second cause rampant speculation. Yet then I quickly questioned, *what if one or both bring bad news?*

The first was written in the printed scribble of someone who rarely writes anything, at least by hand.

> Aurore:
> Yah, well the evening in Guadalupé's got me thinking. Instead of poetry or peridot or distance running, however, I found myself wishing I had pursued our evening's jousting a little longer. Maybe it's your New Yorkie kind of attitude. I never met a woman who could fire off zingers and one liners I didn't

like—even if she habitually remains a pain in the ass.

All of which means I've decided to send a note attempting to engage you in some more mindless repartee here in Santa Fe. I'll be at the Cowgirl Hall of Fame this afternoon at 1:00 p.m., if you feel up to my buying you lunch. Oh, and don't worry, you'll be safe. I don't have any RnR plans or anything like that up my sleeve. I have to get back to my digs and my life of radical-chic reclusion late this afternoon. See you at one?      *Kaliber*

The note just sat there in my hand as my mind wandered. Did I wish to risk a third encounter with this escape artist from the complexities of urban existence? And if so, what was the point? Was I eventually going to get up to some tricks with him just because his unavailable lifestyle didn't threaten my self-congratulatory loneliness?

Alternatively, maybe Aldebaran was the man I should rediscover. He and I went round the moon several times in Cambridge and Oxford. But there was little point to that either. The Zuni erstwhile astronomer undoubtedly would want to continue working at the Northwest New Mexico Visitor Center, while I would insist on remaining 200 miles away in Santa Fe with my own resolve regarding urban sophistication and my daughter's education. And did I even want to commit to anyone at this point in my own escape from reality?

Still, the other note was lying on the couch beside me. The

envelope was black, and I got this strange premonition that opening it was going to unleash some sort of emotional distress.

> *Dearest Aurore:*
>
> *I hope you're sitting down when you begin to read this, as bad news is never easy to assimilate. Yes, it's from your elder sibling Ashleigh, and I'm alive. I know it sounds preposterous and it probably is. Everyone undoubtedly was happy to see me expire. But I'm alive, I'm in New Mexico, I've quit smoking, and I've improved my normally disruptive attitude.*
>
> *I'll save the explanations for later, but if you can get away for 24 hours, we could meet at the Ojo Caliente Mineral Springs Hotel tomorrow around six for dinner and I could give you all the cryptic details.*
>
> *Meanwhile, whether you can make Ojo or not, please keep my resurrection a secret for now. I think it would only do more harm than good to tell Katarina and Kahlo of my untimely exhumation. I wasn't really exhumed, although sometimes I feel like I'm arising from the dead when struggling from bed in the morning at high altitude.*
>
> *But more on that later if you choose to meet me. Send an e-mail response to Blackqueen@aol.com. And*

*remember, my being still above ground on the planet is to remain a secret to all family members and former adversaries for now.*

*A.*

Without my being aware, the note slipped from my hand onto the woven cloth of the couch. Ashleigh alive. I couldn't decide if I was exhilarated or distraught. My Black Queen sister had a way of fouling up almost anything familial, and undoubtedly, I would be tempting the hand of fate even merely entertaining the idea of reacquainting myself with a reincarnated sibling who somehow was out there in the New Mexican ethers.

I had a cup of tea, deliberated, ate a chocolate turtle, deliberated some more, and finally came to the sort of decision that has always led to interpersonal disaster. Somehow, I felt interacting with either of these novel souls would bring inevitable trouble. But then my recent life without any risk had been not much more than a flaming bore.

There was the point that Katarina and Kahlo wouldn't be back until late afternoon or early evening. Their delayed return was just the sort of excuse I always found in publishing to justify throwing over all my scheduled plans to meet some eccentric author. And I convinced myself that what might be gotten away with in New York could just as well be pulled off in Santa Fe.

I decided to risk the modern-day caveman again. O.K. so he didn't live in a cave. But his shack in that remote canyon south of Chaco gave him just enough of an element of mystery and peril I find inexplicably attractive in men. Even though there was little point, I brushed my hair, put on a white baseball cap to go with my white brocaded muslin blouse, jeans, and espadrilles, and set off to a third encounter with Mr. Kaliber Ristraverdé I hoped would prove amusing as well as indisputably provocative.

It was warm enough that he was out on the patio at one of the tables frequented by the quirky mélange of souls one sees having migrated to this adobe vortex of Native American, Spanish, Hispanic, and Gringo cultures. The eccentric escapist had on a pair of small round horn-rimmed glasses, the kind more likely to be seen in Cambridge, Mass, than in the West. The recluse was reading the *Santa Fe New Mexican*, but awkwardly stood up when I arrived, probably not sure if he'd lose points with a woman my age by not doing so. He wouldn't have, but then we needed to do the sort of fraternal hug two people fumble through when unsure whether a full-on body press or French kiss would be appropriate. I was in a crazy enough mood that if the hermit would have tried virtually any public display of affection, it would have been handled with enthusiasm. He was a strange looking dude, but with the same sort of odd magnetism of Chris Cooper's orchid thief who enchants Meryl Streep in the film, Adaptation. I felt like Susan Orlean in the company of a dangerously appealing man a woman should have no business entertaining, if not for conversation, certainly not for more erotic behavior.

"I got your message," I said while sliding into a seat opposite the canyon man with whom I had endured two unusual encounters. It's just like Kahlo usually blurts out in staccato fashion regarding how she has divined something: 'I can't explain it...' But there I was, sitting opposite a man with whom I had done nothing more than exchange moderate verbal abuse. He had a certain look that many women find annoying. Yet with his unkempt hair, face badly in need of a shave, and eyes the color of Western sky blue, Kaliber Ristraverdé had a siren-like effect on me, inexplicable when normally I believe myself rhetorically tied to the masthead when it comes to ignoring any such overtures. He possessed a unique appeal like that of the orchid thief or James Dean in an oilfield. You sensed a lot of arcane knowledge inside that feckless head. And even though I had forcibly developed an intolerant East Coast sophistication, any such normal trump card was no more valuable than a quick wit each time I met his glance. He had the sort of exasperating charisma that rips into a jaded but sophisticated urban female's soul. He rarely said the right things, yet those verbal contretemps had so far merely made me uncomfortable knowing my pseudo-worldliness had little effect daunting this solitary pariah. Yes, I had received his note, and he had the sort of look on his face that conveyed my showing up had all the impact of four minutes of television commercials upon a deaf person. And he knew that I found his insouciance appealing anyway.

"What has brought you to Santa Fe again? Or did you never leave?"

"I drove back to the shack. I had to work on a little claim I have staked a certain distance from my cabin. Sometimes I bring stuff into Santa Fe and sell it."

We were sitting in the shade of an oak tree, and it was unsettling seeing the dappled light on his face because it meant that I shouldn't have worn any makeup. I put my cap on the table, anyway, assuring myself that any physical appeal a woman my age might once have possessed had long since departed. My mind had to be the attraction. "Anything I'd be interested in?"

He didn't have a chance to answer because someone named Carla, who said she'd be our waitress, took our order for drinks. Since Kahlo and Katarina would be arriving back at the Loretto sometime later, I ordered a Diet Coke, while Mr. R asked for one of their famous margaritas. When she departed with hips moving in spray-on jeans, I looked up to see him pursing his lips.

"I'm not sure," he answered, returning his glance from the

disappearing glutes. "You seemed to have some rock-hounding blood in you that day near my shack, so you just might have an interest in what I'm selling. But one thing you learn about mining extractions and locations is that anyone outside the mine knowing about its contents and location is tantamount to everyone knowing. No disrespect intended, but what I pull out of the mine is best kept to myself. Not that you'd tell anyone or try to jump my claim. It's just that secrecy and bald-faced lying are an essential part of successful mining—unless you have armed guards like around a Colombian emerald mine. But even then, your own workers will steal from you. I mine alone, and it stays mine alone."

"I can't say I blame you. No, I wouldn't tell anyone. But then you've heard that before. Besides, I doubt whether you came here to talk about mining, and I know I didn't. We've had two out-of-synch dances and you wanted to see if there could be a little more chemistry than we both thought, right?"

He nodded with the sort of look a man exhibits when you've hit the mark, but the accuracy isn't going to matter one way or the other. We both wanted to continue the dance. But what was the next step, and would we get to it before the music stopped? Both of us knew any potential adventure would be dangerous in the same way women devour chocolates and men nubile women in plural numbers.

"I guess I've always liked dangerous women."

"Speaking of dangerous women, I got a note from the same siren you once almost rolled round with in a Tesuque parking lot."

"Not Ashleigh, because you told me she's dead." I knew the possibility from Sublette, but kept my mouth shut.

"Yes, Ashleigh, who'd be better off staying dead."

"You're joking."

"I wish I were. Unless someone has a macabre sense of humor, another note I got along with yours back at the hotel was written by my late but seemingly also untimely sister. Apparently being underground didn't suit her. Or like both of us, she disappeared from urban chaos to create havoc in a remote realm somewhere."

"Alive?"

"Alive and apparently up for a hot bath in Ojo Caliente. Her note requested I meet her tomorrow night. Maybe you could join us there and further stir up a sibling rivalry I thought to be dead and buried."

Kaliber got a smirk on his face like a man gets who has more than one option for decadence. "Love springs eternal."

"Or hot springs infernal."

Lunch over Rio Grande Gumbo and Chimayo Chicken Salad for me and a Buffalo Burger and Sweet 'Tater Fries for the canyon man actually became more cordial than our first two encounters. Maybe it's because Kaliber had just one margarita and my suppressed but alleged acerbic wit lay dormant because of a lack of any magic elixir. We spent a lot of time discussing gems and minerals. And while there are many tales of gold and other buried treasures evolving out of New Mexico, Kaliber clarified that turquoise, peridot and agate were more likely minerals to be found in arid high country.

Eventually, however, the subject of Ashleigh was too provocative to ignore. If my sister were alive, just what she had done over the last two years as well as what trouble she could cause in the next two were still percolating within inquisitive, like minds.

"You know, I keep finding myself thinking about what happened while I was up in Sublette at a Cumbres & Toltec Scenic Railroad party two nights ago," Kaliber began after finishing the last of his margarita. "I went with this park ranger I know from Grants. The whole do was wild. A lot of booze and dancing and costumes. But the next thing I know someone gets a cell phone call that this journalist, who was along for the ride—and whom I think you once knew better than you found prudent—needs to be rescued. It turns out some woman's tied him to a tree out in an aspen grove near the party. She apparently stole a 12" ruby scepter he had concealed in his trousers and boot and disappeared down into the river valley below."

"I think I know two of the three," I interrupted, shaking my head that not one but two nemeses from my past might have resurfaced in New Mexico. "If the ranger's Chichilticalli and the whiner who was tied to a tree might be Quivira."

Kaliber nodded, as if people from the past have a way of resurfacing. "Yah, as a matter a fact it was the same Quivira Cantrell —or at least he told us you were his former wife. Even though he thinks he can probably write the quintessential treasure hunt story, this woman in all black apparently tied him to a tree and stole the miniature scepter he had found near the Ice Cave."

"Was there anything else unusual about this woman in black?"

"I only saw her from a distance at the party, but I'd say she had hair and eyes the color of obsidian, a gaucho hat with a silver concho band around it, and an attitude. But then who doesn't have an attitude in the West? Come to think about it, she did look like a little bit older and curvier version of the woman I rolled around in the Tesuque parking lot. But the lights were dim, and she had on a lone ranger mask."

"Did Cantrell say anything about her?"

"Yah. He said she had on a strange perfume—some name, maybe like Black Dahlia."

"Black Queen?"

"That's it. And he said when she disappeared down the slope to the river, she threw over her shoulder a word like, 'Adios.'"

"Adieu?"

"Right again. Q-man said she was the only woman he ever knew that used that word when she took off."

"Make that three for three. The woman in black of this disparate trio unfortunately confirms my believed-to-be subterranean sister has failed to honor her death certificate." I sighed as I put my baseball cap back on. "Still, I guess the only way to verify her untimely reincarnation will probably be while soaking in an Ojo Caliente mineral pool."

# A Real Gem

(KETL)

Since I was going to a *kinaalda* ceremony I needed gifts to give Estibalíz's granddaughter. At my age it is better to give things to others, rather than to acquire any more possessions. Over the last year I have cleared a lot of stuff out of my hogan and tipi. But I am disappointed in how much the *belagaana*'s habit of acquiring things over time crept into my life. I don't have that many worldly goods. My life is simple and there is no need to keep much. Books read, blankets saved, eagle feathers rarely worn, all are best passed on to those with more sunrises and star skies before them.

I figured I could give Estibalíz's granddaughter one of my favorite blankets. A thirteen-year-old may not appreciate a blanket right now. Yet over time, when covering up with it on a couch to avoid the winter cold, she will feel the devoted work the Bitter Water Clan woman put into weaving it. A second gift would also be hard to choose for someone so young. I have already given away most of the Glittering World gems I have found and had polished by a geologist friend. But I was going to meet my former park service ranger neighbor Kaliber in Santa Fe, and whenever I meet him, he always gives me several rough pieces of peridot. I could give them to Esti's granddaughter.

My morning was the same as always. I sprinkled corn pollen on the ground and chanted briefly as a tribute to the rise of the sun and then sat in my rocking chair to watch the colors change on the nearby mesas. I have many aches and pains now, and it won't be long before I must leave the world of Changing Woman behind. But the sun still has the same ability to enchant each morning and I am fortunate never to have suffered any noticeable permanent effects over having worked in a uranium mine. I still can walk over sandstone and among sagebrush. Sit with the late afternoon sun coming through the window and read history books written by Native Americans rather than *belagaana*.

I didn't get to Santa Fe until around four o'clock, but that's the agreement I have with the canyon man. If he has peridot to sell, I know he will be at the Coronado Gem and Mineral Shop in downtown Santa Fe at four o'clock on the first Thursday of a month. If I wish to see him, I just show up there.

The shop is crowded. It has displays of everything from meteorites and fossils to crystals, agate, gold nuggets, and many other gems and minerals discovered in the Southwest. Sometimes I put my elbows on a glass case and look down at the many beautiful stones I wish I had found. I have discovered many in my own time. And I will find more. It's a little like tracking. Trackers must keep a sharp eye. Sometimes the face of a gem will catch the light a certain way, or the tip of some sandstone-encrusted agate will appear. You might be walking in the Chuska Mountains and suddenly a spherical rock that is a geode without explanation appears in your field of vision. Inside it might be lined with purple amethyst or rose quartz. I pick up most of them outside of *Dinetah*. The one's I find in the *Diné Bikéyah* I borrow and then put back. Others I sometimes keep, though I know I should honor the white man's lands, as well.

Often in the shop, however, I get a sadness much like going to a zoo. There I wish the animals could enjoy the same freedom I have. And it is the same with the gems and minerals clustered in a shop.

It's exciting to see them all up close, but sad they no longer can share the fresh air and running water found in their original mountain habitat. It is their fate either to remain a secret part of the Glittering World, or to be found by man and relocated to unforeseen confinement. If for some reason Kaliber doesn't come into town in any month, I still spend an hour or so looking at these rare pieces of beauty discovered and taken from amidst the sandstone, granite, and red clay of New Mexico. I plead guilty to enjoying being able to see all at once stones and metals I would never find myself.

The man who runs the Coronado is like any other collector. He likes keeping the rare things he has instead of selling them. But that means always being on the precipice of going out of business. Everyone knows that. Yet the owner, Mr. Vasquez, always buys any peridot Kaliber brings in from his secret mine to sell to private collectors or museums. No one knows exactly where the former ranger's mine is, and he likes it that way.

I think that's him coming down the hall's creaky wooden floor now. I can tell by the sound of his footsteps. It seems strange, but as I've gotten older, certain of my faculties have become more acute and others have begun to wear out. I can't see as well as I used to, and I can't quite hear as well either. Yet both of those senses have become more selective. Sometimes the sounds in the red clay of a man's footsteps—if I don't hear his car or he doesn't wait the polite time before approaching my hogan—reveal who it is. At other times like when I walk to my thinking rock in Acoma, I can still spot a crow on a sandstone outcropping below a mesa.

Kaliber had a backpack more than likely containing some raw peridot inside it.

"*Yah-te-hey*," I said as he spotted me leaning on the meteorite case.

Señor Vasquez was in the office. He knows just whom he can leave alone in the shop without worrying about anything going missing. Neither Kaliber nor I would ever take anything without paying. And Kaliber has made the owner a lot of money with what he brings in.

When Señor Vasquez came out, he brought a jeweler's glass to look at some of the pieces of peridot. I couldn't hear what the two of them were saying, but a few minutes passed while I continued my observations of the wonders sprinkled throughout the shop much like the stars and constellations on a moonless night above the *Dinetah*.

Now some think that Kaliber is greedy, and that he may be getting his peridot from off-limits property. Lots of those who encounter the former ranger tell me they think he's lost touch with reality. I say he's gained it. He has simplified his life down to what is important. There isn't anything he does that is boring or wastes time, as the *belagaana* would say. He is one having come from the outside world that now recognizes the beauty of his physical surroundings.

"Everything alright at the hogan?"

I nodded, tipping my hat, and then putting my hands back on the top of a case. It's awkward for me sometimes, because I don't know what to say to a reader like Kaliber Ristraverdé. He's not like a typical Anglo. And as I approach the long journey to the north I must eventually face, I seem to speak less often than when I was younger.

"Any closer to getting that grant for the school?" he asked. He knows I am one of several *Dineh* who help to raise money for a school teaching the Navajo and Apache languages near Farmington.

"The school was awarded a grant from the Jicarilla Nation Foundation. The curriculum will now offer both Navajo and Apache history and language instruction. The school got 20 new scholarships provided by Kutz Canyon Natural Gas and Oil, too."

Then Kaliber reached out and put a wad of currency in my shirt pocket. It is a ritual we do each month.

"No, you have done enough," I said, taking the money out of my pocket and extending it with my hand.

"Never enough to make up for what I didn't do when I was younger," Kaliber replied. "I never did anything, and now I can." He put the money back in my pocket and held out a little bag with a drawstring I knew contained peridot as a personal gift. "Please make sure the school keeps going. I can never be a Diné or Apache," he added while placing the cash in the bag and re-extending it with both hands. "But I can support their inestimable value to this country."

# The Black Queen

(AURORE)

Kahlo, Katarina, and I all had dinner at the Coyote Café. After her speech apparently first failed during a meeting of Chaco and Government officials, my daughter was now visibly if not vocally over the moon to do with something about her theories. The two were exhausted from impromptu camping the previous evening, and we came back to the Loretto early. Kahlo checked the internet as well as e-mails she sometimes gets from her New York friend Joel, and then went to bed in one of the suite's bedrooms.

Katarina had one of those looks of concern on her face she gets when Kahlo might be in some sort of trouble. Often my mother can be over-solicitous, but now seemed more out of sorts than usual.

"I just hope that what she told them doesn't warrant too much attention," Katarina said, looking up over glasses she had donned to peruse a *Vanity Fair* as a camouflage for her true agitation. "You know how Kahlo gets when too many adults inadvertently confront her. Although she didn't say much at dinner about her sudden clarity, according to this NASA educator she made great progress speaking in a private office with just that same Ms. Morgen as well as Ranger Aldebaran in the room with her."

"What was Chichilticalli doing there?"

"He came to the meeting which was hosted by the NASA lady

to try to determine what sort of kids programs they might initiate. There were about eight of them from the Park Service, Bureaus of Land Management and Indian Affairs, and the Department of the Interior. Kahlo was asked to give them some input on what kids her age might like, but there were too many new adult faces, and she couldn't speak. She got it all out in a private office, however, with just the woman from NASA and that ranger there.

"The problem was that Ms. Morgen apparently left the intercom on and the group in the theater meeting heard and recorded everything Kahlo said. That's all well and good if they don't blab it to the media. But with eight people having heard her revelations—whether those speculations are right or wrong—she could suddenly be besieged by the sort of requests we both know Kahlo could never handle."

I paced back and forth a bit, unsure if Katarina was hitting upon anything of genuine concern.

"Well, you're not going to believe this, but apparently Ashleigh is still alive and wants to meet me tomorrow night at Ojo Caliente. It's all sort of hush-hush stuff. When I first read the note she left at the front desk, I thought it must be someone's idea of a mordant practical joke. But I had lunch with the rock hunter from the canyon south of Chaco and he told me a bizarre story about Quivira and a woman in all black who inexplicably, yet most likely, was Ashleigh. One giveaway was that she was wearing Black Queen perfume, and when she left the scene at a party held someplace along the Cumbres & Toltec Scenic Railroad, she used the word, 'Adieu.' And you and I know that nobody uses that as a farewell but the thought-to-be-late Black Queen, herself.

"The problem if I go to Ojo, is that although you and Kahlo have been away for several days, I'd be leaving after spending just part of Friday with the two of you. Also, Ashleigh asked me not to tell either Kahlo or you that she is still alive, and that she would explain everything in Ojo. I had to tell you, but Kahlo's another matter. Anyway, I'm in a bit of a quandary as to whether to exercise any socially dangerous option that might unearth my late sister."

My mother took off her glasses. "Obviously you have to go. We need to know if my formerly distempered eldest daughter has somehow risen from the dead and is alive and ready to torture some new living souls as well as her own family again. I'll look after Kahlo. She has spent enough time hiking to the furthest-ends-of-the-earth sort of ruins and trails that she should be content for 24 hours exploring the internet."

While threading the corridor up through Española and then the canyons leading to Ojo Caliente, I couldn't get a lot of the complexity of various situations in New Mexico under control. In the Grants Mining Museum I had stumbled upon Chichilticalli, yet his new life of park rangering meant there was little point to rekindling that English affaire. Three times I had encountered the urban hermit Kaliber trying to transmute hunting rocks and drinking from his desolate area south of Chaco into art forms. What was the point of my having invited him to Ojo? And what if he showed up? It seemed like my proclivity for always selecting the unattainable or irrational kept me a woman isolated from the opposite gender, and rapidly losing any middle-aged charms that might avoid the resulting predictable life with two other females. Then what were Katarina and I to do with Kahlo, should what she has discovered be found to have some sort of universal appeal? School could bring further attentions probably causing her stammer and insecurities to grow out of control. And God knows how we would deal with the possibility of microphones and cameras.

Then I told myself I was letting my new life in New Mexico become almost as stressful as my whirlwind daily grind in Gotham. I had to get a grip. I was going to Ojo Caliente, a remote and rough-hewn resort where a woman could boil away her cares in hot pools or lay swathed in steaming Indian blankets with a mudpack on one's face. It would all be good, and I forced myself to believe that any contretemps with which the resurfacing Ashleigh could confront me would be taken in stride. I was going to relax, with or without sister Ashleigh and/or Kaliber Ristraverdé.

I sat in the Hotel's Artesian Restaurant only to see six o'clock come and go on my watch—an old *Printemps* silver-rimmed, white faced timepiece with actual numerals at the hours—I had purchased in Paris years ago. I nervously sipped a glass of Pinot Noir, devoured a piece of bread to hold off an appetite keen from skipping lunch, and tried to keep from looking at the secondhand creeping beyond 6:30.

I told myself to remain calm. There is never any hurry while ensconced in a hot springs resort many miles from the nearest significant civilization. Could Ashleigh really be coming? Or was it all some elaborate hoax? Facing the door was probably not a good idea, since virtually every minute or two I repeatedly looked up to see if a phantom or my disinterred sibling was coming through the door.

Then suddenly, there she was. Ashleigh still exuded her self-assumed regality at 5'10" and in all black. My resurrected sister never did anything halfway. She had on the same black gaucho hat Kaliber had mentioned, but the conch shell band was missing, and she had the black rim tilted low above the perennially macabre whitewashed face, highlighted by black lipstick. Her best feature might still be those anthracite coal eyes she would possess alive or dead. The black silk cowgirl shirt with pearl buttons and black jeans tucked into hand-tooled obsidian cowgirl boots revealed that Ashleigh had put on little weight except in places her suitors always found magnetic. She strode right toward me as if the two of us had last encountered one another a mere hour or so ago.

"Sister Aurore," Ashleigh smiled, giving me a hug that let me know she was truly alive rather than an apparition.

"My thought-to-be late sister Ashleigh," I replied, kissing her on the cheek, the scent of her Black Queen perfume confirming that my sibling had indeed arisen from the dead. "When I got your note, my initial reaction was that someone was playing an elaborate prank. But either I am now in the middle of one of Kahlo's visions, or my elder sister has resurfaced in Ojo for cathartic bathing and an extensive list of explanations."

"Yes, well, I know many of my relatives and former antagonists would rather I had truly been interred, but actually I never was. It was all a ruse I thought to be quite imaginative. Enough so that even the skeptical Katarina was unable to discern either my remaining vitality or secret escape from boring reality."

"Do go on—after you've ordered some of the liquid that eventually puts us all underground."

Ashleigh beckoned the waitress over with a mere look from her pair of obsidian shark's eyes, then after ordering a glass of wine leaned forward on her elbows in her former manner of invading any listener's space for effect. "The official cause of death, as you know, was listed as heart failure. Many believed I had been poisoned, or at least would have lit a votive candle if they could have confirmed such a propitious expiry. Yet I had had enough of the whole bickering family scene, knew I had burned every bridge up and down the Hudson or between the boroughs with acquaintances, and decided disappearance to be the best solution for us all. So I died. Well, at least everyone thought I did, and that my face was contorted enough in death to keep the coffin closed at the wake. Relatives often like to look at their dearly departed, but fortunately in my case, no one felt the need for a last glimpse of their deceased nemesis."

Ashleigh sniffed her Pouilly Fuissé, sipped it to provoke my eagerness for further explanation, and tucked a lock of hair behind her ear. She leaned in further as if what she was about to reveal was for my ears only. "It was all a hoax, of course. Earlier I had asked around in Albany for a doctor having fallen on hard times due to some impropriety. The search produced a shyster who might be amenable to my plan. It was really quite simple. I merely paid him $15,000, and he provided a death certificate detailing my demise from a faulty heart as well as a sealed coffin, so that no further questions were asked. The lack of concern by others played marvelously into my timely demise, after which I merely hared off in the doctor's car—later to be retrieved from Chicago—and simply vanished. A series of Greyhound bus rides later—paid for in cash—and I arrived back in Northwest New Mexico. I shall leave most of those details out for now. But suffice it to say that over the last two years I have experienced a dramatic change of attitude toward all those family members and citizens formerly detested, reputedly due to your dear sister's protracted bouts of stimulants and resultant sugar blues. Yah, I was nasty. And yes, I'll still wear all black. But if you and I become reacquainted over time, my hope is that I can re-intrude occasionally into my all-female family with a lot more decorum and esprit than I ever had for past intolerances. I think I can maintain this philanthropic transformation. But when you've been as obnoxious as I have, the jury shall most probably remain out, waiting for the anathema to return to her original ways."

For a moment I just sat there, shocked that Ashleigh not only was alive and seemingly well, but that there was the unexpected possibility that her entirely disastrous approach to any other human being had altered. Could it truly be that Ashleigh was sitting in front of me, now possessing a change in attitude that might be construed as charitable or kind?

"Was it you who took the Scepter from the party animal I presume to have been Quivira?"

A smirk parted her black lips. "Yah. He didn't have a clue. There was this huge bash up at an antique village along the Scenic Railroad between Chama and Antonito, and I got an invite because a Navajo friend of mine knew the wealthy Native American philanthropist throwing the party. I had on a mask, and my hair is about half the length it was when you and Cantrell were married. Nobody recognized me; nobody knew me.

"You should have seen the look on your former husband's louche face when I stuck the gun in his back. He thought it was all a big party escapade by a woman wanting to get laid in the mountain outback. But it was his nasty sister-in-law resurrected from the dead.

"It was dark, and I took this Cortez Ruby Scepter off him he thought nobody knew about. I didn't even tell Ketl—who told me he encountered Katarina and Kahlo at Pueblo Pintado—that I later added the Scepter to the hidden spot he had put the Mogollon Cross for Quivira. I can't tell you the enormous pleasure I had handcuffing Cantrell to an aspen, then telling him to be patient, that he would be rescued. He always thought he was such hot shit in an argument, and now he was losing both a valuable bit of found treasure as well as his dignity."

I took a big gulp of Pinot. We hadn't even ordered any food, yet I was mesmerized by my sister and her tale of greed, revenge, and various other noxious ingredients of a cocktail only she could concoct. "How did you ever know he was in New Mexico? And how did you know he had the Ruby Scepter?"

Ashleigh pushed her hat up a little, leaned back and uncrossed her still lithe legs as if all part of her bizarre theatrical manner of imparting arcane secrets. "During the two years I've been out here, I've helped out by working as a Native American fundraiser. But everything has been under an assumed name. One of the Navajos I've worked with is the old former uranium miner named Ketl, Kat and Kahlo encountered. I've spent a lot of time sitting on his dilapidated hogan porch staring at mesas, birds, and the early morning sun. Meeting Ketl has gained in value over time because he has an alternative perspective to my jaded one on the intrinsics of life I need to recognize. Like Kahlo, I can't say why. But I like his spirit and over time he has helped me overcome my intolerance for almost everyone.

"One of his favorite cautionary tales or tests, if you will, is to send some hapless visitor on a treasure hunt expedition. He does it as a potential lesson in making the distinction between natural treasures best left alone, and unnatural treasures taken out of the ground by those who value possessions more than any spectacular Four Corners surroundings. He sent Cantrell on a treasure hunt for an ersatz Mogollon Cross—ersatz because he keeps the real one hidden not far from his tipi. I told him I was going to hide a facsimile of his reputed Cortez Ruby Scepter near Ojo for your adventurous journalist ex-husband. But instead, I put it under the same cloth bag near the Ice Cave where Cantrell found the Mogollon Cross. I wanted to see if he would return it to Ketl just as he did the Mogollon Cross. Yet Quivira is no different than many lonely middle-aged men with vestigial testosterone. He failed the test, just as most would. The thought of how much it would bring from an eccentric wealthy collector drove him crazier than betting on the New York Giants beating the New England Patriots."

It was like Christmas or Hanukkah in April. I was getting the sort of feelings for my sister normally associated with siblings reunited. Ashleigh might even prove to have a heart after all.

"What say we rent one of the new private pools under the stars between wine and dinner with more wine? I sort of thought this friend of mine might show up, but he hasn't," I suggested, glad Kaliber hadn't taken up my offer because of the awkwardness of what had occurred with sister Ashleigh two years earlier in the

Tesuque parking lot. "The two of us have a lot to catch up on anyway. I have a feeling a couple of boiled New Yorkers would be a lot more relaxed than lobsters if we soak first and eat later."

Ashleigh cocked her head sideways and grinned. If I still knew my errant sister, she had something up her sleeve.

"I've already rented us two of those private outdoor ponds with kiva fireplaces you can only use after six p.m.," she replied as if one step ahead of me.

One has to pay attention with Ashleigh, though. There is always more left unsaid, much like many Native American rather than Anglo-Manhattan traditions. "Pools, as in plural?"

"That's right dear sister. I wouldn't give up on that late visitor, if I were you—though his appearance might differ considerably from what you expected."

It was the sort of cryptic comment at which Ashleigh was always proficient. I knew not to prod her. That only led to more mysterious hints. So, I dropped it, figuring if Kaliber were to show up, I'd know soon enough, and then we might have to flip a coin.

"So why don't you want Katarina and Kahlo to know of your improbable reincarnation?"

"All in good time," Ashleigh answered, as if everything would be revealed, but not before the requisite protracted suspense. "There is little to no chance you didn't already tell Katarina," she added, staring intently with those jet-black eyes into mine for a reaction I couldn't hide. "But Kahlo's a different matter. I have my reasons, but the little whirlwind would only suffer without an adequate explanation. It might be good to wait until she's back in school to reintroduce the phantom of northwest New Mexico."

Over the next hour my sister filled in more details of the railroad robbery, of her life of charitable fund-raising, of a couple of near misses with long-term male companionship, her change in diet and quitting smoking, and many other particulars of a life appearing more phenomenal for its transitions than adventures.

Then Kaliber walked through the door. He kissed Ashleigh on the lips and then me on the cheek. It was probably accurate to say I was only mildly disappointed. I wasn't sure what I wanted to do with Kaliber at a mineral springs spa where bathing and sexual games often went hand in hand, or pool and room. Still, I had to react in some way, and I found myself perplexed as to what to say to the reclusive reader. I opened my lips, but nothing came out. I felt like Kahlo.

"Aurore," he smiled, pausing for effect while sliding into the third chair of four. "You're probably thinking, 'Why would this dude show up I had invited to Ojo, when he and my thought-to-be-a-goner sister might have similar bathing games planned?'"

At such times, a woman of my age does the best she can to conceal any disappointment. "Well, I'll have to admit, I am just a tad curious."

"Remember," he continued, "Ashleigh and I did get as far as Tesuque Market two years ago."

I nodded, not sure how the two had reconnected, but wishing they had continued any such dance away from yours truly.

"It was only in the last 24 hours we've become reacquainted thanks to *Hosteen* Ketl. When I got back to the shack there was a note on the door. It said: 'Walking up above. Want to pick up where we left off in Tesuque.' And it was signed by your dearly departed sister.

"Now Quivira had told me about the possibility of the bandit in black being his late sister-in-law. But I figured someone like you or one of my ranger friends was just trying to stir up my curiosity with another true gem instead of any minerals lower on the hardness scale."

"Let me guess," I interrupted. "The two of you did more at the cabin than read aloud from Millay."

"Now, now, now," said Ashleigh. "A gentleman never reveals any behavior that might compromise a lady."

"That was no lady," as W.C. might mutter, "that was my sister."

Kaliber pulled his chair a little closer to Ashleigh and put his arm around her. "Sorry, Aurore," he smiled. "Guadalupe's and the Cowgirl Hall of Fame were both good fun. But you and I heading toward any sunset would be like Barack Obama dating Hillary Clinton. We might have a lot to say, but any physical contact might spoil a beautiful friendship."

To say I was disillusioned, again, was only mildly true. Kaliber was probably right, should we have got up to something in a pool. Yet my ego did take a hit that my big sister had upstaged me, particularly since she had risen from her grave to do so.

"Still, not to worry about sibling rivalry," added the man from the canyon. He looked at his watch, then motioned toward the door. "Redemption may be approaching at any minute."

I glanced over at an empty doorway, then back and forth at each of their self-congratulatory faces. It was going to be hard to top my sister's reincarnation. Yet the way the two of them were whispering and smirking was too insulting to be permanent. But to whom could Kaliber be referring? I hoped they hadn't fixed me up with someone I don't know. That sort of thing has all the appeal of losing or winning the Dating Game.

When I looked up again from playing with my napkin, however, Chichilticalli was walking toward the table. But instead of his ranger outfit, he was wearing jeans and a burgundy T-shirt. He kissed me on the lips and shook Ashleigh's and Kaliber's hands.

"I figured you two already conducted a primer over in England," Kaliber winked at me. "And while you and I might have caused some trouble together and regretted it, you and Chichilticalli could just find the second private pool under the stars we rented to be a well engineered opportunity to get reacquainted while eavesdropping on any alternative progress in the next pond."

# Rhymes With Pool

(CHICHILTICALLI)

While driving across to Albuquerque and then up through Santa Fe and Española to Ojo, I had to ask myself if I wasn't trying to recreate a dangerous part of an alternative life I had enjoyed while reading astronomy at Oxford. Even given my brief British education and ability to re-sharpen my wits over time, what was an NPS ranger working at a Visitor Center in Grants, New Mexico, hoping to rekindle with a former New York book editor? O.K. so we had achieved our own *hozro*, as the Diné call the harmony with one's surroundings, fiddling about in the twin university towns of the Muddy Isle. But this was the Third Millennium. And no matter what I may have studied and read, I'm a Native American Zuni practicing simple pursuits while she is from a white Manhattan tribe where sophistication and urban style reach apotheosis.

When I got the phone call from Kaliber, initially I thought his idea of my going to meet Aurore at Ojo Caliente like catching an eagle. It can be done. But if you try, you can end up empty handed or disappointed. What I didn't need is to fail with Aurore Dupín. And she had already intimated to me in the Grants Mining Museum that trying to recreate again what we found ourselves dizzy over in England just wasn't on, as the British might say. I may not be as adventuresome as either Cantrell or Ristraverdé. Yet when it comes to being drawn toward a siren like Dupín, I knew no amount of prayer to the Gods, chanting, or telling myself life in her Santa Fe future fast lane to be impossible, was enough to ward me off from another encounter with the woman who prefers wearing white. Meeting up with Ms. Dupín at Ojo would probably be comparable to the last experience of a male black widow spider. A magnetic female might devour you for dessert afterwards, but what excitement to be had in the meantime.

So, I left the Visitor Center at three and figured four hours of nervous contemplation later I'd probably be flying into the web of the very dangerous woman in white.

Then, there she was, sitting at a dining table with the woman I assumed to be the Sublette *bandita* and Ristraverdé. The two sisters, one in black and the other in white. There was no turning back. Greeting three people all at once like the Dupín sisters and the unpredictable Ristraverdé made me nervous. It had been too long since I had sharpened my wits and traded barbs with anyone at the level of the pale-faced denizens of New York. If I wasn't to be over-boiled in some Ojo mineral bath, there was a good chance a certain Zuni ranger with the Park Service would be scalded by more than one Dupín remark.

"You must be the same Aldebaran I met briefly on the rafting trip two years ago," said Ashleigh, shaking my hand.

"And you could be the Sublette woman in black having induced Quivira Cantrell that an aspen grove is just the place to be before midnight."

"Just the slightest hint of a game with a woman, football, or bookie," retorted Ashleigh, "is enough to excite Aurore's charming former beau's testosterone."

"Sister Ashleigh insists that neither wearing black nor conducting treasure hunts after dark should be thought to be only for the dead."

"And you, dear sister Aurore, with no borealis and dressed in white, are even less innocent than I."

"It saves me from darts thrown by those thought to be deceased yet never having lost the ability upon an unexpected planetary return to cast aspersions. But we digress. I'm sure *Señors* Ristraverdé and Aldebaran did not come here to witness our unexpectedly renewed sibling rivalry."

"Too true," added Ashleigh before turning to Kaliber. "Let's leave these two to their nervous interlude while we pursue our own."

"We'll see you two later for more show-and-tell," added Kaliber while they both stood up and he took Ashleigh's hand.

"A pool game awaits," smirked Ashleigh, "and we shall take our cue."

To say that I was every bit as nervous as I once was while punting on the Cam in England would be an understatement, even for a Zuni. I kept telling myself to relax, that anything Aurore and I got up to in a mineral bath was often the purpose of being in Ojo and would be transitory. That neither of us was committing to combining disparate lives, and that it would be O.K. in a resort like this to take temporary advantage of any potential aqua pleasures, should any such opportunity present itself.

Aurore Dupín was the most alluring yet impenetrable woman I had ever met. One minute you thought you understood her, and the next it was if she had come from some sophisticated urban planet unfamiliar to those from less populous domains. And when you have grown up with the quiet female relatives I still have, you can't get around certain preconceptions of how things should be with any woman, even after a year at Oxford. It was all part of the quandary I maintained of living among a mix of Native American, Hispanic, and Anglo populations. And this mental dilemma even carried over into what should merely be spontaneous aquatic combustion between two lonely souls.

If we had been younger, we might have forgone the bathing suits we changed into in Aurore's room. But I'll have to say, for someone of indeterminate age, Ms. Dupín still has the slender figure and legs of a Marlene Dietrich. Now that I had been back among skin colors like my own in the Southwest again for many years, her pale legs as she slipped into the pool seemed almost extraterrestrial. We had lit a kiva fire, and its warm light undoubtedly made each of us appear as iridescent figures in yellow hues.

We made small talk, or maybe it would be more correct to say that Aurore talked, and I listened. But the clock was ticking, and I'm certain both of us were preoccupied on how anything more intimate might evolve.

She had her elbows up on the pool rim and I was awkwardly doing the same on my side, when unexpectedly a glide through the water brought her to me. Those moments took me back to that grassy area along the Cam River under grey skies when we had become completely oblivious to our surroundings. Now for a brief period in this Ojo Caliente liquid escape, the two of us from opposite worlds elevated core temperatures to match the surrounding liquid heat.

Then came one of those changes in mood you hope to avoid in such romantic surroundings. As quickly as she had paddled over, Aurore drew back and returned to prop herself up again on the opposite pool edge. Neither wished to break the spell, silent in anticipation of the awkwardness everyone dreads.

"I'm sorry, but I just can't do this. Before in Oxford and Cambridge, neither of us had anything to lose, nor were any others involved. But now we are again from two different worlds, you from Grants and I from Santa Fe. And I have a nine-year-old daughter, and you a vocation that will keep you in western New Mexico. Even though the chemistry may remain as intense as it once did in more carefree days, I no longer can put thoughts out of my mind on where all of this would lead. And we both know the answer."

I wanted to respond, but there was little I could say to refute her moment of truth. It was apparent any hopes each of us had had of recreating a halcyon era were evaporating faster than the water from these pools and the West.

"It's a shame, really," she said, glancing a wrist under each eye. "You are a wonderful man, and I'm a fool not to try to make it work. But I'm also a realist, and I know how difficult it would be for both of us. And what all that means in terms of ignoring the future and merely having fun in an Ojo pool has all the spontaneity of an arranged marriage. How would the two of us feel tomorrow? Or the day after tomorrow? Would breakfast be oatmeal and yoghurt, or acorn bread and green chili stew? And what would your mother think of a woman my age wearing a skirt above her knees?" She hoisted herself up on the edge of the pool near the fire, enough so that the moonlight reflected off the wet ivory of that Anglo skin.

I wanted to say anything that might contradict her analysis. But nothing so imaginative was forthcoming. "I booked a separate room because I wasn't sure if you and Ashleigh or Ashleigh and Kaliber would be sharing," I mumbled nonsensically.

She reached out for my hand and we both just sat there with the realization that any sort of romantic inclination would not be overcoming massive cultural and financial differences.

"It's really sad," she said, letting go of my hand and pressing my forearm. "If only we were 25 again."

# The Sleuth is the Medium

(KATARINA)

Aurore is not going to be pleased. But what was I to do once I had interrupted sipping a vodka on the balcony with walls topped by warm *farolitos* and came inside to pick up the phone? The ancient ivories twiddler was left in the Loretto with her vodka and granddaughter using headphones to scrutinize the internet and books. When my daughter left for Ojo Caliente, none of us could have imagined what would unfold in our normally private and predictable lives.

Two hours after Aurore left and Kahlo was in her own investigative world, the phone rang. It was the woman from NASA, Katalyn Morgen. My first thought was that she politely wanted to thank Kahlo for her contributions in formulating some sort of children's program. Yet Ms. Morgen informed me that the Chaco Cultural Center was receiving an inordinate number of calls regarding Kahlo's speculations. One of the calls had come from a young Native American boy in Cibola General Hospital in Gallup. Apparently, he has a speech impediment of a different nature to that of my granddaughter yet the further misfortune to be dying of leukemia.

"I know Kahlo finds it difficult to talk to anyone," continued Ms. Morgen," so what we have done, which we hope meets with and your granddaughter's and your approval, is to filter any media and other calls from those wishing to speak to Kahlo. We have given out neither her last name nor your location and phone number, even though at some point she might be encouraged to respond to e-mails. We have also requested of everyone who attended the meeting in which they overheard her, not to reveal her surname or whereabouts. Obviously, someone has leaked at least some of Kahlo's imaginative work, and for that I can only apologize. However, several of the scientists and officials who were present in the theater when your granddaughter recounted her revelations in the office, as well as a host of others, have asked if she could again come to Chaco and give us more of her thoughts. We realize that there is only one more week until school resumes after Easter vacations, and that of course, any such decision will be up to Kahlo, as well as to her mother and you, whether she wishes to reveal any more of her insightful archeological or astro-archeological speculations.

"In the meantime, the call I mentioned earlier has come from this Zuni child in hospital, who from a preliminary conversation with his doctor we understand will not last much beyond the Easter vacation. After hearing of Kahlo through friends and the television reports, the young patient has asked if it would be possible to speak to Kahlo late tomorrow afternoon."

When Ms. Morgen was finished, and I had told her we would get back to her, I had the premonition that Kahlo's speculations traveling faster than any of us anticipated was going to alter our lives in a way that drives a grandmother to drink more and a granddaughter further to stutter. *The television reports?* What did that mean?

Since I knew Kahlo would not hear if I kept the volume down, I went into the corner where the television screen faced away from my granddaughter, and after hitting the remote button, floundered to one of those arrow buttons that lowers the volume. As I turned on the last part of the six o'clock news, I wondered whether indeed Aurore and I had underestimated the little *wünderkind's* exposition.

A commercial for Xinthracite came on QBC News, and my mind was temporarily diverted to a reassurance that drinking fortunately precludes my taking a lot of prescription drugs that often seem to have a longer page of side effects than remedies. Then a weekend substitute commentator with a smile on her face was introduced.

"Our closing story tonight coming during spring break for many students and others might be more appropriate for the holidays of December. It is an inspirational tale of how a persistent nine-year-old's imagination and inventive mind not only intermittently have overcome a speech impediment, but also have excited the minds of the archeology world as well as hundreds if not thousands of young well-wishers in the Four Corners States and Mexico. At this point, the little we know is that her name is Kahlo, that her adopted Mother—a former book editor from the East Coast—chose her name from the famous Mexican painter, Frida Kahlo. We have also heard through an anonymous source that this nine-year-old investigator reputedly was born of a Mexican mother and Zuni and Navajo Native American father before apparently being given up as a baby for adoption when the mother died.

"It seems that our precocious subject was hiking with her adopted grandmother in northwest New Mexico's Chaco Canyon, when the pair became trapped from leaving the park via the dirt road out due to the flooding of a wash.

"While Kahlo was in the Chaco Cultural Park's Visitor Center, apparently Katalyn Morgen, a NASA educator trying to join with the U.S. National Park Service to set up programs for children to learn about the relationship of astronomy to archeology, was talking to the youngster. Kahlo said she might have some ideas, and Ms. Morgen was eager to hear them. Yet in a theater with eight notables ranging from officials of the Department of the Interior to the Bureau of Indian Affairs to National Park Service rangers and administrators, Kahlo faltered. She began to stutter and could not get her secrets out. The young girl burst into tears and was helped to a private office.

"But here's where our story gets good. With just Ms. Morgen and a ranger named Chichilticalli Aldebaran present, Kahlo began to talk and her stutter went away. She felt comfortable and began to reveal speculations on the purposes of the Great North Road, unique usages of the Great Kivas, possible influences of hydraulics, specifics on pottery paintings, and many other insightful deductions about the Anasazi Native American ancient cities of Chaco, Aztec, and others.

"But what none of the three knew is that Morgen had left on an intercom button after replying to a request to come back to an ongoing meeting in the Visitor Center theater. The scientists, administrators and rangers overheard everything Kahlo said, and apparently were mesmerized. Seemingly, it doesn't matter whether Kahlo is right or wrong. This nine-year-old already has stirred up the world of archeology and inspired hundreds if not thousands of youngsters throughout the Four Corners area.

"It is further reported that after listening to broadcasts beginning as early as this morning, literally tens of schools and hundreds of students, teachers, administrators, and others have overwhelmed the Chaco Cultural Center with telephone calls and e-mails. Schools from as far away as Mexico City and Juarez, and as near as Shiprock and Window Rock in the Four Corners area, have called to request Kahlo to appear and sign autographs, even if she cannot speak. Reputedly major foundations and even a famous former President on behalf of a wealthy software philanthropist with whom he works have called to see about grants helping to establish children's programs that would encourage further educational investigative work by Kahlo and other North American school children.

"All because one young girl could not talk, but believed in the power of ancient civilizations, and in her own willpower to investigate the arcane worlds of the Anasazi firsthand as well as through books and the internet.

"This is Wharton Mirren wishing Kahlo and all of you a pleasant April evening."

"Thank you, Wharton," said a woman in the anchor chair. "And that's our program for tonight...."

In a complete daze, I turned it off, only partially consoled that Kahlo was still happily and obliviously at her computer. For Kahlo to learn of these reactions might be compared to my first concert in Carnegie Hall. Yet I was able to cope, while my granddaughter might not yet, or ever, possess the same faculties for social survival. Her immediate future could be wonderful, or her worst nightmare. And to my knowledge she has not even told them anything of her theories on a missing city, or whatever plural cities she has mumbled about on several occasions. Then again, if Aurore and I could only convince our dear young relation that the whole process presents numerous opportunities for Kahlo to help encourage others like her, with whom she could share ideas. But the far greater fear is how Kahlo will respond to all that attention, all those potential inquisitive faces and cameras, and those intrusive questions that can alter one's life forever.

The next morning I skipped watching any television news, read the *New Mexican* in which I saw a small blurb more straightforward than the TV news piece, and was trying to decide whether to take Kahlo to the Southwest Reading Room or await Aurore's arrival back from Ojo Caliente. My granddaughter was again in her headphones at the computer when I returned from a brief trip downstairs to the shop in the hotel. Often, she listens to music while browsing web sites, and I have learned that she does not respond well to being interrupted.

A half hour later, my daughter walked through the door and after a quick "Hi, Katarina," plopped her bag down in her bedroom.

I noticed that Kahlo still hadn't sufficiently recovered from all the excitement and lack of sleep at Chaco Canyon, because she had put her head down on her hands and had fallen asleep. When Aurore returned from the bedroom and noticed Kahlo still asleep, my daughter veered over and sat down near me in a big southwest décor chair of pine and Indian blanket fabric.

"Well, were you able to boil away your problems, or did one remain in the pool with you?"

"The latter. There was a strange twist. I thought I was meeting my returned-from-the-dead sister as well as our acquaintance from the canyon, Mr. Ristraverdé."

"Let me guess. The whole Ashleigh mystique turned out to be a spoof in poor taste, and the canyon man didn't show."

"Nope. Both showed. And Ashleigh is alive, possibly well, and may even have metamorphosed into a less onerous version of her former self."

"Well, what went wrong?"

"Nothing initially," my daughter replied with a sigh. "I got a long explanation of how Ashleigh had achieved being among the undead and was still gracing the planet. Then Ristraverdé showed up. And that's where the story changes course.

"The canyon man was shrewd enough to realize that the two of us getting up to no good in a mineral bath just wasn't on. That any aquatic frolicking would be nothing more than that, and at least one of the two of us considers herself too old to get up to any such nonsense with a casual acquaintance."

"Wait a minute, dear daughter. You can't just pass over how Ashleigh managed to pretend to be dead."

Aurore filled me in with the long tale of Ashleigh's ruse, how she had turned to philanthropical pursuits in New Mexico, and how apparently our faux-buried relative had called upon Kaliber to rekindle what had begun two years earlier in a Tesuque parking lot.

"But getting back to my dilemma of feeling a third party left out of a game of musical ponds, Kaliber and Ashleigh at the Ojo Hotel's dining room table were both smirking that all would be well soon. Then who should come through the door but the NPS ranger from Grants, Aldebaran. It seems Kaliber had realized that any real chance for my successfully reentering the dating game would be with Chichilticalli. The canyon man had rediscovered Ashleigh, and through her had found out Aldebaran and I had a history of chemistry from our days in England."

"So? What happened to dispel this idyllic setting?"

"Well," my daughter said, shaking her head, "we got in a moonlit private tub, both thinking we could surpass the springs water temperature in recreating the old Oxford days."

"And?"

"Patience, Mamá. I couldn't do it. I just couldn't do it. I told Chichilticalli that I had responsibilities now, and that his life in Grants and mine in Santa Fe would never be a copasetic fit."

As we both considered this odd series of encounters, I looked over at Kahlo. Her head was still down on her hands and tears were streaming down her arms and head bouncing in a manner that telegraphed one of her unpredictable fugues. Aurore went over, gently removed her headphones, and put a hand on her head.

"What's wrong, Kahlo? Something bad on the internet?"

She nodded in agreement without lifting her convulsing head.

"What is it?" my daughter asked, as I jumped up from the couch to join in getting to the bottom of my granddaughter's tears.

Kahlo shook her head, indicating she did not wish to talk.

"Kahlo, what's wrong," I asked. "If you don't tell your Mother and I, we won't be able to help."

"M-m-mom'll never m-m-marry again..." she said while sitting up and dashing away tears.

"What prompted that, Kahlo?" asked Aurore. "One minute you

have fallen asleep while listening to music and browsing the internet. And the next you're in tears. Something must have happened."

"I-I-I turned off my headphones. I w-w-wasn't sleeping. I heard ev-ev-everything you s-s-said about Chi-chi-chichilti-c-c-calli."

"Well, I'm sorry dear, but I'm just not ready to marry the first man that comes my way."

Kahlo stood up and turned toward us. "But I w-w-want my f-father."

"But we don't know who your biological father is," I tried to console my granddaughter as she slumped toward the second bedroom. "The adoption agency isn't permitted to reveal that sort of information."

"I'm sorry that you don't have a father and that we don't know who he is," my daughter added. "I know I'm hard to please and I may not marry. But is there something else, Kahlo? When I came in your head was already down at the computer."

"I heard a n-n-news story on CNN," she answered, putting her hands up upon both ears. "And it's all m-m-my fault."

"What's your fault, Kahlo?"

"I told too much s-s-stuff, and now Ranger P-p-plentyhorn will q-q-quit."

"Why will he quit, Kahlo?

It was then that I realized I had yet to tell Aurore about the intrusive television news she hadn't probably yet heard during her trip to Ojo Caliente.

"B-b-because."

"Because why? Hasn't Ranger Plentyhorn chosen his job at Chaco because he loves it?"

Kahlo nodded in agreement. "B-b-but he said he'd quit if they ever p-p-p-paved the road in. And now they w-will." And with that the little investigator ran in and buried her face in a bedspread covering the pillows on her bed.

As Aurore and I exchanged perplexed glances, I gave my granddaughter a minute to calm down and then walked into her bedroom.

"I know this isn't a good time, Kahlo, but there are two ways you can look at what's transpiring. Either shrink from any tasks that develop from your revelations. Or you can welcome the attention and how it may help thousands and thousands of other kids. I was fortunate, for instance, when my parents encouraged me to continue concert piano playing, when just like you, I was overwhelmed by all the attention and wanted to quit playing forever.

"Unfortunately, the attention, for better or for worse, is probably here for quite a while. But one way of looking at it may be that all your Chaco speculations are in the best interests of children like you everywhere. Katalyn Morgen has phoned to say the contributions you've already made have been enormously inspiring to adults and kids alike. Ms. Morgen also told me that archeologists, administrators, and rangers have requested you come back to Chaco one more time to reveal more of your investigations. That, of course, will be up to you.

"Then a young boy with a different speech impediment than yours is in hospital and wishes to talk to you on the telephone this afternoon. His name is Bobby Atsitsana, and a Gallup doctor has told me the cancer he has most probably means he will not survive much beyond spring break. Apparently after hearing about you on TV, he just wants to hear your voice."

Kahlo didn't move at all, then finally lifted her face a little off the pillow. "I don't want to t-t-talk to anyone," she snorted. "I want my f-f-father, and I'm not s-s-saying anything more about my s-s-stupid ideas."

# A Buried Treasure

(KALIBER)

If there is one thing to be said about my life since I've come to New Mexico, is that living alone in a remote canyon hasn't prevented my meeting several of the peculiar dudes you read about in dime novels, and even the Black Queen herself. Man! For a woman over 50, Ashleigh hasn't lost any of that same dark magnetism she first displayed in Tesuque. I mean the woman stripped down near that starlit Ojo pond like we had known each other for years. Yet her sister was wrong in her guess that the resurrected Black Queen and I had already done some rock 'n' rolling in my shack. While I had a couple shots of Puerto Rican rum, she merely recounted her whole odyssey of deception and theft of her former brother-in-law's scepter.

You might say Ashleigh has a way of saying exactly what she feels, which by now you probably have ascertained is the kind of no-bullshit approach yours truly finds most appealing. Both Aurore and Ashleigh can easily carve up any male should he fail to be truthful. It's like a sixth sense. Except that the Black Queen and those dark eyes could see through any scam or duplicity without even hearing someone deliver more than a few bogus words.

Yet that same intensity carries over into her sexuality and sensuality. Those pointed, sloping breasts glistening just above water line in that Ojo pool telegraphed the aura of a woman who will probably never let chronological age get in the way of a good time. She has *cojones* when it comes to conversation, but plenty of curves to reverse any antagonism that develops during a good argument.

I was worn out when I left Ojo, and she again was to disappear to who knows where in the outback or limited urban centers of New Mexico. But before we parted company, we did have one last conversation.

"What are you going to do about the Q-man's continuing lesson of greed versus altruism?" I asked. "Or is his having lost the Cortez Ruby Scepter enough mental anguish for the big man in his out-West treasure quest? Since you said you'd be on your way early, I called him by cell and I'm meeting him for some late grub at Tecoloté in Santa Fe this morning."

"Good question," she said, positioning her bolero hat atop her head. "I'm thinking it might be best to make it easy for him to get the Scepter back to see what he does. You must admit I have a vivid imagination when it comes to ruses, so I might have just the plan for one erstwhile New York sports journalist who drove my sister and me crazy.

"I figure I tell you where to take him to that big shopping center on Cerillos southwest of town. Then you delay him in the car outside Barboncito Market while questioning what he intends to do for his next treasure hunt. Meanwhile I pull into the lot not far away from your relic of a Subaru or his blue beast Pontiac convertible and make sure that while climbing out of my car and going into the market, you tell Cantrell you saw me.

"You then tell him I've got to have the Scepter somewhere in my car, because I wouldn't leave it in a motel room where a maid might find it, and I wouldn't carry it into the store where the metal could cause some problems with the exit anti-theft devices. You also tell him a friend of yours told him how easy it is to jimmy a car door lock, then go with him and pretend to be jimmying it by using a key I give you while you send him back to look at the trunk lock. I'll leave the Scepter in an oily blue rag so that it looks like I've concealed it should anyone look. You tell him that I've revealed that I always keep it in the rag under the front seat or under the spare tire in the trunk. And if he asks you why you're betraying your recent conquest, you can tell him I've contemplated giving it back to him just to get him to finish his quest and get the hell out of New Mexico. He knows I never cared that much about money because I always had plenty. It won't be long, anyway, before summer football training camps will be beckoning to Mr. Cantrell."

The whole thing went as smoothly as Ashleigh had predicted. I had to be a little careful with using the key in the front door lock so he wouldn't notice while he was inspecting the trunk, and I had to let him find the scepter in the rag. A few minutes after one o'clock the Q-man had a big smile on his face as he was gunning his cobalt Pontiac down Cerillos.

"We've gotta go to Mádrid," he said.

"Why Mádrid? Isn't that a town of hippies and knick-knack shops?"

"Yah, but a couple of guys live somewhere outside of town there that may pay some serious cash for the scepter."

Because I ate my entire burrito with Christmas sauces and three biscuits less than an hour earlier at Tecoloté, I burped before speaking. "How'd you find them?"

"From a pay phone, I called three or four gem and artifacts shops and off-handedly asked about any private collectors who might be interested in rare jewelry artifacts. I did it before I ever found the Mogollon Cross and Cortez Ruby Scepter, because once any sort of object might be reported missing, all the art and gem shops get calls telling them to be on the lookout for anyone asking about fencing jewelry or artifacts. McGarrity in one of his mysteries clued me to how professionals ask in advance rather than after any illegal deals to avoid suspicion.

"Now all I do is stop and make a random pay phone call from a service station and arrange to meet these guys in a discreet location. They look over the scepter I've only vaguely described as a valuable antiquity including rubies and silver, and if they like what they see, they give me cash and that's the end of it. Meanwhile, I'll drop you off in town and you can cruise the main street and the shops or have a beer somewhere."

"Any danger level in dealing with these characters."

"I would think so. But just to make sure they don't pull anything I'm going to have a GPS Ubi-400 taped inside my sock above my ankle. So even if they steal my boots, the device should still be able to locate me. Since you can't check the GPS internet site, I'll give you my cell with the number for positioning checking, and if I'm not back within an hour, you can start looking. Or if you feel up to it, I can drop you off a quarter mile off or so from our rendezvous point and after a few minutes you can walk in to somewhere out of sight to listen and see if you can see the dudes and their vehicle and plates."

"How much do you reckon you can get for it?"

"My guess from conversations I've had is that it's worth more than a million. But I figure if they offer 50-100,000 dollars, I'll take it. I like risk, but only in limited quantities, and whatever they come up with I'll probably just plonk that down on a Broncos-Jets game bet and several other spreads this fall.

"I forgot to mention one more thing. I'm going to be wearing a wire I bought years ago from a tabloid reporter covering the JonBenet Ramsey case. If you can get close enough you could even listen with a transponder and earphone."

Just where he was going to meet these characters was unimportant to me. It was hard enough keeping my mouth shut about everything Ashleigh had confided in me. Sort of divided loyalties, as it were. But hey, this was Cantrell's one shot out West, and I knew it was important for him to come up with something truly valuable. Something that he could first fence without wrestling over altruism versus greed, and then use the proceeds to roll the football game spread dice. Everyone has some unique value they want to collect or sell. I'm lucky because I don't give a rat's ass about treasure, unless high on the carbon scale. I'm just as guilty as Q-man in the sense that I'm a rock and gem hunter and collector. Find me a raw diamond northwest of Ft. Collins, a gold nugget in the tailings of a Gold Hill Mine, or some of the raw peridot I regularly pull out of a disguised location not far from my canyon, and I hoard some of the best pieces. True, I do give some to Ketl to mitigate my collecting habits. But I'm about as pure as a sewage processing plant.

On the other crafty hand, I'm somewhat like Cantrell in that I like risky business. Otherwise, I never would have tangled with the woman sporting black lipstick or her word-cruncher-with-carrot-hair sister. They're more dangerous than any precious stones or minerals, radon gas, or unearthed buried treasure. But I liked the idea of following the big man and trying to hear what goes down in some obscure arroyo or other burned-out remote area southeast of Madrid.

After he dropped me off, I took the same sort of precaution I sometimes used in the jungles of Nam—which I won't mention now because it's a secret I never talk about unless I am forced to call it into play. It then probably took me about five minutes to walk the quarter mile to where from a distance I could first see the two cars. Then I headed up behind a rutted ridge that I figured would conceal me until I could peek to see just where the Q-man and his unpredictable middlemen had gone.

I was just about to give up when I found overlapping creosote and juniper bushes behind which I could remain undetected. It was just like in the cowboy movies, as I parted a couple of branches and suddenly could see the three of them standing below at the confluence of two small empty arroyos. The two dudes looked harmless enough, maybe like a couple of ranchers talking to a neighbor about putting up a fence. But I figure those are the worst types: the kinds that talk as if civilized, then shoot you just because with what you've sold them or told them you turn out to be superfluous to their future. If they're the sneaky sorts who fence stolen goods or jewelry and gems, the fact that you've seen them can prove to be a hazard to your departure. And then they get the cash back they just gave you, as well.

The whole remote transaction thing had a smell redolent of several misfortunate scenarios I had walked into in Nam. Not an actual smell, but rather a morally corrupt odor that first hits your sixth sense as you enter an area. You know something ain't right. And that's how I felt as Cantrell walked toward these two characters, one of which had put a Halliburton metal case down beside his boot. The fact that Q-man was hoping to acquire some real betting money way out here in the middle of nowhere had a similar distinct fatal aroma you sense in the jungle just before someone in your squad gets nailed by a sniper, claymore mine, or booby trap.

The two dudes said something, but I couldn't get the transponder to work. I thought I had blown it, because I tapped the tiny plastic box a couple of times and turned it on and off. But after a few crackles in the headphone, suddenly I could hear Cantrell.

"...Of course," he said before leaning down to pull up his jeans over the top of tan boots people who would never consider hand-tooled cowboy numbers wear in the East or Midwest. "It's not the sort of thing I want to carry in an attaché case."

The one character's clothes looked a little too fresh, as if earlier he was replacing the rings in an old Chevy before tidying up for his second job of acting muscle in clandestine deals. He would have fit right into our Cavalry unit in the rice paddies. The mechanic turned the Scepter over, then handed it to the dude who had a 40-inch waist, but a 34-inch belt with one of those huge silver buckles that telegraph you're from out West.

The heavy-set fellow turned the Scepter over a couple of times, back and forth, then pulled out one of those monoculars gem people use to look more closely for characteristic or flaws. He carefully examined a couple of the stones, scratched one with testing pencils, and then put the end of the Cross in his mouth and bit down.

"What is this shit?" he said with a decidedly ornery look upon a face burned by the sun.

"What do you mean?" Q-man's voice crackled apprehensively in my ear.

"I mean this is a fake," he said, handing it back to Cantrell. "The rubies are nothing more than flawed tourmaline, and the silver is a pewter patina over lead."

"How do you know they're tourmaline and not rubies?" Q unconvincingly asked.

"Rubellite crystals are striated; ruby crystals aren't. The cabochon cut is another giveaway. A period piece this is mocked up to be would have featured brilliant or step cuts." Then he just shook his head like some crazed Viet Cong might when interpretation is becoming burdensome. "If you conducted a Moh's hardness test, you knew that a topaz test pencil scratches tourmaline, because it's only 7-1/2 on the hardness scale, while topaz won't scratch a ruby because it's a 9 and almost as hard as a diamond."

"But I didn't."

"So, you say." The dude shot a glance at the back-up man beside him before angrily looking back at Cantrell. "What all of this means is I think you're trying to scam us."

I didn't learn of the Scepter until after that crazy railroad party when Ashleigh stole it from Cantrell. And when she showed it to me, I didn't even want to touch it because I didn't yet know about Ketl's substitution games and figured it was hot. But when I heard the dude say all that nasty shit, I knew the moment had the same sort of deathly feel that every ominous interrogation situation oozes in Nam. It was the worst type of silence: just like in the jungle when the insects and birds suddenly become silent. You know no matter what you say, your ass is in deep shit.

Cantrell started to stammer about not knowing, and that he must have been scammed. But I knew and he knew he was in big trouble. And I didn't have a gun to save his ass. I just had to hope it was like the rare interrogation when an American grunt is asked about something he can't or won't answer, and his captors in sunglasses decide just to bust up his insides real bad rather than shoot him.

There was always revenge. Yah, that's right. Never mind turning the other cheek. When you see your buddy's jaw get blown off, it doesn't take anything further to incite the old eye-for-an-eye adage. And the scenario down below me decidedly had that sort of feel.

"I don't think we have any more use for either of these fakes, do you, Bart?" the overweight dude said to his partner. "And we obviously won't be needing the contents of this case," he added, picking up the Halliburton.

The thin man just shook his head and pursed his lips. Then he pulled out one of those long silver 44 magnums he must have had stuck in his belt behind and under his sleeveless hunting vest.

"Now wait a minute," Q-man said while backing up slightly. "I didn't know anything more about this being a fake than you did. No one's seen it but me, and I just assumed it's legit."

"Yah, well that's your hard luck, isn't it," snarled the thin man.

The big man nodded to his accomplice ever so slightly.

And that was it. The thin man shot Q five times. The noise was so loud I had to take the wire's earplug out for a couple of seconds. Eighty-twenty they never intended to leave without both the Scepter and the case of money. Dead men tell no tales.

Both put on gloves, then dragged Cantrell over to a ditch and covered him with dirt and rocks. The big dude wiped down the Cross to remove any fingerprints, walked a hundred yards in the opposite direction and stuck it in the ground as if one of those roadside memorials you see for those who can't afford a tombstone or graveyard. Then as they backed up to their car, they used a couple of long piñon branches to wipe away their boot tracks as they went. Wind and rain would soon take care of anything residual.

Initially I had been too shocked to move. The shots had all been fired so rapidly. I figured they'd at least take him somewhere even more remote where I could follow and maybe intercede. But no. They killed his ass as if he were no more than a coyote.

In just the few times I had encountered this big bear of a sports scribbler, I can't explain why, but I felt the guy had a heart most people will never see. Yah, he had his faults, and projected the protective self-involvement of those who their whole lives watch others and describe it rather than doing it themselves. But he did care about the pariahs and misfits that nobody cares about. Yah, he altruistically gave the Mogollon Cross back to old man Ketl and selfishly kept the Cortez Ruby Scepter for himself. But in two months he would have written something nice about some inner-city kid who got his break at a major football university and after playing in the NFL would send his kids to college. Q-man didn't fit in with everyone on the block, but his stories had provoked people to think. That was his legacy. And that's all that can be asked of those unable to withstand the emotions of family life.

Anyway, I let the two scoundrels go on their way, took my boots off, and walked over and retrieved the Scepter. Unfortunately, Cantrell's death would be too hard to explain away. It was better to give him an anonymous burial in the same way he would have slipped into obscurity after his last article.

I quickly used my hands in a soft arroyo bottom with only some chamisa growing in it. I pulled Cantrell from underneath the cairn they had built and after taking the keys, cards, and IDs out of his pockets and global positioning device off his ankle, dragged him into the makeshift grave and placed the Scepter on top of the big man. But I didn't cover him up just yet.

The reason was my chronograph told me that the two assassins had been gone exactly nine minutes and 30 seconds. I cocked my head and listened. Because in 10 minutes they should have been maybe three miles away, just on the other side of Mádrid, heading back north to distance themselves from their recent misguided proceedings.

Ka-BLAM!

I could still hear it, although just barely, as if a distant rifle shot. When the two shooters were departing, I activated a timer I had secured under their car on my way in. Exactly 10 minutes after they left Q-man, the dynamite stick wired to the timer I duct-taped to the gasoline tank did its work. It was just like the pajama sniper that had shot my buddy. He didn't count on my seeing the puff of smoke still floating in the humid air. Nor had he figured out how hard you hit the ground from 30 feet up when someone shoots the palm tree in which you're sitting completely in half. There's rarely a reason to kill another human being. But when there is, religious, racial, or political hatred, greed, avarice, or jealousy inevitably releases the horsemen of the apocalypse. And for those who think they've have gotten away with something, revenge is the ultimate surprise.

# Kahlo Makes the Call

(KETL)

After Kaliber gave me the bag of peridot in the shop, I dropped it off at a gemologist who buys the raw gems from me. I stayed over with a friend who lives in an abandoned place down near the old Lamy railroad station. I needed to hang around Santa Fe for a day to see what private collectors my gemologist friend could arrange to buy the peridot, and then put the money in a Glittering World Education Foundation bank account. We've already been able to build one small school for Diné and Jicarilla Apache young people.

Most visitors would probably shop while they are in the State capital. But usually, I just walk around in the open air and then sit on a bench in the square opposite the Palace of the Governors. The weather must be right, but when I drove in from Lamy, the morning sky had a cerulean color found only at high altitude.

Some of my friends were selling silver-and-turquoise jewelry to visiting *belagaana* under the Palace portico. It's a type of business I could never do, where many Diné charge the Anglos a lot more than they'd pay in Farmington or at pueblo trading posts. But except for the summer, most of the tourists don't get much farther than Santa Fe. And when they see all those Indians sitting in a row under the portico, they think they're witnessing our natural trading and selling at work.

I sit in the square and watch all the people who've never survived on a maize-and-bean diet walk by. The sun warms me up, and often in the afternoons music is played by those releasing spiritual treasures but lacking earthly bank accounts. I like Anglo music as much as I do our own chanting and drumming. At my age, I don't get into town all that often. But spending time in crowded Santa Fe always makes me glad I can return to the simplicity of my destiny in the Glittering World.

"It's Ketl, isn't it?"

I looked up and blocking the sun looked like the old woman I had driven into Cuba. I couldn't remember her name.

"I'm Katarina," she said, stepping to the side a bit so I didn't have to shade my eyes. "You rescued my granddaughter and me at Pueblo Pintado."

I nodded. I knew an Anglo woman her age would expect me to say something. But didn't know what. So, I smiled.

"Do you mind if I sit down?"

I patted my hand on the bench so that she would sit. "Please."

The old woman had something on her mind. But I think she understood about waiting for either of us to say something. We both sat there with the sun high above the adobe walls to the east and the scent swirling around us of caramelized baked goods that Anglos eat for breakfast.

"I'm worried about Kahlo," the old woman said, adjusting her hat to shade her face as she turned toward me.

"She has the burden of being wise beyond her years."

Katarina turned her face back toward the south while our thoughts focused on the little one who has visions.

"A young boy I think you know apparently is dying of leukemia in a Gallup hospital," she said. "He heard about Kahlo's talk at Chaco and wants to have Kahlo call him on the phone. It's something I know would probably prove rewarding to both. But Kahlo doesn't seem to be in the mood to talk to anyone. She is worried about preserving the sanctity of Chaco Canyon. And she doesn't want all the attention. I think a chat—whether she stutters or not—would be helpful both to the boy and to Kahlo. But then I'm not a nine-year-old girl."

"You once were," I answered after a pause. Her remarks are the sort of oblique comments the white people are good at, and to which normally I wouldn't feel comfortable responding. But the old woman was direct, and our similar ages were important in settling any differences while we both neared the end of our journeys. "Each of us has the mind of both child and adult. When an adult is confronted by a problem, the choice of an adult or childlike solution always hovers like an eagle soaring high above. Kahlo has the knowledge of an adult, but the emotions of a child."

"Yes, but eventually we must all grow up. If Kahlo wishes to apply her knowledge from visions or revelations, at some point she must learn to deal with the attention that comes with the territory. Still, she is only nine, and I think her choice is to remain silent right now."

"If you like, I will talk with her. Once I faced the same dilemma, although many years older at the time. There is a cost to revealing you know something others wish they had learned first."

Katarina said very little more. Yet her eyes conveyed that she still possessed the spirit of learning and curiosity of those much younger. For a *belagaana* elder she had an aura of days gained and lost. Few days passed without the old woman learning more from the great wealth of knowledge and experience of her world; others were lost to the insidious curse of Native Americans and Anglos alike: alcohol. Spirits from the bottle always disguise an attempt to end pain, whether from physical suffering, or from mental anguish and the inability to fit in. Those we encounter on the journey of life are never accidental. Nor do such encounters involve luck. They are our destiny. And how we react and learn from them determines much of what we perceive as happiness or unhappiness. I hoped the spirits from the bottle would be defeated before Katarina's youthful spirit of curiosity was overwhelmed by her need to begin the long trip north. She was unusual for an Anglo woman. I felt she would give her last breath to save her granddaughter, and that made me comfortable sitting with or walking beside her.

When we got to their rooms in the Loretto, Kahlo was at the computer. I could tell the electronic box was her best friend in that it made no demands upon her, giving her the pleasure she lacked from others her own age.

"Kahlo," Katarina said while she tapped upon her granddaughter's shoulder. "Guess who's here? Ketl, who rescued us at Pueblo Pintado."

The child leapt up from her chair and put her arms around me. She then removed her headphones and we all three sat down on the bright-colored furniture many Anglos seem to buy to create the same colors we enjoy outside of our hogans and through our weavings. Katarina excused herself to take care of the urgent needs of someone in her eighth decade. But I knew that she wanted to give me an opportunity to talk with the precocious one of ancient visions.

"I think your grandmother told you that a young Zuni boy from our school near Gallup is in hospital with a disease the Anglos call leukemia," I said, looking into the sun streaming through the window. "Before he went into hospital for traditional *belagaana* care, a *Yataalii* conducted a *Yeibechai* curing chant for him. But the white doctors tell that his time to travel to the spirit world will soon come." I then waited a moment for the young one of visions to remember what she had learned of Bobby Atsitsana's call.

"Is Bobby a Zuni?" the young one asked as if a special meaning exists to be among the Pueblo tribe descended from the Anasazi. Then I understood. When I again looked into her eyes, I felt as if through Kahlo flows the blood of both *A'shiwi* and *Nakai*.

"When I visited him, he said he heard about your investigations in Chaco Canyon. He made a wish to the Gods some still believe live upon Dowa Yalanne Mesa that he might meet you or talk by telephone. I told him meeting you would not be possible. But I would try to contact your grandmother to see if you might grant Bobby's wish. I do not know if your destiny involves talking to Bobby Atsitsana or not. That is a difficult decision to make for a young woman whose solitude has helped her gain great wisdom."

"I want to talk to him," Kahlo said, jumping up from her chair. Then when I again gazed at into the rays of the sun streaming through the window, I saw an image of Chichilticalli and what he had described of the child, Argentacruz, and his wife Magdalena when she gave birth on *El Malpais*. Katarina came back into the room and before she could sit on the couch, I stood up.

"I have to go now," I said, not knowing exactly which *belagaana* traditions to honor when leaving.

Kahlo rushed over and wrapped her arms around me. I put my hand on her head. "Both of you must come visit me in my hogan. It is small, but I have a second bed and a couch. I hope you will honor me with a visit, maybe when you are going to Chaco, and it is dry enough to leave by the south road. From there it is not long to my hogan."

Kahlo jumped up and down as Katarina and I shook hands. The look in the Anglo elder's eyes said she, too, wished to say more. But parting gets more awkward the older you get. You do not feel comfortable with the open displays of affection for the young. Just a look says much about whether someone unexpectedly wishes to see you again soon.

"W-will you stay while I call?" Kahlo asked bashfully while taking my hand.

How could I refuse? There was a good chance both Bobby and Kahlo would be rewarded by a talk.

"We can use the speaker phone so you and Grammy can hear."

This was a big step for a small girl from two worlds. But I sensed that with me listening in, she would stutter very little.

Soon the young one had dialed up Gallup. "Is this Bobby?"

"Yes, it is. Who's this?"

"Kahlo."

"Oh, wow!" he exclaimed. "It's Kahlo, and she *has* called like Ketl said she might."

"How do you feel? I know it isn't easy to b-be in the hospital."

"People here are real nice and have helped me a lot. I also have lots of visitors and we have been hearing about you in the news. One news reporter says she thinks you might have a Zuni father. And when I heard that I just hoped that I could talk to you, especially since I won't be able to meet you. My friends all surf the internet and think your investigations are really cool, and so do I. Sometimes in my hospital room here they wheel in a computer on a table and I can check e-mails and look at stuff on Chaco. I love Chaco Canyon. I really appreciate your calling because I know you're real busy right now and all."

"I'm glad you're feeling better. Sometime today or tomorrow I'll send you an e-mail. A-And if you get a chance with the computer, I'd sure like to hear more about your life in the Z-zuni Pueblo."

"I will, for sure. Besides, Mom says I won't be here that much longer. They're going to let me go home, and when they do, I can use my computer in my room."

"I will look forward to hearing from you, Bobby. And if my Grammy and I get out to Chaco again, to visit our friend Ketl—who's h-here right now—maybe we can m-meet."

"Fantastic! Thanks again for calling me, Kahlo. It means a lot even though the nurse says I have to go soon to have some tests made."

"*Yah-tay*, Bobby."

"Is that Ketl on the other phone?"

"Speakerphone. And I heard you say you're feeling better. Kahlo is a very special young woman, and I'm glad you two got to talk. I'll be out to Gallup later today to see you."

"Thanks, Ketl. Oh, and Kahlo?"

"Yes?"

"Is it true that you might know something different about the Seven Cities?"

"M-m-maybe."

"Because they said on the news that scientists and educators want you to talk again at the Chaco Visitor Center, but that you and your Grandmother don't think it would be a good idea."

Kahlo just sat there, and Katarina and I both understood how difficult the heart of such speculations was for her.

"I've talked to kids from Zuni, Gallup, Chinle, and Kayenta, and they've talked to lots of their friends," Bobby continued. "They all hope you keep going with your investigations, Kahlo. I know it's hard, talking and all. Because people thought I had a speech impediment when I talked so loud. Then they found out I have trouble hearing in one ear.

"But if you could possibly do another talk, it would mean a lot to many of the Native American kids I know and me. Even our Mexican grocer says he has seven nieces and nephews in Juarez and Nogales who have all called wanting to know more about you. They admire you so much. It sure would be special to the kids in our schools if you could talk again, even if we can't be there. But if you can't do it, we'll understand. We just hope that no matter what, you know how much your cool explorations mean to at least the Native

American kids out here. Thanks a lot, Kahlo, for spending time to talk to me."

I could tell Kahlo's mind was working like that of an adult, but her speech *chindi* impairing a complete answer.

"I have t-t-trouble t-t-talking to so many p-people," she said, turning away from us to wipe her eyes with her wrist.

"I know, Kahlo. Not to worry. Everyone I know's inspired by what you've done anyway."

"Bye, Bobby," Kahlo said, no longer able to conceal a torrent of tears. "It was sure g-g-good talking to you."

# Black Queen Checkmate

(CHICHILTICALLI)

The winds were up as the two of us stood in the Northwest New Mexico Visitor Center parking lot. Stretched out to the south, *El Malpais* looked just like it has for a thousand years. Strata of grey cirrus clouds that drop no precipitation and merely obscure the high desert sun for less than an hour or two were sweeping overhead from the west.

Kaliber had something on his mind. He seemed more agitated than the occasional hyperactive moods evidenced on our train trip and asked that I meet him outside for a private talk about something that had occurred in Mádrid. It was after hours for the Center, but he had called me before he left the town south of Santa Fe and asked that I wait for Ashleigh to drop him off.

I had done a lot of thinking myself, all of it seemingly leading nowhere. Aurore was on my mind, as were Kahlo and Katarina, and just how my future might somehow be intertwined with theirs. No matter how I looked ahead, however, my destiny still appeared to focus on interactions with visitors to New Mexico. Other than a vestigial interest rekindled by speculations from Kahlo, astronomy seemed a distant pursuit much the same as that of Aurore. Studying the stars might have suited a year in Oxford, but in this millennium,

I felt compelled to regain my sense of Zuni tribal as well as New Mexican life.

Maybe it was atavistic. The Four Corners is a place like no other. One lifetime is not enough to assimilate either its grandeur or spiritual offerings. As a contrast, big city life has a far more dangerous appeal. I miss the witty and complex serendipitous conversations of urban readers who augment the simple things in life with polemics, sophisticated mind games, and subtle humor.

What was I to do, if anything, about my feelings for Aurore and Kahlo, and for that matter, even Katarina? The three Dupíns still invaded my daily thoughts as if leaving them out of my future would be a cardinal sin. Each was special in a unique but somehow intricate way far different than the contrast of the resurrected Ashleigh. There loomed a certain high maintenance having nothing to do with earthly possessions or money. Spending substantial time with any one of the four sirens demanded an emotional roller coaster ride I kept telling myself I was unprepared to make. Any such odyssey didn't fit in with my relatively un-complex and narrowly defined existence. And any of these considerations ignored the dilemma that an acquired Zuni/Oxford education guaranteed a certain schizophrenic quandary over almost any behavioral direction.

At the same time, an anthropologist friend once warned me that the complexity of life on the planet, taken in total, never regresses. Civilization keeps getting more complex, witness air travel, e-mail, and the internet. None will disappear unless superseded by more complex and efficient developments. Having enjoyed an entire year's submersion in the reading, writing, as well as oral comedies and tragedies of England, maybe I needed to extrapolate some of the salient bits into my now less complex existence. Include occasional ventures into further arcane knowledge as well as contact with those who value a clever turn of phrase. A confusing corollary emphasizing that point would be the Dupíns' ongoing connections to my life.

Yet how did I reconcile the thirst for mental growth with a desire to avoid the long devolution into pseudo-sophistication? Neither simple nor complex world completely suited me. And the same could be said of the trio of Dupíns. When away from them, I missed their spontaneous and unpredictable approach to post-cosmopolitan New York life. Yet at the same time, further contact guaranteed certain levels of emotional conflict.

I was undergoing these desultory bombardments while waiting for Kaliber to knock on the locked glass front doors. It wasn't long after his estimated time of arrival, however, that the reclusive rock hunter thundered away on my little refuge of *Malpaisian* Badlands heaven.

"Yo, Chich-man. Some heavy stuff went down in Mádrid."

As we walked out into the parking lot facing the desolate expanse of lava beds to the south, the breezes picked up. The nature of the Wind Gods seemed as if a portent mirroring impending decision-making time.

"Q-man's dead."

"You're kidding."

"No more than an undertaker. He tried to fence that Cortez Scepter and things got real ugly. It's a long story, but Ashleigh hoped to get him to exit New Mexico by making it easy for him to get the Scepter back. He had arranged to sell it for cash to a couple of dudes outside of Mádrid. They looked harmless enough. But those are always the types that kill your ass, whether it's in the city, a jungle, or the high deserts of New Mexico. As a friend of mine who grew up in East Los Angeles used to say, 'Never fear the big man. It's the wiry, thin guy that will knock you down before you know what hit you.' And he was right.

"These two looked like a couple of ranchers. Q-man was wearing a wire and he dropped me off on the way in to meet them, so I was able to climb up above to listen and watch. The one fence man used a monocular and a scratch test and quickly found out the scepter was bogus: flawed tourmaline and silver-covered lead. The other guy pulled out a big silver long-barreled pistol and shot Q before I could do anything. They buried him under some rocks and dirt and split."

"So, they got away?"

"They got three miles or so."

"Just three miles?"

"Yah, while I reburied Q with the Scepter in a suitable grave. I figured it would be better if he disappeared than trying to explain what had happened to the cops. But that's as far as our desperado friends got."

"I don't understand. Why'd they only get three miles?"

"Bad karma."

"If it wasn't for B.B. King bad luck, they wouldn't have no luck at all?"

"You got it. Their day turned from bad to worse."

"Flat tire?"

"A *touch* more. I used a remote-control device to send them to a more challenging level of dealing. They didn't believe Kaliber that he didn't know the scepter was an imitation; I didn't believe Kaliber liked the real nasty shit they dealt him for his trouble. It's sort of like when your buddy in Nam gets his legs blown off after he trip-wired a claymore mine. Your attitude toward whoever did it becomes its own Monster Slayer, as my obscure ancient Navajo relative might say."

"So, it's as if Cantrell just left the state, because few knew he was here and no one but Ashleigh and you knew he had the scepter."

"Yah, No *corpus delicti* and no fixed address for the deceased. I smashed up his cellphone and drove to the Santa Fe Railroad station in Lamy on the way back and buried his global positioning device near there. If anyone checks the web site to track him, they'll think he boarded a freight or passenger train, and by removing the device's battery, any record of where he went stopped being transmitted in Lamy. I also know a place we can hide the cobalt blue beast after we get it in Santa Fe from a side street where I beached it before Ashleigh picked me up at a Cerrillos parking lot. I'll call two guys I know in Gallup. They'll make sure the Pontiac soon ends up in Mexico. Old man Ketl will leave the scepter underground with our late journalist friend to make it disappear for at least a year or two."

"What about the two men? Won't anyone wonder why they blew up in their car?"

"Oh yah. But guys like that won't have told anyone anything about where they were going or what they were after. So, any relative, friend or collector will just think it was some sort of fenced goods or drug deal turned bad. The police will investigate but find nothing and assume the same thing and the case will end up in an unsolved dead file."

"And Señor Cantrell must have left New Mexico."

"That's what Ashleigh said—if anyone should ask. She gave me a ride back from Santa Fe and she's over in Grants right now. We can ask her when she gets here, but I think she said he was heading on to try raising Arizona. We'll have to tell Ketl, of course, but not for a year or so when we'll make it possible for him to retrieve the scepter. Four of us knowing about what happened to Cantrell are three too many. But no one except one gemologist in Santa Fe would ever put two and two together, and he never laid eyes on Cantrell. It's like Cantrell was once a visitor to New Mexico few ever met, and now he is gone."

The two of us then spoke of the Dupíns. Kaliber said that dealing with Aurore and Ashleigh was like a perpetual wait for the other shoe to drop.

He was extolling his 12 hours with the Black Queen in Ojo just when she pulled into the lot. Having heard enough of their games in the spa pool, I didn't yet know from Ristraverdé that there would be more steamy, high blood pressure sessions between the two of them.

When Ashleigh got out of the car, she first kissed Kaliber on the lips, me on the cheek, and then stared at her Ojo partner in spa games. "O.K.," was all she said.

"You've decided?" asked Kaliber.

She nodded, pursing her lips. "Yah. I figure this is New Mexico, not Manhattan, and in order that I don't regress into the shrew I once was, it's important I find a suitable diversion. And you're it. You seem to have elements of danger to which I am drawn, while our recent re-encounter indicates spending time with you is cheaper than paying for massage and more satisfactory than solitary fantasy gratifications."

"You're not going to nag on me about cabin life, or mixing rum with Edna St. Vincent-Millay?"

The Black Queen pursed her lips and shook her head from side to side. "Not at least for a while. This is the new Ashleigh," she said. "I have to find out if I'm capable of morphing further into philanthropic behavior. The trick will be for you to tolerate occasional lapses in my convoluted temperament. You're going to have to assure I stay as relaxed as possible, and since I don't use drugs and can't match you drink for drink, that means a lot of close encounters of the first kind."

"The first kind."

"Yah. That's when you have days during which you seldom reach a standing position except for nourishment, liquid refreshment, or a brief respite to relieve excessive body temperatures."

"Sounds a real challenge, but I'll give it a go," Kaliber answered before pawing the concrete with his boot.

"Which reminds me," Ashleigh said, turning to me. "When are you and that emotionally aloof sister of mine going to throw caution to the New Mexican winds?"

"Mm...maybe not in this millennium. There are just a few problems, like she lives in Santa Fe and currently I'm tied to Grants; she thinks of Kahlo and Katarina as responsibilities I'm unprepared to handle; and I doubt if I could keep up with her drinking habits."

"All of that is merely a huge Indian smokescreen of excuses. You two began your *pas de deux* in England, and rediscovered it still exists in an Ojo Caliente pool. Aurore apparently had misgivings. Yet you can't ignore chemistry at your age. You have to do like Ristraverdé and me: just jump off the cliff."

I didn't reply. I still felt the hurdles insurmountable in their present form. The Zuni part of me was willing to wait for the natural evolution of things. In white people's terms, mine was a cowardly approach. But as a Native American it was a sensible approach to an outside world problem. Decisiveness has never been an overwhelming attribute. Then what if we could somehow resolve the seemingly overwhelming issues? Wouldn't Aurore get bored with my inability to get into complex urban life with the same enthusiasm of a trip to London when you're 25 years old? And would Katarina be able to handle a son-in-law who makes $30,000 a year?

"You two can pretend to ignore each other all you want, but eventually you both have to own up to your own needs as well as those of your daughter."

I looked out at *El Malpais* and wished it could be my ultimate refuge when verbally tangling with strong Anglo women. "How did you find out about Kahlo?"

"It cost me a pretty penny. But cash goes a long way when it comes to having a look at records that identify an adopted child's real parents. Kahlo has made several references either to Katarina or Aurore about wanting her father. And if you're her biological father, you need to carry a bouquet of indigenous cactus flowers or something else suitably romantic to Santa Fe and get down on your knee in front of my misleadingly evasive sister."

All the while Ristraverdé had taken to opening the hatchback of the Subaru and rummaging around inside. He wanted to inject some of his post-Vietnam candor yet realized silence to be the best course of non-action for the moment.

"And besides," added Ashleigh, as the wind whipped the folds of her tailored black silk western shirt, "if Katarina is correct about the conversation Kahlo and that NASA woman had about next Wednesday, there's only one way the whirling Chaco phenom is going to survive. And it has nothing to do with how I will then disclose to her that her late aunt is alive and reformed."

# Curious Children

(KALIBER)

During the next few days I felt the same kind of dangerous enthusiasm I had when leaving Boulder and heading for New Mexico. A vast realm of the unexpected loomed, a high-desert version just as large, but involving an untested relationship with a woman who was trying to morph out of a self-indulgent solitude like my own. Ashleigh was wild sexually. But like me, she was also untamed in terms of sharing with anyone, not to mention the opposite gender.

The Black Queen had made progress, however. And so, I believed, had I. Helping Ketl with fundraising was a start in the right direction. While some might consider her stealing the scepter from the late Quivira a regression, I knew Ashleigh believed that only by distancing herself from the big man could she avoid slipping back into the negative energy of self-gratification. I know, because when you have chosen to cast off everything from your urban past to try to discover who you really are in the outback of northwest New Mexico, it's easy to relapse into morbid self-pity. Ashleigh and I were quite alike in many inadmissible ways. Yet it was that very acknowledgment by both of us that forced one concession.

And that was a hasty search through the ramshackle areas of Grants for a refuge. We needed a small casita nearby, if for nothing more than the vestigial urban amenities we both missed from time to time when roughing it at the shack. But more importantly, at least for an extended trial period, both of us knew that spending seven out of each seven days together would prove volatile enough to destroy any possibility of mutual survival. We had to have weekly trial separations during which two reclusive and abnormally self-absorbed pariahs found out what their tolerance or lack of same for close contact with another human being was. Like Ashleigh said, it had to include lots of rock 'n' roll. But you had to climb out of bed to run, rock hunt, have breakfast, fund raise or any of the other diurnal activities that come at one's own whim when living totally alone. Two characters like us had to learn just what we could and couldn't share with the other remnant from nonconformist hell.

We put down some money on a small adobe casita in the former railroad and uranium-mining center. The place was unfurnished but over time we would outfit it with beat-up relics from weekend garage sales in Grants or Gallup. It was kind of awkward walking through it. I think both of us perceived our Grants second residence to be the ultimate escape from the danger of caring too much for another human being. Still, we were optimistic we could make it work, and driving back to the canyon shack I think we both felt relieved that an escape route had been secured.

"The other big questions involve Kahlo, Aurore, Chichilticalli, and the woman from the grave," she said while negotiating a turn on a desolate stretch of road between the town on the interstate and our little location for radioactive interpersonal research. "I have a feeling that perhaps at least two revelations could alter the little whirling whiz's mindset enough to reduce her speech problems. But the other pending event on Wednesday could cause the diminutive visionary to take off her Annie Oakley gear forever."

"I'm listening," I said, the sleeve of my shirt flapping in the breeze on one of those bright days that telegraph the true bucolic value of the New Mexican high desert. Ashleigh was driving, and as opposed to most incapable of skillfully piloting a vehicle while preoccupied during cell phone use, my new finite partner was quite capable of talking and driving at the same time. But then her faculties were every bit as highly evolved as the perceptive analytical skills of her sister or niece, making Ashleigh capable of doing two things at once.

"The first notion would be for Kahlo to discover her troubled aunt is not dead after all. Hopefully that would relieve her of any guilt she may harbor for having contributed to her aunt's demise. Then if for some unforeseen reason my standoffish sister should agree to cohabitate with our NPS ranger friend—Kahlo's biological father—from Oxford and Grants, I have a distinct feeling the little dervish's speech pattern might take a turn for at least matching that of Hannah Montana. I think sometime after her final divulgence of Chaco Canyon speculations might prove to be the time for me to reappear in my niece the sleuth's soon-to-be-more public life. As annoying as many might have found me in the past, or perhaps will incur in my future persona, Kahlo and I always got along like outcasts-of-a-feather sometimes do.

"The bad news will be all the attention invariably heaped upon her after another round of archeological speculations. The news media are sharks swirling in the ocean of life's potential news shallows, just the slightest bit of blood sending them into a frenzy.

"Still, maybe her reincarnated aunt could offer another pair of sympathetic ears to which she could turn when the pressures of celebrity cause her speech pattern to implode just short of total shell shock.

"Aurore and Chichilticalli are another matter. The two of them taking the same sort of risk we have undertaken might be likened to the possibility of New Mexico becoming a rainforest."

"Yo, woman in black who speaks without forked tongue," I

interjected. "I think your rainforest analogy falls a bit short. Maybe more like the odds of winning a Powerball lottery."

The two of us drove on in silence through the parched ranches and sandstone canyons. That was another element of our newfound enchantment we needed to explore: when to speak, and when to maintain the contemplative silence upon which those who live alone thrive.

During our exploration of adapting to the adult trait of compromise, Ashleigh glanced over at me with those eyes that see into the depths of a like-minded suitor's soul. "Stranger mysteries occur every day in the Four Corners," she said, peering back through the windshield into the late afternoon gloom. "Maybe fate will intervene."

Judging from what I had caught on television in a Grants bar and restaurant during a Monday furniture scouting mission, Kahlo's prospective Chacoan astro-archeological talk—if she could affect at-length speech about anything—was being built up to be a combination of lectures by Madame Curie, Dian Fossey and Sacagawea. The little wonder was facing her biggest test, and the odds were the whole encounter could prove emotionally disastrous.

On Wednesday afternoon the three remaining Dupíns and I gathered with quite a motley yet prominent crowd of archeologists, astronomers, governmental agency types, academicians, politicians, and other interested parties in the lobby of the Chaco Culture National Historical Park's Visitor Center. Kahlo had gone on ahead into the Center's theater to prepare for what could be the most difficult talk of her life. In listening to the woman from NASA who had set up the whole Dupín *wünderkind* exposition, however, great effort had been made to ensure Aurore's daughter could reveal whatever it was she had left in her arsenal of surprises with minimal distraction. Ms. Morgen, Aldebaran and Ketl would be the only three in attendance. Ms. Morgen was to operate an overhead projector, while the other Native American pair would be there to reassure the youthful visionary should her speech pattern become erratic. There would be one camera in the room, a Skycam on loan from NFL games, that would silently broadcast and record Kahlo's speculations as well as travel along an overhead wire to give external audiences an up-close-and-personal view of the miniature phenom.

The rest of those of us whose presence might prove disruptive to coherent speech were either to be seated in the lobby, or outside in parking lot bleachers in front of a daylight visible screen also on loan from NBC Sports.

The not-so-late Ashleigh's plan involved listening in the lobby and then disappearing before her niece emerged from the auditorium. I got the feeling that a few unavailable preliminary shots of dark rum might have put your local rock hunter in a more relaxed state of mind regarding the little wonder's daunting task.

While Ms. Morgen was inside the theater concluding her explanation of how Kahlo's presentation might proceed, a television stage manager in the lobby asked the crowd to quiet down so that several in the production team could hear an in-house transmission of the show's opening and a correspondent's standupper.

"The closing segment of our Children Who Are Curious program tonight involves a precocious nine-year-old who refuses to let a speech impediment get in the way of her thirst for investigating ancient connections between archeology and astronomy," the show's anchor in New York began. "We feel her story and investigations are important enough to devote almost two-thirds of our program to potential astro-archeological revelations she has yet to discuss with anyone.

"For this portion our cameras will take us to the remote Chaco Culture National Historical Park well off the beaten path in northwest New Mexico. The Navajo, or Diné, as they refer to themselves, call the ancient ones that inhabited the cities of Chaco Canyon *Inoote* or *Naassaazi*. Yet from among the tribes descended from the original inhabitants, the Zuni call them *Capaqueslsiliwa*, and the Hopi refer to them as *Hisatsinom*. You may know these ancient peoples by the name, Anasazi. We will tell you more about the Anasazi and what Kahlo Dupín thinks she has discovered about them, after these messages..."

Up on the monitor came a visual indicating commercial messages that pay the bills were to be inserted, then the stage manager in the lobby again asked for quiet.

"O.K., ready for the opening lead-in," a director's voice, from a production trailer outside, came over the monitor, "in...five...four...three...two...one...and take studio camera one."

"For tonight's story of Kahlo Dupín and more on her Anasazi Civilization investigative speculations..." the anchor back in New York's voice continued.

The director's voice overrode that of the anchor's: "Standby for Tsoodzil standupper... In...5...4..."

"...we now go to our correspondent live northeast of Chaco Canyon in New Mexico, Estibalíz Tsoodzil..."

"...2...1, take remote camera 1."

The monitor depicted a side-lit woman with long black hair blowing in the light breezes alongside what had to be the main highway north of Chaco, with Twin Angels Peaks in the distance.

"I stand approximately 23 miles from Chaco Canyon, at the entrance to what in three miles becomes a twisting mainly dirt-and-gravel road separating the park entrance from one of our present-day civilization's high-speed transportation arteries," Tsoodzil's standupper began. "Chaco Canyon also sits adjacent to the Navajo Nation reservation, an area of New Mexico, Arizona, and Utah about the size of New England.

"The remote Chaco Culture National Historical Park and its canyon house the remnants and ruins of many cities of the ancient Anasazi civilization. It is believed that back around 600 A.D. in

Chaco Canyon the Anasazi began to construct what would become an assortment of masonry and log-roofed cities. Their building projects would continue all the way up until the year 1130. Yet less than a hundred years later the Anasazi abandoned these magnificent Chacoan cities. Lack of water or an invasion by other Native Americans remain just two speculations on why the Anasazi may have departed.

"While their famed sun dagger occurring on Fajada Butte and the alignments of buildings to the cardinal directions or windows to light streams during the solstices have been detailed by archeologists in the last 150 years, it is yet to be determined precisely how much the Anasazi knew about any possible further relationships of their architecture to the heavens. Nor have the exact usages of their extensive stone buildings with up to 600 rooms and kivas been determined. That is because the Anasazi had no written history. Although much over the last two centuries has been written about them, just what their purpose was in building these cities out in such arid terrain largely remains speculation."

"It is then that we turn to tonight's subject, nine-year-old Kahlo Dupín. CWAC has learned that our subject reputedly was born on the front seat of a truck in a trailhead parking lot of *El Malpais*, or The Badlands, a huge expanse of lava spreading out like a giant black rumpled bedspread in west central New Mexico. When Kahlo's Mexican mother Magdalena died of cancer mere months after her birth, apparently her biological father, Chichilticalli Aldebaran, a Zuni Native American who once read astronomy at Oxford under a Rhodes Scholarship and now works as a Northwest New Mexico Visitor Center NPS ranger, gave up his daughter, named Argentacruz, for adoption.

"Former New York publishing house editor Aurore Dupín subsequently renamed her adopted daughter, Kahlo, after the famous Mexican painter, Frida Kahlo. When her intelligence and stutter got in the way of forming the friendships normally springing up among young children in school, Kahlo was consistently encouraged by Aurore Dupín and her mother, the famed concert pianist Katarina Dupín, to develop her mind through reading and exploring the internet.

"As you hopefully will hear, Kahlo is quite a detective. Since Edgar Alan Poe is credited with introducing the first detective into literature, and he was a nineteenth century contemporary of the French author, George Sand, perhaps it is fitting that the daughter of Aurore Dupín, Kahlo Dupín, is a modern-day sleuth who has turned her attentions to astro-archeological investigations. George Sand's real name was Aurore Dupín. Poe's first detective was named Inspector Dupín.

"Kahlo set the world of archeology into a quandary when she was asked to present some of her ideas to a colloquium here at the Visitor Center on how a NASA educational program and coordinator might better introduce to children the connection of astronomy to such ancient civilizations. A week ago, in front of a group of imposing Bureau of Indian Affairs, National Park Service, Department of Interior and other officials, Kahlo upon a request to share her ideas began to stutter and was unable to speak about any of her speculations.

"After being accompanied to an office away from the Center's theater, however, our own Inspector Dupín, in the company of her biological father and NASA consulting educator Katalyn Morgen, began to talk nearly flawlessly. What the trio didn't know, is that because of an intercom switch left on, the experts in the auditorium heard and recorded everything, speculations whether right or wrong, archeologists and anthropologists throughout the world have found amazingly provocative.

"The importance is not whether Kahlo's revelations are correct, but rather as our program so often tries to convey, it is the unique insightful progress a nine-year-old inspirational child has made into the world of investigative discovery.

"In that previous Visitor Center office talk, Kahlo revealed ideas which include functions of the Great North Road, ceremonial baths as certain Great Kiva focal usages, the transportation of water through an Anasazi understanding of what we call hydraulics, and even certain meanings of the civilization's pottery painting. No one knows for sure what Kahlo will reveal tonight, nor whether she will be able to do so fluently, given her intermittent speech difficulties. We ask your patience, should she verbally stumble, and her unique speech traits haven't been eliminated from our pre-recording.

"To facilitate overcoming this barrier, she will have just one Sky-cam in the theater with her. Only three others will attend: NASA educator Morgen to operate an overhead projector; and two Native Americans she trusts, her biological father Chichilticalli Aldebaran, and a Navajo elder, Ketl Lizhiní-Shá, to provide any necessary psychological bolstering.

"Rumors abound. Yet speculation is that tonight our youthful investigator through her own unique observations will tie these ancient Anasazi cities to astronomy.

"You may ask yourself why we are spending so much time upon speculations by our nine-year-old subject. The program hasn't chosen to focus on the young investigator just because of her revelations and professional interest in them. The world of children is excited over Kahlo Dupín, as well. The Visitor Center here has been flooded with e-mails and phone calls from schools as far away as Juarez, Mexico, and as near as in Shiprock, Window Rock, Gallup, Chinle, Kayenta, Tuba City, and Santa Fe, all requesting an appearance by Kahlo Dupín.

"As I now raise my hand and our camera pans to the west, south and east, you will get an idea of the interest..."

All eyes on the Visitor Center's lobby monitor witnessed the camera begin to pan to a line of at least 10 yellow school buses to the West and four more to the East out along Highway 550. The raising of Tsoodzil's hand seemed to open the floodgates. The noise on the TV could have outdone a Super Bowl touchdown. Chants began to ring out from open windows, with arms waving various school colors and flags: "KAHLO! KAHLO! KAHLO!" Dignitaries and common folk like me seldom see anything like these noisy youthful explosions except during performances of rock or hip-hop groups and singers, or at high school basketball games.

"As you can see," Ms. Tsoodzil continued when the camera reached the eastern line of buses, "these kids are psyched. The New Mexico State as well as Navajo Nation Police on off-reservation loan are waiting to see if Chaco Culture National Park Center officials permit these enthusiastic busloads of worshippers into the Park.

"KAHLO! KAHLO! KAHLO!"

"If they don't," the correspondent continued, "there are going to be several hundred really disappointed but curious kids that have traveled up to four hundred miles during their spring breaks to see their inspiration..."

The room began to rumble just like in the movies. You could see an enormous quandary developing. Overuse is a big concern in Chaco, witness the difficulty in even driving in to prevent most from visiting. Yet to exclude these schoolchildren who might become the thinkers of tomorrow was a decision difficult to make.

The lobby again quieted down as an NPS administrator fielded a phone call from a ranger at the front desk. "Yes, I understand all of your concerns," he said, putting his hand over one end of the phone and turning to those behind the desk and some key departmental wags. "It's Santa Fe.

"Yes, Governor. Certainly, sir. I think you're absolutely right. I'm not only happy to accede to your wishes but to those of hundreds of others who have informed us that Kahlo must be heard."

After winding up his call from the governor, the NPS official picked up another phone and punched in some numbers. "Captain," he began, as the people in the room listened like the Pope was making a decree. "Let the buses in. Tell the kids from each school…"

The rest of what the NPS official said was drowned out by thunderous applause from those crowding the Visitor Center lobby. I counted at least five concerned faces among them desperately hoping that inside the theater Kahlo would not be daunted by the enthusiasm outside.

Few in the group had probably ever heard of the Zuni 'man-woman' maiden, We'Wha, who in 1886 delighted all of Washington, including the speaker of the House of Representatives, with her charm and demonstrations of arts and crafts. At a charity event, even President Grover Cleveland joined in enormous applause from the audience.

Kahlo is said to possess even greater powers than We'wha. All of us were about to see just what the miniature detective could come up with. The pending ordeal would not be easy for the little whiz I had heard so much about from the Lady in White and the Black Queen. Kahlo was soon to experience the pressures of possessing ancient knowledge in a far more complex modern world.

# Kahlo's Constellations

(KAHLO)
If it weren't for talking to Ketl and Bobby Atsitsana, I wouldn't be here in the Chaco Culture Visitor's Center theater. I couldn't even pay attention to books and the internet over the weekend. Mom and Grammy had both encouraged me to give a final talk at Chaco, too, but sometimes I began shaking just thinking about it. I mean I know I have lots of ideas, but this time there would be far more knowledgeable people there, and it would be televised. What if they thought my ideas were stupid?

I felt like Cinderella brooding about lacking the clothes and carriage to go to the ball. I know I should be able to talk without stuttering, especially if my father and Ketl reassure me. But the mystery of whether I could, found me in bed much longer than usual in the days leading up to our trip. I didn't watch television, either. If I saw anything on the news about my potential talk, it would have just upset me more. I couldn't even eat much while I waited and thought of what might happen.

Then that nice Katalyn Morgen called and reassured me that if I did one more talk about my investigations, that I could do it with just Chichilticalli, Ketl, and her in the room. She said there'd be a camera, but it would be operated by remote control.

It sure was nice of Chichilticalli and Ketl to come and get me and drive me to Chaco. Mom and Grammy took their own car, and that was good, because if I had ridden along with them, they would have given me all kinds of advice on what to do to prevent my speech problems.

If there was just a chance I could do it, more than anything I wanted to for Bobby. And if I could do one more talk, maybe I'd meet some kids my own age who liked books and internet exploration, too. On Monday and Tuesday, I was more confused than ever over being both excited and terrified of being tongue-tied. I even said a little prayer to Zuni Kachinas in the hopes that even though they didn't know me, they might help me in the theater.

While Chichilticalli and Ketl went out into the lobby, Katalyn and I rehearsed on the order of the overhead projection of photographs borrowed from books and illustrations she had had made by a graphic artist. She reassured me by saying that while I would be somewhat lit by an indirect light, the screen behind me would be the primary light source. Chichilticalli and Ketl would be sitting behind each of my shoulders. The only thing I'd be facing would be empty chairs and a dark overhead camera. Katalyn was wearing an earphone through which she told me she could hear the TV director's instructions on when we were on the air. Normally, a TV camera's red light comes on if it is in use, but Katalyn told me that they had turned it off so as not to disrupt my talk. She told me I would have three eight-minute segments to reveal whatever I thought I might have discovered. I heard a lot of cheering suddenly coming from out in the lobby. I was just glad it couldn't be for me because I hadn't even said anything yet.

I just hoped I wouldn't let everybody down, especially Bobby and all the kids he had told me about. Maybe the Anasazi, Mexica, and Zuni spirits would grant me strength.

We had finished rehearsing the visual projections, and the four of us were just quietly sitting there when Katalyn put a hand up to her earphone. "About two minutes until they'll be ready for your talk, Kahlo," she said after listening to instructions from the director. "When you've talked for seven minutes or so, I'll pass you a note when we are just one minute from commercial interruption. And remember," she smiled, "your talk isn't live, it's being prerecorded for broadcast two hours later. So, if you need a pause, that's no problem. And if you start to get nervous, remember you're talking to a group of kids and adults who think your ideas are really special."

I did start to get more nervous, but my Dad reached out and took my hand.

"Remember Kahlo," Ketl and I are both here," he said. "You are blessed with an ability to see things others can't. If you believe in those powers and believe that everyone listening or hearing you later respects you, the words will come. As Katalyn said, pretend you are again talking to the three of us in the office."

I exhaled and told myself just to relax.

"O.K., Kahlo, you can begin talking any time," Katalyn nodded to me.

"Wh-what happened when I first got to explore the Anasazi cities in Chaco Canyon, was, I-I started seeing things I couldn't explain. Everywhere I walked, I remembered all the things I had read in books about what the Anasazi might have thought when they began building cities like Pueblo Bonito. What could be the purpose of the Great North Road stretching 50 kilometers in a straight line to the north? What caused the Anasazi to build their cities where they did? And what was the main purpose of the Great Kivas in them?"

I still caught myself asking whether what I was saying made any sense. But when Katalyn began to project photos of Pueblo Bonito as well as the other cities and then several Great Kivas onto the screen in front of me, it helped me to calm down. The total silence and empty room might be unnerving to certain people, but for me, I concentrated on my dad's idea of pretending I was just in that office like before.

"When I was looking down into the Great Kiva in Pueblo Bonito, all of a sudden I remembered from photographs in books seeing green plants growing in several of the kivas when few were growing in the rest of the canyon, except along Chaco Wash. Maybe that meant there was a water source from below, from springs or former man-made sources. Then I had a vision of the Great Kiva's round floor filled up to the circular bench with water. Within the circle were the two rectangular masonry boxes containing steaming hot rocks and a fire in the smaller box heating more rocks so that the bath waters surrounding the boxes were warm. Anasazi elders were placing necklaces and clothing in the alcoves in the walls above so that they could wade and bathe in the warm water heated by the boxes."

Katalyn kept projecting what I was talking about, and I saw each of the three with me occasionally nodding in agreement. I can't explain why, but those three gave me confidence. I was amazed at how quickly I was able to say my ideas again about the use of the Great North Road, the Coke can and Kokopelli, as well as the possible hydraulic knowledge used to bring water to Pueblo Alto when the Chaco Wash and springs couldn't provide enough water. I was even able to tell my ideas for the meanings of their pottery painting.

The next part was what worried me because I had never told anyone about my astro-archeological ideas. I was glad when Katalyn signaled me twice to wind up talking about the hydraulic visions and the other stuff so that a commercial break could happen.

"That was really good, Kahlo," Katalyn beamed at me as she removed a photo of three pots out of the book *In Search of Chaco* from under the projector. "The director said to tell you everyone loved your talk."

It was lucky for me I spent the first of two commercial breaks organizing my thoughts on what to say about my astro-archeological ideas. I told myself not to worry if they were wrong, and that if not the scientists at least some of the kids might investigate my theories.

"Coming up again, Kahlo," said Katalyn. "You did great the first time...They're ready for the second of your three segments." Then to signal it was time, she reached out her hand and touched my arm.

"Scientists have determined through carbon-14 dating, pictographs, and other methods that the cities of Chaco Canyon were built somewhere between 600 and 1150 A.D.," I began without any speaking mistakes. That gave me courage to go on. "But when I looked at the dates of when the various cities were undertaken, at least seven of them—Casa Rinconada, Pueblo del Arroyo, Casa Chiquita, New Alto, Kin Kletso, Wijiji and Tsin Kletsin—were constructed between 1070 and 1130. After I read about those cities and dates, I unfolded my *A Guide to Chaco Culture* brochure and looked closely at their map of the cities excavated in modern times. I asked myself just why the Anasazi waited 50 more years after they started Pueblo Alto to build more cities? And why seven new cities?

"I started looking at web sites on astronomy to see if there might be any phenomena that might have triggered closer ties to astronomy. The Anasazi already had aligned some of their building walls and windows with the cardinal directions or solstices. Maybe some ties between their cities and astronomy might be important because of their spiritual cosmology. I wondered if anything in the heavens might have occurred around that time so that they began to build more cities.

On the internet I discovered that a Supernova in 1054 four times brighter than Venus was visible at night in the constellation Taurus for almost two years, but *even in daylight for 23 days*. In July of 1054 a crescent moon came close to this Supernova, and while I was hiking to Chaco's Peñasco Blanco, I found out there's a pictograph of the Supernova and moon together.

Another web site detailed a December 3$^{rd}$ annular solar eclipse visible in New Mexico occurring in 1065. Then a third site mentioned that Halley's Comet, which only comes every 76 Years, was *far brighter than normal* in 1066.

That meant there were at least three unusual phenomena in their skies in 12 years. Were these three astronomical phenomena significant enough as reasons for the Anasazi to again begin building new cities just four years later? Were Casa Rinconada and Pueblo del Arroyo begun in 1070 because the phenomena? 'Maybe,' I told myself.

"I thought about how those signs might have been one more reason the Anasazi began to focus more upon a longstanding problem. Water. Even kids know water still may be the most important resource in the West. What if as long ago as 850 the Anasazi civilization recognized water as the most important element in all their cosmology? And began building Pueblo Bonito and its Great Kiva baths as the focal point of their cities? Maybe when they began Pueblo Bonito, there were three water sources: Chaco Wash, a spring somewhere underneath, and run-off from the mesas above captured by now known rock trenches.

"In 1100 the worst century for drought in the area was still a century away when the Anasazi began constructing five new cities. In that upcoming 13$^{th}$ century, the effects of sunspots would heat the earth's surface 1-3°C and would be most intense in 1200. Now that period is called the Medieval Maximum. Narrow tree rings from 1276-1299 tell meteorologists and others that another harsh drought and perhaps cold spell may have made the Anasazi leave Chaco. Modern archeologists write that the Toltecs, Mexica and Anasazi all relocated during that period. Yet earlier, from 1050-1150, the wet and cool weather may have remained an important factor in the Anasazi building cities again.

"Still, I felt there had to be something else. When my Grammy and I visited an Anasazi outlier called Pueblo Pintado, south of here, I had one of these visions I sometimes get but cannot control. We all have visions, but I'm real lucky to remember all of mine.

"I saw seven cities. Yet I saw them north of Pueblo Pintado, maybe in Chaco Canyon. Could the legendary original Seven Cities of Cibola thought to be Hawikuh, Halona and five other Zuni cities and their riches actually have been a different seven in Chaco?

"I began reading *The Journey of Coronado*, a translation of Francisco Vasquez de Coronado's journal of exploration of the southwest and search for Quivira—another legendary destination supposedly having lots of gold and riches. In chapter XI, I found that while already in Cibola, or the modern-day Zuni Pueblo, Vasquez sent Don Pedro de Tovar to explore a different seven cities. To quote the translation, '...they informed him about a province with seven villages of the same sort as theirs, although somewhat different. They had nothing to do with these people. This province is called Tusayan. *It is twenty-five leagues from Cibola.* The villages are high and the people are warlike.'

"If at the time of Columbus, the Portuguese Maritime League also used by Spanish sailors was approximately 3.2 miles, the distance as the crow flies from Zuni to Chaco today still remains approximately 80 miles. I wondered whether Don Pedro de Tovar and his men had found the real Seven Cities, then occupied by Navajos? The explorers returned to Vasquez laden with nothing more than a few turquoises, cotton cloth, corn meal, pine nuts, and 'birds of the country.' What if those Chacoan birds were descended from macaws brought up by traders from Mexico centuries earlier?"

As I continued talking, suddenly I started getting some of the mental backlash that always interferes. It was as if I was dropping all these names that nobody cares about and telling them too much trivia in which they had little interest.

But then Katalyn projected a big circular map of the northern hemisphere's heavens on the screen. When I glanced up and saw the stars, I can't say why, but I was able to compose myself again and forget about all the facts being overwhelming. I had to try to tell what I knew. Chichilticalli, Ketl, and the Kachinas were all still listening. And I hoped Bobby and his friends would be able to hear my talk on a speakerphone before they watched the entire program later.

"Several times the number seven had come into visions I couldn't stop from reoccurring," I continued. "And I asked myself, what if something in the heavens made seven cities important to the Anasazi and later the Zuni?

"All of a sudden while looking at an internet illustration of the stars visible in our northern hemisphere, I felt an electric current run from the back of my head down through my spine and then up my arms. I couldn't explain why, but my eyes became riveted on two constellations right in front of me. As you can see from the flashlight arrow Katalyn is now using to point to them, they are the Big and Little Dippers.

"What had drawn me to them, is that they both have seven major stars. And as Katalyn now slowly revolves the overhead projection of our hemisphere's stars during one point in the year, if you look closely, you will see the Little Dipper, or Ursa Minor, might be pouring water from its cup to the waiting bigger cup of the Big Dipper, or Ursa Major.

"Was this an interpretation that ancient Anasazi astronomers might have perceived, too? Could the Anasazi have made the same interpretation I had? Or could they have believed these Dippers to be signaling the importance of water in their cosmology? Could those two sets of seven stars have had something to do with the legendary Seven Cities?"

A minute earlier Katalyn had signaled me that the second and final commercial interruption during my three segments was coming. Just when I said, "Seven Cities?" she tapped me on the arm.

What she couldn't have known was that although they had told me the Visitor Center would be totally quiet during my talk, suddenly the technical director or someone at the front desk must have accidentally patched in the program's audio to the theater speakers.

"And...remote camera three ready for interviews and Bobby in his Gallup hospital room to be recorded during this break...Take studio camera one in, five...four..."

"Could Kahlo Dupín be right? Could the magnificent Pueblo Bonito, the reputed focal point of Anasazi cosmology, and its Great Kiva have been used for ceremonial baths? And could the mythical Seven Cities of Cibola, have originally been intended rather to be the Seven Cities of Chaco? Or the Seven Cities of the Anasazi?

"One thing we do know, is that there are some very excited school kids and perplexed archeologists in Chaco Canyon this afternoon. For more on some of these initial reactions to Kahlo Dupín's speculative revelations, we now go back out to our correspondent, Estibalíz Tsoodzil, live at the Chaco Cultural National Historical Park Visitor Center."

"For all of you having seen and heard Kahlo," I heard Tsoodzil's voice over the theater speaker, "like the scientists and officials in this room, you probably have questions about what she has already revealed. What about you Doctor Truedson? What went through your mind when Kahlo speculated on Pueblo Bonito, Casa Rinconada, and Tsin Kletsin as just three cities having harbored ceremonial baths?"

"As you perceived, those in the worlds of archeology and anthropology will have many questions as to the veracity of her speculations. Were there three sources for water? And is she correct if they were baths, in saying the rock boxes were used for heating the water? Then why aren't there visible watermarks on the circumferences of bathing kivas? And were the baths year-round? Or not used in winter? Kahlo has done a wonderful job sleuthing, yet unfortunately but necessarily in the world of archeology, lengthy reliable testing must try to decipher evidence for verification of any such speculations."

"Thank you, Doctor...And now I think we have Bobby Atsitsana, the young boy who e-mailed Kahlo and requested she do one more talk, available from his Cibola General Hospital room in Gallup. "Bobby, were you able to hear Kahlo's talk?"

"Wow, me and my friends in the room thought Kahlo's talk was so cool! We're amazed, because all of us use the internet, but it's obvious Kahlo is showing the way to all of us kids who like exploring web sites. We can't wait to see the entire program tonight!"

"Bobby, I'm going to walk outside of the Visitor Center. Even though we've been feeding you the audio portions of what will air early this evening, you can't see what I'm walking toward in the Chaco Visitor Center parking lot. There must be several hundred kids from the surrounding pueblos and cities loudly expressing their enthusiasm..."

'Kahlo! Kahlo! Kahlo! Seven! Seven! Seven!'

"...I hope you can hear them, Bobby. The excitement here in Chaco Canyon is louder than a Final Four basketball game!"

Then the theater speaker went quiet, and I couldn't hear the rest of what Bobby and Estibalíz said. The silence was kind of frightening. I knew it was time to make my final speculations. But Doctor Truedson was right. Everything I had said was just speculation. I didn't even want to tell about the Seven Cities. I didn't want to let Bobby and all the kids down, either. But I could feel my stuttering coming back into my head before Katalyn even signaled me that it was time to begin again what every kid fears: talking to too many people at once. I was scared.

"Coming right up for the last part of your talk, Kahlo," Katalyn smiled. "As you heard from all the kids outside, they're pretty enthusiastic."

I was more worried because of what that archeologist had questioned. He was right. My stuff was just guesswork. I had lost a lot of confidence. Then Katalyn tapped me on the arm.

"Wh-wh-what I did, w-w-was..."

And then I couldn't go on.

I looked over at my Dad and he nodded at me as if I could do it. But when I turned back to the camera, my mouth moved, but nothing came out.

"Give us a minute," I heard Katalyn say to the director through the miniature microphone they had clipped on her blouse. "She needs a short break."

It was strange, but when I looked over at Chichilticalli, all I could think of was if I could ever have a real dad like him. Then I started to get the sort of noises in my head one doctor said might be tinnitus. I just tried hard to keep from crying. I knew I was disappointing everyone.

Then before I knew it, Ketl put his hand on my one shoulder and Chichilticalli on the other. Those shivers went up my arms again. I can't explain it, but this time when I looked at my dad and he looked back with the intensity of a Kachina at me, I calmed down like when I used to run along the path around the Central Park reservoir in New York. All the feedback thundering through my head disappeared like a storm just before a rainbow. I turned back toward the camera and almost all my fear was gone. Katalyn nodded that I could continue.

"There was one thing that still puzzled me about why no one else had noticed what I had about the possible relationship between

Anasazi city building and the Dippers. But an idea finally came to me that might explain why. It was when I was with my Grammy in Chaco a while ago and I told her she could wait in the car while I had to check something out. She had brought me to look at Casa Rinconada, and then when she went back to the car I walked west and counterclockwise around the South Gap trail eventually leading up to Tsin Kletsin. About 300m up the trail from Casa Rinconada there was a big rock on the right.

"Then there it was. A big overgrown mound, just where I thought it would be. From on top of the mound I could see each of Pueblo del Arroyo, Chetro Ketl and Casa Rinconada in a trapezoid. Now everything in my Seven Cities theory might fit. I might have found the seventh city I needed. If I was right, it just hadn't been excavated.

"If people even consider the mythical Seven Cities to be in Chaco, which has way more than seven, they would probably include Pueblo Bonito. But I didn't. I figured it was the ceremonial center of water and separate. Pueblo Bonito might also have prevented anyone from seeing my Seven Cities of Chaco idea."

I looked up at the screen. "Maybe you can see the stars of the Little Dipper Katalyn's projecting." I waited a moment for the audience to look at the alignment of those stars. "Now below it she has projected a potential Seven Cities in Chaco: Wijiji, Una Vida, Hugo Pavi, Chetro Ketl, Casa Rinconada—the possible missing city west of Casa Rinconada, in red—and Pueblo del Arroyo."

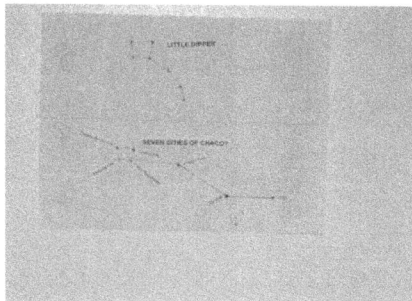

When I glanced around, I could see Katalyn, Ketl and Chichilticalli each cocking their heads to look closer at the comparison.

"What if originally the Anasazi selected their building sites hoping that the Kachinas above could look down and see how they valued their water and ceremonial bathing? And what if Pueblo Bonito—which Katalyn has now inserted into her projection as a green star—symbolized water filling the Little Dipper cup?

"The problem with that idea, those cities are too far out of alignment to be *the* Seven Cities. If the Anasazi had intended for their Seven Cities to match the seven stars of the Little Dipper, why in 1105 would they have started Wijiji where it is, instead of locating it on Fajada Wash south of Una Vida—along the red dotted line in the projection—to match the Little Dipper's handle stars better? And why would the cup be so much smaller than those in the actual Little Dipper's stars? Also, one missing city might be possible. But two I thought probably wouldn't. I got discouraged. Maybe my ideas of the Seven Cities being in Chaco were completely wrong.

"Then I got out my Guide to Chaco map and looked closer. I studied both the Dippers in various positions on different web sites again. It made me remember that the Seven Cities visions I sometimes had, always seemed to include the *Big Dipper*'s seven stars rather than those of Little Dipper. I also went back to the list of Chacoan cities and all the dates when they were believed to have been started. I again confirmed how *seven* of the cities were started not long after three important astronomical phenomena.

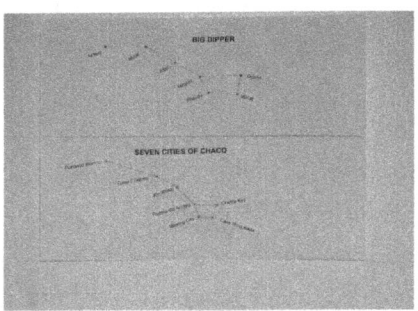

"Then while studying my Chaco map again, it finally came to me. I stared at the Big Dipper, which Katalyn is now projecting onto the screen behind me, and then the map. And suddenly the *Seven Cities of Chaco* seemed to reveal themselves: Peñasco Blanco, Casa Chiquita, Kin Kletso, in approximately the same position as the Big Dipper handle's Aldaid, Mizar and Alioth; and the cities Pueblo del Arroyo, Chetro Ketl and Casa Rinconada matching the Dipper cup's Megrez, Dubhe and Merak. The only problem was, there was no Anasazi city that would correspond to Phecda in the Big Dipper cup's lower left corner. That's when I checked out if there might be an unexcavated city west of Casa Rinconada that might have matched Phecda."

After she projected my Seven Cities speculation below the seven stars of the Big Dipper—including Phecda, and the lines to it, in red

—Katalyn was slowly nodding and smiling at me over the secret she had promised to keep with the illustrator until after I gave my talk.

"Some might question that this potential configuration is enough out of alignment, or the cup too small, to match either Dipper. But to accommodate building these Seven Cities within the walls of Chaco Canyon, with the cup possibly representing both Dippers, could that explain why the cup formed by the cities is too small and the Little Dipper's handle upside down in the Anasazi's Chaco cities? If the purpose was to encourage the Kachinas to keep the water flowing in Chaco Wash, could the Anasazi not only have built their Seven Cities nearby the Wash for water, but also to make them easier for the Kachinas to see their connection to the stars in the heavens?

"I'm sure lots of people will question these ideas because that's all they are. One school kid's speculations on how the Anasazi might have had the stars in mind when they built at least some of their cities. But after Katalyn called me, and Bobby and other kids e-mailed me they wanted me to talk about my ideas about the Seven Cities, I said I would. I just hope no one finds my ideas too weird."

I looked at Katalyn and she raised her eyebrows as if to ask if I were done. I was.

Then I got one of those chills you get when you think you might have said or done something wrong. Maybe what I had speculated would just make the archeologists and astronomers mad. I heard a burst of applause through the theater walls, though. And the kids outside were making a huge racket. All of that should have made me feel better. But it didn't. I just got sad, because now Chichilticalli and Ketl would go back to their own lives, and I would go back to Santa Fe and there would be no more Chaco Canyon mysteries. In a new school I would be 'that girl who thinks she knows everything.'

I asked Katalyn if it would be O.K. if I went to the restroom, and she pointed out a side door I could use from the theater to a hallway to avoid all the scientists and officials in the lobby.

I knew the time had come I dreaded for the last month. I just wanted never to see any more of Chaco or the people who would ask me a million questions I couldn't answer. Even if I could, I'd probably start stuttering. I didn't want to face any cameras or reporters or my Mom, or even the friendly school kids who came all that way to see me. It was all over now. Not only would the archeologists shoot through my theories like Wild Bill Hickok, but Mom and Chichilticalli would never agree to marry each other or even live together. I might never see my real Dad again. I had the attention a lot of kids would die for, and all I really wanted was a real family and a few kids that didn't think I was just this strange little girl who can't talk properly.

A couple of minutes later I changed into some running shorts and an *Atalanta Women On The Run* sweatshirt. It had the Atlanta Track Club's red phoenix ascending from the ashes on it. I felt like I was still in the ashes. I had only run once or twice since New York. But running away from everyone seemed to be my only choice if I didn't want to start stuttering again.

Just after I came out of the restroom, I saw this guy that from what Mom had told me had to be Kaliber. He looked like one of those soldiers from the movie 'Platoon,' or the orchid guy from 'Adaptation.'

"Good job, Kahlo!" he said, reaching out his hand to shake mine.

"Th-th-thanks."

"Where're you going with your backpack?"

"M-m-maybe r-running."

"Running?"

"Mm-huh."

# And Then, There Were Seven

(KALIBER)

It's funny, but I usually have no more than five minutes for anyone under the age of 18. They mean well, but ever since I shot all those Viet Cong probably no more than age 16 or 17 and some of them in nothing more than black pajamas, I haven't had the stomach for listening to kids. That is, until I heard Kahlo talk. Whew! Man, you always hear about prodigies, but when you actually listen to what some precocious nine-year-old's mind has contrived, it's mind blowing. When I ran into her in the hall outside the Chaco theater, I felt like the actor in Shakespeare in Love who reassures that the pages of the script will indeed miraculously materialize. Kahlo was a mysterious visionary in a nine-year-old body.

And I was an eccentric hermit in a 50-something body and mind to whom the Black Queen, through her own resurrection, had now given a second chance. Ashleigh had changed, and inexplicably I knew I was finally going to be able to care about some people other than myself. No more giving peridot and money to Ketl to assuage my guilt. I'd still support his Native American schooling ideas when I could. But I wanted to see more kids come out of their shells like Kahlo was able to do, even if she never could speak so eloquently again. No more Todd Browning's 'Freaks' to be ignored by the likes of those fortunate enough to look 'normal,' whatever that is. Kahlo wasn't a freak. But she certainly was a phenom who was going to have to pay the enormous price of loss of privacy. There would also be her forced submission to the unavoidable stares and snide remarks of those who rather than understanding and appreciating her, would, through jealousy of her successful efforts, treat her with disdain and taunt her as a mental freak of nature. They would be the limited, yet vocal minority further destroying Kahlo's ability to be forthcoming.

The Visitor Center and surroundings, on the other hand, were polar opposites in terms of rampant adulation and respect. It was like the aftermath of an announcement that everyone in a corporation is going to get a massive Christmas bonus. Outside the kids from New Mexican and Arizonan schools were chanting and waving flags; a Juarez Aztlan High School mariachi band struck up the song *Los Laureles*, and even the local Native American kids began to dance when a young girl was singing her heart out like Linda Ronstadt in *La Calandria* from the *Canciones de mi Padré* album. While inside the adults, as if they had to decide archeological truth or consequences before a closing conference bell, were loudly debating the controversial speculations Kahlo had divulged. The din was enormous, phones ringing; archeologists, astronomers, officials, and all-ologists noisily reacting; correspondent Tsoodzil among the omniscient and famous interviewing; fiddlers, the young female singer, and kids from seven to 17 outside wildly dancing, singing, japing, and shouting to Ronstadt's *La Charreada*. Judging by the noise levels Kahlo's speculations had evoked, the world of Chaco Canyon would never be the same.

"Have you seen Kahlo?" Chichilticalli suddenly shouted amidst the noise.

I felt the guilt of someone knowing what he shouldn't, yet not knowing if the clues he possesses should be revealed. "She said she was going for a run. I figured she meant just a quick trot to calm down. Maybe she got back and is outside talking with the kids in the parking lot."

The Zuni shook his head like he had explored all the potential places where Kahlo might have wandered and come up with a cipher. "I thought she might be outside, but she's not. And she's not in here."

"When I saw her in the hallway after her talk, she might have taken off to avoid all the congestion and hoopla. My impression is that the little detective maybe needed to escape to gather herself for the impending media and schoolkids storm. Maybe she ran down the loop to Hungo Pavi to have a think."

Chichilticalli shook his head as if I had chosen the wrong destination. "It's got to be something more to do with one of her kiva baths or the connection between astronomy and the Seven Cities. I thought of the 20-brightest stars, of tonight's full moon, and I even reviewed other constellations. Yet two weeks ago on a bench in front of the Santa Fe Library she told me about her ceremonial bathing ideas, and now she has come up with the possible connection between the Dippers and the Seven Cities. I've been trying to narrow down where she would go to escape all the attention waiting at the Visitor Center. What exact location she would choose that would be most meaningful."

Then suddenly it came to him.

"She's gone to revisit where the Waters should be."

"As in the Big Dipper?"

Chichilticalli nodded slowly and almost imperceptibly. "...Yah..." he said while rolling the idea round in that Zuni- and Oxford-educated mind. "Maybe she's gone to the Great Kiva at Pueblo Bonito. She knows water is the most important element of both the old and the new. I've got a bad feeling about this. She may think she's wrong because of being unable to prove her connection with the Dippers."

"Ashleigh's out in the car. Let's get Aurore and Katarina and Ketl and do a quick recon," I suggested.

"Good idea. You and Ashleigh take your car. I'll get the other three and take ours."

We had left our cars in the employee parking lot behind the building so we could get out. The entire main front lot was alive with an excited crowd of kids singing and dancing and hoping to meet their heroine. The little phenom had done it. But the Zuni was right. The whole thing might be overwhelming to a kid used to talking to no one.

Our headlights further illuminated what the full moon and stars could not on the road seemingly to nowhere. It's probably three miles down the canyon to Pueblo Bonito before the turnaround.

When our two cars got there, everyone silently piled out in the descending darkness and used flashlights quickly borrowed from the Center to illuminate the path ascending to Pueblo Bonito. We all hoped Chichilticalli's analysis proved correct. If the little wonder wandered too far without a flashlight, coyote is always waiting.

After the six of us spread out, a quick combing of the huge pueblo and its circumference revealed nothing. The Great Kiva stood empty in the moonlight. There was no nine-year-old phenom sitting on a wall anywhere.

"Anyone find anything?" Chichilticalli asked while still panning his flashlight round the Great Kiva.

There was silence as each of us realized she wasn't at her speculative center for ceremonial bathing.

"Think, man," I said to Chichilticalli. "You're the astronomer. It's got to have something to do with her speculations."

While others continued to pan with their flashlights, the Zuni paced back and forth.

"I think I've finally got it. Kahlo will be most disappointed over the missing city she can't prove exists. She may have gone there.

"Phecda."

We piled back in the cars and drove round the western turn-around to the Casa Rinconada parking lot. It was a quarter mile up to Rinconada and then west to the potential 'Lost City.' Even Katarina began to pick up her knees. There was a silent feeling among all of us that we'd better get there. The little visionary upset and under pressure ominously felt like a flash flood coming down an arroyo. She could well be desperate and each of us knew it.

Finally, the big rock appeared on the right of the trail, just as Kahlo had detailed in her talk. It was like our search party file had come up on a ridge just beyond the rock. You couldn't tell in the dark if part of the ridge to the right was a mound that could cover what once was an ancient city or not.

At first our scanning flashlights revealed nothing. Then suddenly toward the back of the elevated patch of desert, Kahlo sat cross-legged.

As we got closer, Ketl signed for us to keep our distance and we stopped in deference to her need for privacy. The Navajo and Chichilticalli sat down cross-legged opposite her by what I suppose was a non-threatening ten feet. I knelt on one knee between them, while Katarina stood beside Ketl and Aurore next to Chichilticalli. Ashleigh had hung back the other side of the rock, her thinking being that additional excitement at Kahlo's time of distress would be inappropriate.

After we turned off our flashlights so as not to further upset Kahlo, the whole moonlit scenario, with the occasional distant cry of coyotes and the stars and Milky Way above, oddly reminded me of Sherlock Holmes out on a remote path on Dartmoor in the Hound of the Baskervilles. You could feel the hair on your arms rise. There was an aura around Kahlo, invisible, but you could sense it.

At the same time, her vulnerability was palpable. Kahlo's head was down, and in her lap was a yellow backpack with what looked like some red flower petals on it. Something was wrong.

"Kahlo?" Aurore asked, trying to keep her voice from sounding alarmed. "Are you O.K.?"

The lost detective shook her head from side to side.

"Why not, dear?" asked Katarina.

Initially, Kahlo didn't respond, the agony of her solitude powerful among even the familiar. "I'm sc-sc-scared."

"You're scared?" asked Katarina. "Why, dear?"

"Because I have to g-go to j-j-jail."

"Kahlo, there's no penalty for speculating about the Anasazi," Aurore said.

Kahlo continued to fiddle with the leaves on her pack. "Mm-*huh*," she contrasted by nodding up and down. "I was g-g-going to c-c-confess...But I c-c-can't... I'm af-f-fraid..."

"What are those flower petals you're fiddling with?" asked Aurore.

It was obvious Kahlo didn't want to answer. The five of us stood there not knowing if we should move closer or hold our distance.

"R-red o-o-oleander."

"Red oleander! But I read on the internet that red oleander's more poisonous than white oleander. Why are you playing with red oleander petals?"

"I w-w-won't have to go to j-j-jail. I'm going to eat them s-s-s-so I don't have to con-confess to p-p-poisoning auntie Ashleigh."

"You think you poisoned Ashleigh and killed her?"

Kahlo nodded and we waited for an explanation. "She p-pushed Grammy down the s-s-stairs, and I-I-I-I didn't want her to hurt G-g-gram again."

"I shouldn't worry about those oleander petals you tried to put in my salad," Ashleigh suddenly said upon appearing from behind the big rock. It was eerie, but the Black Queen shone a flashlight up into her face so Kahlo would realize she was alive. "Yes, it's me, dear Kahlo. We were always two of a kind, you and me. It was very bad of me to push Gram, but I certainly didn't mean to push her down the stairs. I was trying to push my way past her—never mind. However, you're grandmother's O.K.—even though perhaps in some danger from her use of distilled grain spirits. We've made amends, and now I want to assure you that your auntie is alive and well and trying to get better in terms of my nasty past behavior."

Ashleigh moved closer to reassure Kahlo she wasn't seeing a ghost. "It wasn't easy, dear Kahlo. But from the dining room I spied you putting those strange flower petals in my salad. Yet after picking the red-colored flora out of my otherwise entirely green salad instead of eating them, I disappeared from our upstate house and paid a doctor to certify I had died of a heart attack. It was unfair to you and everyone else, of course. But as you know, in those days I wasn't particularly concerned with being fair to anyone. Like you, I just wanted to escape. But now I'm alive in New Mexico and Chaco Canyon and hope you can forgive me for my selfishness. At any rate, you won't be going to jail, Kahlo."

Kahlo jumped to her feet, ran the two or three steps to her aunt, and buried her face in Ashleigh's black silk cowgirl blouse. No one knew what to say. It was one of those moments I never have to endure because of living alone. Kahlo was sobbing into her aunt's blouse, and she clung to the Black Queen as if letting go might destroy the illusion.

"Kahlo, there's something else, isn't there?" Ashleigh asked.

We all knew Kahlo's inability to let go was merely the effect of many trying elements in a nine-year-old visionary's life.

Kahlo continued to cry, refusing to pull her face back from the relief of knowing she hadn't killed her aunt.

"Kahlo, I'm alive, you're alive, and lots of kids and inquisitive archeologists would like to meet you at the Visitor Center," Ashleigh said while trying to lean backwards to look at the miniature detective. "They're there waiting to watch the program to start in less than an hour on the big screen in the parking lot. Is it meeting them that's bothering you?"

Kahlo shook her head sideways without removing her face from her aunt's shirt.

"Is it to do with your dad?"

Kahlo nodded affirmatively, then drew her face back without turning around. "I w-w-won't get to see Ch-ch-chichilticalli and Ketl anymore. Mom doesn't l-love my Dad, and he and Ketl l-l-l-live too far from S-S-Santa Fe."

"Well, there's a bit of good news on that front," threw out Katarina, the moonlight glistening off a silver flask she had just lowered discreetly before responding. "Ketl's invited me to visit, and I'm going to take him up on it regularly. You can come with me."

Kahlo didn't move. Ashleigh stroked her hair, but it looked as if nothing was going to appease the young prodigy with the burden of the archeological world upon her shoulders.

"It looks like I'll be able to see you, too, Kahlo," the Zuni surprised us all by adding. He stood up and Aurore put her arm around his waist. "Back at the Visitor Center after listening to your talk, former President Dewitt Parkridge and Peachtree Computer's Will Highgate told me they're forming a new Chaco Seven Curious Children's Foundation. Apparently the two not only were amazed by your talk, but also beforehand heard from Ashleigh all about your wish for a complete home life. They've agreed to a series of NPS fellowships, as well, the first of which they say will go to me so that I can work half time in-and-out of a newly created Santa Fe office, and half of the year in the Northwest New Mexico Visitor Center. Since your Mom's agreed to marry me, there's a good chance you and I will see a lot of each other."

Kahlo moved like a meteorite toward her real-life father.

Just then a string of buses could be heard approaching from round the bend. Linda Ronstadt's *La Charreada* was ringing out of one bus and local high school flags and shouting kids were hanging from the second and third buses' windows. "Kah-lo-Seven! Kah-lo-Seven! Kah-lo-Seven!" they shouted before their sounds faded and their glistening yellow phantoms disappeared down the dark road toward the Visitor Center.

Kahlo had her arms around both her new Dad and Mom. "I can talk! I can talk! I can talk!" she shouted stutter-free. "I can talk!"

"Kahlo," Aurore began while holding her daughter to her. "Do you think you're ready to meet the archeologists, your fans and the press?"

Kahlo nodded, hopping and skipping in a circle before returning to hug her parents again.

"Mm-huh," the sage spanning two thousand years replied. "But kids first."

"Kids first," the six said in unison to the seventh.

END

MORE ON P. J. CHRISTMAN CAN BE FOUND:

AMAZON.COM

P. J. Christman
Paul Christman

YOUTUBE.COM

P. J. Christman

Printed in the USA
CPSIA information can be obtained
at www.ICGtesting.com
JSHW011717270723
45395JS00004B/183